The Revolution
According to
Raymundo Mata

Also by Gina Apostol

Bibliolepsy
Gun Dealers' Daughter
Insurrecto

The Revolution According to Raymundo Mata

Gina Apostol

SOHO

This edition first published in 2021 by
Soho Press, Inc.
227 W 17th Street
New York, NY 10011

Library of Congress Cataloging-in-Publication Data

Names: Apostol, Gina, author.
Title: The revolution according to Raymundo Mata / Gina Apostol.
Description: New York, NY : Soho Press, Inc., 2021.
Identifiers: LCCN 2019059158

ISBN 978-1-64129-183-5
eISBN 978-1-64129-184-2
International Paperback ISBN 978-1-64129-277-1

Classification: LCC PR9550.9.A66 R48 2021 | DDC 823'.914—dc23
LC record available at https://lccn.loc.gov/2019059158

Printed in the United States of America

10 9 8 7 6 5 4 3 2 1

For Arne

Dicit ei Iesus, "Noli me tangere: *nondum enim ascendi ad Patrem; meum vade autem ad fratres meos et dic eis ascendo ad Patrem meum et Patrem vestrum et Deum meum et Deum vestrum.*"

Venit Maria Magdalene adnuntians discipulis quia vidi Dominum et haec dixit mihi.

Jesus said unto her, Touch me
not: for I am not yet ascended to my
Father; but go to my brethren, and say
unto them, I ascend unto my Father, and
your Father, and to my God, and your God.

Mary Magdalene came and told the disciples:
I have seen the Lord and he told these things unto me.

John 20:17-18

Noamla berlemla, mi ra puada vimgoes am at.
Jose Rizal, "Profiles," *Miscellaneous Writings*

Author's Note on the American Edition

In 1998, a fellowship granted by Phillips Exeter Academy allowed me to finish the first draft of what became my third published novel, *Gun Dealers' Daughter,* and begin the first chapter of my next work, based vaguely on a detail in *Katipunan and the Revolution*, the engaging memoirs of Santiago Alvarez, a general in the Philippine war against Spain. I remember the solitude and satisfaction of beginning the text that became *The Revolution According to Raymundo Mata*: the stillness of that spring midnight in New Hampshire, when I began a farcical reconstruction of an anecdote in Alvarez's book—the evening when Emilio Aguinaldo (who will later wage war against the Americans after winning his war against Spain) rides the kalesa with the blind future katipunero Raymundo Mata. I was laughing as I wrote what I thought would be the comic novel's first chapter (it is Entry #25 in the finished draft). There is nothing like the first pages of a new work—when one has finally discarded the trepidation and the horror of beginning—and just begins. The horror of beginning a new work lies in the immensity of its blankness. Any new novel leaves you on your own, worse than on a desert island because it is a desertion and bereftness of your own making. You build toward the angst of those first words, and so the frank release of that first chapter, when you begin, is an unspeakable pleasure, because to be honest: before you begin, it always seems impossible.

For a long time, I had only those first pages. I finished the book nine years later. I published it in the Philippines ten years ago.

Revising the book for this American edition was like that first page: it was simply a pleasure.

This book was planned as a puzzle: traps for the reader, dead-end jokes, textual games, unexplained sleights of tongue. But at the same time, I wished to be true to the past I was plundering. My concept of Raymundo, an actual but unknown historical figure, is cut out of imagined cloth, but I decided to follow his times as much as I could. For me, a powerful reason to write novels like these is that their construction matches my sense of reality. A colonized country is the overt result of various others shaping its sense of self. The novel's multiple voice, which refracts, realigns, repositions texts and viewpoints from awry angles, ruptured plots, confused tongues, and an almost heedless anachronistic sense of the past, is for me a potent way to fathom and portray the unfinished "reality" of such a nation. (And I'm not so sure if this hypertextuality is not true of all nations.)

Here is an example: the notion of the Philippines, in a sense, was produced by a novel. Harold Augenbraum, the scholar on the history of translation who translated Rizal for Penguin Classics, tells me the Philippines seems unique in its enduring yet insolubly mediated relation to its seminal book. The national hero Jose Rizal's first work, called *Noli Me Tangere* (*Touch Me Not*), inspired the mass movement that launched revolution against Spain. That novel was written in Spanish. At this point in history, Filipinos do not read that language. Because we were occupied by America by 1898 and officially ruled by it until 1946, we learn to read in English (at least I have) and speak at least 50 different other languages. I grew up with four languages: Waray, Tagalog, English, and Cebuano; at this point, I consider the first three of those native tongues (my spoken Cebuano is still funny). I was required to study a fifth, Spanish: but my learning of it was much removed from actual practice. Thus, Filipinos must read in translation the novel that begot us. It's no wonder that, in my view, two things shape the Filipino: puns and Jose Rizal. The Rizal Law of 1956 required the reading of Rizal in schools—but it did not require reading him in the original. In a further spin, many of us study his novels in another colonizer's tongue, English (as for me, I first read the *Noli* in Tagalog: one more colonizer, so the joke goes, for those not from Manila).

The essence of a country like the Philippines is that it seems to exist in translation—a series of textual mediations must be unraveled in order to reveal who or what it is. More precisely: it exists *in the suspension* of its myriad translations—it is alive in the void of its ghost-speeches. In this way, for me, Filipinos embody a definition of the human: a translated being. It seems to me we are all always only on the cusp of being understood, or understanding ourselves.

This novel in many ways is about recovery. The recovery of a text, a body; the recovery of a hero, a history; the recovery of a country, a past. It was miraculous to me how writing this novel was such a joy: when I began writing it in earnest, I looked forward to writing it every day. The power of Rizal, and the power of this history, is that these genii are inexhaustible: we must be glad for the patently unfinished and infuriating history that Filipinos have—in this way, it seems Filipinos must represent the complexity of everyone's incomplete and indeterminate selves, and our endless, surprising resurrections.

Gina Apostol
New York, New York

Editor's Preface

I had not read General Mata's journals when I spoke last year to a Mürkian psychoanalyst about the possibility of hysterical abreactions occurring on a national scale. This was during a lull at a conference at a floating restaurant on Manila Bay (or was it a fish market in Kowloon?—I can't keep those junkets straight). There was a full moon, and we could see the marble columns of a colonial building nearby—a monstrous wreck that gave the shantytown around it a nasty glamor. The scholar was an unshaved blonde, the kind one often meets at academic conferences. She was expounding on independence movements as "macroscopic examples of aggressivity in the analysand" while she fondled some frangipani and picked through the pectorals of a Peking duck.

It struck me as she manhandled vertebrae and munched on the fronds, or vice versa, that academic blondes are aggressive bores.

To compare our revolution—the crux of our history—to some hysterical patient on a hypothetical couch was just icing on her slanderous cake.

But what did I have to offer her as evidence of the irreducible reality of our history? I knew no scholar, no text, not even a comic book that spoke of the Philippine War of Independence without disturbing solipsism or deeply divided angst. It's a history that invites neurotics to speak up.

It's no great surprise that it ends up a vulgar patient in obscure neo-Freudian journals.

When the publisher Trina Trono described to me the Raymundo Mata manuscript—an excessive term, perhaps, for the mess she held up in her hands—I have to say I was skeptical. She held up an assortment of unpaginated notes and mismatched sheaves packed in a ratty biscuit tin and stuffed in a tattered medical bag, the edges of the papers curled up in permanent rust.

Then she thrust into my hands another stack, a neatly typed translation, with notes.

But even then.

I was not persuaded.

In my experience, the voice of the revolutionist is clouded by conflicting purposes.

He is vulnerable to the cynicism of a world that by the time he is done has sadly changed.

Our revolution failed.

Let's face it.

We drove off a Spanish empire that had already given up the ghost then the Americans beat us to a pulp.

They had guns.

We wore slippers.

Who are we kidding?

Everyone acknowledges we got it worse than Vietnam, and the Battle of Manila Bay was way back in 1898.

We lost big time.

Why else do we have postcolonial conferences except to invite everyone to pick at our scabs?

Typically the revolutionist's memoir emerges when the hero is beyond innocence—when the dream is dead. The gap between the irreducible (the mad flipflop fever, the trauma that cannot be spoken) and the speech that cradles it (unnaturally chronological, with suspicious clarity, and keloids of rancor garnished by footnotes) is only natural.

After all, as the blonde scholar said, and I quote with disgust: "the gap between language and reality is the bane of the human condition."

Unquote.

However, in the histories of our revolution, this is magnified by the speaker's own acceptance of his Fall. We're left with the pathos of which he cannot speak, a rotten trick, if you ask me.

This is the tragic underlying note of all our histories. And so I felt this familiar troubling pain, below the diaphragm, near the liver, when I picked up the tin-can journals of Raymundo Mata, now conveniently stashed into this fine translated state.

My surprise was great as I read on. That the storyteller is, I must admit, flawed, maybe mad, does not diminish my faith in his story.

In fact, his madness amplifies its truth.

Estrella Espejo
Quezon Institute and Sanatorium
Tacloban, Leyte
December 17, 2004

Translator's Note

It was difficult to approach this text with calm as a translator. It is linguistically deranged. One notebook was in spastic code, squiggles and symbols that I think were Japanese characters, hiragana or katakana—I don't know anything about Japanese. The halting, hallucinatory rendition of those moments arises from the fact that I could barely understand what he was saying.

Interspersed throughout his papers are sheaves that seem to be his private diary, written in the throes of his insomnia (he was well-known for his nocturnalism; there is that sordid legend in his hometown about certain bestial acts he performed in private, in bat caves; I won't get into that here). These intermittent outpourings are mostly in General Mata's first language, a curious variant of Tagalog. They portray an admirable grasp of vulgarisms, licentious metaphors, off-color puns. Throughout the diary his prose is remarkably "quotidian," some call it "rakishly colloquial," not to mention "peevishly colonial." As has been said at that last conference in Kauai (or Kowloon, who cares): "he favors loose speech when he writes on loose leaf . . ."

Neat antanaclasis there, Professor Estrella!

But the challenge was to translate the richness of Raymundo's tongues into singular, common English. I tried my best.

In this way he can sound shockingly modern, with an almost lurid Byronic passion. The lapses in civility that bedevil the text may include my own frugal powers of speech. Trust me, I found faint comfort in the vulgate of our times.

Dr. Diwata Drake refers to some of these passages in her justly celebrated [criminal] monograph on the [purloined] Mata papers (but I believe she has since returned those translations). She discusses the suggestive instances of "frustration, aggressivity, regression—the triad of resistances that mark revolutionary pathology," but really, if you think about it, he was probably drunk.

The original papers are not pristine. Some sections have been lost forever. A few remnants are decidedly fantastical, destined for the dustbin: e.g., a set of tyrannical memos that may be direct transliterations from an ancient Indo-Malayan script that for some reason exists otherwise only on a copper jug dug up in Palawan, or Palau.

Curiously, critics from Yogyakarta have both denounced the script as inauthentic as well as demanded that jug's return.

At the same time it seems that Raymundo's manuscript is not entirely innocent of transgressions on the Arabic, though mainly in regard to suspect nouns, e.g., odd mutations on terms for grape derivatives, also of words for "fig." Raymundo has spatterings of Waray (errant strains from his unknown mother?—a tragic story[1]), pidgin and random Cebuano, as well as nominal, surly Ilocano. Elsewhere cryptic notes of Cavite-Chabacano occur, fruity, with a slightly buttery-chocolate taste, good for pork but not fish. In short, a grand Babel of the Filipino soul marinates in the manuscript like some wet mix of adobo, pancit, and lugaw.[2] [3]

It's important to note that his Tagalog, erudite as it is (especially

---

1 Oh the transgressions, you can call them that, on the life of his sad mother! The late lamented Leyteña, Maria Tarcela, or is it Marcela—whom Caviteños fail to acknowledge as the crux—the heart—the haunting ghost in young Raymundo's story—as is the case of all Filipinos and their mothers, if you think about it, really. (Estrella Espejo, Quezon Institute and Sanatorium, Tacloban, Leyte)

2 Ah how I remember the luxury of lugaw as a kid, whenever I was sick in bed and stayed home from school—my mom's specialty, flavored with cinnamon and molasses. Those are the moments I remember most about my robust nanay, maker of sinanlag and ladler of hipon (not that bland Tagalog bagoong!)—her own art, mix of shrimp and chili, with the occult taste of the sea and the earthy residue of baptismal fonts! Not this damned watery vileness—this cheap, mealy mash, this glum slime—that the nurses keep giving me! I have fragility of the nerves, not gum disease: can't I get real, decent rice, at least! (Estrella Espejo, ditto)

3 Fragile nerves! You're a spastic imbecile. I mean, a special ambassador. (Dr. Diwata Drake, Anaheim, California)

when he deals with anatomy), is irreversibly contaminated by the Spanish.

General Mata's use of Spanish must be addressed if any reader is to appreciate this text at all. In 1896, as we all know, Mother Spain was no welter of fabulous ambiguity. Spain was the tyrant of the islands.

Since 1521.

It's true that chunks of conservatism regularly fell off like rotting teeth from the obsolete dentures of the King of Spain. And yes, Spain had commanded the islands by indirection, if not misdirection, via the Viceroy of Mexico, for three hundred seventy-five years—give or take a few months of British occupation of Manila and Cavite (coincidentally, twin rebel *loci* of our hero's childhood).

The worst were the friars—the actual rulers of the islands. At times the only Spaniards in far-flung parishes, the feeble *frailes* kept feeling like Kings.

Sure, some note the religious orders did have their de las Casas[4] [5] [6] [7] [8] types: missionary warriors or navigator-scientists, third sons with ambition in their hearts.

---

4 Really, Ms Translator? Who are you kidding—we had no Bartolome de las Casas in our *sucesos*, no eloquent curser of the conquistadores. We had Padre Damaso and Padre Salvi. Scalawags! *Demonio!* Spoilers of women and faith! Whose side are you on, Ms. Translator?? (Estrella Espejo, ditto)

5 Uuuh. Professor Estrella: Padre Damaso and Padre Salvi were fictional characters created by the hero-novelist Rizal. Though, true: Spanish priests were the devil. And that is the *summa* of Spanish history in the Philippines. (Trans. Note)

6 True! Father Damaso and Father Salvi are brain-children of Rizal, just like the country! Ah, how Rizal portrayed the truth. Just look at the demon friars' spawn, the deathly pale mestizos all around us! Diyos ko 'day! A ghostly people created in ungodly lust! Though I do like their *cochinillo*, t.b.h. (Estrella Espejo, ditto)

7 Uuuuh. Rizal was a mestizo, Professor Estrella? (Trans. Note)

8 Ah, there's the rub. That the country arises from fiction, but this makes the demons no less true. Such is the fate of fantastic Nation. (Dr. Diwata Drake, Copenhagen, Denmark)

In sum: after 1492, when they finally kicked out the Jews, the dregs of Spain's anti-Semitic soldiers found themselves with nothing to do (some were even Jewish). So says the Basque historian Salvador de Madariaga. Many of them took on the cassock and found their notions of grandeur satisfied in a coconut and banana-strewn archipelago, filled with ripe papayas to their hearts' content. They learned the island languages but kept their own tongue. Dictionaries of Chabacano and Pangalatoc and Waray abound, scribbled by nosy, lonesome friars, when they weren't torturing the natives to fetch them water, make them paper flowers, or sculpt their wooden Christs. Not to mention indulging in bedroom affairs (yes, yes, Professor Estrella: they were scalawags and rapists, for whom the above papayas are only metonyms for their ripe lusts!). When the Filipinos came into their own as people of the faith and wanted a piece of the sacristy for themselves—demanding to become priests of their own parishes—hell, no, said the friars. When Filipinos wanted to own their own lands, hell, no, said the friars. When Filipinos began to write their own books, oh no, you don't, they said.

It was the *frailes* who agitated to condemn those fin-de-siècle writers and local printers and native priests and mestizo rebels to death.

However, rebellion in this pelagic not-yet-nation was not so peculiar.

For instance: in 1896, the Filipino rebels' nemesis, Miguel Primo de Rivera, at the time a twenty-six-year-old colonel of the Spanish army in Manila, went on to become the dictator of Spain (1923-1930)—clearly, a premodern type.

Miguel Primo de Rivera became the jailer of the existentialist philosopher Miguel de Unamuno and antecedent of the historical fiasco Francisco Franco. Primo de Rivera turned out to be a thoughtless crusader not only against the insurrectos, as Filipinos were indiscriminately called by the katsila,[9] a.k.a. *coño* (as Filipinos

---

9 Filipinos used the term katsila, or, in the orthography of the time, *kachila*, to refer to both the Spanish person (Castilian/castellano) and the Spanish tongue. Even today, katsila types in Manila are simply called, without irony, *coño*. (Trans. Note)

indiscriminately called the katsila)—but also against his own people, the Spaniards. This comes as no surprise except to all of us who could care less about history.

Should it comfort Filipinos to know that an enemy of their liberators was direct progenitor of a whole bloodline of fascists, founders of the Falangist Party, so that Filipino revolutionaries are linked to saintly anarchists, radical victims, and lovely socialists such as George Orwell, not to mention impotent dilettantes, such as Hemingway?

It should, but this late in history—*que se joda?*,[10] as my mother would say.

And so it is that the nineteenth-century Spanish of this memoir's heroes has about it the romantic fervor of a steamy liaison with a voluptuous mistress—a whole sauna bath of soggy metaphors. Raymundo Mata's prose possesses the Spanish of incipient *amor*: faintly medieval, awash in cultish linguistic sulfur. The academic language of the revolutionaries marries anarchic spleen with romantic chivalry, giving birth to deeply troubling progeny—that is, anti-clerical Masons who went to church.[11]

It is not necessarily to my complete dissatisfaction that the rigors

---

10 Do all mothers have an unconditioned way with words to show their unconditional love, Mimi C.? *Que se joda.* A pungent phrase from my childhood. For my mom, may she rest in peace, that meant, *I do not care, do as your conscience sees fit!* And so I would learn not to disobey—except in my dreams. Later I learned the words meant something else. In this way my mother condemned me, nga birat ka, or silibanco pa man, buot dida, inday, in loving tones that made me buotan: that is, a beloved though bruised daughter. Ave Maria! (Estrella Espejo, ditto)

11 Ah, but is it not so that the cases of our affection are also matters of our split [mis]identifications, Professor Estrella? The above church-going anti-clerical Masons are specimens of humanity, are they not, just like our contemporary Filipinos: who are homophobic gay-lovers and matriarchal misogynists? As a wise proverb of an otherwise secular genius goes: *That he is a trinity tells us even God is empty—a divided self* [Claro Mürk, *Proverbs III*]. (Dr. Diwata Drake, Manila, Philippines)

of history have divorced the country from the Spanish *lengua*.[12] [13] But some regret what was lost in that linguistic divide, namely, a rather large bulk of the nation's patrimony, maybe fifty kilos' worth.

As for the particulars of the Spanish begotten in Raymundo Mata, or misbegotten as the case may be: as we all know now, since Dr. Diwata Drake, late of Magdalen College in Oxford, now gallivanting around the globe, already blabbed all about it before we went to press (but I shall not expound on that here, as the klepto lawsuit is ongoing, I have nothing to do with it)—the general was brought up in a priest's kumbento, in the home of his uncle, an island-born half-katsila of the cassock, committed to Christ.

True, the uncle, called *Tio U.* in this coded diary, seems to have been only a coadjutor, a lowly assistant priest. Who knows what axes this unpromoted man had to grind? He and his brother, Raymundo's father, were mestizo *coño*—sons of a Basque policeman, of the Guardia Civil, and his lowland wife, a businesswoman, specifically, a vendor of lamp-oil. The lowly status of Raymundo's uncle among the Spanish religious orders does make scattered pieces of faith in the papers even more affecting—signs of a nephew's filial piety: e.g., Raymundo Mata's litany to the Latin names of Mary (Entry #12), and so on.

But more interesting: the boy was educated in the theater.

From birth, Raymundo Mata was immersed in the world of make-believe.

His father, Jorge Raymundo Mata, a.k.a. *el genio* Jote, was the priest Tio U.'s beloved wastrel brother—an itinerant actor in provincial melodramas.

Who ended up a bandit.

---

12 A colonial dish of ox tongue, made by my mother with tons of peppercorn and olives. Cooks from other regions—and they know who they are—ruin it with sugar. Shame on them! (Estrella Espejo, ditto)

13 Yes, Estrella, one may call that *lengua* a suspect yet indivisible part of the Filipino stew simmering in the tongue—smothered with soy sauce and garlic, braised later in an American brew: English. (Dr. Diwata Drake, Manila, Philippines)

Sad, but true.

His mother, the Leyteña, Maria Tarcela, or Marcela (her legend remains cloudy), was an actress of religious dramas, Shakespearean follies, and plagiarisms of Alexandre Dumas, *père et fils*, all couched in the fatalisms of the era's faith.

She died young.

This might explain the similarities in morbid sensitivity between Raymundo and another orphaned son of theater, Edgar Allan Poe of America.

In any case, it's no surprise that the language of religious street drama—moro-moro, pasyon, senakulo, all the detritus of the vulgate Bible—infects Raymundo's speech like dengue.

Muddying up the issue are obfuscating whiffs of ancient Roman gas and wanton allusions to classical Greek—indecently undigested. This curse of nineteenth-century syntax was the crap of *latinidades*, the Spanish era's grammar schools of shifty curricula often denounced by its privileged victims. Asides of florid oratory, leaps into Solomonic metaphysics—all of these were hard to stomach, much less translate. Add to this the irritating lapses into indigenous, oracular speech—

I tried my best.

In particular, Raymundo favored the diction of Pontius Pilate, a role he is said to have played several times in Lenten passion spectacles with quite a dash.

His years of furtive education as a bastard child in a baptistry added layers to his style, the effects of which my own speech has yet to banish.

I presume that many of the "set pieces," unusually incoherent paragraphs of disturbing resonance, may have been cribbed verbatim from some philosopher of note, perhaps of the Spanish Enlightenment (though some maintain that term is an oxymoron). He had a freakish memory even as a child, according to Caviteños—those well-meaning citizens on that revolutionary mass off of Manila Bay.

However, it may be, as Professor Estrella suggests, that Caviteños are particularly ill suited to recognize genius.

There is the issue of his night-blindness, a mild yet creeping debility that he seems blissfully to ignore through most of these confessions, a clear triumph of his (manic) will. Tragically, he succumbs to darkness, his old friend, only toward the end, mainly in the guise of sloppy handwriting.

In the center—or, if you will, eccenter—of all of this is the character Raymundo Mata himself.

The man you will find in the manuscript has no approximate precursor in the annals of the revolution, perhaps even of humankind.

The original sheaves are a bunch of papers in multifarious guises—some handwritten, some typed, some in fine script, some practically illegible, some in green ink, some in that crust of sepia drool, with a kind of spiderweb-splatter of time's ink draining from the grainy scrawl.

It's worth no one's while to pillage that mess: but it rewarded my time.

The problems this text presents to a translator are obvious.

Beset in almost each sentence by a question of literary provenance, obscure native diction, and Raymundo Mata's increasingly frightening schizoid tendencies, I gave up and took long meditative walks.

Nevertheless, we the future owe him gratitude.

Curiously Raymundo Mata reverted to English in the latter parts of his journal. At first he seems to write as if testing the waters, in baby-step English if you will. In the end Raymundo mastered English, but English raped him.

You'll see.

Mimi C. Magsalin (pseud.)
B.A. History, University of the Philippines-Diliman & Smith
College; Ph.D. Comparative Literature, minor Asian Studies,
Cornell University (not yet a.b.d.)

Addendum*

First of all, I'm not blonde. Yes, I read the Finnish-Peruvian philosopher retired to the jeweled coasts of Provence—Claro Mürk.

Guilty!

I would wish that crime on my enemies!

However, more pertinently, I'm an American. Of mixed heritage. A Midwestern mongrel. But I'm Filipino on my mother's side. Okay, half-Filipino on my maternal grandmother's side, but the Viking ancestors in my father's Milwaukee line might add Eskimo, so there!

Blondeness is only a pharmaceutical indulgence in my family.

In other words, and I never confessed this to anyone but my first love, who then promptly abandoned me: I'm a bottle blonde, Clairol Spungold #34.

That I have a nervous disposition, I will allow.

As Mürk says, and I paraphrase, to each llama his own symptom.

My papers on the psychoanalysis of the Filipino independence movement are no accident as my own analyst has betrayed to me. The seed was my experience in the Wisconsin public schools. I wanted so much to be part of their group—the dairy-damaged cretins who pulled at my brunette braids and once hung me from the gym rafters in a rug while singing the theme song from *Fiddler on the Roof.*

I'm not Jewish, I kept saying; but I was in a rug, and they couldn't hear me.

My interest in the Philippines was inevitable.

The country has a history of self-loathing that may not be necessarily unfounded.

Estrella Espejo, a scholar from that academic oasis a.k.a. the Republic of Diliman, is a case in point. Her form of victimhood has sad physical reverberations. Let me state here, once and for all, that the publisher Trina Trono asked me to take over the reins of Estrella's editorship as Estrella unraveled from the strains of her malaise.

There was no boat on Kowloon harbor, no bamboo to attack, no Peking duck—all desperate delusions handy for her version of the world.

She was on leave from her university, and who knows what fever dreams she had in her snow-bound apocalypse during her sabbatical in Kalamazoo, wrapped up as she was in the parkas of her estrangement and typing her letters to me with numb fingers, "as moribund in whiteness's spiritual ice as the Abominable Snowman," quote unquote. Estrella was attending a conference and emailed me that winter from a hotel room in Michigan.

She had read my papers on the revolution, e.g., "Sublime Paralysis: Sadomasochism in Mabini's *Decalogue*" and "Sticks and Stones: The Masonic Fetish," chapters of my monumental, unfinished tome, *You Lovely Symptoms*, tentatively subtitled *The Structure of the Filipino Unconscious, Not Really a* Langue, *or a* Parol[e].

She admired my "way with footnotes," as she put it.

Let me add that while Estrella herself, like classic hysterics, resists analysis, she is fatally attracted to pathetic versions of quack therapy.

The signs of creeping astasia-abasia were evident when we first met at that diner in Kalamazoo to discuss perplexing features in the Mata manuscript. She repeated to me—she had flown in from her sickbed! from her historic hometown of Tacloban! to attend this cold, cold, cold, so cold! conference—and I imagine she did not mean only the weather. She spoke in the quivering staccato of seasonal-affective disorder that only a depressive from the tropics will fail to recognize.

It was so critical to her profession, if not her health, she said—to attend this midwinter panel on postcolonial dread.

Yes—it was she who contacted me.

I was innocent from the start.

Just check her sabbatical calendar on Google!

At the diner, a nondescript, strictly Americana affair of lino-leum tables with warped, dust-eaten edges and tin-can vessels for cheap utensils, Dolly Parton coming from the jukebox in the corner, Estrella could barely move her fingers to enclose her hamburger. Pickle relish and mustard kept jumbling out from her fist. I told her it was only a sandwich, not a battle with imperialism. Eat! By the time the ruins of ketchup and lettuce practically reduced the deli waitress to march us out of the premises, Estrella could barely walk out the door.

It seems that random encounters with Western forms cause out-breaks of her illness: she can take Philip Morris cigarettes (especially menthols) but has adverse reactions to Hershey bars. She is allergic to Texas but not New York. She has done very well in Paris. As if in a trance, she kept humming to all the songs on the jukebox—The Eagles, The Carpenters, and especially Journey: she sang the chorus of *Don't Stop Believin'* with a yodeling throb. It was quite affecting. (I believe other symptoms, such as her pronounced and chronic Rizal-fetish—not to mention her brain-damaging, feral regionalism—may be traced to this disease.)

I took her to my apartment, and it was there that I read the man-uscript in the hours before I called 911. I was mesmerized. I confess: I was galvanized into scholarly activity. Estrella was sleeping, pros-trate on my futon, and as long as she looked as if she were breathing I left her alone, holding on to my lead Mongol Pencil #2. I clutched page after page with intolerable desire. Here was a document worth my while: filled with misconstructions of the ego and malaprop-isms of time, affections unnarcotized (banyan trees get more time than the revolutionary Cry of Balintawak—genius!), autistic lists, moving digressions, classic psychopathologies of the tongue (typical of the Filipino, who has an irritating penchant for puns), and, most important, a pervading obsession that baffles the most tolerant prac-titioner, the patient listener.

That patient listener is I: it is I who was meant to edit this volume, not that noisome narcolept on the bed. I called 911 when I realized at three a.m. that she had stopped snoring, and when I put my ear to her mouth there was no sound, no wind, no sign of life. One of the symptoms of her illness, when brought to an acute point, is an involuntary blockage in her trachea. This is a typical offshoot of astasic stress. Trust me, I know whereof I speak. To this day she believes I tried to smother her when in fact I saved her life. But I will explain all this in court (*see* "Verizon Wireless Statement").

Estrella needs to seek a therapist. I hope she gets a good one.

Dr. Diwata Drake
Milwaukee, Wisconsin
August 15, 2005

MANILA CHARACTERS:
A TRANSLATOR'S ABECEDARY OF
THE REVOLUTION OF 1896[14]
By Mimi C. Magsalin (pseud.)

Acrostics and Anagrams

Part of the fun of being a revolutionary was making *anagrams* of your name to hide your identity from Spain's Guardia Civil. E.g., *Oxicam* for Diego Moxica, rebel leader in Leyte; *Damolag* for Magdalo, that is, Miong, that is, General Emilio Aguinaldo of Kawit, Cavite, first president of the Republic; and *M. Calero* for Marcelo [H. Del Pilar], prolific journalist, tireless reformer, and workaholic, byline Madrid. Jose Rizal, the great novelist-hero, author of the romance that begot the nation, did not bother with games and gave himself the most boring Boy Scout *epithet*, Laong-Laan—Ever-ready. Still, the canny secret society of the Katipunan used Rizal's codename as password. Particularly confusing for Guardia Civil who were dyslexic. As for *acrostics*, jokes or slips enlightened raw intelligence: zeal aided luck.[15]

Americans

During the Second World War, destroyed more Philippine libraries and historical matter than Spaniards did during the entire revolutionary war of 1896. At the time *Americans* destroyed Manila in 1945, the islands were both U.S. colony and ally.

---

14 The reader may skip this glossary and flip over to it occasionally as the need arises. On the other hand, it's best to be forewarned. (Trans. Note)

15 Aha!! This acrostic reads: *J-o-s-e R-i-z-a-l*! Jokes or slips enlightened raw intelligence—my foot! The Philippine national hero, writer of the novels *Noli Me Tangere* and *El Filibusterismo*, eye surgeon, polyglot, traveler, martyr, does not deserve being only the butt of a joke, Ms. Translator, Mimi C.! Even worse, introduced only by footnote! Rizal is the center of all things Filipino—though also the undeserving punchline of all things Filipino. To speak his name is to honor the nation. (Estrella Espejo, Quezon Institute and Sanatorium, Tacloban, Leyte)

Andres Bonifacio

The Supremo. Founder of the secret revolutionary society, Katipunan, that eventually overthrew Spain (with brief help of Americans) in 1898. Killed in August 1897. *R.I.P.!* The first and foremost katipunero—i.e., revolutionary. Also called The Great Plebeian. The Great Plebeian was a Great Reader. Nice slogan for a library. Think of other variations: "Supremo—the Supreme Reader!" Et cetera.

Artemio Ricarte

Never surrendered! Refused to pledge allegiance to United States in 1901, exiled to Guam with the *Sublime Paralytic*. Ended up running a turo-turo in Yokohama, serving pancit and adobo to expatriates. His return to the Philippines during Japanese rule in Second World War is very complex topic for a novel.

Balagtas

A.k.a. Francisco Baltazar. Filipino poet. Wrote in Tagalog. Author of *Florante at Laura*. Rizal loved him. Not to be confused with balagtasan: oratorical poetic jousts invented by drunken people.

Blumentritt

Street in Manila. End of jeepney line that begins at Novaliches. Also, Austrian ethnologist (1853–1913). Friend of the Filipino People. Famous letter-writer, especially to *Jose* Rizal. Also sent postcards.

Cryptolect

Secret language a group adopts to prevent others from knowing its business; useful in revolutions and adulterous emails.

Cryptolepts

Psycho readers, *qu'est-ce que c'est?*

Cryptomane

The revolutionaries were in love with codes; they were *cryptomanes*. *Cryptomanes* take pleasure in both art and function of ciphers (not to mention the thrill of being in the know). Do not confuse with *cryptolepts* (deranged people who think everything is in code).

Doctrina Cristiana

First text ever published in the Philippines [c. 1593] containing evidence of indigenous Tagalog script, called Baybayin. So important to national patrimony is kept it in the Library of Congress of the United States.

Emilio, a.k.a. "Miong"

That is, Aguinaldo. Of Kawit, Cavite. First president of the Republic. Childhood friend of the hero Raymundo Mata. Did Aguinaldo kill *Andres Bonifacio,* the Supremo? Who knows? Water under the bridge.

Epifanio de los Santos

Longest avenue in the Philippines. Site of rebellion: also called EDSA. Also, former National Librarian. Invoke full place-name to make knowing remarks about texts, reading, revolution, etc. etc.

Epithet

Second most popular way of honoring heroes (most popular: street signs). Good for quiz shows and crossword puzzles.

Fiesta

Some chronicles note that at times revolution was like a happy *fiesta* (party for the patron saint)—with pintakasi (featured cockfights), gambling, and lots of communal engorgement of free foodstuffs. Enemy cannons provided fireworks.

Fil-Am

Filipino-American. An ongoing conundrum: Is it easier for a rich man to go through the eye of a camel than it is for a *Fil-Am* to understand his parents' country? While the known fact is—it is easier for a camel to go through the eye of a needle than it is for a married child of a Filipino green-card holder to enter the United States! See also *Nora/Vilma Complex*.

Fire, Insects, and Worms, plus Wars and Typhoons

After *kleptos*, great enemies of national heritage. See also *Americans*.

Forgers

Bane of Philippine historiography. Scholars consider some documents to be entirely *forged cryptolects*, such as the un-fact-checked but otherwise fascinating *Minutes of the Katipunan*—not only a possible *forgery* but also completely in code! Talk about criminal genius! Though *forgery* is, okay, a felony, aren't such attempts also an extreme form of *cryptomania*, a kind of love for the revolution? *Forgers* muddle up an already muddled history, but at least they're not *indolent*.

Gom-Bur-Za

One more revolutionary password of the secret society. Also, *neologism* and portmanteau.

Graciano Lopez-Jaena

Propagandist, reformist, orator. Author of "Fray Botod" [Friar Rotten], moral tale that's not as funny as its title sounds. Visayan; wrote in Spanish.

H

Middle initial of Marcelo del Pilar, leader of the Propagandists. Still have no idea what it stands for.

Heidelberg[16]

Flowers floating from *Heidelberg*, Germany, to Manila Bay are a physical impossibility. I think.

Hitler

Grandson of Rizal.

Incunabula, Filipino

Not a lot around. See *Fire, Insects, and Worms, Etc.* See also *Americans*.

Indolence of the Filipinos

Pet peeve of colonizers. The hero Rizal wrote a whole essay refuting it, proving he was industrious. Devote an entire postcolonial graduate seminar to it, called *Industry or Indolence?: Retrospective Recrimination in Current and Colonial Attitudes toward Bla Bla Bla* [name your symptom here].

Jose

Rizal, of course. His first novel, *Noli Me Tangere*, revolutionized art and nation. His second novel, *El Filibusterismo,* is an art-novel miserably read as political tract. His third novel, *Makamisa*, is unfinished. Font of Wisdom, Holy Grail, Martyr Most Prolific, Seed of History, Origin of Words. A bit short, however: only 4'11.

Katipunan

The revolutionary secret society, organized by *Bonifacio*, the Supremo. Glorious name, now an Avenue. Means "association": from verb *tipon* (to congregate). Possibly a completely made-up

---

16 "To the Flowers of Heidelberg." Oh, that poem of the hero Rizal about missing his homeland in the cold climes of Germany while he studied to be a medical doctor so he could fix his mother's cataracts! I sympathize! The temperate climes are Nature's diabolical pox! (Estrella Espejo, ditto)

noun, that is, a *neologism*. Full name of the association: Kataas-taasang, Kagalang-galang na Katipunan ng mga Anak ng Bayan. By the time you finished swearing this mouthful, you got arrested.

Kleptos

One more damned virus of Philippine history, shame on them. Books and manuscripts about the revolution, especially primary sources, have been prey to *kleptos*. A famous case of *klepto* is the theft from the National Library in Manila of the final draft of the *Noli Me Tangere* in Rizal's own hand; and who knows what other manuscripts have been feloniously fondled? Not even the novel's injunction—*Touch Me Not*—dissuaded the thief—who, of course, being *klepto*, had to not only touch it but steal it.

Krag

Civilize them with a. Krag-Jørgensen rifle, the American soldier's weapon of choice in the Philippine-American War (1899–2013), epilogue of the 1896 Philippine revolutionary war against Spain ("Why can't this memoir have only one war instead of two?!" a referee of an acclaimed academic press exclaims, "I'm so confused." So was the nation, lady, so was the nation!). Jaunty motif in a musical wartime slogan, "Civilize them with a Krag!" The Americans were also fond of another weapon, the Colt .45. However, since their imperial misadventure in Manila in 1899, Americans vowed never to subjugate other nations with false alarms of democracy, benevolent assimilation, etc. etc.

Lacuna

Do not confuse with Laguna, a province in Luzon and Jose Rizal's birthplace. Also, a general in the Philippine revolution, first name Urbano.

Mabini

See *Sublime Paralytic*. Sadly, now a street of brothels and murky infamy.

Magsalin

Matronymic of Crisostomo Ibarra, hero of Rizal's *Noli*. His full name was Crisostomo Eibarramendia y *Magsalin* (surname was Basque, cut to Ibarra, for short). The name *Magsalin* is a pun. It means the infinitive transitive verb "to translate" as well as "to transfuse," as in blood. Which makes sense to Filipinos. Rizal's novel about Ibarra *translated* history into fiction and *transfused* a patient (nation) with fresh blood.

Masons

Godless.

Neologisms

Another device of cryptolepts and revolutionaries; also a symptom of certain kinds of brain damage. *Katipunan* may be a *neologism;* so, too, the Tagalog word for freedom, *kalayaan*. Queries the polyglot Rizal to his brother Paciano as he translated the tale "Wilhelm Tell" from German into Tagalog: "I lacked many words, for example *Freiheit*, liberty. The Tagalog word *kaligtasan* cannot be used, because this means that formerly he was in prison . . . I found the noun *malaya, kalayahan*, that Marcelo del Pilar uses. In the only Tagalog book I have—[Balagtas's] *Florante*—I don't find an equivalent noun. The same thing happened to me with the word *Bund—liga* in Spanish, *alliance* in French. The word *tipanan* . . . does not suffice." Excuse me, ehem, Dr. Rizal: Katipunan, anyone? Why could he not think of a word easily coined by the Great Plebeian, *Bonifacio*?

Nora/Vilma Complex

The tendency to think in binaries. As in: if you are not for superstar Nora Aunor, you are for star-for-all-seasons Vilma Santos. If you are not for Vilma, you are for Nora. For instance: if you compare the great actress Nora to a durian, you are insulting Nora. If you compare Vilma to a durian, you are insulting a durian. That is the point of view of a Noranian. If you compare the great actress Vilma to a durian, you do not know what you're talking about. That is the point of view of a Vilmanian. The *Nora/Vilma complex* applies to debates on: girl/boy; class/race; etc. Also, Tagalog versus English; Filipino versus Fil-Am; Rizal versus Bonifacio. Ditto the debate on revolutionary founder of the Katipunan Bonifacio versus everyone else. (Other binaries: Tagalog/Cebuano; Morena/Mestiza; Pangak/Coño; the following are not binaries but *reify the concept of binaries*: Mutt/Jeff; Betty/Veronica; Pugo/Togo; etc.) The Aguinaldo/Bonifacio debate gives off a fishy odor in the Aguinaldo camp. In the Bonifacio camp, the debate is tragic. If you speak against Aguinaldo, you are echoing the prejudice of the Americans against Filipinos at the start of the twentieth century. If you praise Aguinaldo, you are defaming the memory of Andres Bonifacio. If you like Bonifacio, you're a patriot. If you don't know who he is, you are likely *Fil-Am*.[17] [18]

Novena

Nine-day prayer consisting of a series of metonyms. Raymundo Mata's curious *Penitential Novena to Zajir Solé*,[19] addressee in dispute though sense of guilt is obvious, is unfinished.

Our Lady of Antipolo

Patron saint of travelers. *Fiesta* of *Our Lady of Antipolo* was popular day of pilgrimage. Always a good time for katipuneros, disguised as

---

17 Ah, Ms. Translator: I see what you are doing. As you speak of binary thinking, decrying the destructive binary of Filipino vs Fil-Am, you enact binary thinking! A clever stratagem in your neurotic speech: a shrewd *Borromean knot*, if you ask me. But as a non-binary octoroon, I denounce it. (Dr. Diwata Drake, Paris, France)

18 Hehe, Dr. Diwata. Mea culpa. I cannot resist. (Trans. Note)

19 Aha!! That anagram does not escape my eagle ear: Zajir Solé = Jose Rizal! Again! Gotcha, Ms. Translator! Good one, though. (Estrella Espejo, ditto)

devotees, to hold meetings. Also a good excuse for them to drink basi, tuba, lambanog, and all other kinds of rice and coconut-suffused alcoholic drinks during meetings. No wonder no one really knows whatever happened at the election fiasco at the Tejeros Assembly.[20] Or at the momentous Cry of Balintawak. Etc. etc.

Pedro Paterno

Original balimbing, i.e., most consistent traitor among brains of the nation. An elegant Filipino among reformists in Madrid, mocked by Rizal for being "rich and vacuous fop," *Paterno* beat Rizal to printer's press by publishing first Filipino novel (Rizal proclaimed it a dud), titled *Ninay*. Those who played footsie with Americans during American Phase of the Revolution (Paterno, Arellano, Pardo de Tavera, Araneta, et al) became oligarchs of the nation, with too many streets named after them.[21] [22] [23] [24] [25]

---

20 Oh, Tejeros! Site of the treacherous insult to the Great Plebeian, Andres Bonifacio, whose defeat in this original sin of an election fiasco, so common now in our corrupt times, not just in Manila but even in Georgia and Mississippi of the United States of America or Brazil of the other Americas!—this election anomaly was preface to the great hero's assassination, damn you, Miong, a.k.a., General Emilio Aguinaldo, later first president of the Republic! Murderer! Traitor! (Estrella Espejo, ditto)

21 A breathtaking analysis, Mimi C. I love your fine, direct, empirical point here! (Estrella Espejo, ditto)

22 Ah, Estrella. How do you solve the problem of that differential space, of deference and defiance, among leaders of yet-unborn Nation? That is a question Paterno, Aguinaldo, et al, present in Mimi C.'s "breathtaking analysis": how to gaze upon the (albeit also likely venal) Filipino master caste (in class, money, or learning) who are simultaneously mastered by The Master—yoked under the colonial bond? Does that differential space— the wrenched cry even among those with obvious upper hand—signal the crushing force of colonization or the demonic curse of empathy? (Dr. Diwata Drake, Kolkata, India)

23 I mock your differentially spastic—coconut, Dr. Diwata! Ulol na apologist ng may-kapangyarihan. (Estrella Espejo, ditto)

24 Sub-altern! Mon semblable, mon frère! (Dr. Diwata Drake, Paris, France)

25 Tuyaw! Gunggong! Uwat! (Estrella Espejo, ditto)

Phases of the Revolution

Like the moon, creates confusion. Though many trace the seeds of war to the Cavite Mutiny of 1872, the Philippine Revolution began with the Revolution of 1896—the war against Spain. Then comes the Pact of Biak-na-Bato, between Spain and the Philippines, which leads to the revolutionists' exile to Hong Kong. Third comes U.S. Commodore George Dewey, who shipped the revolutionists from Hong Kong to Manila during the American Phase of the Revolution, when Filipinos defeated Spain with American guns and set up the Malolos Republic. The fourth phase of the revolution, the Philippine-American War, is tragic. The final phase—

Plagiarism

Form of flattery.

Puns

Enough already.

Quioquiap

Evil; throw him into history's dustbin but make fun of him first. Counter-reformist Spaniard Pablo Feced was an enemy of Spanish reformists and Filipino writers of the Propaganda Movement. *Quioquiap* was his poison pen name.

Retana, W. E.

Evil; Rizal disliked him. Historical irony: *Retana* ended up in control of many of Rizal's papers.

Schoolhouses

Rizal's obsession; what he built in exile in Dapitan. Much admired by Rizal's fan, Raymundo Mata.

Sublime Paralytic

Sublime *epithet*. A genius cripple who directed war from his rattan rocking chair a.k.a. butaka. Reason for his famed paralysis: unknown. Hero Most Admirable: like *Ricarte*, refused to pledge allegiance to the Americans. Exiled to Guam, died in grace. See *Mabini, Apolinario*.

Tanaga

Popular Filipino textual form. Unlike the balagtasan, moro-moro, *Urbana at Feliza* epistolary manual, *Doctrina Cristiana*, novenas, zarzuelas, medieval romances, folk legends, riddles, slumbook pages, etc., it is not mentioned in this manuscript. Now it is.

Unamuno, Miguel D.

Existentialist Basque philosopher. Born 1864 in Bilbao, Spain, died 1936 in Salamanca, Spain. Liked Rizal. Really, really liked Rizal. Couldn't decide what to call him: Tagalog Hamlet, Oriental Don Quixote, Filipino Christ, Tagalog Christ-Quixote, Compendium of History, et cetera. Also called The Indecisive Spaniard.

Valenzuela

Now a town in Bulacan. Dr. Pio *Valenzuela*'s famous visit to Rizal in Dapitan indirectly led to the hero Rizal's death. Oops. Dr. Pio Valenzuela's companion on that fateful visit was our memoir's hero, Raymundo Mata.

Writing Memoirs

Popular form of exculpation, axe-grinding, factoid-making, score-settling, self-immolation. Some categories of memoirs include: Fun Facts, Prison, Published-When-All-Relevant-Witnesses-Are-Dead, Sublime Analysis, Second-Try-Because-First-Testament-Was-A-Disaster,

Minor Character, Musician, Unclassifiable.[26] Other types (comparative) are: Mirror Memoirs; Duel Memoirs; and Plain Conflicting Memoirs. The Philippine Revolution has been the subject of all of the above.

X
Not the best option when signing your name in blood.

Youth
Raise high thy brow serene.

Zamboanga
The town of Dapitan is in the province of *Zamboanga*, on the island of Mindanao, southernmost and second largest landmass of the archipelago. Very far away from the capital, Manila. Rizal was exiled there in 1892. Site of famous meeting between heroes Raymundo Mata and Jose Rizal.

---

26 In order, from *Fun Facts* to *Unclassifiable* respectively, these are some examples from the Philippine revolution: memoirs of Santiago Alvarez, Artemio Ricarte, Emilio Aguinaldo, Apolinario Mabini, Pio Valenzuela, Antonino Guevara, Julio Nakpil, Raymundo Mata.

Reading and Writing:
Some Notes on the Author's Patrimony
By Estrella Espejo

*"Since the beginning of the colony, boldness, deceit, and
acrimonious speech have had a foremost seat, but greed is today
the dominant passion in the white people. Their needs are
many and there are few means of satisfying them."*

Okay, okay, so let the blonde scholar have her say.

Yes, it is I who showed her Mimi C. Magsalin's translated text.
I have yet to recover from my error.

On my hospital bed here at the sanatorium among the coconut
groves of Leyte's storied beaches, where Douglas MacArthur the
general landed in triumph and Ferdinand Magellan the circumnavi-
gator landed only to die, that's what he got, killed by us, the Visayans!
Hah!—may I add a few remarks on imperial commentators.

It may surprise some to know that the above insightful statement
came not from nineteenth-century Filipino reformists Graciano
Lopez-Jaena or Marcelo H. del Pilar. Not even Dr. Jose Rizal, the
national hero, executed by the Spaniards in Bagumbayan for his
"pernicious" first novel, was so explicit.[27]

No, the author of the above was a Spanish military official, probable antecedent of our glorious hero Raymundo.

---

27 The Spanish government's indictment of Jose Rizal, dated December 26, 1896, is a
curious type of tyranny: literary criticism sentenced him to death. Instead of proving his
treason, the indictment goes on about his writing style: "His harangues *bla bla bla* are full
of clichés *bla bla bla* [italics mine] . . . is neither a competent writer nor a profound thinker
bla bla bla. The products of his pen *bla bla bla* betray a most imperfect command of the
language *bla bla bla*." The judge-literary-critic finds most offensive the defendant's ability
to speak Spanish. *Note:* Rizal also spoke French, German, English, Italian; he conversed
with a bunch of Bavarian medical students in their common language: Latin; however,
he failed to finish his last novel, begun in Tagalog, and he never learned the fine language
of my birthright that Magellan's own scribe, the venerable Italian Pigafetta, found fit to
decipher: that sophisticate's tongue, Waray.

General Juan Manuel de la Matta occurs in history as the author of a report to the governor and captain-general[28] of the islands on February 25, 1843.[29] Thus the life of the Matas [Mattas] in the Philippines begins with *writing*. Each Mata [Matta] shares pet peeves.

Born in Kawit, Cavite—birthplace also of Miong, a.k.a. General Emilio Aguinaldo, later first president of the Republic—Raymundo Mata spent a cheerful youth swimming among mangroves, shitting in the Binakayan river with his boon companions, Miong and Candido Tria Tirona, a.k.a. Idoy, and discovering his manhood with the most loyal and beloved confrères, Benigno Santi and Agapito Conchu (with whom in grammar school he formed this memoir's precious triumvirate, the Three Musketeers of San Roque).

His childhood, of course, had an ominous frame—the legendary Cavite Mutiny, precursor of the Revolution of 1896.

But during the Mutiny, he was only a kid, munching on guavas.

An infirm boy whose disability became his ironic claim to fame, Raymundo was bullied, *siempre*, in elementary school, at the Escuela de Niños, and at grammar school, the Latinidad de Jose Basa, where he met the tragic Agapito, his first love, and the saintly Benigno, his last friend.

It is unlikely that he saw his future, unrequited *amor*, Rizal the bookworm, in the hallways of the Ateneo Municipal when he transferred to that more prestigious high school in the capital, Manila. By the time Raymundo arrived in Manila, Rizal was a success in Europe,

---

28 As noted in Blair and Robertson, *The Philippine Islands, 1493-1898*. Volume 52, 91. All quoted passages above are from pages 91-111 of that volume.

29 The date corresponds to such celebrated incidents as the Battle of San Juan, which began the Philippine-American war in 1899; and the more modern Revolt of 1986, which overthrew the dictator Marcos and his wife Imelda, La Abuelita Loca (not a good representative of the Warays, by the way)—history recycles glory in mysterious ways. But what the hell's in the tsokolate tablea during the month of February??!

toast of the reformists in Madrid and Barcelona, of Spaniards and Filipinos alike, globetrotting medical student who published novels in Berlin and Belgium and traveled even as far as New York, in America (where he thought the nation's industry was marvelous but its slave-history a disgrace).

But like Rizal, the young Raymundo was a mad scribbler at the Ateneo—he jotted juvenile sentiments in diaries, wrote bad plays, inscribed love letters to witchy women, and made tsismis—puerile, unworthy gossip!—about his rabble-rousing male friends, in code.

If one thing characterized the hero Raymundo Mata, it was his gift for idolatry.

In August 1896 Raymundo took up arms against the "white people," having joined the secret revolutionary society, the Katipunan, five months earlier.

No less than the founder of the Katipunan, Andres Bonifacio, the Supremo, swore Raymundo into the Society (his old childhood friend Miong also came along, but that's another story).

Raymundo, inexperienced in both love and war, was barely out of his teens in 1896—bookish, dreamy, and night-blind.

Not an auspicious recruit.

(In fact Miong later claimed he did not really want him along at the initiation rites of the Katipunan, because, quote unquote, even as a kid Raymundo was a loon. On the kalesa leading to the initiation, Miong made jokes about his friend's redundant blindfold, and their small altercation before the Katipunan blood compact was not a good sign.)

Raymundo put his life into the revolution. In fact, he gave it to the cause. It's not so clear exactly what he did.

His role in revolt has been shrouded in obscurity.

Until this memoir.

A boat ride he took with Dr. Pio Valenzuela to see the ophthalmologist and novelist, Dr. Jose Rizal, was a disaster, so say judgmental historians.

But in the memoirs, as you will see, Raymundo made much of his short acquaintance with the martyr.

Just like his descendant Raymundo Mata, the Spanish official General de la Matta of 1843 lambasted Spaniards—Filipino Spaniards in particular, that is, whiteys born in the Philippine islands, also known as *Filipinos* (today's Filipinos, as we know, were not originally Spanish cookies—shame on you, Spanish biscuit company, go to hell![30]—since Filipinos were at the time called *indios*, not to be mixed up with Indians, who actually called themselves Pequots or Mashantucket or Lakota, not subcontinental "Hindoos"; and so on and so forth in this mindless game of history tag).

Among the jewels of intuition in the 1843 Matta Report are Matta's characterization of his own people, his indictment of the Spanish clergy, his prophecy of violent doom if Spain failed to make reforms, and his malice toward lawyers—sentiments also applicable to his descendant.

Of the Spanish friars [Matta notes with impartial sagacity]:

> [Their] gross manners, stupid pretensions, and exactions
> from the chiefs of the provinces and the gobernadorcillos
> and notables of the villages occasion anger, quarrels and
> discord which disturb the quiet of the inhabitants, distract
> and embarrass the authorities, and nourish those indis-
> creet and tenacious struggles in which all lose.

Thus, as early as 1843, in a nutshell General de la Matta summarized the demons of Spanish dominion, the friars, that prefaced

---

30 Traveling in Spain, you will still find, manufactured by the devilish Artiach Biscuit Company, *con autentico chocolate negro*, "these authentic Filipinos, cookies dipped in dark chocolate that you can eat with your friends. You can put these Filipinos in the fridge, they are delicious." *Que horror!* Savagery and cannibalism in the grocery aisle! But, as always, no one is surprised.

all sorts of rants against Spain during the time of the revolution—among both Spanish civil servants and the revolutionaries who opposed them.

General de la Matta, of course, was no revolutionary, so his secular venom is remarkable.

Whereas, to our modern ears, the anticlerical rage ("indiscreet and tenacious") of Raymundo Mata (or even of Rizal, for that matter) is trite, obsolete, commonplace—the spite of subalterns.

So goes the sad march of history—the wars we waged become tiresome tropes, and blood spilled turns into flesh only in the words of unexpected men.

General de la Matta goes on:

> It must be kept in mind that ambition is wont to affect the Spanish people transplanted to these distant and hot climes; that arrogant presumption is their distinctive characteristic . . . The hot climate especially contributes to captiousness and the development of vehement passions.

Even including the unnecessary asides on Philippine weather, Raymundo Mata himself would not have described the captious Other more pungently [Spanish guardia or American colonel]—their greedy "ambitions," their "arrogant presumption."

Such descriptions of the enemy from the enemy himself are revelatory for all readers of Raymundo's memoirs.

The words of General de la Matta, precursor of Raymundo

Mata,[31] [32] [33] allow us to see, once more, darkly, the reality of oppression and the justice of Raymundo Mata's war.

Not much is known of Raymundo's view of the American Phase of the Revolution, a.k.a. the Philippine-American War. Captured by Americans, Raymundo was in Bilibid jail until 1902, apparently collating these memoirs in between bouts of water torture.

I assume that the haphazard nature of their compilation, still to be fully comprehended, attests to the squalor and terror of his last days.

Did he die in jail?

No one knows.

One Francis Saint Clair Watson, or Clair Watson Saint Francis, a British journalist or American G.I., who cares, he's racist, was the last to see Raymundo Mata alive.

---

31 This ingenious detail is instructive—that General de la Matta, Spanish *intendiente* and thus enemy of the people, is ancestor of the protagonist Mata. I urge Estrella in this moment of oracular sanity to pursue her analogy. The 1843 Matta Report is a *mirror text*—the words of the Other that allow us to pierce a knowing of that which eludes and exculpates, hides and always seeks: the Rapscallion Self. In this way knowledge occurs by distortion—for a mirror is never truth, and yet *for a while* it relieves us of the burden of not knowing (*cf.* Mürk, *Parables I*, "The Speculum"; *cf.* "The Shape of the Sword," an Argentine *ficción*). The actual, complete text of the 1843 Matta Report—craftily cobbled above from disparate portions of the document—is racist, anti-Filipino, and vicious. And yet from antipathy how strange that, according to Estrella, truth arises. Estrella, isn't it both a genetic and symbolic marvel that Mata contains within himself the Enemy, his ancestor Matta, so that the Self "like a vertiginous Russian doll concatenates into a delirium of recuperated animosities, a precious history of revulsion" out of which truth erupts [Mürk, *Random Sayings*. Eds. Dux, Drake, et al.]? In short, it is possible that *we are whom we despise*, and sadly vice versa. (Dr. Diwata Drake, Kalamazoo, Michigan)

32 I have no idea what you're talking about. You are gobbledygook to me. (Estrella Espejo, ditto)

33 I propose this question—and I propose it timidly, as I am still a graduate student after all these years, doing only a minor in Cornell's Asian Studies Department: Are we kind of forgetting that General de la Matta and Raymundo Mata may not be related? (Trans. Note)

An interesting footnote is that he was jailed not for sedition but theft, possibly a clerical error.

What Raymundo left behind are a bunch of papers, messy and a bit of a pain, a few cockpit debts, an empty leather medical bag, and books.

A distinctive quality of this war was its reliance on *reading*—literacy was the charming obsession of many a revolutionary.

Annoying foreign observers such as Saint Francis Clair Watson, or Francis Clair Saint Watson, said Americans came to "civilize" the "natives." Of course, this is an irony not lost on a single Filipino forced to read all three hundred forty-two pages and nine hundred ninety-nine thousand words of *Noli Me Tangere* in high school! (And *I* had to read Rizal in translation, in Tagalog—but Warays will do anything for the nation.)

The American Revolution had farmers and dentists. The French Revolution had a mob of lawyers.

Our prime mover was a poet.[34]

The Philippines may be the only country whose war of independence began with a novel (and a first novel at that)—Rizal's *Noli Me Tangere* ("Touch-Me-Not").

Our notion of freedom began with fiction, which may explain why it remains an illusion.

Rizal's own modest reading of the aims of his novels at the time of his 1896 trial, in which he rejects the life of politics, must be completely ignored as the muted ravings of a rational guy who did not want to die.

---

34 Take note: he was also an ophthalmologist (an occupation that some rashly view as a *figure of speech* for his poetry's surgical attempts). His Austrian friend Blumentritt, so conjoined in spirit with Rizal that they liberally shared metaphors, has noted that the country's ills were a "cataract" and Rizal was their surgeon. This memoir of the night-blind Raymundo Mata is significant in this respect: it is the lengthiest extant chronicle by a patient who consulted Dr. Rizal. However, one must not blame Rizal for Raymundo Mata's subsequent woes—the patient's errors are his own.

The Supremo Andres Bonifacio, founder of the Katipunan, the secret society, was a fan of Rizal, worse than a Noranian. It is now understood with some regret that Bonifacio's raid on the Manila arsenal at the outbreak of war, which led to the Supremo's hurried flight to Cavite—and sadly his death (damn damn damn the Caviteños)—may have been a literary allusion: inspired not by careful military planning but by the gunpowder plot in Rizal's second novel, *El Filibusterismo*, or *Sedition*.

Hence, its doomed, though inspiring, failure.

By 1896 readers were risking their lives all over the place to smuggle pamphlets and decode anagrams of heroic names. Membership to the Katipunan rose dramatically with the publication of the first (and last) distributed issue of a newsletter, *Kalayaan*. Histories of the war refer constantly to memos to the warfront, distributed decalogues, intercepted letters, confiscated libraries.

It is said that unread peasants gained revolutionary passion via the recitation of pasyon, the holy narration of the death of Christ. The peasant katipuneros were vessels of material text as much as of their unworldly God.

Lastly, an argument in a printing press led prematurely to revolt. *It's a truism that our revolution existed—and lives on—as text.*

One revolutionary, Juan Maibay, relates reading aloud the published principles of the Katipunan to a bandit, Matandang Leon Matulis,[35] [36] in the middle of a jungle at the height of wartime before finally initiating the thief into the revolutionary society.

---

35 Estrella, if you are referring to the story in Santiago Alvarez's *The Katipunan and the Revolution*, please note: the revolutionary who initiated the bandit (who became General Luis Malinis by the way; the tulisan Matandang Leon had already died in the war's first skirmish, near Balara) was Genaro de los Reyes, not the medicine man Juan Maibay; and the event occurred after breakfast in someone's home, not in the swamps of Makati. (Dr. Diwata Drake, Makati, Philippines)

36 Juan—Genaro—Luis—Leon—who cares. It's the thought that counts. (Estrella Espejo, ditto)

See Entry #42.

And of course many of the unfortunate mysteries and miserable lacunae in the war's narrative occur because bibliokleptomaniacs abound, lurking in the stacks of dim libraries.

One notes below a passage from a text Raymundo admired as a boy:

> There is between savage and civilized life an "irrepressible conflict." Where the hum of human industry is heard, with villages, churches, schools and manufactories, there can be no forest left for buffaloes, bears, and deer. Civilization was rapidly supplanting barbarism, and the savages were alarmed.

Such anti-colonial, pro-environmental sentiment appears in *Lives of the Presidents of the United States of America*, a book read and re-read by Raymundo, also a fixture on the shelves of Andres Bonifacio, the Supremo and Great Plebeian; referred to in a letter by Jose Rizal, National Hero and Martyr of Bagumbayan; and even annotated by the brains of the revolution, Apolinario Mabini, the Sublime Paralytic; but not heard of at all by Miong, a.k.a. General Emilio Aguinaldo, later first president of the Republic—the Only Non-Reader of the Bunch!

And look where that got him—ambushed by the Americans!

Texts such as the above must have stoked the reader Raymundo Mata's revolutionary hatred for "churches" and enflamed love for exotic wild animals, buffalo and deer (non-existent in Manila but *que se joda*). Raymundo could not help but side with the "alarmed savages" in the above book, with those victims of nineteen-year-old George Washington's genocidal hunting rifle in 1748 (an English long-rifle used in the Americas' wars against Indians, precursor of the Krag). Such identification with Native

Americans, through *texts*, must have been a guiding light for our heroes—

Then why the hell they were so easily duped by Commodore George Dewey and the murderous Krags of the Philippine-American War of 1899 is what I want to know![37]

---

37 It is true that an 1867 translation of John S. C. Abbott's popular history of American presidents was in the Supremo Andres Bonifacio's library (confiscated by Spanish authorities when the secret society was unmasked). But please note Abbott's unenlightened description of the "savage" Indians: "They . . . resolved, *Satan-inspired* [italics mine], to sweep every vestige of civilization from the land, that this continent might remain *a howling wilderness* [I decline to annotate this last resonant phrase in this American volume, emphasis mine, written decades before the memorable words spoken about the Philippine province of Samar by U.S. General Jacob 'Howling Wilderness' Smith in 1901]."
It is wishful thinking to imagine that the Filipino heroes identified solely with the Indians. In fact, their interpretive lapse and ardent identification, with the likes of George Washington, were tragic [*see* "The Purloined Krag," my online monograph in *Postcolonial Retrospection: Studies in Stereotomy Volume II*, still in painful reconstruction; I posit instead an *inter-framing* in the *crosshairs* of the Philippine-American War, in which the rebel must pellucidly situate himself as *both* Washington *and* Indian, a difficult acrobatic performance]. Who knows, dear Professor Estrella—educated Filipino rebel leaders perhaps *misread* Abbott's American history? Even Rizal, in his equivocal way, said of America that she was the most likely "rival" to Spain if war ever did come, but "acquiring possessions beyond the seas . . . [was] against [America's] traditions." *Sic.* Heroically, Filipino rebel leaders saw themselves as the American George Washington brandishing a revolutionary gun. When sadly, on the Other hand, in the eyes of the Americans, they were "savage" Indians soon to be slaughtered by the U.S. Army. Thus, shit happened. (Dr. Diwata Drake, Plymouth, Massachusetts)

On With the Book!
By Dr. Diwata Drake

Claro Mürk, the renowned archeologist of the unconscious, in defining the Self, astutely revisited what Galileo on his deathbed said of the earth: *it moves*.

What is a book?

It's in flux.

What is a man?

An unfinished tome.

And what's the state of the postcolonial country founded on the image of another's desire?

Undone.

So let's get on with it already.

I enclose here, perhaps rashly, the urgent progress of the manuscript, warts, queries, and all, a history of a book deferred and interrupted.

We cannot wait any longer.

This work, annotated by yours truly—a mongrel, mixed-race foreigner, true, an American-born professor formerly of Magdalen College, Oxford, now on [voluntary!] sabbatical—and translated by, okay, a too-young Fil-Am grad student, born in [unknown Filipino place-name], educated in Manila and Cornell, not quite a.b.d., and, sorry, randomly interrupted by that whiny, I mean, wily, Waray, fulsome scholar of nationalism, Tacloban-born-and-bred, Estrella Espejo, who first presented details of the ms. at a conference in Milwaukee, not Kauai, while on sabbatical—rest in peace, Estrella! in your sanatorium!—this work, *The Revolution According to Raymundo Mata*, is a pre-emptive text, one might say.

We publish it before judgments settle and understanding congeals.

We publish it in haste as advance copies of the book have inadvertently leaked out. (Contrary to others' blind insinuations—the culprit is still at large.)

And already critics promote vile rumors.

I will attempt here a brief calming note.

Yes, it is true that a pall hangs over this manuscript, a tragic tale of both loss and recovery. Yes, especially in its midsection, from Entry #33 onward, it is an adventure story without a corpse, a mystery without a detective, an autobiography without a cause.

Be patient, read on.

No, it is not true that the original manuscript has completely disappeared.

Reader, keep calm.

We possess fine translations.

As the publisher Trina Trono says: it is a hazard of history.

Trina Trono advises all concerned that the actual manuscript in the fragile forms of its slapdash conception is forthcoming, she is rummaging through her personal effects given the violent passing of some abominable typhoon, she has lost contact with—and the line was a bit garbled—she has lost Internet service, et cetera, et cetera.

Do not worry—in Manila, something *always* comes up.

But the future cannot wait forever.

So we present this bundle, a small cosmogony, one might say, of indecisions and revulsions.

An uncertain universe, true—but what else is there?

Pardon its unglamorous state therefore, the scratches in its margins, and this unappeased aporia, appalling in its own way—patched up as our enflamed reading progressed.

Critics of the pirate copies have decried "a paratextual prolixity . . . that tears at the Filipino soul but holds on to its stitches," a bitter calumny.

If you will notice, by the end of the document we were silent (or at least those of us with tact kept our mouths shut).

Especially in the latter entries, we made it clear Raymundo Mata spoke for himself.

However, the reader will observe that the beginnings of the

journals, Part One and some sections of Part Two, embody awkward morphologies of larval textual forms and other distressing aspects of the memoirist's gestational phase.

In short, scripts and scraps of botched and fractured texts begin the story.

We deemed it best to address those spirited voids—hence, the footnotes.

Some of us, you will agree, were more lucid than others.

In these first sections the writer seems to test his strengths and finds unwitting, at times unwilling, vessels for his verbiage.

Francisco Balagtas, a.k.a. Baltazar, the eminent Tagalog poet, plus a slew of dead French novelists writhe in their graves, trifled with, preyed upon.

Let them squirm.

Like any biographical tale this text contains false starts, red herring, dead ends, mysterious trails.

The patient reader will embrace the flapping embryonic gills, the infant passages from which Nation emerged, including alphabet games, morality plays, Catholic litanies, and frank delusions.

Bless that reader.

May she meet us one day in paradise, or maybe a book club in Queens.

The rest may proceed at your own discretion.

Those who wish to begin elsewhere, say at Entry #21, when Raymundo finds the weapon of language in Manila, or even later, at Entry #25, a critical moment of initiation, may do so.

Go ahead. The text exists at your leisure.

Tumble through it as you wish, but please do not blame us for your concussions.

Finally, a quirk of this text is that it includes an editorial unraveling.

Filipino scholarship has an endemic originality: it is stained by passion.

You will note a chronological set of querulous attachments, a marked departure from critical protocol that some experts of the advance guard have assailed with paltry wit as "a scholarly dissipation," "not academic arrangement but derangement," et cetera et cetera—and so it is that their gross applause provides ground for this edition's remarkable candor.

Enclosed herewith are the underbeams of the text's construction—a rumbling exegesis by email, anathema, and dyspeptic scrawl (o writer, you know who you are), which I am loath to qualify or condemn without a lawyer nearby.

Caveat lector.

However, I suggest that this construction is no different from what anyone has vaguely divined about the world: that history is a devil's brew of the three I's—*I, I, I!* Among others: innuendo, ideology, and idolatry.[38]

Let the reader embrace history as it lies: *ecce homo.*

Here's the book!

---

38 Not to mention imitation, invocation, and inspiration. (Estrella Espejo, Quezon Institute and Sanatorium, Tacloban, Leyte)

The Revolution According to Raymundo Mata

by

Raymundo Mata

Part One

~~~

A Childhood in Kawit

In which the hero learns the alphabet—Spends time with play-mates Miong and Idoy at idyllic Binakayan stream—Recites Balagtas at precocious age—Enrolls at Escuela de Niños—Reads a lot—Recalls Terror of Cavite (also known as Cavite Mutiny)—Records history of family—*Mother, a Visayan artist, dies of tuberculosis—Father, dramatist, actor, and fan of Cavite Mutiny's Padre Burgos, flees Kawit—Uncle, assistant parish priest of San Felipe, brings up abandoned child*—Enrolls at Latinidad de Jose Basa—Meets best friends Benigno Santi and Agapito Conchu—Passes time with fruit bats—Alludes to Rizal's historic *Noli*—Meets father, in disguise: the Cavite bandit *el genio* Jote[39]

---

39 A few notes on hero's paternal grandparents (his maternal ancestors being unaccounted for), not mentioned in the memoir nor gleaned from files in Sevilla, Spain; Valladolid, Spain; and the Departmental Archives of the Basque Pyrenees, Spain—instead, a bountiful harvest comes from family interviews: in Binakayan, Cavite; Quinapundan, Samar; and Vacaville, California; and from telltale gaps in the hero's account, not to be ignored:

Raymundo's grandfather, Raymundo Mata Eibarrazeta, was said to be a soldier (half Basque, all bravado) whose ancestors hailed from the Spanish Pyrenees. Storytellers of Kawit, Cavite, narrate that the elder Raymundo had a checkered career in the Spanish militia and retired with his temper intact in the environs of Cavite's ports, married to a Chinese vendor of lamp oil. True, none of this is corroborated in documents in Sevilla or Valladolid—no mention of one Raymundo Mata Eibarrazeta of Jaca or Kawit occurs in official lists—worse, the memoirist's Chinese ancestry is completely erased, as usual. For authenticity, we rely on the hero's recall and the [dubious] accounts of inflammatory Caviteños. (Estrella Espejo, Quezon Institute and Sanatorium, Tacloban, Leyte)

Entry #1

love my father's yellow stream buttnaked green coconut open to surprise cuckoldroaches-dancing-in-a-cone Porkrind-Chronicles salt-weep of fish Emilia [*sic*] Christmas lights Padre Mariano Gomez (r.i.p.) my gonads! indios Jorge Raymundo Mata scabs lanzones deeply ripe mangoes navel-orange thighs[40] [41] [42]

---

40 Raymundo Mata begins his diary with gibberish. This can only be Katipunan code, the secret weapon of the secret society. The list's complete meaning remains a mystery, though one discerns the name of one of the three martyr priests—Mariano Gomez—friend of the Mata family and beheaded by Spaniards in that incident that foretold the revolution, the Cavite Mutiny of 1872. The priest's name occurs almost in the same breath as that of the future general's father, Jorge Raymundo Mata. Thus, this opening refers to the family's connection to the Cavite Mutiny. Town lore proclaims that the Mata brothers, priest and actor both, had been involved in the uprising, using dramatic disguises to foment revolt. (Estrella Espejo, Quezon Institute and Sanatorium, Tacloban, Leyte)

41 Katipunan code or not, there is method in this madness. Globular shapes are classic imago of the pre-mirror stage: the maternal mangoes, not to mention the direct reference to navels, show the general awash in *vagitus*—"the infantile cry" way before the mirror stage—"the first stammerings of speech" [*vid*. Mürk, "Message to the Antibes Plenary," 1953]. Of course, the reference to the father is an obvious (and, to be honest, banal) allusion to The Father. (Dr. Diwata Drake, Kalamazoo, Michigan)

42 The text begins with the following list: "*ama rillo, bukong nabuko, cucurachas, chicharon de* Chirino, *daing ng daing*, Emilia [or Emilio, handwriting unclear], *faroles*, Padre Gomez, etc etc . . ." My guess is that General Mata, a child at the time as the clumsy handwriting shows, plays an abecedary game (*a is for amarillo*, etc.) lifted from school exercises and common to bored children. His alphabet is unfinished; the last word is *naranjitas*. His game is marked by ingenious, though childish, puns—hard to translate. He code-switches, as in "ama," which means "father" in Tagalog but 'she/he loves' in Spanish; "Rillo" is a town from Castile-La Mancha, studded with little streams, or rills. *Amarillo*, of course, means the color yellow. My rough translation of his trope, *ama rillo*, connotes the crudeness of his humor. Similarly, the wholly Tagalog *bukong nabuko* may be interpreted as personification (*nabuko* denoting chagrin, uncommon to buko, young coconuts) or rhetorical emphasis (as in "chagrined chagrin," an annoying tautology). An occult allusion to Russian aristocrat Nabukoff is abject and must be avoided. However, the vulgar imagery of the surprised-open coconut is inescapable in the phrase. In this case, I made compromises but kept the ambiguity intact (I think). My own favorite translation is "saltweep of fish"—*daing ng daing* in the admittedly more accomplished Tagalog. I consider my phrase a fine evocation of the young Mata's wit. I could not duplicate its lyrical malady. (Trans. Note)

Entry #2

January 20, 1872[43] [44] [45]

---

43 This is, of course, the year of the Cavite Mutiny, vestigial phase of the revolution of 1896. The *Calendar for Manileños* corroborates the year. But the *Calendar* is unreliable (it has no bibliography); so I checked Agoncillo's *Revolt of the Masses*. Hah! The exact date of the Mutiny. (Trans. Note)

44 On this date, fiesta fireworks went off near Manila, specifically Bilibid, a jail town visible at the time from Cavite (now obscured by miles of videoke bars and the diesel belch off Southern Luzon Expressway). Philippine-born soldiers (a.k.a. insulares) of the Spanish arsenal in Cavite mistook fiesta noise across Manila Bay as a signal for battle (but why?!), and so began a sorry *motin*. A bourgeois riot, similar to the Boston Tea Party instigated by American-born British merchants. Some historians call this "the first labor strike" in our history. I call it katangahan, yes, *idiocy!*—typical of the tragic absurdities that bedevil the province of Cavite. The mutiny ended up killing *Gom-Bur-Za*: three innocent priests of varying tendencies: Mariano Gomez, Jose Burgos, and Jacinto Zamora—their unmerited deaths are further proof of the errors of Cavite! (Estrella Espejo, Quezon Institute and Sanatorium, Leyte)

45 Clue: *three-syllable dvandva used as Katipunan password.* Answer: *What is* Gom-Bur-Za??? And why was it a revolutionary password? *Because* Gom-Bur-Za *mattered!* No one (except *certain invalid scholars* mired in primitive spleen) disputes the importance of the Cavite revolt (just as few would portray the Easter Rising of 1916 only as some drunken Irish mayhem—though some have tried). The rise of native clergy threatened the Spanish orders. Of course, while Filipinos hated the clergy, they also wanted to become priests. A common schizophrenic polarity. The real problem, Estrella, is that Filipinos revere *GOMBURZA* as if each priest-martyr were equally marvelous. Whereas the facts of the Cavite Mutiny are a glorious case of dysrecognition and mis(taken)identification. Every Filipino should take a stab at interpreting their mess(age). In "The Garrulous Garrote: What *GOMBURZA* Says," I point out that the priest-triad Gomez-Burgos-Zamora is, yes, a pancit mix, a noodle combination that will never cohere. The triplet priests, each of whom has nothing to do with the others, are a *symbolic knot*. Sure, Padre Mariano Gomez, aged saintly reformist, was by then retired and unjustly arrested. And Padre Jacinto Zamora was just a *jugador*, an unlucky gambler innocently caught in the scene of the mutiny. No wonder he lost his mind at the scaffold: he thought all he'd been doing during the mess around him was losing at cards! But it was above all Padre Jose Burgos, the Philippine-born prodigy, radical heresiarch—*he* was the genius provocateur, prelude to the overbearing genius, Rizal. His talents as orator, philosopher, and elegant blasphemer—the panoply of his skills—give lie to the notion of equality among this Holy Trinity. Father Burgos is the center of tragedy in the Cavite Mutiny. Thus, *GOMBURZA* was no salutary unity and singular heroic entity but, yes, a split identity, a bad *yoke*: sad fate of the signifier. But that does not lessen its importance. (Dr. Diwata Drake, Clyde, Ohio)

Miong, Idoy, and I[46] went off to the banyan grove. We played the game *Guess What the Branches Look Like, Tanga!* Stumps of gnarls and tangled crosses. Corpses, scimitars, and rocking chairs.

Buta ka, buta! Butaka.[47] [48] [49] [50]

We went to the river—our usual games. Tuktukan again— Miong's favorite sport. God, Miong has huge eggs like a dinosaur's, an auroch's. Where does he get them? I lost at tuktukan again. My eggs are always too—weak. Then we went on a hunt for wild guavas. We shot all the green ones into the water. They made plopping noises like shit. Then Miong took off his pants under the sampaloc trees.[51] [52] We're like that—nature is our arousal. We raise

---

46 Future Katipunan generals Miong, a.k.a. Emilio Aguinaldo, later first president of the Republic, and Idoy, a.k.a. Candido Tria Tirona, were the memoirist's earliest pals. Idoy was Raymundo's cousin who died a hero in the First Phase of the Revolution—the war against Spain. "The river" is most probably in Binakayan, the barangay near which stood the house of Raymundo's splenetic Spanish grandfather from Jaca. It is pleasant to consider the heroes enjoying a leisure moment by the Binakayan streams. This reminds me of my own times in my mother's hometown when I learned to swim in Barugo's river, my long, wet hair buoyant with freshwater minerals, stray Coca-Cola tanzans, and soft, calcareous sediment that I belatedly realized was, well, not hygienic. Those were the days. (Estrella Espejo, ditto)

47 "Buta ka, buta!" Or did he say *batuta ka*, phallic symbol, meaning *You are a police baton, a guarda civil's tool?* Butaka, I know, is a rocking chair. I failed to translate. (Trans. Query)

48 You are blind. (Estrella Espejo, ditto)

49 Pardon? (Trans. Query)

50 *Buta ka* means: *you are blind*. In Waray. (Estrella Espejo, ditto)

51 Curiously, in an episode not noted in these memoirs, the Caviteño Idoy, a.k.a. Candido Tria Tirona, died "under a sampaloc tree" [Calairo, Emmanuel, *Cavite El Viejo*, 133] attacked by Spaniards while he was "resting" [*ibid.*] after the bloody Battle of Binakayan. For this mortal disruption of his siesta, Idoy is called The Martyr of Binakayan. In revolutionary memoirs, "resting" was the second most common trope. ("Marching bands" is the fourth; "pintakasi," special cockfights, runs a strong third.) Blood is barely mentioned. Spanish officers "rested," troops "rested," page after page is filled with "resting." Not a single memoirist talks much about the experience of killing; but all talk about "rest." The foregrounding of this pastoral scene mirrors the fantastic resting that lines revolutionary memoirs like hemp, as if events proceeded in narcotic haze. What is repressed? Death. (Dr. Diwata Drake, Redwood, California)

52 Dr. Voodoo, why talk of blood when it has not yet been shed? Isn't it enough that one

our butts in the air and watch insects flower under our shadow for hours. Shadow under our flower for hours.

I guess you could call it Eden.

I followed shit. I mean suit.[53] [54] [55] [56] [57] Shitting is like yawning. Transitive compulsion, mathematical. Yawn and the world will yawn with you. Shit, ditto. I took off my shorts. Schoolboy style with the front

---

breathes through hoary tubes and has wires in the heart, and that the body performs its dance of vapors beyond the soul's consent? Why destroy peace? The boys are sunbathing by the river: let them be. (Estrella Espejo, ditto)

53 The pun on shit and suit is mine, but it matches the vulgarity of the original. *Kitchen Spanish*, as Rizal called Cavite's *chavacano* (rough or vulgar) speech. Neither Spanish nor Tagalog. If I were to translate word for word Raymundo Mata's language in these early passages, the reader would give up in despair. My facsimile of his playfulness possesses my errors, but I retain his allusiveness, his shifts in tone, and the somewhat lunatic energy of his observations, not to mention his puns. With at least three languages at every Filipino's disposal, Raymundo Mata can pun at least seven ways in one phrase. That's simple math. Thus far, I count five languages in the diary—Spanish, Latin, Tagalog, Waray, and Cavite-Chabacano. (Trans. Note)

54 In a letter to Ferdinand Blumentritt, his sedate Austrian mentor, Rizal did not seem to have much faith in the mixed-up vocabulary of the people of Cavite. Evidence of Rizal's views of language rests on his correspondence with the Austrian (I discount for the moment the views in the *Fili*, being fiction). No one knows what kept the ethnologist Blumentritt at home. A sensitive *malade imaginaire*, he failed to meet Rizal anywhere in the hero's mad dash around Europe in the 1880s: they met only once, in Blumentritt's Austro-Hungarian Bohemia. Despite their heartrending bond, the friends spent only forty-eight hours, max, in each other's company—and so it seems we have the European's hypochondria to thank for the copious, homoerotic correspondence that survives. In one of those endless letters, Rizal made a matter-of-fact list of Filipino languages to satisfy Blumentritt's scholarly questions. Next to Cavite, Rizal simply noted: *español de cocina.* (Trans. Note)

55 Homoerotic? Shame on you, Mimi C.! Just because you have the power of the pen in the modern age does not mean every word is a phallic orgy. Friendships between men in the nineteenth century produced affectionate, loving, fond epistles of, well, gayness, but that does not mean they were gay! May Rizal's heterosexual hex vex you from Banahaw! (Estrella Espejo, ditto)

56 Mimi C. did not say Rizal was gay. She said the letters were homoerotic. (Dr. Diwata Drake, Berlin, Germany)

57 Same difference. (Estrella Espejo, ditto)

buttons, no strings for me. Karsonsilyos[58] [59] are for old men and babies. When I got my pants with buttons and snapped one shut—it was better than holy communion! Now it's kind of ordinary, a habit. I mourn the world's changes, especially my own. I pulled my pants down.[60]

I sat silent. Still. What freedom. What colors and shapes and dragonflies like embroidered signatures on a handkerchief. What cool wind, dapping at my butt like a Saint Peter, fisher of men. I could not help but sing.[61]

Bird who has freedom to fly. Cage it and it cries. How much more for country so pretty. Who should not wish to go beyond? Pilipinas whom I love like a lady. Nest of my tears and sorrow. My goal, to see you really really free.

Entomological fulmination in immobile rectitude. Wings absorb my scientific stupor—thoracic addenda, luminous. Sputter and spiral,

---

58 This trope, Filipino Spanish-ism for underpants (*calzoncillos*), recurs in the memoir. Filipinos liberally fucked with Spanish words: metonym, metathesis, etc. etc. (Trans. Note)

59 I used to put on my grandfather's old pants just for fun; then my mom beat me up for my "wild ways." *Una jovencita varonil.* I was a disgrace. One summer, my brothers wore odd loose trousers without buttons, we also called them karsonsilyos, when they turned twelve, special dispensation for their late circumcisions. They paraded their swathed, tortured bodies as if they were Cassius Clay or something, and I envied their loutish look—their rite of passage with their weird pants. On the other hand, they did look like a bunch of circus animals on display, strutting around town in their underwear, not indecent, but sad. (Estrella Espejo, ditto)

60 If he got this orgasmic about buttons, what would he have done with zippers? "The anal stage" is a lurid misconception. Crude terminology based on finite contingencies (i.e., the human body) brought psychoanalytic thought to an impasse. We now understand that Freud's *theories* are sound, but his *words* were disgusting. Raymundo here is in what has been pejoratively referred to by prurient, ignorant, non-Mürkian analysts as an *anal crisis* but which we in the twenty-first century realize is just one in a healthy continuum of linked, random, and eternal neuroses. "What are the three facts of the human condition?" an interviewer once asked Mürk in a Helsinki spa, where he spent time in the aftermath of that fateful Antibes Plenary of 1977. "I have three words for you," the savant replied in the languor of Finnish sulfur, a tanned and floating oracle: "Neurosis. Neurosis. Neurosis." (Dr. Diwata Drake, Bali, Indonesia)

61 The statement indicates that what follows ("*Bird . . . really really free*") was set to music, perhaps a nursery rhyme. Many words were indecipherable; they seem smeared with some offal; plus, the handwriting shows this was written in a hurry. Decoding the lyrics, given the lacunae, I translated verbatim as much as I could. (Trans. Note)

tiny hallucinations of God. I do not mean Bathala.[62] Bathala not tending to hallucinate, rather empirical in his approach, sensory persuasions ruling. But church God has a certain unstable abstract mindset. Hallucination of church God, I mean, the vitrine splendor of insect wings.

To catch wings in commotion is impossible.[63] [64] Even as I watch, I change the facts of nature: there and not there, in that moment. I take down for my killing eye—the one that always

---

62 Raymundo Mata invokes Bathala, the Tagalog name for God first mentioned by Chirino, a Jesuit chronicler of the 1600s. Rizal disputes the term Bathala three times in his letters to Blumentritt. (Some scholars, in this postmodern world that disrespects the dead, blaspheme that the hero could have been wrong.) Rizal queries the term again in his annotations of the history of the Philippines by an official living in Mexico, the *Morga*, in which through anguished footnotes the hero Rizal re-examines colonialism via a colonizer's blurry lens. He is so earnest in the *Morga*, so angsty, so personally crazed with bitterness against the katsila, I like it better than the novels. Rizal writes to Blumentritt: "It was two years ago that I told [Pedro Paterno, Filipino expat in Madrid] I was surprised that no Tagalog knew about the word Bathala. He then showed me a dictionary [*sic*] . . . [Chirino's] translation of the saying [*bahala na ang May Kapal*] is not correct." Rizal was clearly annoyed by the Jesuit Chirino's lapses: Rizal pre-cursed Orientalism and bore Edward Said's pet peeves way before his time. An unbearable burden, if you ask me! Woe to the lonely avant-garde! If Rizal is correct in his argument, that Bathala was an error by the Chirino, yet one more form of Orientalist idiocy rather than a genuine indigenous term, then Raymundo Mata's reference to Bathala is erudite—learned from school, not from shitting. I'm sure he's hiding a revolutionary code somewhere—maybe "Bathala" is some kind of password? (Estrella Espejo, ditto)

63 Revolutionary password?!!? I will explicate the above act for those undamaged by ideology's miasma. Raymundo imitates his friend Miong and takes a shit by the river. As Raymundo shits he sings (and cribs from the anachronistic anthem *Bayan Ko* [c.1898], for no good reason—what was going on here, Ms. Translator?) and indulges in "feeble forays into zoologic insight" [Mürk, *Mapping the Libido*, vii]. Raymundo is observing insects (later he notes their colors with lyrical precision: "bluebottle, greymottle, veinsottle") with minute attention that signifies a latent obsessive-compulsive schema in his psychic apparatus. This does not surprise me. (Dr. Diwata Drake, Vienna, Austria)

64 I would be the last person to question a renowned scholar such as Dr. Diwata, but I'd like to note here the hardship of translating texts—the *terror*, as she has once noted, of the linguistic abyss. Of course I make mistakes. All translators are confronted by territories for which they have no signposts, no cartographic schemes. As for *this* passage—it is a hypergraphic coil, a cacophone of contrapuntal tones, rich in its obscurity—I tried my best. Dr. Diwata should at least understand my situation before she throws stones, I mean footnotes! (Trans. Note)

sees—the half-moon-script of ladybugs. Their wings flap madly into odd stasis, into the optical fallacy of a lunar phase. Then, there's the candor of dragonflies.[65] Flimsy tracery of their wings, exposure of their slim volitions, pulse-maps available for all to see. I catch the radiances of flies. Bluebottle, greymottle, veinsottle—they have a filthy intimacy with the river's shades of green. I snatch ants at their trade, watch spiders lay their traps. Ant equals bird plus pepper.[66] [67] Ant plus parrot equals penis. That is the declension of the word *langgam*. I hear mosquitoes speak bad things[68] about me. ZZZ. ZZZ. Splat. That's what they get. "Gossip sucks blood." Note to killer's eye:[69] put that in your

---

65 Reminds me of my mom's hometown, land of the morning shit. They had outhouses, no plumbing, so one had close encounters with nature. And on those road trips people took during my lost summers (when inland trucking had an entirely unmerited glamor), on Pantranco buses that passed through San Juanico Strait, the Bicol region, Southern Luzon—on those trips sometimes we had to improvise. I learned geology this way—the rocky grounds of Samar, volcanic grasslands of Bicolandia: the path to Manila littered by an organic gleam. I'm sorry, where was I? (Estrella Espejo, ditto)

66 Exact meaning unknown, but the declension may go like this: *langgam* means ant in Tagalog but bird in Cebuano; *pikoy* means bird—specifically parrot—in Waray but penis in Cebuano; *utan* is vegetable in Cebuano but slang for penis in Cebuano and Hiligaynon; the word for pepper, *sili*, in Hiligaynon means, yes, penis in Waray: a delightful round-robin of phallic syllogisms going from language to language via natural ephemera. The polylingual Filipino has no other recourse but sophistication—and a dirty mind. (Trans. Note)

67 And the winner of the award for the dirtiest mind? *Cebuanos!* (Estrella Espejo, ditto)

68 Aha. I see. The mosquitoes who "speak bad things" are the frailocracy, rabid eaters of nineteenth-century Filipino flesh. The imagery of killing mosquitoes (i.e., friars) is original—much better than the reigning insect trope—that Moth and the Flame fable that the young Rizal (and copycat Aguinaldo, too) kept invoking. Enough of that already! Sorry, Rizal—but that Moth story was boring. (Estrella Espejo, ditto)

69 "The killer's eye." Is that a reference to "mind's eye," as in Wordsworth, or Shakespeare? Did Raymundo Mata read Wordsworth or did the translator? Mürk, in his reading of Freud, understood that language is at the heart of the self's opacity. If it is impossible for us to say what we mean, how much more problematic is a translated country? If language defers meaning rather than provides it, what static arises in this bouillabaise? This text is exemplary in that it teaches us that we must always read with this axiom in mind—we will never *know* history, but in the meantime we can always blame the translator. (Dr. Diwata Drake, Vence, France)

diary. Neat phrase. Thus, how do I? Maybe not Eden: but taking a shit is an education.[70]

What would King's World do without shit? It is true that shit gives me power. Shit leads the world to me. Shit mesmerizes the Kingdom.[71] [72] [73] [74] But I'm modest enough to know that I am expendable. Shit is their cause. I mean, my rear is just means, no end. I am contingent. Shit is necessary.[75] [76] Philosophy hatches warmly in my bowels.

---

70 I know there are haters out there (*see* above), but I enjoyed working on these passages. Raymundo is scientific yet lyrical, which academics, who do not understand poetry, fail to appreciate. His wordplay was fascinating to read and challenging to translate, for instance the image "half-moon-script" of ladybugs ("*pagsusulatang mala-biyak-ng-buwan . . .*") to describe the flutter of their wings. I hope others enjoy my poor attempts at parlaying this energetically tactile yet philosophically absorbing section. (Trans. Note)

71 Ahh. I get it. *Filosofong Tae.* Heisenberg in the *hornal*. The dignity of Boethius's *Consolation of Philosophy* is at stake here. There it is again: he says "King's world." Then he capitalizes Kingdom. Pun on his name Raymundo. "Rey-mundo." King-world. Now I'm getting Mimi C.'s point, how she had to resolve the translator's dilemma. Let me see. Hmm. Puwitic poet. Now I'm looking for the puns, the language shifts. Is "killer's eye" a pun on his name: "Mata"? "Mata" means eye, in Tagalog, but he/she kills, in Spanish; as well as bush, as in *mata de pelo* (head of hair). Et cetera! Raymundo, the Mata-d'or—golden(killer)eye. Or Raymundo, Goldenhair-*surpr*-Eyes. Ad insanitum. Mimi C. is right: translating must have been a challenge. My head aches. I need to rest. (Estrella Espejo, ditto)

72 Estrella, you saw what I was trying to do, thank you. (Trans. Note)

73 You're welcome, but I have a migraine. (Estrella Espejo, ditto)

74 So you were trying to convey disturbed puns in Raymundo's text by creating your own? An anomalous though unavoidable process, as another jocose philosophical jack has pointed out: "to translate is error; to forgive, hogwash." [Mürk, *Practices XX*] (Dr. Diwata Drake, the Maldives)

75 Give her a break, Dr. Diwata. You know she is still only in graduate school, though her linguistic talent is a mature genius. At least she puts in the effort—I give her the grade *bueno*, more or less B-. (Estrella Espejo, ditto)

76 *I am contingent. Shit is necessary.* The ophthalmologist Rizal has nothing on Raymundo's in*sight* here. Recognizing *shit* as *meaning*—in which what seems "nothing" is "all," and what is [empty] is [full]—is more revolutionary than going to war for mere country. Raymundo is a fine folk phenomenon. What do Filipinos call the wise fool—Juan Pusong? Juan Tamad? He has the blissful ignorance of the incidental sage: ". . . since every pen is no penis, and every id no idiot" [Mürk, *Aphora XIV*]. (Dr. Diwata Drake, the Maldives)

All this is cavil as you notice. I dilly and I dally. I zig and I zag. All prologue and introduction, tactical ploy, oiling up the barrels, testing the locks. There's a rock stuck in my gullet like a bullet. There's a load in my cannon like a toad. O jesusmaryjoseph mea culpa I disgraced your God, only two minutes ago. Mea culpa. O that those two minutes were back I intercede without blemish shame blame oooh dammmmn. All-Powerful one, Friar Most Holy, Aggrieved and Aggravating. Salvame! [77] [78] [79] [80]

O Francisco Bulag-tas,[81] salvame!

---

77 I think I'm on a roll. I think I'm getting it. This passage, dated January 20, 1872, the Cavite Mutiny, is a metaphor. "There's a rock stuck in my gullet like a bullet. There's a load in my cannon like a toad." Raymundo refers to pent-up anger of the generation after Padre Burgos, rebel-priest executed in Cavite. As I noted, the Cavite Mutiny was a sorry excuse for a rebellion (slightly less pathetic than soldier mutinies that ring shopping malls with bombs at Christmas). However, its consequences were not insignificant. The Mutiny became an alibi for Spaniards to round up any suspected rebel—student, priest, or *cochero*—loitering on the street; they exiled merchants and *marineros* both. The aftermath was so traumatic to honest Filipinos everywhere that, for instance, Jose Rizal's father forbade his children, all eleven of them, except Paciano who was already in hiding and Concha who was dead, to use the following words in conversation: "Cavite, Burgos, and *'plibestiro'* [filibustero]." His father's injunction scarred Rizal, ten years old at the time. For him, the Mutiny was a sacral wound (somewhere by the lumbar plexus). In 1887, he dedicated his first novel to "the three martyred Filipino priests" and in 1891 his second novel to *filibusteros* (seditionists) everywhere. Thus, born of Cavite's trauma, Rizal's novels sparked revolution. (Estrella Espejo, ditto)

78 Dear Estrella. Excuse me. Ehem. "The load in my cannon"? A metaphor for the Cavite Mutiny? He's talking about constipation. Could it be said that from the Cavite Mutiny Jose Rizal begat novels, while Raymundo Mata begat shit? Alternative meanings abound. (Dr. Diwata Drake, Kalamazoo, Michigan)

79 Is this what they teach in—where are you from?—Kasilyas, Arkansas? Dumi-dumi, Delaware? (Estrella Espejo, ditto)

80 Isn't it enough that I had to translate this Chaucerian bawdry, its knee-jerk anticlerical tropes, and the triteness of its toilet jokes (any five-year-old can spout the *bullet* [bala] and *cannon* [kanyon] puns), but will you guys stop it already? (Trans. Note)

81 "*Bulag*-tas": a blasphemous pun! According to Raymundo's relatives, "Bulag" (Tagalog for blind—while in Waray bulag means split or apart) was the merciless pet name given to young Raymundo in Binakayan; it is not clear when his debility surfaced. Balagtas, on the other hand, was the foremost Tagalog poet of his time. Raymundo's incontinent

Sing, Raymundo, sing!

    Inside and outside, my country in despair

Betrayals are reigning

Genius and goodness are thrown to the air

Sorrowful bowels irritating

    Good deeds are hammered down

To the abyss of seas that moan

Talented faeces are off and blown

Buried without cornerstone

    But the sly and bad of heart

'Neath a pure throne hides a fart

And to those with beastly art

Sweet incense is offered.

Sing, Raymundo, sing!

Omni—po—tent—ehem. Ehem. Ohoommmmmmm.

Raymundo:

Treason and evil take the lead

While goodness bends over

Bulag-tas:

Holy reason's so hung over

        Only tears are shed.[82] [83]

---

bluster is not becoming of a hero, shame on him! On the other hand, I myself cannot fail to blush at memories of a Catholic girlhood, when we pinned a number of mean names on a whole rosary of sorrowful classmates. Bless me, Father, for I have sinned, against skinny Albino (a.k.a. *Wild Gamao*), sickly Miguel (a.k.a. *Green Muhog*: Greensnot), and, last but not least, my slow, deceased cousin Bibot, whom we just called *Mongo*, for short. Mea culpa. (Estrella Espejo, ditto)

82 The original passage relies heavily on the Tagalog romance, Balagtas's *Florante at Laura*, with which the future general is clearly familiar. A gestational text, that is, a text that has shaped national identity, the poem *Florante at Laura* fascinates even wayward souls. *The sly and bad of heart 'neath a pure throne hides a fart*—I was ashamed to translate his imbecility. However, Raymundo accomplishes what he sets out to do—he illustrates in sweating, panting rhyme the sweating, panting act—and while the onomatopeia is barbarous, the achievement is clear. (Trans. Note)

83 Francisco Balagtas (1835–1863) a.k.a. Baltazar was a Tagalog from Bulacan whose work was universally admired—by Spanish priests and Filipino readers alike. This is

Entry #3[84]

Raymundo Mata
Escuela de Niños, Section Atis
Kawit, Cavite

"The Terror of Cavite"

Six years ago, terror struck Cavite. One day, I was quietly bathing by the river and playing tuktukan with Miong. The next day, dead ducks and the ash-flesh of fruit floated on the river. The Guardia Civil burned and looted Kawit. Children ran for their lives with chickens, servants, carabaos. The Guardia Civil was worse than the cholera. Every house in town was empty. I saw Miong fall on his head, running with the maids. (He has never fully recovered from the brain damage.) They took my uncle into the convent's courtyard, under the buntis trellis. They said he was the culprit.

---

because of his work's grand abstract symbolism, another term for *I don't get it!* The damsel in distress plot of *Florante at Laura* could be seen as: subversive code for dark oppression (Las Islas Filipinas = Laura, the raped virgin, etc.), or entertaining Cervantean romance. Filipino komiks versions highlight its bondage themes. Rizal was a fan of his poetry (I prefer the komiks). Rizal quotes Balagtas fondly, as an acolyte might allude to a master, in his novels and in letters to Austrian ethnographer Blumentritt.

The balagtasan, on the other hand, had nothing to do with Balagtas. I recall the balagtasan contests during rainy patriotic holidays on the island of Leyte, that heedless land of the typhoon path, when the sinewy mists of the shadow-poetry jousts held sway. Ah, the balagtasan rhyming contests, which the exotic vowels of Tagalog, that foreigner's tongue, easily accommodated, while consonants allowed for ample versification! The forbidding poetry competition had a vitality that did not measure up to the cunning of the eponymous lyricist. The rules of balagtasan were actually invented by a twentieth-century group of bored Filipino bards in a coffee shop. And yet it tells you something about the vocal energy of our indolence. The balagtasan adept's fame rests on marvelous oral improvisations. The poems in print, on the other hand, just sound like cold leftovers. (Estrella Espejo, ditto)

84 A few early sections of the manuscript are academic effluvia—well-preserved school essays in schoolboy script. (Trans. Note)

The fake priest, the mestizo, who instigated the Mutiny. What the hell? He's a real priest![85] [86] [87]

I hid in the pigpen under the house, with the sawdust and mud. They poured urine on his head, they threw his books out the windows. The books hit his ears. His chamberpots rained on the grass, on his poor books.

After destroying the sala, they set fire to my uncle's garden. Roses, kaimitos, kalachuchi, banyan. Razed to the ground with a sweet, oily aftersmell that lasted for weeks. Jackfruit trees with swaddling spines, mango branches heavy with fruit, guavas, their easily fried leaves—they were all toast for the wind. Fruit trees burned with anomalous perfume

---

85 The family refutes the accusation that his uncle, Tio U., was the Filipino in the costume of a priest who instigated the mestizo soldiers of Cavite to revolt. First of all, he was a real priest. Second, it was his brother the actor who liked costumes. In sum, the mutiny was just an excuse to loot the old priest's garden and terrorize him in his own home! (Estrella Espejo, Quezon Institute and Sanatorium, Tacloban, Leyte)

86 When one makes of one's identity a performance, is it still one's identity? Regarding this paradox of the human, Mürk pondered in the *Parables*: "If a llama sees his furry shadow in a forest and says, that is I, is he still a llama?" (Dr. Diwata Drake, Cuzco, Peru)

87 It is tempting to consider the role of the priest's brother, the actor Jorge Raymundo, a.ka. *el genio* Jote, as the costumed man in a priest's outfit who exhorted revolt during the Cavite Mutiny. But no reliable records but gossip from Spanish friars of the time and a plotline from Alexandre Dumas give evidence of such a disguised rebel. (Trans. Note)

under which we dreamed[88] [89] [90] [91] [92] for days. Roasted flakes of mango peels, flints of rose-thorn embers, ashes of bamboo hearts—the burned ground smelled like the mulch of flowers from the May parades.

For us kids, it was an orgy of fruit-gathering. We tasted the merits of scorched guava versus wood-burned papaya. We hurt our lips. Chafed our cheeks on barbecued kalamansi and blackened chili blooms—saplings from the south, my uncle's favorite among the plants in his garden[93]

---

88 It's true that I, when I smell a ripe guava, am transported instantly to those days at my grandfather's riverine home, and my being chokes—I am suffused, half-deafened—with memory, so that the term "homesick" contains within it something deadly, a visceral "sick"-ness, and I need to get back to bed and lie down and weep for the loss of things. All for a guava! (Estrella Espejo, ditto)

89 I'm not sure. The word "dream" may be an analytic cue, where language gives away reality. This "academic effluvium," if not a literal dream, portends a fantastic memory. The wondrous specificity of its content possesses a healthy irreality that may suggest a retrospective text. Is it possible that he did not write this when he was ten? And in what language was this, Ms. Translator? (Dr. Diwata Drake, Cuzco, Peru)

90 It is, let's see. How odd. It is in English. (Trans. Note)

91 Dr. Diwata, again we must differ. After all, you're a cynical bastard, while I'm an acolyte of truth. Why must this be "wondrous" rather than actual? My experience tells me that fruit, in sensitive souls (a notion perhaps foreign to you—o foul-hearted Fowl!), produces a "wondrous specificity." It is indisputable that tropical fruit has an insidious reality. (Estrella Espejo, ditto)

92 Ah. So I am the Fowl? Oh Starry-eyed Mirror, *espejo* most gullible—you are the Gull. I do not dispute truth when I talk of dream. I point out only the provocative qualities of the boy's recollection, or anyone's recollection for that matter. If you ask me, "dreams" are facts; it's being awake that's overrated. (Dr. Diwata Drake, Vence, France)

93 Unpunctuated, as usual. (Trans. Note)

Entry #4

That was the beginning[94] [95] [96]

---

94 *Diyan nagsimula.* Original phrase in emphatic Tagalog. No period. A grammatical and existential mystery. Is it a clause that stands alone? Wherein the schoolboy essay "The Terror of Cavite" is the antecedent of the subject-pronoun *diyan*? Or maybe the demonstrative pronoun is an expletive—*There began*—awaiting its nominative, the force that through the green fuse makes sense. Or consider the verb *nagsimula*—sole action, past tense. But then again: if you view it as a suspended, helping verb (as in, *nagsimula mag-almusal? nagsimula manguto?*: he began . . . breakfast, he began . . . picking lice) there are so many intriguing predications, permutations of possibilities. So much depends. (Trans. Note)

95 Grammar *is* the existential mystery. We exist *only* in language—our tragedy is that it is not enough to make ourselves whole. "The unconscious is structured like a language; the conscious, on the other hand, looks a bit like certain funny little Andean goats" (Mürk, *Miscellaneo* XXIII). (Dr. Diwata Drake, Lima, Peru)

96 Oh shush! There is no mystery here. It follows "The Terror of Cavite," the beginning of the hero's political consciousness—his personal Cry of Balintawak, or storming of the Bastille, if you wish. The piece is the single expansive testament to the Mutiny in revolutionary memoirs. Rizal, ever traumatized, barely refers to it in his letters, and in an autobiographical fragment ("Memories of a Student in Manila"), he does not mention it at all. Of that pathetic Mutiny, I will concede this—the Caviteño Raymundo's radical prose uniquely recaps history. A shrewd eruption here: *Diyan nagsimula.* There it began! Prophetic! Visionary! If only other memoirists had such eloquence: the brevity! the pith! (Estrella Espejo, Quezon Institute and Sanatorium, Tacloban, Leyte)

Entry #5

p 3 Cunegonde; garden

p 3 Idoy's namesake? Ha ha[97]

p 10 "en un lugar de la Mancha cuyo nombre no quiero acordarme"

How the Portuguese[98] Made a Superb Auto-Da-Fe to Prevent Any Future Earthquakes, and How Candido[99] Underwent Public Flagellation

After the earthquake,[100] which had destroyed three-fourths of the city of Lisbon,[101] the sages of that country could think of no means more effectual to preserve the kingdom from utter ruin than to

---

97 Idoy: Candido Tria Tirona, previously cited cousin and future general, martyred under a sampaloc tree after the Battle of Binakayan; a.k.a. the Hero of Binakayan, because he died; estranged from Raymundo in their adolescent years. (Estrella Espejo, Quezon Institute and Sanatorium, Tacloban, Leyte)

98 Craftily, the budding satirist Raymundo substitutes "Portuguese" for "Spaniard," and "auto-da-fe" for "burning of Cavite" in this picaresque romp that he wrote when he was only ten! The prose, one must admit, is a bit dense—but what clever allegory! What sarcastic semblance of his weeping country's fate! (Estrella Espejo, ditto)

99 Here, Raymundo makes his cousin Idoy, a.k.a. Candido Tria Tirona, his fable's hero, though later in the memoir he fails to mention at all Candido's doomed valor in the actual war. In fact, he forgets Candido altogether. Clearly, this section is a prophetic paean *to all victims of war!* This is the diarist's strategy: he hides true meanings in patriotic symbols, and makes of the intelligent reader an undertaker, a patient digger of his buried pieties. Me, to be honest—I'd rather just attend the funeral. (Estrella Espejo, ditto)

100 Sad and portentous reference to the monumental 1863 earthquake in Manila that killed Archbishop Pedro Pelaez and destroyed Manila Cathedral. Young Padre Burgos, future martyr of the Cavite Mutiny, took over Pelaez's duties as canon of Manila, setting in place a chain of bitterness among the Spanish religious orders, who resented the Filipino's rise. One might claim that Burgos's exalted position led to his death by envy in 1872. Thus, the earthquake, indirectly, set up conditions for the "quake" of revolution years later. (Trans. Note)

101 i.e., Manila. (Estrella Espejo, ditto)

entertain the people with an auto-da-fe,[102] it having been decided by the University of Coimbra,[103] [104] that the burning of a few people alive by a slow fire, and with great ceremony, is an infallible preventive of earthquakes.[105]

In consequence thereof they had seized on a Biscayan[106] for marrying his godmother, and on two Bulgarians[107] for taking out the bacon of a larded pullet[108] they were eating; after dinner they came and secured Don Felipe Enrile,[109] and his pupils Candido and Miong,[110]

---

102 Human barbecue; *lechon de tao*; obviously a metaphor for the conditions of tyrannous ruin then settling on Raymundo's beloved Cavite. (Estrella Espejo, ditto)

103 Perhaps a corruption of Calamba, Rizal's birthplace?—as if "Calamba [Coimbra]" were a metonym for Rizal, who is in his own person a "university," thus "University of Coimbra," metonymizing Rizal himself, makes sense in this sly legend. (Estrella Espejo, ditto)

104 What are you talking about, Estrella?? Coimbra is a city in Portugal, where a great earthquake also happened—the setting of Voltaire's great, anticlerical Englightenment novel, *Candide*. (Dr. Diwata Drake, Paris, France)

105 A stroke of genius! A world of invention here, in this ironic statement on the tribulations of such people as Raymundo's priest-uncle, tortured by the Guardia Civil; also of Rizal's mother, who was "roasted on a slow fire," so to speak, as she marched in chains barefoot from Calamba in the burning Laguna heat, a sight that also traumatized Rizal as a child, just as the traumatized Raymundo had watched soldiers burn his uncle's garden. (Estrella Espejo, ditto)

106 A typo? Biscay is on the wrong continent, a site in Iberia. Or does he mean Biscay's Filipino 'sister,' the province of Nueva Vizcaya—capital: Bayombong? My vote: Bisayan—an allusion to Raymundo's lamented mother, a talented Waray actress. (Estrella Espejo, ditto)

107 i.e., perhaps Bul-anons (as in Boholanos—a notoriously vagabond, lovely people). (Estrella Espejo, ditto)

108 i.e., *lechon manok*. [*sic!* I know, I know, you Spanish-language nerds—chickens do not have mammary glands! It's a Filipino joke!] (Estrella Espejo, ditto)

109 Don Felipe Enrile: Raymundo's revered *maestro* at the Escuela de Niños. Also lauded for his kind heart and intelligence by Miong, i.e., Emilio Aguinaldo, in his *Gunita* (though the learned *maestro* seemed not to have done the dropout Aguinaldo much good). Precocious Raymundo dedicates his ingenious labors here to his teacher. That he shows his esteem by burning him to death only reveals a boyish sense of humor. (Estrella Espejo, ditto)

110 Schoolboy humor: comic allusion to two classmates. (Estrella Espejo, ditto)

the one for speaking his mind, and the other two for seeming to approve what he had said. They were conducted to separate apartments, extremely cool, where they were never incommoded with the sun. Eight days afterwards they were each dressed in a sanbenito, and their heads were adorned with paper mitres. The mitre and sanbenito worn by Candido and Miong were painted with flames reversed and with devils that had neither tails nor claws; but Don Felipe Enrile's devils had both tails and claws, and his flames were upright. In these habits they marched in procession, and heard a very pathetic sermon, which was followed by an anthem, accompanied by bagpipes. Candido and Miong were flogged to some tune, while the anthem was being sung; the Biscayan and the two Intsik who would not eat bacon were burned, and Don Felipe Enrile was hanged, which is not a common custom at these solemnities. The same day there was another earthquake, which made most dreadful havoc.

Candido and Miong, amazed, terrified, confounded, astonished, all bloody, and trembling from head to foot, said to themselves, "If this is the best of all possible worlds, what are the others? If we had only been whipped, we could have put up with it, as we did among the Binakayan-ons; but, not withstanding, oh my dear Felipe! my beloved master! thou greatest of philosophers! that ever we should live to see thee hanged, without knowing for what! O my Crispulo, thou best of men, that it should be thy fate to be drowned in the very harbor! O Miss Di-Ganda, you mirror of young ladies! that it should be your fate to have your body ripped open!"

They were making the best of their way from the place where they had been preached to, whipped, absolved and blessed, when they were accosted by an old woman, who said to them, "Take courage, boys, and follow me."[111] [112]

---

111 This lively section was a challenge to translate from its decrepit original. The antiquated, convoluted syntax (e.g., "they were never incommoded with the sun," bad passive-voice habit of Romance languages, when all he meant to say was, *damn they froze to death*); outmoded details, which I kept intact (e.g., *sanbenito*, garments worn by criminals sentenced to burn by the medieval Inquisition); and other obsolete ingredients tested my poor powers. I hope I have not added nor detracted from the oracular ideas that glimmered in this section. (Trans. Note)

112 I note the translator's disclaimer above—as if you could not tell this apart from Chapter Six of Voltaire's *Candide*, translated into English and easily downloaded from Google! As for my esteemed colleague, I will have to point out that Estrella Espejo's ejaculatory interpolations on this text are wrong once again—wrong, wrong, wrong!— serial misreadings of a woeful kind. Inexplicably, the young Raymundo's manuscript inserts Voltaire's *Candide* word for word, except for substitutions of random names in the manuscript [Don Felipe for Pangloss, Miss Di-Ganda for Cunegonde, etc.]. Yes, he is precocious—but a precocious plagiarist! However, "oracular," the translator's term, is, in my view, also correct. It would have been impossible for Raymundo, a sensitive boy in late nineteenth-century Philippines, not to see the parallels to his country's condition in the anticlerical satire he's writing down word for word; just as it is impossible for Estrella not to read Raymundo in the paragraphs from Voltaire. You will find translations of *Candide*, a.k.a. *Candido*, even in Pangalatoc or Ilocano in Manila's antiquarian bookshops (Estrella's errors, on the other hand, need not proliferate). Thus, despite herself, Estrella's "misreadings," her anachronisms, are accurate. It could be, who knows, a reading that did ring in Raymundo's bones. "Anachronism is to the unconscious what honey is to bees or sounds are to syllables—we read in desire, not in time" (Drake, Dux, and Ménårdsz, Eds., *Readings of the Rhizome: An Annotation of Claro Mürk's Parable IV* [The Garden], page 21). (Dr. Diwata Drake, Vence, France)

Entry #6

Finished Cand. Volt. is a genius, Narrative has just discovered Steam Locomotion. Gave me the Shivers, my heart raced, Reading the book. Even now I remember Lines and images, my nerves on Fire. A Bludgeon, a Lashing—the rage and magic and fury of Words. I fell into a Fever, I read it over and Over again. Many good lines, esp. Martin. I like Martin. Did Cand. pass Manila? Seems trip from Paris to El Dorado, Venezuela, back to Germany via Span. vessel could go Manila galleon route—will trace map. Tio U. angry. My eyes, cost of Kerosene, not good for Health, bla bla bla. I know he is only concerned. His concern breaks my heart, but I ignore it. He put a poultice on my eyes, Threatening. *You will go blind*, he said. Mabubuta ka, buta. Blind from ecstasy, I thought I would Vomit. But I am already blind, I said! I cannot see at night! Still, Tio U. keeps leaving Books around, as if Forgetful. Looks at me, I think with a Wink. Now, he left Cerv. *Cuyo nombre no quiero acordarme.* Burn the books of my foolish youth, oh ye of good faith, the noble Gentleman said in delirium. I remember his face bloated by whip-lash, tortured by the Span. I remember every day. How many days to heal his burns? How many mornings and nights did we press the oil and herbs on Tio U.'s sick and tortured don quiXote Face? How long did we pray to his indifferent G.? My mind fails at the mea-sures of our fear. I fill with hate. *Coños!* Then I open up a page—we hauled everything back, every ruined and mauled thing; and it is as if nothing happened, I'm sipping barako and falling in love with a paper girl, Cunegonde. Ms Di-Ganda. Damned son. Damned nephew. I'll burn in hell.

This Cerv. is funny. Can you believe—[113] [114] [115]

---

[113] Entries #5 and #6 are clearly contiguous, but they appear on separate sheets, so I made them separate entries. These sections are faithful to the physical sequence of the papers: but it is I who numbered each separate piece of the manuscript. (Trans. Note)

[114] However, on the back of #6 are some crossed-out paragraphs, perhaps a discarded section for another typical school essay, "*Mi Familia*" (see #9). I append it in its entirety below. One understands why the writer trashed this piece: it presents details just to get them over with, in dull declaratives ("He did . . . he came . . . he was"). He does not seem inspired by the particulars of his father's life, though I would like to know what happened to his joyous great-uncle Jorge Luis, "*el vagamundo de Jaca!*"

"Everyone called Papá *el genio* Jote. His full name: Jorge Raymundo Mata Eibarrazeta. When Papá was born, he had a big head, like Napoleon and also like his great-uncle Jorge Luis, a fiddler and a man of ill fortune. So Papá came out looking unbalanced, brain-heavy, and at first he wasn't named in case he died. Then they named him after his Papá, the old soldier, and his great-uncle Jorge Luis, a bagpiper from the Basque mountains. Papá grew up handsome, broad-shouldered, and wild. He had a katsila nose—too big for his fine features, much admired. He was generous, impatient, and a good mimic, like his great-uncle Jorge Luis, a clown who stowed away with swine and pineapples on a caravel. Papá had a way with languages. When he went off to Manila, he came home with prizes—for extemporaneous speech, Latin, classical declamations. He was an interpreter, not a creator. (The poems he later gave my mother were other people's odes, some written by his late great-uncle Jorge Luis, a poete maudit ["*un poeta loko-loko*" in original—Trans.] and perfumed dandy.) He fell in with a group at the university that dreamed of *La Gloriosa*, but that was also not original: it was The Liberal Age in Spain. The vogue was to hate the friars: it was only later that hate was necessary. My father, *el genio* Jote, liked giving speeches. He was good at it. He had a very good memory. Then he got expelled. So much for the liberal age, *la gloriosa*. God Bless Rey Alfonso! And Rajah Malitic and Lakandula! And my Great-Great-Uncle Jorge Luis, the vagabond of Jaca! At home, my father had nothing better to do but raise a storm. That's how Papá discovered the holiday plays." (Trans. Note)

[115] Here lies Raymundo's genius. This biographical nugget is in the wastebasket, not the entry: "if reality is in the seams, where does fantasy abide?" [Mürk, *Queries for Ménârdsz at the Analytic Arboretum*, Antibes, 1967]. (Dr. Diwata Drake, Vence, France)

Entry #7

This story, of the Gentleman from La Mancha, comes back to me in parts. Mamá played Dulc. I could have been three. Very pretty, in the green dress. She couldn't walk anymore, but she was the most beautiful woman in the world. They sat her in a chair on stage, a movable butaka. Papá was the Gentleman. The plot comes back in bits and pieces as I keep reading. It's not much fun to read if you already know the ending. Dulcinea fans herself to death. That's what it looked from backstage, where I watched Mamá. Papá on a bed, shouting with dignity: "Burn the books of my foolish youth, oh ye of good faith!" Something like that. Props (patched-up porcelain bowls, faded embroidery on shawls), open-air mosquito stages in dirt plazas, a fly circling the ugly fruit of a jackfruit tree[116] [117] [118]

---

116 *Langaw lumalaway sa langka*: feeble English fails to assimilate the lyrical nature of this fetid matter. Sorry. (Trans. Note)

117 The Mata family declares that Raymundo's mother died in childbirth. "He killed his mommy; that's why he was nuts" is the prevailing wisdom among that warped, typically Caviteño clan. The passage belies their claim: Raymundo remembers traveling with his player-parents until the age of three, at which time his actress-mother died of tuberculosis. (Estrella Espejo, Quezon Institute and Sanatorium, Tacloban, Leyte)

118 This entry had many crossed-out lines, and I append them as #8, next page. (Trans. Note)

[Entry #8 (lines crossed out and/or heavily edited from #7)]

[series of crossed-out details about mother's eyes, punctuating fairly random sections of #7][119 120 121 122] "People remember her eyes . . . Their strange haunted look still follows me around. They were gray: color of rocks at low tide . . . They devoured her face, took up space in people's memory . . . Must have been the first thing I saw—her eyes in pain, distended. [series of morbid statements] An awful thing to begin life knowing you are hurting another . . . Her blood. I see her blood . . . She washed her handkerchiefs herself when we were traveling. I thought all women breathed blood . . . [childish notions of gender] Boys and girls had differences . . . Mamá had milk, Papá had mustache; Mamá had blood, Papá had tears . . . Mamá coughed blood from her mouth . . . blood poured from her tummy . . . Papá

---

119 Phrases in brackets are my own condensation of writer's main topics in this section. (Trans. Note)

120 "Condensation" is a fine term, Mimi C. This bracketed section, The Dream of Mother's Blood, is perhaps the most significant of the documents presented so far. The unconscious makes signal moves in the kid's elisions. Does the boy erase what he does not wish to confront—his mother's slow death and his perceived role in her dying? In any case, my heart goes out to Raymundo. Not to contradict my esteemed colleague, but the Mata family members may be correct: Raymundo's mother died in childbirth. Note the hallucinatory "blood [pouring] from her tummy." He had psychotic visions, watching her as Dulcinea to his father's Don Quixote, etc. It is likely that at that point in time, she was already dead! (It does not really matter if he did or did not watch her as Dulcinea: what's vital is that this image recurs, a misplaced recollection.) The above elisions—ghostwords—tell us more about the boy's state of mind than any other matter in the journals thus far. If that ruthless proverb is true, that "it is the world of words that creates the world of things," then what ghostworlds do erased words create? And do we really want to know? (Dr. Diwata Drake, Salamanca, Spain)

121 Do *we* really want to know? (Trans. Note)

122 I am pulling out my nose hair, tearing out my earwax, at the insane insinuations of that *salamanquera*, Dr. Diwata (Man)Drake—are you on drugs? You're the psycho! Why can't you let him be, life and legend as we make it, and not muddy us all up in the gummy mucous of your sublime?* (Estrella Espejo, Quezon Institute and Sanatorium, Tacloban, Leyte)
*I mean slime. (Estrella Espejo, ditto)

cried and cried from his nostrils and his eyes . . . There are pros and cons, and I can't tell who I want to be."[123] [124] [125]

---

123 I beg your pardon, Estrella. You mistake me when you insinuate that I view "psychotic" as pejorative. Some of my best friends are psychotic. I use the term as it accords to Mürk's astute taxonomy of personality. In a magisterial lecture, simply and elegantly known in English as "The Theory," the famous Finn from Lima, Peru, in enigmatic prose that, unfortunately, also sounds like Woody Allen on acid (Finns aren't really known for their clarity, plus Claro Mürk had that Peruvian thing—kind of a Carlos-Castañeda peyote-killed-my-brain brand of humor), established his tripartite *Strüctür of the Hüman(ité)*. Incidentally, orthography, for Mürk, illustrated the "[de]sign of the arbitrary," a central tenet of his handwriting. Some texts classify his taxonomy into "the neurotic," "the psychotic," and "the pervert"—but I understand Mürk himself had always regretted those particular translations. These *Strüctürs* are basic to *Hüman(ité)* and are not necessarily pathological, Mürk explained, unless, he said, when applied to full-blooded Scandinavians, "who are all a bunch of damaged neurotics." Claro Mürk, as we know, was bi-cultural, among other bi-identities. (Dr. Diwata Drake, Naantali, Finland)

124 In extremely small, extremely hard to decipher handwriting, the following passage ends the entry, but the handwriting indicates the thought was distinct from the main text, a spider-scrawl of grief: "I guess even now I mix up Mamá's death with her many deaths on the stage: which is the illusion? It's hard to ask that of a boy, and for a long time I could not escape the sense that Mamá would come back, take off the pretty stage dress, and boil barako for me." (Trans. Note)

125 Psychotic or not, these lines say that your petty catfights, Estrella and Dr. Diwata, are not worthy of the boy Raymundo's grief. (Trans. Note)

Entry #9

Raymundo Mata
Latinidad de Jose Basa
San Roque, Cavite
"My Family"

His father disowned him. Publicly, in the plaza. Don Raymundo Mata (it's said he clipped his surname, Mata Eibarrazeta, to fit the badge on his uniform) whipped his son, my Papá, *el genio* Jote, through the fiesta crowds with the blunted leather of his old Guardia Civil lash. Some say it was a cynical drama, a ploy to keep the family's lands. It worked. My grandfather, God Bless His Soul, was a peasant's son from the hills of Jaca, in Spain, a displaced soldier from the Pyrenees who never returned to his cursed hills. Yes, he missed Jaca's barren mountains and the drunken wine brawls that contaminated his stint as a barman in a neighboring mountain town, Aretxabaleta! The old man hated Cavite's lushness, the gleaming untouched Bay. Ah—Jaca. Now there was a town for you! People in Jaca broke their backs for grain to grow! They waited four years for the next rain! You think your lives are miserable? Hah! People do not understand life if they do not know how it was in Jaca!

I myself dream of going to Jaca one day, not to mention the red wines of the mystical village, Aretxabaleta!

For his oldest son to become a scholar, not a soldier, that was unfortunate—but to be with actors and *demonios*, that was dumb.

It was the second son, my uncle, Tio U., who kept the peace. He's the hero of this story. When my uncle was born, no one noticed his awkward head, a family trait, or the vague look of his soulful eyes. Except for his feeble eyes, he bore nothing from his father, who knocked furniture over in blind rages.

My gentle uncle watched the rampage, with useless shame.

My gentle uncle followed in his brother *el genio* Jote's footsteps, but he never caught up. He didn't have the guts, the stamina, or the katsila nose. His was a bit bulbous, more like a hill than a monument. But *el genio* Jote shared his adventures with his brother. He took his little brother to the dances, the fencing matches, the debates. The younger boy read the books *el genio* Jote read. My uncle even memorized my father's speeches, not knowing they were generous helpings from the letters of Montaigne. In the end, it made sense: priesthood became my uncle's calling—the vicarious life.

The brothers' paths forked.

The university kicked my father out, but my uncle succeeded, in his own way. He was no trailblazer. Tio U. took the synodal exam and patiently waited for the results. They gave him a small parish, San Felipe. It was really just a cul-de-sac, and he was only an assistant, a coadjutor, though his grade could have made him curate. But he never complained. "Not everyone can be Burgos," he said with a hint of bitterness. (Yes, he meant the famous canon of the bishopric of Manila, May He Rest In Peace!) He liked his church because from the windows you could look out on the Bay.[126]

I would like to conclude this essay to explain once and for all that my uncle did not encourage the soldiers of San Felipe to riot. Tio U. took care of me when my father left. It pains me to hear the slander. Beat me up again, but my uncle the padre is no *filibustero*.[127] How

---

126 The hero's early identification with the conservative, God-fearing uncle is typical of a child's sentimental progress—later, Raymundo's shift from devout nephew to agnostic radical is not so different from modern-day Manila teenagers, who might wake up Opus Dei one morning and turn Maoist by nightfall, give or take a few strolls along EDSA. (Estrella Espejo, Quezon Institute and Sanatorium, Tacloban, Leyte)

127 After the Cavite Mutiny, suspected subversives (*filibusteros*) were under surveillance, but life became normal. For instance, future Katipunan general Don Mariano Alvarez, implicated in the Mutiny, became town mayor of Noveleta (his son Santiago became Raymundo's pal at the Latinidad de Jose Basa). Don Jose Basa, once exiled to Guam, returned to establish a famous private school of (lame) secondary education. Don Jorge Raymundo Mata, a.k.a. *el genio* Jote, the hero's father, was hunted down because he was one of Burgos's *compares*, part of his barkada, so to speak—the Guardia Civil being unaware that he was really only a bad dramatist. After the Mutiny, *el genio* Jote never returned to Kawit. It's said that he remained incognito in the mountains of Maragondon,

could he turn traitor? He was a scaredy-cat. He could never be a man like my Papá, his brother. He didn't have the spirit, the gonads, you know—*huevos*. That's just his character. He's a man of God. Why would he disguise himself in a priest's outfit[128] [129] [130] and incite insurrection in Burgos's name? He was a man of faith in more ways than one. Yes, he met Burgos—but who hadn't, in the narrow alleyways (and I use the word narrow with double senses!) of that college they attended? He did think Padre Burgos was a bit—tense. Too wound up. A northerner, you know: Tio U. was uncomfortable with

---

allegedly a lithe, cross-dressing bandit. All records—plus vicious rumor—seem to indicate, however, that his flight may have been—well—flighty, occasioned not by *filibusterismo* but *cervantismo*, romantic grief. But in the 1890s, the legend of the revolutionary bandit, *el genio* Jote, took on a certain glamor among Caviteños. (Estrella Espejo, ditto)

128 As noted, a prominent rumor was that, to frame the genius Filipino canon Padre Burgos, scheming friars bribed another Filipino of Spanish descent to disguise himself as a priest in the hours leading to the revolt and so implicate native clergy as conspirators in the soldiers' riot. The similarity to the plot of trumped-up conspiracy in Rizal's novel, *El Filibusterismo*, is not coincidental; the "decoy episode" is also a favorite of fine *fin-de-siecle* melodramas, including my favorites, Sherlock Holmes mysteries and the anarchist novels of Eugène Sue. Raymundo categorically refutes that his uncle was that decoy Filipino priest of Spanish descent. The Mystery of the Cavite Mutiny's Unknown Curate is unsolved to this day. (Estrella Espejo, ditto)

129 Conspiracy theories, also known as outbreaks of paranoid-schizophrenia in the public realm, are symptoms of meltdown in a diseased society. Conspiracy theories abounded in both camps—Spaniards believed all *filibusteros* were evil Masons and native clergy were all subversives. Filipinos believed that every Spaniard was out to get them. Of course, the Spaniards *were* out to get them, but the fact that the substance of Filipino paranoia was true is not the point. The psychoanalytic historian's concern is that the patient (colonial Filipino society) acquired an obsessive pathology, symptom of trauma. To cure it of paranoia's lingering effects need not require rooting out paranoia itself (a symptom that may never go away, *even when the direct cause, the Spaniards, are gone*, which, of course, proves pathology) for "freedom is cognition in a cage" [Mürk, *Exercises* IV]. The cure is ceaseless analysis, which may simply be the burden of being alive. As for the paranoia of the tyrant: power is an illness not even constitutional amendments can cure. (Dr. Diwata Drake, Zurich, Switzerland)

130 Nonsense! The Philippines is not a patient, and you, Dr. Frankenstein, are no nurse. (Estrella Espejo, ditto)

the type.[131] [132] But the Guardia Civil knew they were wrong to lock my uncle up. As proof—the court returned to Tio U. his material goods (what was not torn and burned) and his land. (True, he had to retire and never got the parish of his desire, Kawit, but that's not his fault.) Now he lives a quiet life taking care of his old father, the Spanish *veterano*, basking in the good esteem of his peasant neighbors, for whom he writes letters and interprets canon law. I rest my case. The End.

---

131 It's true Burgos was a northerner: from Vigan, Ilocos Sur. But like Raymundo's Tio U., Burgos was the son of a Spanish militiaman and a Filipina mestiza—one-eighth "Filipino," if you want to be *meticuloso* about it. Burgos, a mestizo like the hero Raymundo Mata, literally threw in his lot with his motherland—his mother's country. Something to think about. The rebellion of the mestizo world, as Filipinos call its hybrid society of mixed souls riven by colonizers—mulatto or Creole being alien phrases—marks the trauma of this revolt. (Estrella Espejo, ditto)

132 On the other hand, hybridity is the violent lot of history. Cf., Frederick Douglass, or Homer A. Plessy. (Dr. Diwata Drake, New Orleans, LA)

Entry #10[133]

[. . . She[134] lured my father into her bastard world, that unseemly place—the dramatic stage. He became obsessed with mounting increasingly more ambitious plays. Not content with religious

---

133 Not knowing whether I should insert this otherwise clean, intact Tagalog fragment, which Raymundo separates into its own page, in an apparent state of incompleteness awaiting further inspiration, I keep it in its place, next to the "essay" (#9). All indications (the same boyishly careful handwriting; lined paper; complex sentences mixed with periodic phrases) show that the fragment may be part of an essay (#9) that he had meant to be a full autobiography, cut short by the fervent, touching digression, *apologia sua Tío U.*, the sweet defense of his uncle. (Trans. Note)

134 Family memory does not deal kindly with Raymundo's mother—after all, she's an in-law. Her origins are ridiculed but only guessed at ("ay, Bisaya—siguro Waray!" was their laughing response to me when I asked—ignorant regionalists!). Mixture of orphan slattern and provincial diva, she was, like her husband, a mestiza whose itinerant beauty indicates she may have been of the priest's-seed caste, that disgusting trend in nineteenth-century Philippines. They met when she played Mary Magdalene to *el genio* Jote's novice Jesus, but what's intact through the Mata generations are not the details but a historic ribald innuendo about their meeting—which says more about the family than about the couple, if you ask me. Disowned by his father, the delinquent Don Jorge Raymundo Mata, *el genio* Jote, eloped with his *dulce estranjera* and took their talents on the road. When she died, c. 1870s, he left his son with his loving, long-suffering brother and disappeared, apparently inconsolably bereaved (though that may be a family fiction to mitigate his paternal failings). As a dramatist, he was bombastic and therefore much in demand. (Estrella Espejo, Quezon Institute and Sanatorium, Tacloban, Leyte)

mysteries, my father dabbled in diabolical myths. One, about three witches who predict a regicide. Another, about daughters who abandon their father, a foolish king. In others—monsters created out of air by a bookish wizard; and fairies who fall in love with an ass.[135] His realism was dangerous. People saw allegories in the smallest speech. When the old king raved in blind madness in the thunderstorm, the weeping audience saw their country betrayed; when the witches cackled about assassination, the audience cheered. In all of them, my mother's delicate cough and tear-dimmed eyes, the stain marks of her talent, possessed their souls. She coughed artfully in all his fables, which grew so probable for everyone else that priests were ready to squash my parents' brief career, but not without first demanding a free performance. No one noticed that it was she—she was reason for each script: if you note Papá's stage directions and plaintive speeches, they were all written with her in mind. He wrote them *to keep her alive.* He was lucky. His eyes were going bad, a genetic malady, or maybe his heart was weak—his househelp noticed

---

135 The fluid conflation of his father's plots with other, more famous texts is not a surprising case of anxious influence: "How unbearably progenitive is the wit of the unconscious?" The answer was Mürk's most famous remark: "It's criminal, my dear Pedro." [Mürk, *Queries for Ménardsz at the Analytic Arboretum*, Antibes, 1967] (Dr. Diwata Drake, Reading, England)

that he failed to see her blood: though it was true that he wept at her growing, infinitely labored, distracted ways. She was an actress: even unto death, she wished to act. My father, the playwright, made art out of sorrow, out of his intolerable recognition of his beloved's slow deterioration. In his last play, *Maladie Cama-Sexual*, also known as *La Remontada*, I note remnants of the drama *La Dame aux Cam-elias*[136] [137] (especially in the title)—but also I sense his terror, in the figure of Tarcelita Gaucho of Leyte, the tragic banditwoman of the secret excre—][138] [139] [140] [141]

---

136 Popular nineteenth-century play, imported from France; the playwright, Dumas *fils*, was not only part-black but illegitimate, which made him doubly irresistible to revolutionists, who were sentimental, like many radicals. (Estrella Espejo, ditto)

137 Dumas *fils* was the great-grandchild of a Haitian slave and her French-nobleman lover, grandchild of Napoleon's foremost general, later Napoleon's enemy, and son of France's best-read novelist, that is, the actual heir of *The Three Musketeers* and *The Count of Monte-Cristo*. Thus, the French contribution to Filipino letters must be situated in its mulatto context—or not. (Trans. Note)

138 Hybrid, schmybrid! French novels translated into the Spanish (and some into Tagalog) were popular among the nineteenth-century bourgeois classes. This explains both Raymundo's diction and his weepy sensibility. Even his bastard Shakespeareanisms have a French perfume, as if translated from some Parisian *feuilleton*. I regret that we somewhat owe our revolution, not just colognes and overpriced scarves, to France. For further information on the connection between Filipino revolutionary emotion and French intellectual movements, including the French Revolution, see my incisive paper, *Francophone Philippines: A Bibliographical History from 1789-1899—Bourrienne's Napoleon to Turot's Aguinaldo* (unpublished). Or actually, just do what I did and look up the list of books in Rizal's library. Such is the bastardy of the revolution—its library drowned us in Europe's sewers while our souls—nurse, nurse, I just want my lugaw filled with luy-a, right now! (Estrella Espejo, ditto)

139 Uhum, ehem, Estrella. I believe lugaw is a Chinese dish, and ginger was indigenous not to Leyte but to India. Nothing is entirely one's own and singular. (Trans. Note)

140 Does not make my desire any less mine. (Estrella Espejo, ditto)

141 As if in mid-cough, the description ends. Borrowed symptoms, imported syndromes: how much of our parents' tedious destiny do we ingest? Raymundo's dramatic delusions, his manic literacy, not to mention the precocious hypermnesia of a world not his own—like an organic fallacy, Raymundo's ills sweetly shadow his parents' lives. But here I agree with Estrella: who are we to speculate and spy, to cure him of his sorrows? "To seek a cure is our lasting fantasy; only in analysis do we vibrate and speak" [Pedro Ménárdsz to Claro Mürk, addendum to *Epistles* No. 54]. (Dr. Diwata Drake, Kalamazoo, Michigan)

Entry #11[142]

"El jardin de las lenguas que se bifurcan"[143] [144]

---

142 What follows is another gestational text, a vestigial gill of language, passionately religious, that permeates the memoirist's childhood. (Trans. Note)

143 That is, "The Garden of Split Speech" or alternatively ". . . of Forked Tongues." The title indicates this piece is either a moro-moro drama or pasyon play, in this case a riff on the biblical Agony in the Garden. (Trans. Note)

144 *Moro-moro:* costume drama with boring Manichean themes, usually involving the bloody deaths of Muslims, whom Spaniards called *moros*, happily transferring their prejudices upon their colonies. Hate this drama—so black-and-white. *Pasyon:* Lenten seasonal play that followed the ups and downs, mostly downs, of the life of Christ. Love this drama—so people-oriented. The plebeian Christ is symbolic of the suffering of the Filipino people. (Estrella Espejo, Quezon Institute and Sanatorium, Tacloban, Leyte)

Miong: *Si, tu. Tu mi engañar*—[145] [146] [147] [148] [149] [150] [151] [152] [153]
Idoy: Oh God, my Lord—don't say that wor—[154]
Miong: It is written. The cock crows and thrice you will—
Idoy: Don't say it. Blasphemy. Jesus Christ!
Bulag: Is this the man? Are you the King of the Jews?

---

145 Roughly—*Yes, you. You will betray me.* The Spanish solecisms here [e.g., *tu mi engañar*] indicate knowledge of Chabacano, Cavite dialect mixing Spanish, Mexican, and Tagalog in Babel-like mash. Variants of this language include Ermita-Chabacano (now extinct); Ternate-Chabacano (born of Mexican escapees from the galleon trade); Cavite City-Chabacano; and Zamboanga-Chabacano, which mixes pidgin Ilonggo, Cebuano, and other Visayan languages with even more pidgin Spanish, resulting in a not-so-pidgin headache. (Trans. Note)

146 Chabacano: mixed languages brought over by Spanish-galleon delinquents from the New World around the seventeenth century. But what's the point of bringing up all the differences, Mimi C.? All were just infestations, espasol germs of *español*! (Estrella Espejo, ditto)

147 Well, true, but these men were also laborers, sailors, and servants whose wandering lives and dependent dreams are also ours. (Trans. Note)

148 Oh, yeah, how I wish for myself that traveler's life, the vagabond freedom of ancient boat-sailing. But I am tied to a hospital cot, with only a sliver of Panalaron Bay on the horizon, meager portion of my ambition—my malady undiagnosed, my dreams unbowed. (Estrella Espejo, ditto)

149 Young Raymundo is well trained in his father's art—melodrama. He casts Miong [Emilio Aguinaldo] as Christ-figure rather than betrayer. This is ironic since it is Miong, in 1897, who betrays the Plebeian Christ, a.k.a. the Supremo Andres Bonifacio!! Idoy's challenge, "Die, oh Moor," is a rash prophecy of Miong's future infidelity. Bastard! (Estrella Espejo, ditto)

150 Your forays, Estrella, into irrelevant, wasteful dudgeon fray my patience. Your invalid state is sad. Please take your medication. (Dr. Diwata Drake, Milwaukee, WI)

151 Irrelevant? Wasteful? I speak of the death of the Supremo, the plebeian hero of the Katipunan—not of the bourgeois Rizal, heroic as he is, or of this—this—blind dramatizing bat of an aesthete—dramatist—this Raymundo—and you call me irrelevant? *Utak-mestiza! Mongrel brain!* Just because I lie here in a dead-end sanatorium, you think you can silence—! *Putragis! Bulag!* (Estrella Espejo, ditto)

152 *Yawa nga de puquis!* (Dr. Diwata Drake, Chicago, Illinois)

153 Oh no you don't! Crucify her! God Knows Hudas Is You! (Estrella Espejo, ditto)

154 The original states: *Oh dios, Bat-hala mio. No midigo esa palab*—. (Trans. Note)

Miong: *Putragis! Bulag!* [155] God Knows Hudas Not Pay!

Idoy: *Caramba!* My sleeve is shorn!

Miong: *Yawa nga de puquis!* [156]

Idoy: Aaaah! Take that! Infidel! An arm for a pocket, shin for a sleeve!

Miong: It is true—your God must be—the one and only—

Idoy: Die, oh Moor, and know that Prince Vilardo, Count of Andalucia, has once more plucked the feathers from the infidels' infamous—.[157]

Bulag: I wash my hands.

Idoy: Oh no you don't. Crucify him.

---

155 The original states: *Putragis* [expletive, variation on *puta*, i.e., a not so good woman]! *Bulag* [taunt on his blindness]! (Trans. Note)

156 More likely, Visayan variant of Chabacano. It is not a kind of fruit. (Trans. Note)

157 Fancy play-acting here. Lifted bodily from medieval romances popular especially among old Spanish priests, who had to approve the plays and thus shaped the archipelago's dramatic tastes. We can trace current drama, e.g., noontime serials and *telenovelas*, to the tastes of those robust, barely educated Basque and Catalan and Castilian priests long ago who lorded over the leisure hours of the colonies. It is the single Spanish legacy we can be grateful for! I especially love the current imports from Venezuela and Korea, though I must say I also keep in delicate wrappings my old Betamax tapes of that classic serial drama—*Marimar*! (Estrella Espejo, ditto)

Entry #12

LETANIA DE NUESTRA SEÑORA[158] [159]
De Senor Padre Butete[160]

Kyrie eleison. Christe eleison. Kyrie eleison. Christe, audi nos. Christe, exaudi nos. Pater de coelis Deus. Miserere nobis. Fili Redemptor mundi Deus. Miserere nobis. Spiritus Sancte Deus. Miserere nobis. Sancta Trinitas unus Deus. Miserere nobis.

Sancta María. (Holy Ship of Christopher Columbus!)[161] [162] [163]

---

158 "Litany of Our Lady." I did not bother translating the Latin passages. In rough pencil, Raymundo injected indecipherable phrases (noted in parentheses) into his Latin exercises. I could only glean their possibilities. (Trans. Note)

159 Correct, Mimi C: no need to bother translating dead words! As part of the miseducation of Filipinos, Latin was the coin of shallow learning. Instead of teaching modern Spanish, the priests preferred obscure Latin. The more rote and useless, the better! Catholic jargon = soup for the Filipino soul. This section is a portion of the *Doctrina Cristiana*, or mumbo-jumbo of the faithful. I give the grade of *sobresaliente* (excellent!) to Raymundo's efforts of translation. How well I remember my own time in Mrs. Cruzada's religion class, writing down every single cardinal virtue and capital sin, with corresponding definitions in polysyllabic vocabulary (noting however that ignorance was no sin while knowledge was no virtue in religion class; but anyhow with fortitude I practiced my penmanship). In the meantime Mrs. Cruzada ate ice candy and asked to bite into our chocolate American snacks if we had any. This, I noted, was gluttony, *gula*, but I gave her my imported M&Ms anyway, out of charity, *caritas*. In the end, my religion grades under Mrs. Cruzada were *sobresaliente*! (Estrella Espejo, Quezon Institute and Sanatorium, Tacloban, Leyte)

160 The renowned author of the *Doctrina Cristiana* was Reverend Father Gaspar Astete. *Butete* means puffer fish. Hahaha. Good one! Bravo, Raymundo! (Estrella Espejo, ditto)

161 The random translations that dominate this "prayer" are signs perhaps of a feverish cholera epidemic going on at the time [1883], though the text offers no explicit comment on his illness. Raymundo again fell victim to this disease nine years later [1892] when cholera struck him in Manila. (Trans. Note)

162 Jokes are a sign of the unconscious. What lies here in this outbreak of hysteria, this gleeful lingual rampage upon the Virgin Mary's names? What's with the tongue so firmly in cheek? What's he trying not to bite off? (Dr. Diwata Drake, Kalamazoo, MI)

163 Your head. (Estrella Espejo, ditto)

Sancta Dei Genitrix. (Holy Genitals!)

Sancta Virgo Virginum. (Holy Redundancies!)

Mater Christi.

Mater Divinae gratiae.

Mater Purissima. (Holy Cats!)

Mater Inviolata. (Mother in a Can?)

Mater Intemerata. (Mother Most Tameme!)

Mater Immaculata.

Mater Amabilis. (Mother Most Speedy!)

Mater Admirabilis. (Mother Even Speedier!)

Virgo Prudentissima. (Holy Bank!)

Virgo Veneranda. (Mother of Venereal Balconies!)

Virgo Fidelis. (Virgin of Dogs!)

Speculum Justitiae. (Specolorum!)

Sedes Sapientiae. (Seder of Knowledge!)

Causa nostrae lactitiae. (What??!!)

Vas Spirituale. (Spirit of Vesicles!)

Vas Honorabile. (Honorary Vesicle!)

Vas Insigne devotionis. (Why the Hell This Chain of Vesicles?!)

Rosa Mystica. (Porn Star Name!)

Turris Davidica. (David the Circumcised?)

Turris Eburnea. (After-Effect of Circumcision?)

Domus Aurea. (House of Aureoles!)

Foederis Arca. (Pubic Arch!)

Janua Coeli. (Freakish Coil!)

Stella Matutina. (Star of Comedians!)

Salus Infirmorum. (Hospital Bed!)

Refugium Peccatorum. (Icebox!)

Consolatrix Affictorum. (Queen of Pain!)

Regina Patriarcharum. (Queen of Chauvinists!)

Regina Propletarum. (Queen of Gobbledygook!)

Regina Apostolorum.

Regina Martyrum. (Queen of Sado-Masochists!)

Regina Confessorum. (Queen of Tabloids!)
Regina Virginum. (Queen of Virgins!)
Regina Sanctorum omnium. (Whatever!)

Agnus Dei, qui tollis peccata mundi . . .
Ora pro nobis!

R: Amen. (Finally!)

Entry #13

May 16, 1884

Noli me tangere: caseated organ of a purple hue. Six inches and counting, enflorescing. Explosive pulp, a bit cheesy. Nigh: left femoral stigmata; tender to touch. Necrosis *in croce*—doctor says to rest it in peace. But oooooooh. The Lollipolypalooza. It won't stop its dance! Bless me father for I have sinned may I do it again?[164] [165] [166]

---

164 The shifts in tone keep surprising me: from the stiff, public diction of the school essays to these private sheaves of purplish waste, this time spattered with medical lingo. Raymundo uses his Latin resourcefully. In any case, I'm just the translator. I only play with the dice I'm given. P.S. "Lollipolypalooza" contains the extravaganza of dialects he indulges in here; I refuse to repeat the mess of his pungent phrases. (Trans. Note)

165 The second journal to which Raymundo attaches a date: this time, it is the year Rizal began writing the *Noli*. Of course, Raymundo in Latinidad de Jose Basa has no clue what Rizal, six years his senior, was scribbling in Europe (though they seem to be reading the same books). Even a few of Rizal's friends thought he was writing a medical treatise—and were annoyed to learn it was just a romance. "Noli me tangere" also referred to a doctor's caveat for dying sufferers full of contagion—"don't touch [this patient]." The line originates from the Catholic-Vulgate gospel of John. Rizal used it as a beautiful metaphor for the canker of colonization. Raymundo's kinship with his hero is explicit in this section's fine allusion to Rizal's historic novel. (Estrella Espejo, Quezon Institute and Sanatorium, Tacloban, Leyte)

166 Onanism nurtures obfuscation. In this case, the clues are obvious. "Six inches . . . a bit cheesy" and the final apostrophe to the Divine: this is a young boy discovering the pleasures of jacking off. Catholic ritual, of course, lends this otherwise dull routine its meaning. Masturbation occurs not in the action itself but in the *act of confession*. The power of Catholic taboo lies in its use of *words*. The solitary act has no *reader*, thus no point: the "masturbator" has yet to exist. He comes into being, authorial and anxious, when he (voluptuously) speaks to the Father, a.k.a. The Other, a.k.a. The Big Other (not to be confused with *the little other*, a distant cousin somewhat removed). This is how "language . . . constitutes the self into the symbolic order" (Mürk, *Epithets* LII). However, I do not recommend it to everyone. (Dr. Diwata Drake, Kalamazoo, Michigan)

Entry #14[167]

Name: Raymundo Mata

Nickname(s): Mundo; Paniki; Bulag; Buta (but stop calling me that)

Father: Don Jorge Raymundo Mata Eibarrazeta of Kawit, a.k.a. *el genio* Jote

Mother: Doña Tarcela Delgado of Leyte[168]

Place of Baptism: Santa Maria Magdalena, Church of Kawit, Cavite Viejo, Cavite

Grade: third year at Latinidad de Jose Basa, San Roque, Cavite

Best friend(s): Agapito Conche; Benigno Santo[169]

Favorite Hobby: Reading; Picking lice[170]; Exploring the Forest[171]

Favorite Song: None

---

167 The entire page is part of a so-called "slumbook," term used in the American era, also known as *libro de memorias* in the Spanish times. Filipino school children filled up self-illustrated autograph books to remember classmates by. Raymundo's *libro* is disheveled, with dedications from irrelevant classmates; I preserve here only Raymundo's page. (Trans. Note)

168 This is the only direct reference to his missing mother's family name and provenance. (Estrella Espejo, Quezon Institute and Sanatorium, Tacloban, Leyte)

169 Agapito Conch*u* and Benigno Sant*i*: town layabouts and future *suspechosos*, destined to be arrested by the Guardia Civil. Many years later, Agapito Conchu was executed at the Fort of San Felipe, one of the *trece martires* of 1896 (Thirteen Martyrs of Cavite). Benigno Santi was last seen with Raymundo in 1902 at Bilibid jail, prisoner of the demonic Americans. Bastards! Americanos! (Estrella Espejo, ditto)

170 Raymundo declines to add to this list the talent for which he was much admired by his peers: prophecying the results of cockfights. He was miserable at other games, such as tuktukan. His wanderings in the forest were secret, but now legend. It is said that his eye condition made superstitious gamblers believe he was something of a cockpit savant; the losers, of course, just beat him up. (Estrella Espejo, ditto)

171 Site of dream, or *traum*. Always useful to italicize, if possible. (Dr. Diwata Drake, Vienna, Austria)

Favorite Book: *Sa Martir ng Golgotha* by Juan Evangelista[172] [173]
Favorite Color: Purple
Favorite Author: Eugène Sue (especially *The Mysteries of Paris*)[174]
Favorite Place: Bazaar La Aurora
Favorite Letter: K[175] [176]

---

172 An original and masterful Tagalog novel, as suspenseful as a *telenovela*. What a young polyglot he is, reading classics in Spanish and Tagalog with versatility! (Estrella Espejo, ditto)

173 *El Martir de Golgotha* was a popular Spanish novel, translated into Tagalog. Such plagiarized editions were common at the time. (Trans. Note)

174 As the opening of the Suez Canal enlivened trade, more French novels translated into Spanish became available. Books, however, were expensive. Raymundo's stash indicates that his family was a) at the time well off; and b) romantic. Eugène Sue is an unjustly forgotten writer of political triple-deckers, the bestselling novelist of his time. My own favorite is his stroke of moral genius *The Mysteries of Paris*. Highlights of Sue's novels include wealthy princes who turn out to be socialist reformers; whore-mistresses; twin orphans separated from birth; serial killers; evil Jesuits; hunchbacks; dwarves; and long-suffering foot soldiers of the Napoleonic wars. In fact, not too different from our contemporary television and komiks masterpieces, except with anarcho-syndicalists. *The Mysteries of Paris* traces the travails of rich radical adventurer Prince Rodolphe, who in disguise foments rebellion among the Paris slums. Any connections to *El Filibusterismo* are inevitable; Rizal admired Sue and read him in both French and Spanish. Not even Victor Hugo escaped Sue's reach: *Les Mysteres de Paris* influenced *Les Miserables*, which in turn influenced elaborate Broadway extravaganzas, which just goes to show that, happily, popular art does not evolve. (Estrella Espejo, ditto)

175 Raymundo's fascination for the trivia of the literary arts, e.g., letters and types, was pronounced. As the entries flow into his adolescence, anagrams, acrostics, coded texts, and other puzzle word games abound. (Trans. Note)

176 Ehem, Ms Translator: the letter K is not an autistic typographical obsession. It is romantic love for the revolution! In San Roque, Raymundo Mata has just met the short-legged but soulful sister of Agapito Conchu, code-named K in this journal. In this retrospective text, he conflates romance with his future, undying love: the nation—that is, K—the Katipunan! (Estrella Espejo, ditto)

Entry #15

I sat in the banyan grove, listening, just in case. Light was falling, the world was going blind.[177] [178] [179] My cue for movement was the faint rustle I began to hear—a feathery fidgeting one could detect only out of long silence. The bats were stirring from their cave,[180] telling me I should begin my walk back home.[181]

---

177 In reality, Raymundo *was* going blind: my understanding from his indifferent relatives, still living a stone's throw from the Republic's Memorial to Independence, in Kawit, is that as a young boy he could see well in the day but had a degenerative nightblindness, a debility now labeled *retinitis pigmentosa*. I empathize with his sense of loss, the symptoms of a possibly genetic ailment over which he has no control. (Estrella Espejo, Quezon Institute and Sanatorium, Tacloban, Leyte)

178 First overt textual reference to blindness, apart from Uncle's Admonition ("Tio U. angry. My eyes . . . ," *see* Entry #6). One hazards the view that blindness at this stage may have been *hysterical*, and I don't blame him. I can only make empathic guesses. Certainly, there are many things this youth might wish to be "blind" to: unrequited love, an absent father, a socially castrated uncle, a dead mother, and a grandfather from Jaca. The cases in which a hysteric's fetish progresses from organic truth are myriad. The human body is not just a vessel, it is an *accomplice* (*cf. Epithets* XLIV). (Dr. Diwata Drake, Kalamazoo, Michigan)

179 Isn't "the world was going blind" personification for dusk? (Trans. Query)

180 This is foreshadowing. In late 1897, after rebel successes in Cavite, the revolutionaries retreated in despair from the fresh onslaught of Spanish colonel Miguel Primo de Rivera and his redoubled forces. They found refuge in paniki caves, dark and sulfurous regions distressingly familiar to one among Aguinaldo's men—the stoic, blind soldier Raymundo Mata. This camp was the famous Biak-na-Bato, last refuge of Emilio Aguinaldo's troops in the First Phase of the Revolution—the war against Spain—and site of the first peace pact, with Spain. It was during this long, sad march that Raymundo received his general's stripe. After Biak-na-Bato, the rebels took the money from the pact, settled in Hong Kong, and with the arrival of the Americans a year later renewed their rebellion, the Second Phase of the Revolution, only to confront the treachery of their American "friends"! This is how it came to be that Raymundo Mata wallowed at the end of his life in the American jails, lamenting his travails in these memoirs. Bastards! Americanos! (Estrella Espejo, ditto)

181 In Raymundo's memory, the rebels' retreat to Biak-na-Bato was suffused with an atmospheric trail of bats—symbol of the darkness into which the rebels would descend after the (temporary) surrender of Aguinaldo's troops to Spain, and the still darker, grim fate that awaited them in the next phase of revolution, against America. (Estrella Espejo, ditto)

But as I climbed off the banyan's gnarled branch, that is, its ghost tree, there he appeared. Bernardo Carpio, Diego Silang, Padre Pelaez—all the heroes of the past rising from the ashes. Or, better and infinitely wonderful, Padre Mariano Gomez, hallowed be his name, who baptized me in stealth (so my uncle says). It was my father—but it was also all of the men[182] of my uncle's stories. Dark, benevolent, and hunchbacked. This man was dressed in rags with a basket of rambutan in his hand.[183] He was skulking to the ground—he crouched, startled. He was dressed as a woman. He did not speak.[184]

Of course I knew him as my father because of his crinkling brow, protruding upper lip, giant katsila nose, and my own eyes: bright, broad-lashed, and stupefied. He was the funeral figure in the portrait in my grandfather's home.

He looked like me.

Except he wore a dress.

---

182 Raymundo nostalgically names a number of heroes for whom I have fond though spotty recall. *Bernardo Carpio*, the only man in the list who never lived, is a superhero in a significant, therefore unread, tale, a giant chained to a cave; the trembling in the cavern as he pushes at his chains explains why the country has volcanoes. Bonifacio liked him; Rizal alludes to him in his novels; geologists are not that into him. *Diego Silang* was an Ilocano rebel who terrorized the Spaniards, though his wife, Gabriela, of course, was the actual fighter. *Padre Pelaez*: saintly Archbishop of Manila who died among the ruins of the Cathedral during the 1863 earthquake (*see also* Entry #5). *Padre Gomez* [*see also* Entry #1]: family friend of the Matas. In the end, disturbingly clerical images indicate the boy was still his uncle's nephew—conservative, Catholic, and devout. I can't wait for him to turn rebel. (Estrella Espejo, ditto)

183 Perhaps a dream. Consequent to the Masturbation Entry (#13), this scene might be viewed as displaced guilt from his joyful habit of jacking off. Or not. What comfort is there when heroes reveal their humanity in gross ways? A lot. The transvestite detail has intriguing psychoanalytic possibilities. As for erotic matters such as rambutan (hairy, vaguely pubic, a squamous aside) and bat-cave fetish (need I mention cavernous holes, and the freaky furry creatures disgorging from them?), I shall leave their psychic design to the reader's imagination. (Dr. Diwata Drake, Kalamazoo, Michigan)

184 Dr. Diwata Drake, I have one word for you. Quack! If I weren't tied to i.v. tubes, with abasic despondency and a still undiagnosed lung problem, not to mention weird epidermal eruptions right now, like fish scales, on my arms, I'd be rushing to Kalamazoo to give you a piece of— (Estrella Espejo, ditto)

He, on the other hand, had no idea who I was.

I took a step forward, he took a step back. I looked back at the emerging, slow flurry of the bats, rising from behind us like ominous ashes. My father followed my gaze and looked with attention at the dark creatures.

"*Paniki*," I whispered.[185] [186]

The name came out of the lowering forest like a sigh of trees, a part of the day's progress. As darkness comes, sounds gain precise trajectories, geometries in space that I can trace, like compass points. For me, nature has a comforting orderliness in the dark. Birdcalls have their logic, insect wings move in reasonable hum. Nature's purposes are clear when sight is gone. I understand that this is not true of most, who are scared by night's secrets—except for this man, my father, whose glance without fear tested the flight of bats with responding radar.[187]

They hovered above us now, as if bidden by their name.

He now looked at me with the same thoughtful glance he gave to the night fliers. They had an awkward way of flying, these blind pilots—not from lack of skill but from habit, their sense of space's immensity that they rightly claim for themselves. Reeling wings, like drunken birds, pointless rocking, zigzagging then "righting" themselves up—their

---

185 "—*Paniki, sabi ko . . . etc.*" Fruit bat is an approximate translation of one of the species known in the Philippines generically as paniki. Whether Raymundo uses the term as vocative, addressing his father as demonic apparition, or nominative, naming the actual bats, is ambiguous. In any case, flying vermin appearing with long-lost fathers is not a good sign. (Trans. Note)

186 Most probably the golden crown flying fox, *Pteropus vampyrus*, found only in the Philippines and once swarming over central and southern Luzon, in the days before concrete condominiums ruined its habitat and the view from the (also diminished) esteros. If I might add, "blind as a bat" is not scientific; bats can see, but it's more convenient for them to navigate by sound because they're *weird*. I had to learn all that in high school biology, when really, all I wanted was to play bulangkoy. Ah well, those were the days, how our youthful prisons become charmed memories. (Estrella Espejo, ditto)

187 The use of the modern acronym radar [from *r*adio *d*etection *a*nd *r*anging] is an inspired translation from the antiquated Tagalog. (Trans. Note)

bumbling aviation mimicked the trembling leaves, the rustling wind in the woods, a cunning shadow-like presence. They opened their mouths as if to scare us—a feral yawn that doubled as sonar scream. Then they flew off, leaving us to our thin radars of recognition, our infinitely weaker human ways of connection.

"Paniki,"[188] [189] [190] responded my father.[191] "My poor Bulag."[192]

"No. Not Paniki. My name is Raymundo," I said, the retort in his presence I've always wished to speak.[193]

---

188 The text implies that this term paniki was a boyhood nickname of the hero. The state of the manuscript indicates many pages have been lost, and the scenes that began this name-calling are not told. (Trans. Note)

189 Aha! A telling reference to the hero's nom de guerre. Raymundo was attached to fruit bats perhaps because of the "blind" creature's metaphoric (or is it metonymic, this part of my education always confuses me, in the same way I've always mixed up Nashville with Memphis) relationship to the author's degenerative eye disease. (Estrella Espejo, ditto)

190 Names are the most arbitrary among the plots that frame us; simply responding to our "names" is an act of repression. What's hidden and slips in response to the question, "who are you," is intolerable: *I have no idea, someone else gave it to me.* The typical Filipino name—the ones that conjoin the Spanish with the American (e.g., Cherry-Pie Morena, Dimples de la Cruz)—inscribes old struggles in daily speech. But at least they're funny. (Dr. Diwata Drake, Foggy Bottom, Washington, D.C.)

191 This section, The Dream of the Bat and the Father, is the boy's third hallucination. Another psychotic break, wrapped in historic tissue. It's no surprise the boy was prone to visions, given his orphan troubles. That these spells of lunacy have a coherent literary quality is, to my mind, more disturbing. Perhaps it underlines for us the paralyzing fact that, above all, neurosis is *word-bound*, and it spooks me to think one day one will submit to the mind's intolerable whim—when in dementia language becomes "a shuddering excretion of pustulant dreams" (cf. *The Mürky Manifesto*, tract written by renegade students of Mürk, led by the Colombian-Latvian translator/critic Pedro Ménárdsz and known collectively as The Mürky Mürks, expelled from Mürk's Analytic Arboretum in Antibes in 1968 for a bizarre episode of mud throwing and an "ecstatic abandonment of science," one of them even pinching me as he exited. The Ménárdszian minion left a ruby streak on my cheek, shaped like a soggy rhombus, which sometimes stings even now, a phantom palm). (Dr. Diwata Drake, Foggy Bottom, Washington, D.C.)

192 As previously noted, Raymundo was fondly called Bulag, especially by his boyhood friends. His code-name in the revolution, though, was Paniki. (Estrella Espejo, ditto)

193 This seems to be a Good Dream. As opposed to the Bad Dream, the Good Dream "names" (so to speak, but not really) traumas. The boy's trauma seems to be that he is unknown to father, and vice versa. This kind of dream leaves you refreshed, wide awake,

The message of his image: he was alive.

I went after him, but he was gone. I ran back home, bats tracing my joy in dark reels, flying upside down like drunks. But when I reached the windows of the kumbento, and I saw my uncle's dark figure, like a paniki himself, outlined in hunched fatigue, as if reading, I stopped. Would he believe me? And anyhow, what did it matter? It was this grave, nerve-wracked man who had taken me to his burdened heart—it was he who loved me like my father.

Tio U., I saw him dressed like Apoy Yaka, an old lady, he carried a basket of rambutan.

And what is your evidence that woman was he, my son?

Because he ran away when he heard my name.

---

and unaccountably happy, as if your dilemma, by this "naming," has been resolved. The Bad Dream, of course, is whatever makes you a mess. It's true that on any day the Good Dream could become the Bad Dream, and vice versa. The problem with The Mürky Mürks, according to Mürk, in his "Letter to Ménårdsz" [Mürk's *Epistles* No. 54], is that they believed language of *any kind* was a virtue, whereas, as we should know, it will always doublecross us. The reddish stain on my cheek, a welt of consciousness, traveled with me that entire summer, though on that day I, too, chased the Mürky Mürks out of the arboretum—faithful to my mentor, betrayer of my love. (Dr. Diwata Drake, Villefranche-sur-mer, France)

Ay, bulag ka talaga! [194] [195] [196]

---

194 Chronologically, this entry seems to have occurred or been situated during vacation months (March through May) of 1885. A year later his uncle sent the chastened boy off to Manila, in anger over Raymundo's alleged truant exploits in San Roque, wandering off to bat caves and forests when he should have been memorizing the litanies to Mary at the Latinidad. Thus ended the San Roque chapter in his life. (Trans. Note)

195 The issue is why? Why does this dream occur at this point in his life? He is undergoing puberty; he dreams of manhood; he exercises freedoms he has never indulged in before; he is sexually volatile, experimental, and confused. Various signs of repression fly about: a healthy, accepting homosexuality? chronic onanism? Or perhaps the bats (in this dream mere background) are in fact his real subject, the foreground of his reverie: i.e., *putas*, or *mga babaing mababa ang lipad* [low-flying women, for which bats are also metonyms]. The question remains: what was he doing in the banyan tree? The forest's association with the father—a masked rebel, a skirted bandit, a wanderer in exile whispering secrets in his ear—comes off as ruse: Disguise. No alibi is an accident, so says the savant. Just as, on a national level, what erotic *jouissance* is encoded, nay, gleefully discharged, in the aggressive battle with the colonial master—masked here in the banal skirts of doomed romance, this melodrama between *pére* and *fils*? (Dr. Diwata Drake, New Orleans, Louisiana)

196 Oh. My. God. Dr. Diwata. My kidney's going spastic, my knuckles are cracking. Kill me now with your speculative saecolorum, Dominus vobi-scum! You're worse than the mumbo-jumbo of the friars! This is a heart-rending meeting with the boy's long-lost father, a moment of affection, of familial reunion! Where's your humanity, your sensitive side: you vampire, you black-hearted, malnourished—bat? (Estrella Espejo, ditto)

Entry #16

"The Legend of Travestida"

Always the double, always the mirror[197] [198]—I was in his clutches: the Man of No Return. He was my father, but he was also my mother; he was the womb and he was the grave.[199] [200] He wore a striped jacket with dutiful cravat, like that worn by Atenistas:[201] a ready-made tie clipped to his collar, a vulgar insincerity. He looked man-made, not wrought by God. Even his trade was contrived: a fruit-seller in the wilds, where wild fruit held dominion. His jacket did not match his floral skirts, with their green-and-violet

---

197 *Siempre doblando, siempre espejándose.* An interesting switch to puerile Spanish, which seesaws through these early sections, at times in random scribbles, at others in packed passages with excess fat. (Trans. Note)

198 Does the writer mean "I" is always doubling and mirroring itself? Or does *doblando* [*sic*] refer to the Man of No Return? The Self's sentence, it is true, is a dangling modifier. In any case, it is interesting that Raymundo recreates his father's apparition in picaresque form, this time as a quixotic encounter starring a transvestite. (Dr. Diwata Drake, Manila, Philippines)

199 Oh who cares about your mambo-jargon, Dr. Diwata?! I liked best the Shakespearean allusion: "the earth that's nature's mother is her tomb;/what is her burying grave that is her womb" [*Romeo and Juliet*, 2.3.10-11]. (Estrella Espejo, Quezon Institute and Sanatorium, Tacloban, Leyte)

200 Please explain the significance of Shakespeare? (Trans. Note)

201 Students at the Latinidad and his next school, the Ateneo, probably studied Shakespeare, you know, translated into Spanish, of course, hence the allusions! I just love these wordplays in the text, don't you? Makes me think of my college classes with that demon teacher, Profesora Magdalena Rama. Aroint thee, witch! I still hear her condescending cackle in my dreams, most pronounced when I could not explicate in class the stupid significance of the pounding of the gates in *Macbeth*. It's funny how abuse grows on you. Profesora Magdalena was my worst nightmare, with her silver bowl-cut of a Hamlet-wig—come to think of it, she had sunken cheeks with big dark eyes, too, she looked like a skull—but her enunciation was golden, a gliding stream: she spoke like the Holy Spirit, from the diaphragm. O Profesora Magdalena Rama, where art thou now? Dead! Most famous student of the Ateneo was, and still is, Dr. Jose Rizal—and it was downhill from there. Raymundo, after his serial truancy at Latinidad de Jose Basa, arrived at the Ateneo a full decade after Rizal. (Estrella Espejo, ditto)

lace. Nobody was fooled. I spied him from a heart's-width—the length of my sight; my uncle was right. I was blind. In that case, he fooled me. Maybe he was my father; maybe he was my mother. He spoke my name.

"Fruit Bat."

But how do you know who I am?

You left me before I even learned to read, and now you mock my longing.[202]

Love is not what I want from you, but it is my right.

He did not stay. He left me with ten admonitions:[203]

"1. Beware of dogs. 2. In certain temperatures, watermelon is poisonous. 3. Love your neighbor as yourself; when you are moved to kill him, don't. 4. Also, never pick a fight with printers, boat porters, and ladies. 5. Penetrate beyond illusion. 6. Never drink of the sap of the paraiso bark in the month of April. 7. Beware the seed of the paho fruit, fleshy and fulvous; the lanzones fruit, when burnt, acts as pesticide. 8. Whosoever takes up arms for love of country is as a babe suckling at his mother's breast and moves in harmony with nature. Also, if you don't look back at your past, you're a pest. 9. August, the month of Caesar, is a good time to go to war. 10. Now I know why women wear skirts."

He left, taking everything with him, even the rambutan in the basket. Over the course of years, these are the bandit *el genio* Jote's reported acts of bravery, which I enumerate briefly to save lamp oil:[204] disarming a Guardia Civil in Noveleta while said enemy was

---

202 The text is garbled here, but the sentiment, as translated, is, I believe, faithful to its plaintive intent. (Trans. Note)

203 There are three known decalogues arising from the revolution: Andres Bonifacio's; Emilio Jacinto's; and Apolinario Mabini's. This, *el genio* Jote's Decalogue, is the fourth. The rebels liked counting in tens, like the god of Moses. (Estrella Espejo, ditto)

204 This is perhaps figurative: Raymundo found it hard to see at night, though many witnesses, especially young women and cockpit gamblers, attest to his quite lively vision during the day. (Estrella Espejo, ditto)

eating a baduya (flavored banana) in 1896; stealing a horse in the dead of night and serving it to troops in Naik by morning, leaving only a note (but this may be apocryphal); offering lunch to the wounded Supremo (going by in a hammock) near Limbon;[205] [206] helping a woman out of a ditch in Balara; acting as courier in multiple instances in the trench lines between San Mateo, near Manila, and the revolutionary forces in Cavite; picking juicy pakwan to offer troops exhausted by battle in Imus. In all these comings and goings, *el genio* Jote remained incognito yet appreciated, rumored and ineffable, and impossible to interview, such being his vaunted modesty,

---

205 Raymundo refers to the revolution's early days: cohorts of Miong, a.k.a Emilio Aguinaldo, Magdalo general of Kawit, raided the Manila leader Bonifacio's camp in Limbon. Mga Hudas! Traitors! After the election fiasco of Tejeros Assembly, the men of Miong arrested the Supremo of the Katipunan for treason, among other lies. What do you expect of Caviteños! Philippine history has never recovered from this tragedy. Raymundo attests that his father heroically offered a guava to the bloodied Bonifacio, Supremo of the Katipunan, who was carried to trial in a duyan—a frail, swaying hammock! This moving incident, of *el genio* Jote meeting the Supremo, is like Veronica meeting Christ, except with a Guava instead of a Shroud, and it occurs in no other Filipino text. How nice that the son offers this evidence of his father's patriotism. The reference to Limbon is confusing: if this were written *before* Raymundo moved to Manila to study at the Ateneo in June 1886, then this is a *flashforward* to the Magdalo raid in Limbon in April 1897 (eleven years later). This proves my suspicion that this narrative is not anachronistic but polychronistic, that is—proof of the bad food in Raymundo's Bilibid jail cell when he was writing this under custody of American G.I.s! Not to mention the water torture he endured! Oh the inhumanity! Bastards! Americanos! (Estrella Espejo, ditto)

206 By the way, the noble use of waterboarding in the G.I. jails was beautifully explained in an admiring description of an American hero of the Philippine-American war, the court-martialed Major Edward Glenn: "Major Glenn was highly commended by his superiors for his good work. The major was a relentless interrogator. As an aid with uncooperative officials, he used a method of duress called 'the water cure.' The uncooperative official was spread-eagled on his back and the end of the hose was run into his mouth. The other end of the hose was connected to a water faucet. Water was poured into the victim until he swelled up and thought his guts would burst." The effusive chronicler goes on to say: "American Army surgeons later testified that the water cure was not lethal in itself, although they did admit the victim might expire from heart attack or sheer fright during the procedure." Bastards! Americanos! (Estrella Espejo, ditto)

but most of all his slipperiness,[207] [208] his astonishing mystery. He also raised a ruck[209] [210]—

---

207 "Slipperiness": one more analytic cue. Let us note that Raymundo develops this scene of the father in two types of text. Here, as so-called romance, that is, fiction; and in previous, Entry #15, as diary—non-fiction. In diary form, the father is a Good Dream—equivalent to such benevolent *padres* [fathers] as Padre Gomez and Padre Pelaez—while in the romance, please note the rancor—his father is suspect, he is "slippery." In fiction, the son gives way to bile: "You left me before I learned to read and now you mock my longing." This is an abandoned boy's riposte to a deadbeat dad. Very likely, truth is hiding in the tale. Significant, then, is Raymundo's sophistication, his mature experiment with difference, with forms of narration. To unload the load on his mind. It's as if, in this "multifarious" tome, Raymundo is aware of the curiously shapeshifting effects and uses of story, to recall Truth. (An important trope is his verb above: *to read*.) Awareness of multiple viewpoints *within one person* is unprecedented in revolutionary memoirs. Instead, what we have is dueling versions *among different persons* of the same dismal scenes. I would say that among the bloodiest battles in the history of revolution are those between *dueling memories*, in which each side imagines only his single stubborn version is true. However, Raymundo portrays here the awareness of the split being, through his doubled father—the duel that dwells within. (Dr. Diwata Drake, New Orleans, Louisiana)

208 Split? Dear Diwata—Raymundo's father is not a banana. (Estrella Espejo, ditto)

209 The text reads: *Nag-alsa ng gu*—. Raymundo does not finish the passage nor write legibly. I deduced the following fragment—*nag-alsa ng gulo* (he raised a ruckus). What do you think, Estrella? (Trans. Query)

210 I suggest *nag-alsa ng gamit*—or *nag-alsa-balutan* (packed his bags). Rebel refugees who scrambled out of Manila and into the towns of Cavite after the disastrous August 1896 battles in the capital were called *mga alsa-balutan* by the Caviteños. Although the phrase may as well be *nag-alsa ng buhangin* (blowing in the wind). (Estrella Espejo, ditto)

Entry #16a[211]

Kawit, June 19, 1886[212]

Dear Son,

I hope you are doing well. Someone a concerned correspondent a good friend tells me that you are doing too well [*sic*], he says he's seen you at the Botica,[213] imbibing who knows what and shooting the crap with well-known wastrels like a damned indolent youth. Beware the gossips at Botica Luciano! Remember what happened to your father. Please do not f—.[214] That witch in a skirt carrying a basket of rambutan that you saw by the "bat caves" during vacation, I say again, that fright—that fright was not your father you came home with a fever [*sic*]! And what were you doing in the bat caves anyway! Whatever he said disregard [*sic*]. Your father— may he rest in peace—he is gone. Do not f— like him. You have always had a strong imagination I blame myself [*sic*]. I allowed you to stay awake at night reading books and now see what we

---

211 This letter bleeds from the backside of Entry #16, "The Legend of Travestida." In hasty Spanish, with run-ons but much affection. The tortured priest-uncle, now a robust farmer, is more of a rustic than a writer. The only entry in these journals not by Raymundo, included here because it's about him. Anyway it was in his mess of papers. (Trans. Note)

212 Rizal turned twenty-five exactly on this date. Raymundo is not yet seventeen. (Estrella Espejo, Quezon Institute and Sanatorium, Tacloban, Leyte)

213 Three popular student hangouts in San Roque, Cavite, were the pharmacy, owned by the Chinese mestizo Victoriano Luciano; the bookshop Bazaar La Aurora, next to the Botica and owned by Antonio San Agustin; and the cockpit, of course. Luciano and San Agustin will become two of the Trece Martires (Thirteen Martyrs of Cavite) killed at the onset of the revolution, along with Raymundo's beloved friend, Agapito Conchu, *R.I.P.!* Happily, in this journal, Agapito is recalled, thus revived and lives. Such was not the case for Luciano and San Agustin. However, their fate is memorialized in the town's modern name. (Estrella Espejo, ditto)

214 *Filibuster* was the scary, four-syllable word, worse than fucking. (Trans. Note)

have reaped. You are going blind. In more ways than one. Beware, my son. Take care of yourself. Your condition can only degenerate if you do not follow God's will mark my words [*sic*].

Blindness is not only physical it is spiritual my son [*sic*]. My concerned correspondent says your illness is God's judgment on you bla bla bla but have faith. The God of love is with you I pray—be warned—there are forces of evil out there my son terrible occasions for sin avoid them [*sic*]. Beware your father's fate a good man with bad judgment of his peers,[215] God have mercy on his soul. Remember your Lolo is a katsila, a veteran policeman with rank and honor. Yes I know he's going nuts but that's not his fault. If you only knew what syph—I mean that—well, cholera—can do to the brain! And even if our name has diminished our pride need not.

I am sending a ticket for a passenger boat to Manila. Take it from Cavite Puerto. Mang Rufino[216] will pick you up go with him in peace, do not resist [*sic*]. You will be enrolled at the Ateneo everything has been arranged [*sic*]. You will live at Señora Chula's boarding house on a decent street Calle Caraballo please check the address. She has taken care of many good young men of Cavite God bless her generous soul. May the Jesuits straighten you out so help you God [*sic*].

Much love,

Tio U.

---

215 The priest-uncle Tio U. refers to the father's association with the *filibustero* Padre Burgos, though some family members insist that the letter in fact warns about the father's lapse in marrying a non-Caviteño ("bad judgment of his . . ."). It seems at this point that Raymundo was enamored of a young woman (Lady K?) while hanging out with a disreputable barkada, his gang of low repute. The priest-uncle preferred him to go into orders. Ateneo was their compromise. (Estrella Espejo, ditto)

216 Rufino Mago, or Magos, of Binakayan and Cavite City. Later in these journals, this old servant reappears in the hero's fateful journey to Dapitan in Zamboanga. (Trans. Note)

P.S. I'm sending your favorite a bag of lanzones and baby man-goes still green from the garden and a handful of guavas I urge you to burn your books except for the novels. Which I would like to have back [*sic*].[217]

---

217 As noted by Professor Estrella, this singular memoir came together finally while Raymundo was in an American jail, circa 1902; however, as I have taken pains to point out, the *physical manuscript* is multifarious. There are odd and various sheets; in degenerating handwriting and polyglot styles; all bunched in a tin can—nestled as Raymundo's executor had abandoned it, in an old leather medical bag. The bag also contained crumpled trash, random paper, as well as worms. I have ordered it chronologically as best I could. As he grows into adulthood, bursts of retrospection occur, less so in his immature texts. Gradually, the sense of time in each section becomes lucid. Altogether, the result, yes, is an inconclusive carousel of the words (and worms) of Raymundo's memory: yet without a doubt it unfolds a man's, and nation's, story. (Trans. Note)

Part Two

Provinciano in the City

In which the hero arrives in Manila, denounced for truancy and
"imbibing"—Becomes a sexual deviant—Learns 'real' Spanish
at the Ateneo Municipal—Hates his boardinghouse—Describes
Lady K, of the short legs and ample modesty—Nurses a broken
heart—Feels like hell—Is scared shitless by Father Gaspar—Is
cursed by a book—Observes Agapito's secret passion—Shares
doughnuts and chocolate with a cripple, among others—Prefers sex
to sedition—God punishes him for not becoming a Mason

Entry #17

So this is what it's like. Boats, cobblestones, esteros.[218] Eating walnuts from paper cones while leaning against the wall.[219] Horseshit
on streets, bats in trees. Chinese men, hair like kite-tails, selling
paper by the handful. While the women smell of fish and look like
angels. (There are also innocent girls I better not touch.) Rats. Spitting, spitting everywhere, a carnival, a contest of spitting. Good one.
Got it smack on the curtain of the carretela.[220] [221] It smells here. It
really does. Rotting fruit, guano, shrimp-fry, mud, and the awful

---

218 That is, swampish rivulets flowing from the Pasig River. A term still used today to
denote waterlogged and still swamp-smelling ancient portions of the city. (Trans. Note)

219 *Cucuruchos de almendras habang nakasandal ha pader*. In these sections on his arrival
in Manila, the young diarist from the provinces favored Espangalog, street-talk variant of
Spanish and Tagalog (with some Visayan). (Trans. Note)

220 *Tumpak ha tela de carretela*: his **prepositions** verged on the Visayan, though **nouns**—
especially for manufactured goods, as in *tela* (cloth, or curtain: *telon*) and *carretela* (horse-
cart)—were Castilian. **Adverbs** (e.g., *tumpak*) mainly Tagalog. (Trans. Note)

221 The linguistic hash has its logic. That **nouns**, easily imported elements, should be
Castilian makes sense: in the American-centric century, for instance, Filipinos logically
called a refrigerator just *Frigidaire*; to take a picture is *to Kodak*—the commercial noun
is its being, commerce constructing the being of the colonized—no need for translation.
Prepositions have always been bane the of language-learners. Here, the Visayan
preposition *ha* signals the dominion, unheralded but ubiquitous, of regional, migrants'
languages in the nation's soul. As for the rampant Tagalog **adverbs**, bubbling up like
undigested walnuts-in-a-cone, they are the crunchy dregs of Raymundo's mishmashed
linguistic tract. (Dr. Diwata Drake, Zurich, Switzerland)

offal[222] [223] [224] [225] that clutters the streets—trash, trash, trash, even in front of Don P.R.'s mansion: it's a city of garbage. Not to mention the Germans and Dutch by the waterfront, their perfume made me cough. I packed so quickly I'm not wearing the right shoes: I'm wearing Chinese flipflops[226] and carrying a carton suitcase, like a peddler. So this is Manila. Damn that letter writer. I could die of dysentery from everyone's phenomenal phlegm.[227]

*

---

222 *Bastos na basura*: Raymundo's endless wordplay is obsessive. (Trans. Note)

223 I would hesitate to say that some pathology of the tongue possesses Raymundo Mata. But obsession might be normal, especially among Filipinos. These psychodynamics of the everyday can wrap anyone in phonemic warps: alliteration, anagrams, et al.—play abounds in anyone's daily speech. Best to view linguistic play as humorous weapon, not disorder. In such subjects as Raymundo Mata, the slipshod work of the colonial unconscious joins with the exuberance of language acquisition to make of the linguistic mess of one's daily life, well, a form of art. (Dr. Diwata Drake, Schaffhausen, Switzerland)

224 Ha! Speaking of puns, Dr. Diwata, I have three words for you: *Psychobabaw*! (Estrella Espejo, Quezon Institute and Sanatorium, Tacloban, Leyte)

225 Ah, indeed! *Touché*. I urge you to read my opus, Professor Estrella—the grand offshoot of my work with the great Mürk in the aftermath of that sad fracas, the Antibes Plenary of 1968. I sided with him, my mentor, and betrayed my love, true. But it was all worth it! Read my book *Your Lovely Symptoms—The Structure of the [Un]Conscious, Not Really Lang[ue] or Even a Parol[e]*, and it may explain your fine phrase. These are the symptoms of your peculiar desire, couched in your pun: **Foreignism, Judaeo-Christianism,** and **Tagalism.** To wit, psychobabaw [etymology]: *Psycho*, foreign [in this case Americanist] slang, short for psychopath!, pronounced: sigh-koh! *Babel*, or *babble* [hence, psychobabble], obvious Biblical allusion. *Babaw*: Tagalism, a local epithet, pejorative adjective, meaning shallow! What's enfolded in your triple-decker pun? *Your lovely symptoms, fractured, fragmented, [w] hole!* (Dr. Diwata Drake, Schaffhausen, Switzerland)

226 *Chinitong-chinelas*: another nonsensical neologism; racist. (Trans. Note)

227 *Nakakapatangang nganga*: gross. (Trans. Note)

Entry #18

"Dagobert the Coward,
Or, Memoirs of a Student in Manila, 1886"[228] [229]

"To hell with secret lists, jousts in the dark on my white horse—rescuing not maidens but my hot-coal hands, my feverish limbs." So resolved Dagobert the Coward on his way to speak her name. The great nineteenth-century swordsman, Conde de Monte-Buntis, held by the hand the sweet prepubescent Lady K, damsel of fan, cowl, and comb,[230] [231] of paper flowers and leaden pen, of short legs descending from endless stairs, Manila mantilla in disorder, but no one dared notice (she was only fourteen). Dagobert looked downcast at her feet, step by step descending: embezzling desire. The Count held

---

228 "Si Dagoberto, Ang Duwag, o Memorias de un estudiante en Manila, 1886." Short-short story written in some kind of frenzy: it has no ending and no apparent beginning. Worse, it is written in Espangalog, that collegiate mix of Spanish and Tagalog (freely interpreted here). (Trans. Note)

229 In the year 1886, Raymundo moved from San Roque, Cavite, to the Ateneo de Manila, sent down to the city by his uncle. An extant letter notes why (*see* Entry #16a). As this entry notes, the anonymous poison pen was most likely one of the Aguinaldo brothers, Crispulo or Miong ["the vain and vertical Meditabundo"], who wrote to Tio U. of Raymundo's truancy, about his being "seen at the Botica, imbibing who knows what and shooting the crap with well-known wastrels." Damned nosy busybodies these old heroes were. (Estrella Espejo, Quezon Institute and Sanatorium, Tacloban, Leyte)

230 Here, Raymundo shifts from Tagalog to Spanish: from *del pañuelo y la peineta, de las flores de papel y la pluma de plomo*, then back to nonsense Espangalog. I have endeavored to do it injustice (i.e., translate): *binting binibini sa escalerang hagdang no hay hanggan . . . de pie de paa descender desear ¡o mi! de desfalcar . . .* The last-mentioned verbs occur as if pilfered from a thesaurus, in alphabetical order. (Trans. Note)

231 Yet meaning is, in many ways, clear: this story is an abject tale of growing heterosexual, normative desire: the boy socialized into his world's hierarchies. However, most delightful is a glossary of adjectives, a series of antonomasia—my favorite is the stupefied horse, Atontado. Perhaps a game in his Spanish grammar copybook, like his abecedary that begins the diary, Ms. Translator? (Dr. Diwata Drake, Florence, Italy)

her in perpetuity, in impunity, in insolence.[232] [233] [234] *Ecce homo*: he, Dagobert, would put an end to that.

But first: what were his weapons? Item: a subjunctive and morbid heart. Item: lots of adjectives. Item: allusions to Virgil and other classical sources. Items: loquacious, nose, dwarfishness.[235] Item: a bag (more like a paper cone, a cardboard cornet) of walnuts.

Second: what were his obstructions? His own heart, his speech, his knowledge, his smallness, his history of powerful vacillation.

Thus Dagobert went to war, with a cardboard cone of words[236]— stupefied, tedious, fugitive, brooding, and anxious. His loyal horse, *Atontado*, gleamed brightly on the grass, a ruminant pillow. His young squire, *Enojoso*, a bit thick-skulled, had the monotonous habit of flicking his right shoulder like an epileptic, but Dagobert couldn't afford any better. Knights with good posture were hard to find in modern times. *Fugaces*, his plural patrons, a pair of evil twins, had faces like Romans

---

232 Typical of Raymundo's juvenilia: Latinate words overpower even his Tagalog. (Trans. Note)

233 Yes, I was overpowered once—it's true, I loved him, he of that angelic frenzy, that ideological righteousness, my love. Pedro Ménårdsz, that Colombian-Latvian firebrand, prophet, leader of the eventual outcasts of Antibes, the Mürky Mürks. True, I was once on the side of his genius, on the day he took us hostage, in his thrall, during the Antibes Plenary. I did not expect my response; he had never even bothered to flatter me. I was just taken. For a moment, I believed he would relieve me of the knot, the burrowing borromean knot of my desire—in which my tripartite parts, Filipino, American, and Filipino American— might find solace in the Ménårdszian solution to identity, which had bounds, not just gaps. But it was not to be—I could see the fallacy in my love, the apostasy of answers. There was no way to pleat my parts into ironed and orderly design, like the Catholic uniforms of my childhood. And so we chased him out, chased him, chased him, chased him out of the garden of the Antibes Plenary, chased him out along with the rest of his fantastical heresiarchs, the Mürky Mürks of 1968. All I have is this throb in my cheek, where once his acolytes pinched me, as they fled. It still hurts. (Dr. Diwata Drake, Vence, France)

234 Uh. Huy! Psst! Psst! Dr. Diwata, Dr. Diwata, are you still there? Snap out of it. Huy! Psst! (Estrella Espejo, ditto)

235 The Spanish trio is: *locuaz, nariz, pequeñiz*. (Trans. Note)

236 *Cucurucho de palabras*. (Trans. Note)

but no idea how to ride a horse; thus they paid Dagobert to under-take adventures while they sat safely at home, picking their teeth (but with what elan, what carious excavation!). Ah, as for the vile, the ven-triloquial, the vain and vertical *Meditabundo*—arch-rival in horseplay, doppelganger from the Dolomites (via Kawit). *Zozobra*, the cackling witch, was perhaps less treacherous than Meditabundo, his old friend.

There was a time when Dagobert and Meditabundo[237] bathed together happily in village streams, catching fireflies, egging each other by the riverbanks with furious concentration, with affection. Dagobert remembers how his tender eggs were so often cracked and broken because Meditabundo always cheated in the game. Medit-abundo needed to win. He needed to be boss, even for an eggshell. The Tuktukan King.[238] Dagobert, wise for his young years, understood his friend's frailty, and his fingers shielded his crushed eggs[239] in vain. Dagobert, though a coward, never cried.

Now as they set off, separate but simultaneous, on the way to Zozobra Castle, to vanquish the power of the Count and so free the pale menarchal maiden, Lady K, Dagobert was not so sure of Meditabundo's

---

237 Meditabundo, meaning "brooding," seems to be conflated here with Miong, that is, Emilio Aguinaldo, later first president of the Republic, Raymundo's old childhood friend by the Binakayan streams. Idoy, a.k.a. Candido Tria Tirona, is also a likely suspect, except that he is not known to be "brooding"; he was more of a bruiser. (Estrella Espejo, ditto)

238 Tuktukan, from Tagalog tuktok (to peck), the shameless game played with eggs and string, occurs again here in Raymundo's story—a trope in the diary. Boys tied a string around their waist and an egg around the string's other end. Making vulgar pelvic motions, hands off the string, boys "egged" each other until someone's shell cracked. Boys on the sideline made bets on who would "crack" first. Prominent scene in *Makamisa*, Rizal's alleged third novel, features a competitive game of tuktukan. The game is still popular in organized events, such as family reunions and corporate bonding parties. (Estrella Espejo, ditto)

239 Filipinos, in their ancient pastimes, had no Freudian hang-ups. Swiveling one's crotch to crack someone's "eggs," visible play of virile humping as a form of leisure activity, became "obscene" with the arrival of the Spaniards. One good reason for the revolution against Spain was that the Spanish were "k.j.": killjoy. One imagines an Eden of orgastic foreplay in prehispanic Philippines, a fabulous paradise of innocent phalluses in the world before Magellan. (Estrella Espejo, ditto)

goodwill. First of all, it was Meditabundo who had written that evil letter to his Uncle U. that took him away from Sir Ever-Ready and Sir Good,[240] [241] just as life was getting interesting. Second, here he was on a damned quest for a girl with short legs, in a city with dwarfish memory . . .[242]

---

240 You wish. (Dr. Diwata Drake, Patagonia, Argentina)

241 Agapito and Benigno, Raymundo's pals from San Roque, soon to transfer like Raymundo to Manila. (Trans. Note)

242 *Una ciudad que nunca duerme, que sueña como un duende* [awkwardly literal: city that never sleeps, dreams like a goblin]. (Trans. Note)

Entry #19

Number 15, Calle Caraballo, 1886 [243]

If I were to retrace my steps down those cobbled lanes, sidestepping memory's potholes, leaping over nostalgia's waterlogged carriage ruts, I would find myself before a latticed window of capiz-shell ruin,[244] [245] not too different from others around it—a mix of elegance and atrophy, the kind of squalor that ennobles many recollections of students returning from Madrid to Manila. I was no foreign traveler, a mere provincial in the city, but I borrow from their passages my current nauseous sense of disorientation (or it could be the effect of this moldy pan de sal, damn the Guardia Civil, I mean, American G.I.s). Houses with thatched roofs and wooden buildings with metal railings stood together on that street. The beauty of buntis trellises, those steel commas of geometric window art punctuating this modern city's spectral homes, framed kerosene images of studious labor and hid the wildlife within.

Señora Chula took good care of us. A hospitable widow from our

---

243 Located *extramuros*, outside the walled city (*intramuros*). Rizal's boarding house, circa 1873, was a few houses down, a corner establishment against the Pasig River. (Estrella Espejo, Quezon Institute and Sanatorium, Tacloban, Leyte)

244 *Las ventanas de concha.* Capiz shell was the preferred lattice material for Spanish-era windows, native and charming: translucent nacre squares in harlequinade or chessboard patterns. (Trans. Note)

245 My own heart's bitterest memory is my return to my grandfather's old home—by the riverbanks of Barugo—and I saw the house's ancient wood, broad narra stairways, and, most of all, the sliding frames of its antique capiz-shell windows (with which I used to run over dead moths and beetles back and forth, back and forth on the ledges' sliding frames, on those endless boring summer vacations)—I saw it gutted beyond remembering and replaced with glass jalousies and concrete: to Americanize! My mother, a winsome diva whose practicality was her unsuspected strength, slapped me and said—just be glad you have better plumbing. But Ma, can't we have both—beauty and a bath!? The family's past is vanished. Chilling essays of corrupt self-knowledge lie in the remains of ruined homes. Later in Raymundo's memoirs, shell divers from the island of Capiz, after which the old-fashioned décor is named, appear briefly, a pair of patriotic mariners whose lives echo the romantic symbolism of the cast-off windows. See my monograph on their forgotten escapade: "Mermen of the Deep [Deeps of Filipino Oblivion, That is]," *Provinces: Essays on the Dis-[Re]membered,* 2–40. (Estrella Espejo, ditto)

province, always carrying a book of novenas and whispering to her gods, she had proud pectorals and a benevolent rump. Agapito showed me the hole in the wall, where we had a good view of the novelties of the widow of Noveleta. I believed stooping to look through it was dastardly and inconvenient, and checked it out only twice a day.[246] [247] [248]

I preferred La Jovencita Varonil (name withheld). She had a sweaty mustache and limber pelvis and liked to play tuktukan with the guys. It was her innocence I liked, the way she did not care if I bumped against her torso or crammed my palms against her haunches, the better to declare her victories. I would crack eggs with her forever, though she laughed at me, rightly so, because I was clumsy, pumping against her boyish hipbones, and I always preferred to lose, distracted by her shaking body. She climbed trees like a tarsier, swam like a dog, and ate like Agapito: who chewed with his gums showing. She was not sultry as much as cadaverous. Everything about her was disreputable (including her precocious hairy armpits), and so, doubly enchanting.

Oh Manila! That first boarding house on Calle Caraballo swarmed with swampish fevers and disgraceful tumors—all mine. The suddenness of my situation fed my rash passions, so I excuse myself—abruptly disgorged as I was, barely sixteen, from the provincial games of the all-boy's schoolhouse in San Roque. Where before I thought mostly of

---

246 Can you please excise, Mimi C.? Should we foist on our young readers this unexpurgated view of [pornographic] heroes? (Estrella Espejo, ditto)

247 More to the point, the unexpurgated view *before* our heroes, that is, the fine rump of Señora Chump. Oh, Estrella, must we be so prim? Why so proper now, after wading through his shitty episodes, masturbatory declensions, troubling hallucinations? Were our heroes immaculate conceptions? Did they not have eyes? Hands, senses, passions, well-oiled organs, wet dreams? Et cetera, et cetera. (Dr. Diwata Drake, Stratford-upon-Avon, England)

248 Not sure if I agree with either of you. Personally, peeping Toms creep me out. However, I am no divine expurgator, like Saint Luke or Saint Mark. I am only a translator and do my best to render faithfully the hero's Word. (Trans. Note)

the cockpit, now I thought only of the henhouse. So many women, in narrow proximity—at night, only a plywood-inch away! La Jovencita was only one among other, less alluring nieces of Señora Chula. The pious Anday was her grumpy maid. Flat-chested (but what of that? her modest aureoles like meteor dust on earth's thin camisa provided mutable compass points, disarranging and disturbing, as she cleaned and grumbled all day long). Murmuring the rosary in the vulgate (the more vulgar the better). Huge bun on the head, thicker than guano buns on trees. Titay, the cross-eyed four-year-old, Anday's bastard child. One day her prince will come. Above all—oh.

Agapito's sister.

Lady K—who sometimes visited.

Silence is best among the unworthy.

My fellow inmates were indifferent scholars and creative bullies. If only Tio U., mild-mannered lover of Cervantes, knew he'd thrown me into this bestiary, worse than the blanket-tossers in *Don Quixote*! He would weep, he would rush me back home, in person.

Señora Chula's son, "Leandro,"[249] [250] [251] [252] [253] was a rake and rep-
robate in the mold of Roman centurions, but more stupid—he
organized a riverbank picnic the week I arrived, and while I was
trying to keep my footing in the clammy mud he pushed me in—
in jest. He tried to drown me in the Pasig then had the gall to save
me! From the magnificent bosomy widow Señora Chula he earned
a mother's embrace, and as for me, the nearly drowned weakling,
she sent a look of pity mixed with scorn. The beasts around me
laughed. "Leandro" was tall, broad-armed, muscular—the type
women pretended not to stare at then whispered about when he
was gone. (Some nasty neighbors lay the obscure paternity of tiny,
humpbacked Titay at his feet, the brute.) In his presence women,
even his cousins, had a simpering fatuity that was never lost on
him: he treated them with a nasty joviality—a particularly masculine candor—and they playfully tapped their fans against his
boorish chest, giggling at his insolence. He was four years older
than I and two heads taller.

---

249 The writer uses quotation marks around names. Maybe Estrella knows their
identities? (Trans. Query)

250 Voyeurs and felons! As a kid, I always hated bullies like them and never gave them
valentines. I have no idea who these beasts in quotation marks are. I hope they died in the
revolution. (Estrella Espejo, ditto)

251 Interstitial characters such as "Leandro," "Florencio," and other quotation-mark cretins
occur in various memoirs of the heroes. Once the war begins, these names disappear unless
they *become heroes* (e.g., Miong, who becomes President Aguinaldo). Where did the quotation-
mark characters go? Minor martyrs, obscure traitors, passive shopkeepers, wild gossips, brave
wives, foolish girlfriends, and, hard to take, *Filipino soldiers of the Guardia Civil shooting their
own*—these also populated the villages, towns and *arrabales*. The array of victims, victimizers,
and kibitzers were all one after the revolution. This gamut had to pick up the pieces of the
battered country when revolution failed. The origins of modern postcolonial governments
perhaps lie in these names. It's likely that we descend not from "heroes" but from these "beasts
in quotation marks," as Estrella calls them. (Dr. Diwata Drake, Jaca, Spain)

252 That's okay for you to say, Miss Kalamazoo: I'm no descendant of beasts. You forget—
it's your kind, the whites, that killed the heroes! (Estrella Espejo, ditto)

253 And it's your kind, the deranged—oh, why am I even answering your email? (Dr.
Diwata Drake, Jaca, Spain)

I hated him.

"Florencio" from Batangas was "Leandro's" sidekick, capable, kind, but easily misled. He had a knack for memorizing but a measly conscience, as small as a rat's. In private, when we were alone (we shared a room with weeping "Moises"), he treated my miseries with sympathy and asked me advice about Latin; but in company with "Leandro" he slouched like an oaf and beat me up. "Moises," a new boy like me, was always away on the weekends, picked up by his knock-kneed, sentimental Chinese mother who could not bear to have her only son gone from home. He treated his weepy Mama with contempt, laughing at her bent-over, shuffling walk with his companions; he didn't tell anyone that whenever she left, he cried. He was a storehouse of vulgarity and, stout from his mother's end-less noodles,[254] [255] [256] was good with his elbows, cudgeling the small boys under "Leandro's" watchful eye. "Moises" did not last long, and "Arcadio" took his place, another cretin, a future criminal with bad teeth.

Soon it happened that when they learned of my debility (my Botica Luciano eyeglasses were a giveaway) they'd lure me out at night, and I, the fool, was tricked. On the pretext of "gathering

---

254 Long-lipe [*sic*] pancit: Raymundo uses English here; lone Saxon phrase in these Castilian sections. (Trans. Note)

255 Interesting pattern, Mimi C.: you re-translate the English into English. One deals with "native" terms in various ways. **Re-Englishing** is a structural corollary to **Obvious-Footnoting** and **Annoying-Renaming**.

    Obvious-Footnoting: Ex. *Nanay* [footnoted as "the Tagalog equivalent of Mama"] or *Sinigang* [footnoted as "clear broth flavored with tamarind and ginger"]—as if Filipino readers never heard of their Nanay who keeps on making sinigang. **Annoying-Renaming**: ex. calling kalamansi "native lemon" or puto "native rice cake." In turn, the reader is temped to declare, *it's a goddamned bibingka, you native morón!* Academic notes expose a structure of colonial neurosis. They seem confused about their implied reader—the unknowing foreigner? that rare breed, the Filipino who reads footnotes? The automatic slip, of course, privileges the foreign reader, stand-in for the colonial Master. (Dr. Diwata Drake, Babil, Iraq)

256 Here's one more structure of colonial neurosis for you, you hairy mongrel: **Footnote-within-Footnote**—["hairy mongrel": *mestiza-balbon*]! (Estrella Espejo, ditto)

santol" or "catching fireflies" they would strand me in the middle of the dark street to be cursed by coachmen and left to die, prey to vehicular monsters, a blinkered ass. For them it was a game, blindman's bluff. Someone would always rescue me from my terror as horses approached, just in the nick of time as carriages passed—usually my roommate "Florencio," who would hold out his hand and guide me to the curb. With weeping gratitude I followed his lead, despite my anger and humiliation—but not before all of them had their fill of gagging on their knuckles, rolling on the cobbles with their evil glee.

Then there were their other victims, names too lamentable for recall, except for the soulful Agapito. For some reason I ended up their leader, which wasn't much of a consolation. That house's disturbing divide—devout women crossing themselves twenty times a day for the smallest reasons, contrasted against those demon louts—haunts me still. I rose with saints and ate with sinners, a miserable communion. Fortunately I mingled with the zoo only when school was over, the sunset shading our exhaustions. (Plus, "Leandro," an overstaying scholar who finally got kicked out of school, was soon too tired from his job as printer's apprentice at the Frenchman La Font's to rough up anyone with usual valor.)

By the second term I found a place closer to the college, on Calle Magallanes, and, informing my uncle that location was the reason, I left that cursed house, with fond memories nevertheless of the view from my window of the river Pasig, the startling aroma, like fabulous squid, of women at their ablutions, and the drops of sweat on a feminine mustache, perpetual and livid, an oily gleam.

Entry #20

Dear Q—,

Until now I am not forgetting the labor of yours, that on waking at morning is your rising with litheness, your making the cross, your getting on knees and praising God, thanking him that you he kept from common danger . . . God is the first sound from your lips, the first thought of yours.

I see your form enchanting, the kindness and modesty that is shining through your walk and your entire conduct, that is seen in your churchgoing and your listening to the sacred sacrifice.

Today I see that your bosom is open, and I gaze at your clean heart, that is following the sacrament to which you are boiling the rice with full love, the God of love that you hold in your hand, that offers to the powerful Father remembrance, respect for his high power that He is wielding over the world . . . [257] [258] [259]

---

257 Raymundo shifts to pure Tagalog for no clear reason in this unfinished paragraph. This formal language, quite different from the casual language of the early entries of Part I, occurs nowhere else in the text and is reproduced below. Raymundo's original, in straight, stylized Tagalog with hispanized spellings and the Tagalog's trademark verbal indirection, full of Predicates but no Subjects and too many Gerunds reads (and I translated literally and faithfully above):

"*Magpahanga ñgayo'y, di co nalilimutan ang casipagan mo, na pagca guising sa umaga'y, malicsing babañgon, sasandatahin ang cruz, maninicluhod ca't, magpupuri sa Dios, magpapasalamat at iniadya ca sa madlang pañganib at pinagcalooban nang buhay na ipaglilingcód sa caniyang camahalan sa arao na iyon Dios ang unang bigcás nang labi mo, at palibhasa'y Dios ang unang isip mo.*

Aquing natatanao ang cauili-uiling anyó mo, ang cabaita't, cabinhinan na nagniningning sa iyong paglacad at boong caasalan, na ipinaquiquita sa pagtuñgo sa simbahan, at ipinaqui-quinyig nang Santo Sacrificio. Ñgayo'y, naqui-quita cong bucás ang dibdib mo, at natatanao co ang malinis mong puso, na naquiquibagay sa sacerdote na inihahain mo nang boong pagibig, ang Dios nang pagibig na hauac sa camay, at iniaalay sa di matingcalang Ama, alaala't, galang sa mataas niyang capangyarihan, na ipinag-hahari sa sangdaigdigan." (Trans. Note)

258 Mimi C.! This literal overlay of Tagalog's gerund-orientation onto English syntax is an astonishing commentary on the ordinary anguish of translation—or its impossibility. Almost as bad as Nabokov's unreadable *Eugene Onegin*, your "translation" willfully ignores rules of English to give Tagalog's verbalism its prominence. This is an *in*version of the norms of translation—when originalism is the goal, not clarity. Versions of the self, as one can see from any "translated" text, are thus often *sub*versions: if it's in language we reveal our Self to an Other, we are mutated, broken, mis-presented when we code-switch, in our attempt to be heard. (Dr. Diwata Drake, Clyde, Ohio)

259 Mimi C.! Goddamnit, do your job already: be polite! I just want to understand: if you need

Until now I do not forget your industry,[260] how you wake in the morning and at once rise with eagerness, with the sign of the cross, genuflecting and praising God, thanking him for keeping you from harm and giving you life to serve his love on that morning and every morning God is the first sound on your lips as God is your first thought.

I see your charming figure, the goodness and grace that shines through in your walk and your whole demeanor, as when you sit in church and listen wide-eyed to the Sacred Sacrifice. Now I see how your heart is open and I look at your pure soul, and what is that which you hold in your hand—it is the God of Love—throbbing with high power that He wields over the world—and to which you offer your remembrance and honor.

What is that which you hold in your hands—a god of love throbbing with power, the majesty he wields over the world—to which, in my dreams, you offer tender memory and respect. I keep seeing your bodice open, your pure chest, rising and falling,[261] [262] as you sit

---

English, use English. (Estrella Espejo, Quezon Institute and Sanatorium, Tacloban, Leyte)

260 This second passage seems a tentative translation, in Spanish, of the first, except that towards the end, once again, Raymundo surrenders to juvenile vulgarity, which I deplore. These pages could be a copybook: a diligent, schoolboy exercise. These are among the last of the diarist's gestational pages, that is, birth-language pangs of this memoir. (Trans. Note)

261 Raymundo, now situated in markedly bourgeois, collegiate society, hive of the colonial metropole, pictures the "pure" woman, virginal, genuflecting: a lady with no trace of a vagina. Quite a contrast with the largesse of good, provincial Señora Chula. This is the image, a feeble idolatry damaging to all women, that urbane nineteenth-century writers perfected into inanition in characters such as Rizal's vacuous Maria Clara. In Raymundo, we have revolution in another guise. His peculiarly hybrid tongue—provincial and metropolitan, regional and Tagalog—liberates him as he attempts to violate catatonic modesty inherited from Christian virtue. Good for him. (Dr. Diwata Drake, Clyde, Ohio)

262 Yes, Dr. Diwata, but should his revolutionary eye do so at the expense of her heaving chest? Oh, it's not that I object to radical desire, but pity the suffering of translators—their damned conspiracy with masculine ways! This is the trouble with translation—I keep getting entangled in crimes of the patriarchy, especially in these sections of romantic dalliance in the nineteenth century that populate his adolescent journals. So on top of that, the risqué hero challenges the orthodoxy with vulgarity, so that not only his grammar but also his acts are flecked with misogyny, leavened by (rape-like) passion. (Trans. Note)

in my church, wide-eyed, mouthing a holy sacrifice. Now I see your enchanting form, your goodness and grace shining through your gestures, your shy walk towards me.

In my dreams.[263] [264] [265]

Why should God be the first sound on your lips and the first thought in your heart? Open the day, Q—,[266] in another way. Your holy gestures are wasted, eagerness lost on air: making the cross, genuflecting, sighing and thanking—a Ghost. Think of a different Body—that which sighs, thanks, kneels, and rises up in eagerness: to be with you, double-you. Your charming body, grace and goodness in your entire demeanor, your shy walk. Walk towards me. Bless me, E—. Be good to me, R—. T—, shed your grace. Oh Y—, why not?

Until now I think of your industry, your litheness, as you get up and grasp it as you would the cross—lateral and literal benediction; then you genuflect, you pray, you kneel, *o dios*, the first words on your lips

---

263 Not to mention, Mimi C., his demonic incursions here on the good manners and right conduct of Urbana and Feliza, the Emilies Post of nineteenth-century Manila. The epistolary form and especially the obsolete Tagalog used in the beginning allude to texts on manners such as *Pagsusulatan ng Dalawang Binibini na si Urbana at Feliza* (*Letters between Two Women, Urbana and Feliza*, 1864), etc. But Raymundo is no gentleman! Bastos! (Estrella Espejo, ditto)

264 Dear Estrella, your own allusion, i.e., to the Victorian etiquette guru Emily Post, presents a lovely dilemma in these footnotes. For after all, Urbana and Feliza antedate the annoying Posts. Some would say your charming recidivism, the use of Western allusion to punctuate your patriotism, marks your subjective richness: the world is your oyster, and you devour it with a plate of salt. In our indiscriminate age, you and I have traversed the colonial and back. We eat the world raw at our own risk, colonial subjects one moment, voracious master of many cultures the next. This is our wealth, our privilege. (Dr. Diwata Drake, Baltimore, Maryland)

265 Emily Post-It that, *bruja*. Speak for yourself. I eat oysters with kalamansi—not salt! (Estrella Espejo, ditto)

266 Various letters of the alphabet are scattered in this entry with the randomness of letterpress types crowding a printer's drawer. These were leaden metals in which the alphabet retained an obdurate physicality: what was it like when you could hold the phantom phoneme, like a heavy key, in your hand? (Trans. Note)

(you lick your lips), *o dios*, the first thought on your mind (you close your eyes).

It's like church: a holy sacrifice. You the devout devour the mass by heart, the pauses, parts, and breaths, the unspeakable and righteous act. You shame the grace of an angel, you fit the form of shyness, as you hold it, the god of love, in your hands . . . [267]

---

267 *Pagsusulatan ng Dalawang Binibini na si Urbana at Feliza* was an etiquette and morality manual. This is anything but. Raymundo writes a rapturous (rapist!) love note, addressing anonymous virgins to make much of time. I repeat: Bastos! (Estrella Espejo, ditto)

Entry #21

Number 17, Calle Magallanes, from October 1886

I was a poor student. My years in the cockpit at San Roque did not prepare me for this new world of the city. I was only good at spelling. Because I have a weird mind, the priests said, like a letterpress. My Latin was so-so, but my Spanish was terrible despite all those nights spent reading. Turns out, I read books without thinking, only for the feeling, the way words strike my soul; I should have examined their tenses, their syntax, the exceptions to the rules! Who cares if it's true that Don Quixote de la Mancha suffered like Christ—if I wrote the *esdrújula* without an accent, I should be punished. I counted with pleasure the slaps on the forearm, the stings in the palm, all my transgressions whipped out of me. Yes, yes, take them away, my errors, my base conjugations! Let my welts swell up—the pus of lapsus—the easier for me to caress my wounds, stigmata of learning. Somehow it heightened the thrill of knowing—that I learned the masculine nature of all Greek words through lashings and earned the subjunctive case with my own blood.

I practiced my lessons everywhere. Riding the carriages, walking home, I looked for exercises of my prowess, grammar gymnastics. I translated songs, even conversations, in my head. I copied out whole sections of books in Spanish. Even the most boring, the numbing novenas, the etiquette manuals. I enjoyed the act of copying, rounding out words in my own hand, finding out verbs in the act, sprung from the cages of their conjugations. I translated Tagalog into Spanish, and once, just for fun, Spanish into Tagalog (an ad, I think, for a Minerva press, and I added a drawing, too, a piece of pleasant pulchritude I embellished extravagantly in art class). Soon enough I progressed. And I remember that day when Father Baltazar, an oratorical mollusk with languid limbs, instead of throwing the book at me, grunted, with a kind of animal surprise, when I declaimed—backwards!—the imperfect subjunctive of the verb *matar* in perfect simulation of his own screech. *Tu mataras . . . él matara . . . ¡espero que yo te haya matado!* [268] [269] I gained thirty-two lashes instead of the usual octuple for my flawless display. Who knows what would have happened if not for the insuperable pedantry of Father Baltazar?

I understood then the sinful triumph of suffering for pride, not ignorance.

I slept well that night (as long as I did not touch my forearms, which throbbed from knowledge). Even now my skin flushes, my beard trembles, when I remember my victory, the look of admiration, albeit violent, in the invertebrate priest's eyes.

That look occurred spasmodically among my professors, I recall.

The next year, when I was no longer in his class, scholarly Father Baltazar would greet me in the hallway with that gaze of an epicanthic worm, a look that on his part passed for affection, and I, always taken aback, would mumble *Salve* and rush on to my next class.

In Physics and Mathematics, on the other hand, I was only so-so. In Biology I had fun with nomenclature, in particular, and other aspects of taxonomy. In music I was a dunce.

I remember Father Melchior because he reminded me of fish

---

268 *You killed . . . he killed . . . I hope that I have killed you!*: shout-out to Raymundo's killer name, an elegant catenation of grammar and desire. (Trans. Note)

269 Grammar and desire: language's unconscious threat yoked to the explicit plot here of language acquisition. A frisson occurs in the text from that most delicious of couplings: when the conscious and unconscious both speak the hero's name: *¡espero que yo te haya Mata-do!* Part 1 of these diaries has exposed Raymundo's primal texts. In Part 2, Raymundo begins his switch to the Master's tongue. Education is the double-edged sword in histories of colonies, but most especially the getting of the Master's Word, rape and reward both, benefit/bane: *what gives us speech kills, thus we are.* Language-acquisition becomes this Gordian knot in what seems an insoluble puzzle of identity. In the Greek legend of the knot, for King Gordius of Phrygia and Alexander the Great the reward for untying is dominion over Asia. Alexander the Great, in the consummate simplicity that marks the monster, simply cut the knot with his sword. It's a cliché to wail, *There is no Alexander's sword for the knot of colonial language.* The colonized endlessly confronts the wound of identity, and dominion over Asia will ever be deferred. But what if one just Becomes the Monster—just cut that knot with the umbilical sword, and so admit with Mürkian calm *that fixed identity you seek is an illusion anyhow*—Master or Servant, none of us cohere and all of us are fractured by a gaping lack? And so a terrible bemusement—that the state of the colonized is the state of all—beguiles our waking hours. (Dr. Diwata Drake, Galatia, Turkey)

in my hometown—a plump shiny mackerel,[270] with fat funhouse flesh glistening with grease. Everyone said he was an "invert," but a jolly good one he was, whatever an invert was. Free with the ferrule but judicious with praise, he taught me drama, and it was like some animal stirring in me, a sleeping asp or hibernating cobra, that the Spanish plays aroused, and I possessed an organic alertness, a weirdly physical response, to the scenes of dying courtesans, masked bandits, epicurean buffoons, and polyglot witches that populated that dreamlike course. In truth I was happy to leave that class when the term was done—so disconcerting was that feeling of fervid love for things that had no right to be familiar, as if I were in heaven, or some alternate place of damned repose.

But the enduring influence was Father Gaspar. He was the only *indio*,[271] a pathetic sycophant when the need arose—hence his tenure in that space, enlightened in some areas but, let's face it, narrow in the ways that matter. At the time I did not appreciate his timidity, the way among masters infinitely inferior to him in intellect Father Gaspar played the second-rate fool, a brown, skinny Sancho Panza and receiver of their vicious jokes. He taught first-year Latin, his skills dooming him to the illumination of principles in the *Doctrina Cristiana*. I must say, the required material of his skimpy syllabus flattened his genius. But I learned under his pious indulgence to

270 *Una caballa brillante ... rechoncha ... cuyas es camas esperpénticas ... relucen con grasa:* here, Raymundo's Spanish is spotted with awkward phrases—it's like translating a symbolist on speed. (Trans. Note)

271 Spanish caste terms are particularly troubling for a translator of nineteenth-century Filipino society. *Filipino*, the term that stems from the mongrel multiplicity of a fantastic history, did not exist then as we know it; it is a post-revolutionary spoil. In Raymundo's time, people were coded not only by how much Spanish blood they had in their veins but by where and how they got that blood. *Peninsulares* (from Europe) were Spaniards born in Spain: highest caste. *Insulares* were Spaniards born in the islands: also called *Filipinos*. *Indio* is how Spaniards denoted all Filipinos without Spanish blood: an ignorant and pejorative solecism, transported from their errors in America. So what then should a translator do? Take on the Spanish prejudice by using the denotative term "indio"? Or translate it colloquially as "Filipino"? A tragic agon of colonial pain lies dramatized in quotation marks. I took the path of least resistance and just footnoted. (Trans. Note)

return to childish reverie and recall the past (short as it was; I was only seventeen). We repeated all the lessons of the Latinidad[272] [273] in a single term, and with each prayer re-learnt I reviewed entire childhood episodes along with Latin declensions: there were so many hours for daydreaming in that redundant class I could have written this autobiography[274] several times over, in the genitive, the ablative, the infinitive, ad infinitum. I learned later that Father Gaspar was writing a dictionary of ichthyology, his field of expertise, being from a southern island, but so far he had only reached *abalone*. Even his personal life was a shambles. But there was something about this priest, with his truncated talent and wistful look, that recalled to me the inside of certain clams: he was a washed-out shell. It's not for his lessons that I owe Father Gaspar my . . .[275]

---

272 As noted, at the *latinidades*, such as at San Roque, pupils were taught only Latin, a dead language, as if Spanish were some kind of hidden mystical key to a garden barred from them, and Latin was its barbed wire—landmine of learning. Having learnt the power of education from their colonies in the Americas, Spain did not systematically teach its language in the islands, though novels and magazines proliferated in Spanish, and there is evidence that Raymundo, a savant, gleaned a jumbled heap of meanings from his random youthful readings, from books scattered about by his wily uncle. A refreshing quality of novelty imbues Raymundo's prose here—his sudden transport into a living world of words, of comprehension with bright leaves. It is to be noted that a central demand of the shortlived, if not shortsighted, Filipino Propaganda Movement (1880–1895) was, oddly enough, the teaching of Spanish in public schools. (Estrella Espejo, ditto)

273 Isn't it easy for us to call the Propaganda Movement "shortsighted," rather than one in a continuum of a nation's progress? As if the flaws of the U.S. Articles of Confederation, e.g., were destiny, not contingency. "Nationhood" arises in jerky motions—more akin to awkward crablike lunges, sometimes backward or sideways, at times forward—and we pat ourselves on the back or claw at our wounds with the prosthetics of hindsight. When no nation is ever so prescient, or exceptional. (Dr. Diwata Drake, Philadelphia, PA)

274 Material evidence suggests that various fragments of this journal were written—or conceived—years before his stay in Bilibid jail where Raymundo was last seen in public, under the custody of the Stars and Stripes. My tendency is to view each section as psychologically true to its chronological placement, though the circumstances of its collation—whether or not Raymundo had time and energy to revise, redact, embellish these tracts years later, as Dr. Diwata has suggested—is matter for future scholars' endeavors. (Trans. Note)

275 Like many of these college entries, unfinished. (Trans. Note)

Entry #22

From April to December, the same year[276]

A bit short, eyes expressive and ardent at times, at others languid, she was pink-cheeked, with a smile enchanting and provocative that showed pearly teeth. A form like a sylph, a figure that, let's say, for want of a better phrase, cast a spell. I've seen prettier women but none more tempting.[277] They wished me to draw her, but I excused myself; I did not believe I could do her justice. They kept at it. In the end I obliged; I drew her with clumsiness, with the charm of a clown. No one noticed the flaws of the simulacrum except myself. I played chess, or was it checkers?, with her fiancé. It must have been my distraction—I kept looking at her, no, she kept praising me, no, I had no idea how to play, parlor games were not part of my education in the cockpits of Cavite—anyway, I lost. From time to time she looked at me, making me blush. I couldn't concentrate. In the end, talk turned to novels, and at least on that point I could play with advantage. Soon it was time for her to go back to her college, saying goodbye to us all. I returned to my boarding house, and I did not think much about that day. The next week I saw her again, from afar, with her fiancé and other young women.[278]

---

276 The year is 1886. This section is a collage of events, surprisingly coherent, in flowing Spanish. (Trans. Note)

277 The opening lines here, so eerily similar to episodes in Rizal's *Memorias de un Estudiante de Manila*, have a disturbing effect. If it weren't for the tone of burlesque romance, non-existent in the self-portrait by the grave young Rizal, I would have sworn this buffoonish entry were a direct copy. (Dr. Diwata Drake, Chawton, England)

278 I prefer this side of him. I disagree with Dr. Diwata: he's no buffoon; he's urbane. This drawing-room Raymundo is *muy simpatico*, and I'm happy to note that he's quite repressed. (Estrella Espejo, Quezon Institute and Sanatorium, Tacloban, Leyte)

I changed boarding houses.[279]

At her college during visiting hours I saw her with my sister[280] [281] who had become her intimate friend. I, having nothing to say to her nor having had much of the honor of her acquaintance in the days past, did not offer more than a ceremonious and mute salute,[282] like an ass. She answered my knuckle-headed gesture[283] with admirable delicacy and grace.

I returned to La Concordia[284] on Thursday.

---

279 Casa Tomasina, on Calle Magallanes, Raymundo's second boarding house, was a shell of its former self by the time Raymundo left in 1892: one by one young men left its wooden porticos to pursue the glittering scar that was Europe. Raymundo, though of Spanish descent on his wretched paternal grandfather's side and so seen as "privileged," was always in financial distress and limited by his uncle's conservatism: all he saw of Europe he got from *El Mundo Ilustrado*, a monthly magazine. (Estrella Espejo, ditto)

280 The text says *hermana*, a first reference to a sister. Did he have a sister? (Trans. Query)

281 Raymundo had no sister. Maybe it meant "beard," someone in cahoots with his infatuation. (Estrella Espejo, ditto)

282 The text reads *mudo saludo*, with a deleatur penciled in over the *d* in *mudo*, changed to *l*, that is, *mulo saludo*. My solution incorporates both terms. The inferior alternative was "mulish salute." (Trans. Note)

283 The phrase does not occur in the original, which goes: "*no le dirigí mas que un ceremonioso y mudo [mulo] saludo al que ella contestó con una gracia y delicadeza admirables.*" However, her "admirable" delicacy implies his recognition of his rudeness, and my translation supplies the psychological truth he could not speak. Plus, he may not have known the Spanish word for "knuckle-head." *Torpe* comes to mind. (Trans. Note)

284 A long way from the Ateneo, requiring a meandering banca drive (one must imagine travelers then going by river, not road, which transforms one's concept of Manila), La Concordia College in Santa Ana was a convent school for women, favored by Manila's merchants and the provincial bourgeois. Figures in Rizal's novels, such as Maria Clara and Cecilia/Marcela, the heroine of *Makamisa*, went to such convents, and flighty *colegialas* today are their dismal descendants. Rizal himself frequented these girls' colleges as a gentleman caller when he was a student in Manila. I concede to Dr. Diwata that Raymundo's details, in fact, have an almost hallucinatory resemblance to Rizal's memories of his youth. However, this is proof that college narratives, whether in 1876, 1886, or 1986, have decidedly limited thematic variations: e.g., the barkada-gang-of-friends theme, the waiting-in-the-vestibule theme, the nosy-aunt theme, the gift-giving theme, the wilting-souvenir theme, the lovelorn-look theme, and, of course, the heartbreak theme. (Estrella Espejo, ditto)

As we talked I began drinking the sweet poison of love. Her glances were terrible, so sweet and expressive; her voice was melodic, as if a spirit haunted her speech. Soon a languid ray penetrated my heart, and I felt as if I did not know myself. And why did hours pass so quickly, and I had no time to enjoy them? In the end, when the clock struck seven, I bowed to her, and my friends and I returned home.

I returned the following Sunday. The night was a torment. I had made a charcoal sketch to make up for my first awkward experiment with her figure. It ended up being a sketch of a dog, but it was the best I could do. She arrived with a bag of walnuts, and I presented the charcoal. She exclaimed her delight, while she kept munching the walnuts. She was so devilishly enchanting, even with her teeth cloying from the brown sugar—her sweet, molasses-slimed smile.[285]

My visits continued. I restrained myself, nay, prohibited my heart to love, because she was promised to another, not to mention he was a better chess player. But I told myself: Perhaps it is I whom she loves? Perhaps her love-match, made for the future, had been an infants' amour, in which the heart had not yet been open to know true love? Nevertheless, I told myself, I am neither rich nor handsome nor gallant nor likely to call anyone's attention; and if she did love me her love must then be true, not built on vain and mutable foundation. But even so, I took upon myself the discretion of silence, and until I saw certain proofs of affection between us, I told myself I would not submit to her yoke nor declare myself to her.

The next Sunday I carried a clay bust, this time of a bantam chicken. It was the best I could do. She almost cried from ecstasy. She offered

---

285 *Una dulcísima sonrisa de* kalamay: the lone Tagalog word, for solid brown molasses, sticks out in this Castilian section, which shows Raymundo's fine progress as a student of Spanish. (Trans. Note)

me an artificial flower she had woven herself, placed carefully on my hatband, a paper symbol of her love.

Another day. I went alone to her college, carrying letters for her, as well as a chicken wire dangling figurine of a horse. It was the best I could do. I felt perverse for some reason and asked the malignant nun at the front desk to send my gifts up. That day I received a note saying she was put out that I had not waited. I decided not to reply. When I visited next, she came down with a serious and formal air, I bowed to her, she barely answered, giving a slight inclination of her head, without smiling, and went on to join another group. I was left all alone, on my indifferent bench, playing with the multi-colored silken cat's cradle, which I had devised just for her, made of seven scraps of my forlorn hatbands. It was the best I could do. Towards the end of that dolorous visit, she came up to me: happy, talkative, and shedding charm the way deciduous trees shed shade. She entertained us deliciously with her delectable conversation. As night fell, the moon rose majestically, and once again it was time to leave.

In time vulgar and deceitful gossip spread that our yet imaginary and embryonic love was, in fact, real; in all quarters our relations were spoken of and decided as fact when between the lovers we had declared nothing clearly except through glances and, on my end, the morose representation of a felt puppet, slouchy and a bit lumpy, made in her image but in truth looking sadly like a rodent. It was the best I could do. I saw her every Thursday and Sunday, and she, on receiving me, was always enchanting and attractive, capturing my heart that still denied complete surrender.

One day when an aunt and some others decided to make flowers for I do not remember which saint, waiting for me to pick them up later, I did not arrive at her college. I was ill. The next day I saw all the ladies wearing their church mantillas and waving their paper fans, there by the landing on the staircase. She was simply yet gracefully dressed, with hair loose and a smile on her lips.

—You have been unwell? she asked in a sweet voice.

—Yes, I answered, but now I feel better, thank you for your concer—

—Oh, last night I prayed for you, fearful that something bad had happened!—

—Thanks, I replied. If that is the case then I would prefer to be sick forever, if by doing so I had the happiness of being remembered by you: even death might be a blessing.

—What? she asked, you wish to die? That makes me sad.

Ay! How sweet was our conversation!

Ah! Happy times: how they wrench my heart!

Oh! Erase from memory that which should give joy but instead revives misery and desperation!

That Christmas, back home on vacation, the banks of the streams seemed melancholy, pondering many things and concentrating on none. I saw rapid waves carry branches torn off from trees, and my thoughts, wandering other regions and fastening on distant objects, took notice of nothing. Then I perceived a rumble, I raised my head and saw, wrapped in a cloud of dust, a number of carriages and horses. With violence my heart beat, and I turned pale. I stood by my horse on the narrow dirt road. There I waited.

There she was in a carriage passing by with her fiancé and other women from La Concordia. She waved at me, smiling and fixing her shawl; that's all I saw and nothing more. And the car passed in rapid shadow, leaving nothing but a horrible vacuum in the world of my affections.[286]

---

286 "*Un horrible vacío en el mundo de mis affecciones.*" Compare to Entry #8: "for a long time I could not escape the sense that Mamá would come back, take off the pretty stage dress, and boil barako for me." It's interesting that Raymundo's second heartbreak possesses emotional language, distinct feelings and deliberate expression, whereas the first one (mother's death) is a series of detached details. I can't help but think that the horrible vacuum is, in fact, the first one: and that all others are only *una rapida sombra* ("a rapid shadow") of early pain. (Trans. Note)

Entry #23

Psigotar om Berlesdy[287] [288] [289](*Rludoar om Nonocsy,*[290] [291] ——————————

---

287 Aha! Finally: the Katipunan entries! I was wondering when the secret language of the revolution would reappear. All that love stuff: boring. Coded signs here indicate Raymundo's fear of capture. After his failed romance, he turned to serious business: the work of patriotism. Makes sense, especially since he's in Manila, seat of the Katipunan. But what the hell does it mean, "psigotar om berlesdy"? Perhaps an anagram? "Pigs— or goats—bleed something something"? A revolutionary warning against informers? (Estrella Espejo, Quezon Institute and Sanatorium, Tacloban, Leyte)

288 Beats me. *Rludoar om Nonocsy?* Sounds fishy, or maybe Finnish. While this section is mostly in Spanish, a few odd words occur in cipher. In no language I can fathom—and I've shown it to all the guys I know at Cornell, an entire soccer team made of international graduate students, including Lebanese. No one can figure it out. This cryptic message is one of the mysteries of Philippine historiography. (Trans. Note)

289 Bah! Elementary, Watson! They are anagrams, possibly Katipunan notes. Or revolutionary Masonic cipher. Anyway, figuring it out is easy if you act like Sherlock Holmes. Haven't any of you translators read him? You should. The first line reads: "Pigs seem too broadly r—" ; the second line continues the first: "(R)—otten dead Jesuit Indians." The entire phrase must be: "Jesuit Pigs Seem Too Broadly Rotten. Dead Indians." Gobbledygook, yes, but passwords need not make sense. That's why they're passwords, *idiot*! "Jesuit pigs" must be code for spies. "Dead Indians" must be rebels. This encryption is preliminary—but it will keep scholars at work for decades. Great find, Mimi C.—the beginnings of Raymundo's Katipunan diaries. (Estrella Espejo, ditto)

290 Estrella: please don't get mad—but does it matter that the date is 1886, Raymundo's Ateneo years—six years before the Katipunan was launched? Maybe it's a collegiate joke, Pig Latin? (Trans. Note)

291 Oh shush, Mimi C. Is heroism a mere prank? Of course it's connected to the Katipunan! Generals of the revolution have mentioned codes in their memoirs: this is one of those Holmesian ciphers beloved of nineteenth-century secret societies, such as the Masons, from which the Katipunan (and Arthur Conan Doyle) heavily borrowed. (The Katipunan's passion and dignity, of course, were indigenous.) Masonic rites of secrecy thrilled the revolutionaries. The Masons were notorious cryptolepts, code fetishists (as well as ghoulish graphic designers). Thus, in Raymundo's diary, we see evidence of Masonry's baroque obscurantism and frankly enigmatical tricks, from which derived the Katipunan's cumbersome initiation rites, for instance. (Estrella Espejo, ditto)

————————————→ a.k.a., Profiles in Bastardy)[292] [293] [294]

Case A
Bamofmi R.[295] [296] [297]

19 or 20 years of age. Originally from San Roque, now at the Normal School. Visits occasionally to drag me to Mass. Father, a fisherman; mother, a fish vendor. Favorite food: fish.

Religious dreamer, more of a follower than a schemer. Humble sodalist of the Legion of Mary. His looks are not prepossessing: pug nose and brittle hair. Dry pimply skin scaly from his years in the sun, on his father's fishing boat. Perhaps eczematic. Wants to be a teacher like his idol, Don Felipe. He's a plugger, sticks to the straight and narrow, a hermit crab crawling sidewise to his goal. My heart goes out to him. He's a good friend, faithful though unimaginative, with a nervous agitation that marks sincere men.

---

292 I get it. *Psigotar om Berlesdy* = Profiles in Bastardy. The cipher is in English! Just check the letters: then decode. Cheers. *Rludoar om* . . . Studies in?? But still—why in English? (Dr. Diwata Drake, Reichenbach Falls, Switzerland)

293 Oh thou cryptic doctor—good one! S = R; I = O; G = F; et cetera. I get it! Thanks. (Trans. Note)

294 Am I the only one out of the loop? What terrorist signals are you sending? (Estrella Espejo, ditto)

295 Therefore, if I am not mistaken, *Bamofmi R.* could be—*Benigno S.*! This section is a serial monograph on his contemporaries. The following, then, are probable suspects, I mean subjects, in order: Benigno S[anti], Emilio A[guinaldo], Candido T. T[irona], Juan C[ailles], Pedro P[aterno], Agapito C[onchu]. He begins and ends his list with his two great friends from San Roque, his John the Beloveds—Benigno Santi and Agapito Conchu. Except for the fop Paterno, all are from Cavite. Other actors are mentioned in passing: the pious Crispulo [Aguinaldo] and the treacherous Daniel [Tirona]. (Trans. Note)

296 Uh, Mimi C., you're missing the last one. Case G, who has no name, just an initial. (Estrella Espejo, ditto)

297 Oh, yes, Case G. That, too. (Trans. Note)

A steadfast romantic, known as *Ipot* for his disasters with women. Also an ascetic, a Jerome in the desert. He'd starve himself into purity if his mother, bless her, didn't keep sending him baskets of food, which he always shares. She sends excellent Raw Oysters and average Fish Snacks.[298]

Defects: Smells a bit of shrimp fry.[299] [300] [301] Any deviation into the original, the strange, freaks him out; does not have the stamina for candor, much less stomach for jokes. It's because of his devoutness. An ideologue for the Virgin, a cabalist of the saints, flogger of his sins. I observe him carefully because it's a mystery how someone so punished by God can so love Him (he's a bit ugly; Bamofmi, I mean, not God, though who knows?). One wonders if Christian piety arises from self-loathing, deepened by his misplaced feeling of depravity. Poor Bamofmi! He prefers whips for Christmas. Bless me, Father, for I have sinned. *Confiteor Deo omnipotenti. Mea culpa. Mea maxima culpa.*

One drink and he cries to God for forgiveness.

A bummer at parties.

Good Qualities: Worships women, though like many here not immune to the adventures of Don Juan Tenorio (believe me, I've been in line with him among the damned at Fonda Iris). Fine, if

---

298 *Talangka: sobresaliente; Torrones de Tulingan: pasado.* (Trans. Note)

299 Rough translation of *may anghang bagoong.* In patches of prose, the Spanish student regresses into Tagalog. (Trans. Note)

300 "Regresses" is a key word. It is always useful to note when the writer returns to native speech, which is when he touches upon the authentic self. (Estrella Espejo, ditto)

301 *Touché*, Estrella. It is, of course, an amusing fable that "native speech" always equals "authentic self" in that insight that in our days passes for political propriety. As if the "authentic self" had a single character, speaking only one language and in correct syntax to boot. Whereas perhaps it is less tempting but more analytically productive to imagine the self as a jumbled aggregate of fragments and bits of languages, "foreign," "native," and others, a signifying soul wantonly spliced: especially the Filipino soul— so tugged about into linguistic quarters who knows where and when which of its languages—Tagalog, Spanish, English, Waray, and so on—will draw blood? (Dr. Diwata Drake, Dobbs Ferry, New York)

perfunctory, memory. Nice handwriting. Possesses without stint an organ of veneration (somewhere by the liver, where sighs diffuse). Best of all, he has the ardent soul of Saint Francis, though no birds settle on his shoulders. Instead, they—ipot.[302]

Case B
Anotoi E.

I have always been under his thrall. Small build, Chinese eyes, quick temper. Brooding. Moody. Of a landowning, pious family. Mother hard-working, chief of *cigarreras*[303] [304] whose energies surpassed her simple birth. Father, deceased, former mayor (rival of Cemdodi's dad). Let's face it, a dullard in the classroom, but with a winning personality, an easy, unaffected way with men. Despite his slightness, he was always our class president and pet of *maestros*. He took me in hand ever since I began to walk, in those times of cholera when we believed the world was doomed. Though his brain got squashed in that mutiny near Kawit. (He has yet to recover from that fall.) He acts like the older brother I do not have, boxing me in the ears whenever he feels like it. I did everything he did and still have this instinct—to curry his favor, as if certain one day I will lose his regard forever. It's a terrible feeling, my abiding, satisfying, and anxious complicity in all his distractions.

He demands love, and I carry it like a foetal cord, a strain in my blood.

Anotoi E. was, and I confess with regret, the worst bully and

---

302 Ipot: the organic sheddings of our feathered friends, occurring at times in pointillist pellets, Pollock-like runs, or fine impressionist shades of shit. (Trans. Note)

303 Cigarette makers. Implies that mother was a factory foreman. Notes on class status occur in these sections. (Trans. Note)

304 Class, of course, is the signal issue in discussions of the revolution, metonymized in the class(ic) dichotomy *Bonifacio versus Aguinaldo*, that is Peasants = Redeemers versus Petty-bourgeois = Betrayers. Race is less remarked upon. Raymundo, as a petty-bourgeouis Basque-Filipino-(ghost-Chinese) *cuarterón*, quadroonish or mestizo type, from landowning, military, and lamp-oil-selling castes, is, I'm sorry to say, destined to mess up. Let's see what history reveals. (Estrella Espejo, ditto)

an awful cheat—but he never got caught! Even when his mischief was at my expense (that poison pen letter to Tio U.: a form of high-jinks for him: joke!), I forgave him. He's a man of daring. And so we follow. When his father died, he left school at fifteen with a convenient excuse. To have an adventure. Bought his own boat by the sweat of his brow and began a fine seafaring life selling fishnets, thatch, and bamboo prows.

Now he's a little mayor, Kapitan Noimf![305] Ready to go to the top.

Good qualities: Bold decision-maker, coiled to act. Not hampered by introspection or given to remorse. The past is a clean slate of his good intentions, and the future is a gift. Devoted friend. Patriotic.

His brother Csorputi is a saint.[306] [307]

Defects: A troubling sense of gloomy self-regard,[308] even I must admit. It leads him into bursts of moodiness over real and imag-ined slights, often directed, rightly, at the Guardia Civil, but also at his old companions who befriend others, at men better educated

---

305 Ah! Niomf = Miong! Hah, Dr. Diwata, now I get it—I, too, have deciphered the code! His childhood friend Miong, a.k.a. Emilio Aguinaldo, later first president of the Republic, became kapitan (mayor) of Kawit at a tender age. Also a school dropout, when his father died. Miong left school to help out his mother, the young widow Trinidad Aguinaldo y Famy. But it's not clear that he was any good at learning anyway. (Estrella Espejo, ditto)

306 Crispulo: Emilio's older brother. A devout Christian. Initially opposed to revolt and the Katipunan because of its Masonry but became a disciplined soldier. Killed right after the historic [dubious] Tejeros Assembly of 1897, in which Emilio was elected [sic] president, while Bonifacio was demoted [cheated] to minister of the interior [and even that seat was taken away!]. Emilio was "elected" while at battle; Crispulo insisted that Emilio swear his oath and stay in Tejeros—he offered to take his post at war. Emilio agreed. Sure enough, Crispulo was shot. He died in battle in his brother's stead. In an interview with the historian Agoncillo, Aguinaldo is "visibly affected" when he mentions his late brother. (Estrella Espejo, ditto)

307 Did his brother's death feed Aguinaldo's callous betrayal of Bonifacio, who challenged him at Tejeros? Aguinaldo's brother Crispulo died to uphold the election at Tejeros Assembly. So under ancient grudge slips brotherly guilt and self-loathing: twin emotions of survivors, of war and other traumas. (Dr. Diwata Drake, Kawit, Cavite)

308 *Un amor propio, incómodo y meditabundo*: periodic phrases proliferate in this section. (Trans. Note)

than he, at mestizos flaunting women he wants, at foreigners with advantages he covets, and a million other matters, at times so trifling I cannot immediately discern them, though in a series of events I've shared with him fleeting moments of borrowed bitterness, over provocations and aggressions I must say I barely noticed but pretended to feel. Perhaps because I'm an orphan, obliged to cultivate oblivion, I try to get rid of it—that gruesome gnawing on the bones at the world's injustice.

It can cause goiters.

Curiously abstemious, don't know what to make of that.

For a long time I've kept these disloyal feelings to myself and now feel guilty and relieved both at giving them words.

Case C
Cemdodi L. L.

Man of brawn. Father, former mayor (rival of Anotoi's dad); mother, schoolteacher (my aunt Juana, a devout woman—she named him after the hero in Voltaire, though sadly, like his brother, he was no scholar, though as we can see, learning is no impediment to the masses' regard!). Robust even in youth—strong-armed, muscular. Defended me in that skirmish in my first month in Manila. He knocked "Moises" out for good and the kid went back wailing to mother in Tanauan with a black eye. Cemdodi was only visiting. "Moises" never returned to the boarding house. I had no trouble with "Florencio," "Leandro," and the boys of Calle Caraballo after that. He believed it was his duty as my cousin to fight for me. Otherwise, I can't shake off the feeling that he treats me like a loser, that he's ashamed. His parents are bigshots. My father is either dead or a bandit. Plus, I'm practically blind, a nighttime imbecile. How could I, his own cousin, end up a basket case?

I will never be worthy of his respect, which makes me want to kick him in the butt.

How he became best of friends with Anotoi E., son of his

father's bitter rival, is town legend. Now they are so thick it makes me sick.

His brother Demoat is a weasel.[309]

Good qualities: Simple-hearted. Loves Cavite. Loves his family. Hates Spaniards. The one-dimensional virtues are his: loyalty, obedience, piety. Chastity, not so much. His courage is profound (though shortsighted), his loyalty enduring (but canine). I love him as my elder, but he's exactly my age.[310] Hearty drinker.

Defects: Simple-hearted. Gains convictions by habit, not reflection; his truths are dog-eared. These are not necessarily defects—but they're a drag. Killer boxer, however, so one should never mention any of his defects to his face.

Case D
Chuem C.

French charmer. Phony. Schoolteacher with the pose of a *remontado*—but the heart of a bully. Everyone likes him, taken in by his stranger's *langueurs* and amazing, eight-inch mustache, oiled and greased with ritual passion (the envy of Efepoli, who has twice his heart). He avows a shrill, vocal fealty to Cavite that anyone else

---

309 Daniel Tirona: Candido Tria Tirona's younger brother. Pairs of brothers are a war trope. Familial bonds drew people to battle. Daniel took over his brother's troops when, like Crispulo, brother of Aguinaldo, Candido died early in the war. Candido died in the Battle of Binakayan, before the fiasco of the Tejeros Assembly. A student in Manila when revolution broke out, his brother Daniel had never officially joined the Katipunan, which explains why he could so easily degrade the Supremo. It was Daniel Tirona, the lout, who at Tejeros challenged the Supremo Bonifacio's fitness to be leader of any government—he challenged even the Supremo's right to be minister of the interior, when it was Bonifacio who had founded the secret society, organized its passion, inspired its growth—damn you, Daniel Tirona! You're a wart on the nation's undersole, a crippling boil! (Estrella Espejo, ditto)

310 Mathematically confused. If Cemdodi LL is Candido Tria Tirona, he was six years older than Raymundo Mata. Raymundo has a mutable notion of his age, situating his birth year between 1862–1872, convenient for the historical dramas to which he was witness and symptomatic of the mental concussions rebels were heir to in those dank and pestilential American prisons! Bastards! Americanos! (Estrella Espejo, ditto)

would find suspicious, except Caviteños. Who knows where his family came from—from the sewers of Paris or the fine houses of Binondo. A bastard child. In any case, he has good qualities.

Good Qualities: Possesses the capacity to throw in his plight with that of present company. Others would call that sucking up; but many view his acts as profound—an honorable empathy. He cherishes kinship, family, the slightest of ties. His nervous system is that of a hound: his loyalty to friends is feral, and his enmity is equally tedious. In this case, he is most like us: blessed with a deep sense of community and a fierce covenant with those of our blood. Tribal. So we, his chosen family, welcome him with open arms: because he is not ours, and yet he chose us.

Was he product of a viscount-merchant's squandered youth? orphan of a Bruges perfumer? Who knows? Has the ability to make of ignominy an attractive mystery: life is a game of luck he has won. The schoolchildren, his charges, love him—but it's not clear whether they are mainly fascinated by his prodigal mustache and foreign tongue. Good drinker.

Defects: Same as above.

Case E
Padsi P.

Around 30 years of age. I was proud to be introduced to him, at first, seeing as he was of a generation and kind not my own. Lawyer, of medium build. Smooth hands reeking of French cologne. Spaniard by affect, Chinese by blood. Budding (but elegant) Judas. *God Knows Hudas Wear Fine Clothes!* Well-dressed voluptuary of Binondo. Piano player. Envy of young Manileños, hero-worshipped by us provincianos. *Tu un daldalero!*[311] Urbane, talkative (ay, stop it already,

---

311 Perverse, ungrammatical Espangalog here. A form of Cavite-Chabacano? Translation: He's a huge talker [*tu* = you (Spanish); *daldalero* = talker (Tagalog, from daldal: to talk)]. (Trans. Note)

my God![312]), frequent traveler to Madrid and Barcelona. Knows many people—M. Calero! Pablo Feced![313] Hung out in Paris with Juan Luna! Drew his family chest himself! I'm most jealous of his conquests among women, though I would not decline possession of his books.

Good Qualities: Successful in his field. Nice shoes. Persistent (trait most obvious in his dealings with women). If ambition is a virtue then he's a saint. Fluent though legalistic Spanish. I must admit my own sounds falter, I still can't lisp. Good at chess. Fine drinker, but mysteriously leaves before it's time to pay: got to admire talent like that!

Defects: Vain. Pompous. At worst: substitutes fine tailoring for true refinement. Noamla berlemla, mi ra puada vimgoes am at.[314] [315] [316] A liar, one can't really trust him. Lots of girls fall for him, especially the superficial ones. I hear rumors Lady K. likes him, though she is engaged to another. Let that flirt go to hell! Will stab a man in the back as befriend him, if need arose. Relationships are calculated costs.

He will go far. Let's say, in a dispute, he sees the chance of his

---

312 *Agi, saba na daw, por dios por santo mio!* Odd outbreaks into Visayan are also habitual and perplexing. (Trans. Note)

313 M. Calero (a.k.a. Marcelo H. Del Pilar, the tireless journalist) and Feced were enemy combatants in the Propaganda Movement: Pablo Feced was the notorious Quioquiap, nasty castigator of indolent Filipinos in Manila's conservative dailies. *Feces*, is what I call him. Bastard! Spaniard! (Estrella Espejo, ditto)

314 *Noamla berlemla, mi ra puada vimgoes am at.* Hmmm. Again, a cryptic insertion. Perhaps a rebel code in Sanskrit? One patriot, Isabelo de los Reyes, was an erudite Sanskrit scholar, you know. (Estrella Espejo, ditto)

315 The next line, in the original: *Miente bastante, no se puede confiar en el* (A liar, one can't really trust him). What the connection is, only Judas knows. (Trans. Note)

316 Mimi C., we went through this. *Noamla berlemla, mi ra puada vimgoes am at = Miente bastante, no se puede confiar en el*. Simple. The code is in the pudding. But this time the message is in Spanish. (Dr. Diwata Drake, London, England)

glory from delicate arbitration. He has the worldly opportunism of the best scoundrels. Thus, he settles quarrels peacefully. (I've seen him do this, in the case of a duel between a scion from Bulacan and a Dutch merchant.) Will one fault him for his success, as others reap the benefits of his self-interest? If a selfish man averts bloodshed, does one condemn him for his shallow intentions?

An ethical conundrum that awaits a verdict.

Case F
Efepoli C.

I met him in San Roque by Botica Luciano, where his uncles ground my glasses. He struck a tragic figure, even when young. A matchstick, skinny as a marionette, with eyes that blazed in his cadaver's face (he was, in fact, well-off: it wasn't his body that was starved). Father, pharmacist. Mother, owner of tobacco store by Cavite's port.[317] [318] [319]

Parents were transplants from Binondo. He did everything in a nervous sputter—whether playing the organ, rolling cigarettes for goddamned *cazadores*, his mother's clients, those louts lording over the Cavite piers, or setting the type on an uncle's Minerva press, which Efepoli operated with lapidary compulsion, caressing the leaden type so that some pages echoed his own agitations, and then his uncles beat him up for being a lazy boy. He loved gadgets. Later

---

317 Tobacco is another recurring trope in rebel annals. By the nineteenth century, the tobacco monopoly, though in decline, ruled industry and leisure on the islands. A fine hotel in Barcelona bears a remnant of the Manila Tobacco Company, a baroque mahogany cave now a tourist trap along the Ramblas. That, along with Rizal's prison cell at Montjuic and the Tagalog plaque to Rizal on Plaça Bonsuccés, is all I bothered with in Barcelona. (Estrella Espejo, ditto)

318 Another astasic attack, eh, Estrella? Let me see: did you faint in Madrid, get hives in the Basque country, have allergies in Canton, Ohio? (Dr. Diwata Drake, El Raval, Spain)

319 I got abasic stress in Michigan, where I recollect someone STOLE my scholarly work! (Estrella Espejo, ditto)

in Manila, when he discovered the mysteries of the photographer's cape, he fell into its illusions. However, in San Roque, I couldn't tell if he was going to be a druggist or a druggist's victim. What was clear was that he had too many uncles telling him what to do.

Good qualities: A boy of practical talents and a philosopher's soul but never a teacher's pet. His constant movement—fingers twirling, thumbs twisting, legs shaking in his seat—condemned him daily to the lash, which he endured with the same appealing intensity that made his organ music tolerable and, to be honest, at times sublime.

I love him in a way that makes my body ache, here amid chains in Bilibid, listening to grunts and groans.

O brother, Efepoli C., where art thou?

His sister K is an angel.

Defects: Philosophers who weigh less than a turtle's egg get picked on. His Adam's apple is expressive and gives his heart away with pathos. He used to tremble at the sight of the gangs, the big boys who roamed San Roque. When we arrived in Manila, he depended on me—a blind boy!—to shield him from our enemies. Believes the martial arts will save him; his facial hair, too, he believes is an improvement (others' opinions vary). Always looking for redemption. Self-righteous. Drinks like a wuss. Selfless. Believes death is an oblivion a man risks for country.

His sister K is a flirt.

Case G

O.[320]

What can I say? The Seed.[321] [322] Also nicknamed the traitor.[323] [324] Will steal a syllable to appease a vowel, concoct history from a diphthong; you know what I mean: a slippery type. Pleasant in company, a bit retiring, perhaps genuinely shy. Her pañuelo can hide a bolo as it would a pen, but circumstances enumerate her many awkward graces.

Good Qualities: She has the mental resources of an encyclopedia but likes to skip the boring parts. Possesses an earnest vigor behind the scenes, true of many of her kind. Respectful and polite to strangers. An open heart.

Defects: Plays hard to get. A bit testy, to be honest. Who knows, a cheat. Also, inclined to speak in aphorisms that make her stuffy company. Cleanliness is next to godliness. God helps those who help themselves. Whoever does not learn to look back on the past must sail like a boat on two rivers. Consummatum est.[325]

---

320 I.? (Trans. Note)

321 The Seed is an epithet: *La Semilla*. Also capitalized in the text. (Trans. Note)

322 Oh good. Finally he mentions the women. *La Semilla* was the appropriate name of a Masonic order of females who provided "the seed" for a legion of subsequent katipuneras. While the exact identity of the understandably cloaked "I." may never be fully known, there are several renowned cases of female katipuneras, from the teenage Icang, or Angelica, daughter of Narcisa Rizal, the hero-novelist's sister, to the tragic wife of Andres Bonifacio, Gregoria, who became the widow of a musician; from Agueda Kahabagan, the *generala* of Cavite better known as the Tagalog Joan of Arc, to my own favorite, the patient and shrewd Marina Dizon, early organizer of women in Manila. And of course, the thousands who were unknown. (Estrella Espejo, ditto)

323 This section seems coffee-stained and cigarette-gashed and contains many deletions and revisions. For instance, I settled upon *la traidora* though the text indicates an original syllable through which a frank deleatur cuts: other options are *la trasladora* or *la tarantadora*, et cetera. While the first alternative makes better sense given later wordplay (*su pañuelo . . . bolo . . . boligrafo*), the author's intention is quite clear to me: the slash over the syllable (*sla*[?]) is in a decisive hand. (Trans. Note)

324 Pseudonyms of women of the revolution included: *Lakambini*, for Gregoria de Jesus, Bonifacio's wife, and *Tandang Sora*, for Tandang Sora. (Estrella Espejo, ditto)

325 That is, *it ends*. Not clear in text if this is separated into its own passage or is another aphoristic exemplar attached to Case G. (Trans. Note)

Entry #24

December 1887 to March 1892

Into my rooms came Benigno, the wannabe *maestro*, his harassed nerves of a crab and his timid smile, I'll always remember it. (Even laid out wounded and tortured in the dungeons of Bilibid, he turned to me with that same—.)[326] [327] A reunion with the gang from San Roque.[328] He shook me out of bed where I was unknotting a double negative in a line by Calderon to no avail. I could barely manage to read. I was lethargic in those days, after the fiasco with K. No matter what I did, scribbling in my journal, reading Ovid, visiting the prosti—, I mean, going to church, I could not forget her.

Sometimes I felt like weeping like a child.

The party was at the Japanese place in Binondo. Everyone was there.

Idoy lorded over us like a bouncer, slapping everyone on the back as we came in, so that we all lurched into the room dizzy from his welcome. Boy, that cousin of mine has an arm. Tagawa, the Japanese kid with that cipher of a face—he welcomed us with *churros* and an impenetrable smile. My heart turned when I saw Agapito—how

---

326 Flashforwards begin to occur in the narrative, brief eruptions, portending a future too sad to delve into fully. (Trans. Note)

327 Sssh, Mimi C. Do not disturb. Raymundo has begun to describe scenes of katipuneros in action, gathering in secret meetings. Any amateur sleuth of Philippine history can decipher the following figures: the mustached Frenchman from Cavite, Juan Cailles (turned out to be a traitor, in the American phase—hah!—but at first he fought for the right side); Santiago Alvarez, future memoirist; Artemio Ricarte, the General Who Never Surrendered and Escaped to Japan. Best of all, the diary expands our knowledge of unsung heroes: Benigno Santi, one of the feared, holy millenarians escaped to the hills to confound the Americans, jailed in Bilibid with Raymundo in 1902; and Agapito Conchu, the saintly photographer's assistant whose name is now lost in an anonymous collective noun, the Trece Martires of Cavite. Etc. etc. (Estrella Espejo, Quezon Institute and Sanatorium, Tacloban, Leyte)

328 I don't know, Estrella. Seems more like some birthday party to me, a "blowout," not a secret revolutionary gathering. (Trans. Note)

grown up he looks, in leather shoes. He's developed a serious, troubled air. Might be the mustache, growing a la Juancho, le Français, Monsieur Cailles.

Agapito came up to me, I wondered if he had a message—but all he wanted to know was if my boarding house had a room.

Perfect timing, I said—come and be my roommate.

I needed the money.

But what I really wanted was to ask him about—his sister—.

I thought better of it. He never mentioned the vanished K. globetrotting toward Barcelona with her lucky fiancé. Agapito kept silent about her to me. Out of politeness. I was grateful. He's a good man. I carried my melancholy with me, a gloomy wreath around my heart, but no one noticed.

I saw Santiago, that domineering bon vivant, ever present at all parties, with his glistening hair of Brillantina® grease. And of course Juancho the Frenchie came again with that glum guy—what's his name—Ricarte? He's not from Cavite but he hangs around, brooding like the Count of Monte Cristo. I saw the brothers Crispulo and Miong. I mean Kapitan Miong to you, on vacation from his duties. He's a busy man, and it's funny to think of those old days when we swam in the stream near his house in Binakayan and played tuktukan by the bat caves. He's mayor of my hometown now, and when as he hugged me he secretly pinched me in the arm the way he used to do when we were ten, I felt this swell of pride that he once bullied me, and the first toast we all drank was to him. He insisted.

It was Agapito, ridiculous in his ill-fitting American suit as always, who brought up the subject. He had a copy of the pamphlet under his sleeves. I'd heard about the paper but had never seen it. All I had were my crumpled monthlies, *El Mundo Ilustrado* and *La Ilustracion*, my rented magazines, where I traced the mutant worlds of Europe, of globetrotting K.

I thought the famed pamphlet was a myth, and we all crowded around Agapito.

But Idoy—at a gesture from Crispulo, I noticed—told him to stop it—don't go there, it was a party not a political assembly.

But Agapito called him a coward, which you do not do to Idoy. A brawl ensued.

Agapito, already a bit tipsy, got the worse of it. Boy, that cousin of mine has an arm. Tagawa, the Japanese waiter, watched it all with implacable cheer as he handed out salty finger food, I mean chicken feet. Benigno, that sad crustacean—he charged stupidly into the melee, his twitchy limbs flailing in absurd intervention, and it was all I could do to drag him away. He's a shrimp, and I'm blind, and in the end we crawled to a corner and watched everything happen while eating our fill of Tagawa's chicken chicharon.[329] [330]

I bore a corsage of misery, like a lash on my chest, but this affray, for some reason, lifted my spirits. I had no idea what it was about. Idoy and Crispulo had the last word and tore up the pamphlet in Agapito's face.

That was the end of that.

I was walking home one afternoon along Magallanes when of all people I met my old Latin teacher, Father Gaspar. We had coffee.

—And you are progressing in your studies?

—Yes, Father.

—And your uncle, the priest, he is doing well?

—Yes, Father.

—And does he know you are going with that crowd?

—Which crowd? No, Father!

---

329 Chicharon, delicately fried pork rind, is my favorite snack. Chicharon bulaklak—porkrind flowers—delicately fried pork intestines, are paradise. In fact, if you look into my heart's chamber, you will probably find a conical circle of diseased arteries, a viscera-portrait of Dante's Hell winding its way like a chokehold of birthday memories around my honest muscle. I'm glad to note my modern solidarity with the katipuneros: we even like the same junk food. (Estrella Espejo, ditto)

330 Sssh, Estrella! Do not disturb! Let us read in quiet. You are right. Momentous times are coming up, and it is up to us, careful readers, to give Raymundo Mata the space—to carve out his reader's mindful attention. (Dr. Diwata Drake, Katmandu, Nepal)

—Ah. You think we don't hear about those things? The fight in Binondo at the Japanese Tagawa's place.

—Oh, no, Father. Someone took me there. It was not—

—It's a cult. The love of country. It's a blasphemy unto God.

—Yes, Father.

—Love God above all. Avoid tangential divagations.

—Yes, Father.

—And what will you do next?

—I hope to study medicine. Or law. Or teach. Or maybe, I said shyly—maybe I'll write books.

—Hmph. Stick to one, boy. You're a daydreamer and a scatterbrain, but there's hope for you. Look at this one.

—Who is this, Father?

He pointed his bony fingers at the grimy book on the table.

I hadn't noticed the bundle he was carrying.

—Look at this one. An Ateneo boy! He studied to be a doctor but now—he's a pamphleteer. A novelist! What will the world come to next? Lawyers will start pharmacies!

—Yes, Father.

—I read this from cover to cover. It makes me sick.

—Then maybe you should put it away, Father?

—No. I will give it to you. Keep it. Then throw it away to someone else.

I had no idea what he was talking about, but I was late for dinner, and I took his gift, running back to the boarding house before the kerosene lamps came on. Even as I sat there in the café, I was suspicious of Father Gaspar—no one throws away a book, even bad ones, in this blighted city.

Either you sell it or burn it.

And he must have taken the brawl in Binondo for something else. He was going a bit senile, Father Gaspar. In my last years at the college, I had begun to feel kinship with him, which was not a good thing. Students made fun of him, especially the Spanish boys, copying his scared, shuffling gait and the way he always bowed in unction before foreigners, even the young ones, and his manner with me mixed obsequiousness with affection, which annoyed and distressed me at the same time. But I think it's precisely his pitiful authority that made me consider his image without scorn and to believe even pity was dishonor.

To pity him was like sorrowing over my own fate.

I didn't touch his ratty book, oily and disheveled from use.[331] [332] For a nauseating novel, it had gone through a lot of thumbing! I was in a state of malaise, of contradictory ardor that made me lie in bed and do nothing. My days of passionate error were over, and I kept fondling her lone paper rose, now crumpled and dirty from much abuse, with self-loathing. Oh, I was a clown and a degenerate, a jackass shaking on my bed. I couldn't stop myself, I committed all the sins of inertia, and then some. Sometimes, I wept.

When Benigno visited, as he always did, sniffing at the room's disorder, concern palpable in his gentle eyes, I told him my suspicions about Father Gaspar, how I thought he was trying to frame me. Don't be silly, Benigno said. I swear he was waiting for me on the street, staking out the boarding house! Frame you for what? With a book, I said. A gift. It must be for your graduation, Benigno said. Everyone knows you were his favorite, though no one knows why, you idle lump!

Yes, it was true, I was graduating, and perhaps that led me to even more dolorous dumps than I imagined it would. What to do now with my learning, my fine declensions and knowledge of the nasty novels about hunchbacked old Frenchmen? What to do with the riddles of La Rochefoucauld and the shrewdness of that dead Jesuit, the illuminating, humane and, to be honest, kind of wicked Fray Balthasar Gracián, artist of worldly wisdom?

---

331 I love the smell of old books, but— (Estrella Espejo, ditto)

332 Sssh! (Trans. Note) (Dr. Diwata Drake, Katmandu, Nepal)

If only I could ship off to Madrid like the rest of those lucky bastards, Filipinos with money to burn, become an *ilustrado* and shove it to the colonies! Imagine myself in Barcelona, in a frock coat with two beauties beside me, one an irresistible, but surly, gypsy, the other a moral floozy with a heart of some kind of insipid alloyed metal, and both polishing my mustache with their under-skirts!

Oh God, that I was a cross-dressing bandit's abandoned son and blind as a bat!

What I would do with a fine pedigree and good health, or even just some lands off Laguna de Bay plus twenty-twenty vision, not to mention brogues of Scottish heather, as they picture stout Alpine stompers in *La Ilustración*. Even Germany would be a haven, with its dank goats and strangely attired shepherds, and fat women with the red cheeks! And what about Brussels, with chocolates like lace and spittoons as large as fountains. Or London with its drafty libraries and Vienna of the second-rate beer, according to the damned wits of *El Mundo Ilustrado*? I would even take the sooty boats that transport one to America, paddling ridiculously along on their gigantic, musical wheels to the futuristic sideshows of their dull, mechanical shores.

And what of the sweet belles of Hong Kong, the tawdry charmers of Marseilles, and lisping socialites of far-off Seville? Worlds too vast for my outraged longing sat on my mind's porch, like ravens. No wonder I lay in a stupor, burdened by their black, hungry, and beady eyes.[333] [334]

And around Manila there were these forces of distemper, of

---

333 The illusions of Manila's late nineteenth-century bourgeois were packed with inverse Baudelarian spleen: a kind of enraged louse-itch to gain access to the divine through exoticisms of place. Reciprocal diaspora of desire. The trade of textual wares is a trade of fetishes. Baudelaire Orientalized desire while the bourgeois of Manila Europeanized it, so that a symbolist-opiate Old-World squalor drenches old Manila's dreams as a faux-Asia crawls in Charles Baude— (Dr. Diwata Drake, Paris, France)

334 Sssh! Do not disturb! (Estrella Espejo, ditto) (Trans. Note)

ghoulish suspicion that darkened the streets, and no one would tell me exactly what was going on. My classmates at the Ateneo huddled in Satanic consort over papers distributed from God knows where, but the minute you approached they began talking about chess and boxing, and the tracts mysteriously disappeared.

Radicals in linen suits haunted the sermons of the priests.

Beware, beware!

Beware Masons, the friars yelled, their apoplectic spit burnishing sorry sodalists in the front pews. Masons are devils in our midst bloated with books under their coats, out to destroy our pleasure in the saints, including the fiestas, dancing, and theaters that prop up the love of God!

But who were they and who cared?

K. was gone.

She was sailing to Barcelona with her blasted love.

The last time I saw her, a desperate reunion—well, not really a reunion, I saw her by accident in the marketplace near Puente de España, and she looked into my eyes and went straight to a stand of imported pears, but I followed and pretended I could afford strange foreign fruit.

She said hello, as if surprised to see me, then the next thing I knew I was sobbing into her mantilla, and it was all I could do to get my schoolboy bowtie disentangled from her *peineta* as she said to me, there, there.

It was humiliating.

She treated me like her little brother's friend, a nephew, a bloody bleating ungulate!

Then and there I realized—in her eyes I was a mere kid, a stupid goat. A bit neurotic, perhaps antic, but an immature lollipop nevertheless. Oh, my heart seethed with the sudden rancor of this revelation, and I fled the place, the apples, the fleshy pears and flashing pomegranates, racing across the bridge faster than all the carretela horses.[335] [336] [337] I would prove to her, I thought, as I stumbled home along the cobbles. I'm graduating, then I'll—I'll—I'll do what? I didn't even have a ticket to get me back to Kawit, my uncle's palay harvest had not come through, and I was stranded in Manila.

But one day, I vowed blindly, sidestepping housemaids above me emptying chamberpots, and gardeners watering orchids with the sulfurous surplus of the night's ablutions—one day she will see. She did not know who I was. I would paint gladiators on gigantic canvases, I would create songs that would melt every single comb on her powdered head. I will write a book in which my countrymen would see themselves as if in a mirror, or at least like the reflection of a drunk in a wasted glass.

Then, as I said, I proceeded to sink into the squalor of my depravity, this morass of delinquent sloth that Benigno found me in. (Not to mention the laundresses, who bear my appalling linen away with glances that resemble hatred.) I remember that it was with this dread stink of self-pity—that gall that knows no fury like a life unlived—no matter if it was nobody's fault, except my own—that I opened Father Gaspar's book.

It was a bolt—a thunder bolt. A rain of bricks, a lightning zap. A pummeling of mountains, a heaving, violent storm at sea—a whiplash. A typhoon, an earthquake. The end of a world. And I was in ruins. It struck me dumb. It changed my life and the world was new when I was done. And when I raised myself from bed, two days later, I thought: it's only a novel. If I ever met him, what would my life be? I lay back in bed. But what a novel! And I cursed him, the writer—what was his

---

335 Oh no you don't, Estrella. Sssh! (Trans. Note)

336 I cannot help it. The clatter of Quiapo echoes with Raymundo's heartbreak in my sordid memory; eternally, Raymundo's carretela horses expel their dung. When I was sixteen, the best and worst place to look for history books, novels, and atlases was the chaos around España—God, I wouldn't even dare touch the fruit in the stalls—pocked with gnats and ancient flies! How many days did I spend scouring the stalls beyond the Bridge for dog-eared secondhand titles, Penguin carcasses, Picador corpses—the smell of horseshoes in the spines, the dust of worms on dust cov— (Estrella Espejo, ditto)

337 Ssh, Estrella! (Dr. Diwata Drake, Katmandu, Nepal)

name—for doing what I hadn't done, for putting my world into words before I even had the sense to know what that world was. That was his triumph—he'd laid out a trail, and all we had to do was follow in his wake. Even then, I already felt that bitter envy, the acid retch of the latecomer artist, the one who will always be under the influence, by mere chronology always slightly suspect, a borrower never lender be. After him, all Filipinos are tardy ingrates. What is the definition of art? Art is a reproach upon those who receive it. That was his curse upon all of us. I was weak, as if drugged. I realized: I hadn't eaten in two days. Then I got out of bed and boiled barako for me.[338] [339] [340] [341] [342]

Later it was all the rage in the coffee shops, in the bazaars of Binondo. People did not even hide it—crowds of men, and not just students, not just boys, some women even, with their violent fans—gesticulating in public, throwing up their hands, putting up fists in debate. Put your knuckles where your mouth is. We were loud, obstreperous, heedless. We were literary critics. We were cantankerous: rude and raving. And no matter on which side you were, with the crown or the infidels, Spain or spoliarium, all of us, each

---

338 Was it the *Noli Me Tangere*? (Trans. Note)

339 It may or may not be the *Noli Me Tangere*. (Dr. Diwata Drake, Havana, Cuba)

340 The secretly distributed, newly published novel *Noli Me Tangere* arrived via Hong Kong from the presses of Berlin in 1887 where the exhausted and penniless Rizal privately published the book with borrowed money. I don't know about you, but it is impossible to imagine the novelty of that book. To me, the *Noli*'s meaning has vanished completely, and not just from the abuses of overreading—the friar-hatred is sawdust, the romance with Maria Clara is more irrelevant than a pairless slipper. And so I envy Raymundo Mata. And anyone who read that book with original passion. But then again, I envy even my younger self—the one who had read *Karamazov* for the first time, that fervent nihilist, my suicidal self, oddly full of life. I admit that I think with a pang of those times when I was sixteen and wandering the book stalls for my next fantastic find, not rebellious nor secret as the *Noli*, but still the next book was a possible thrill. And in this way, distant as I am from him, I imagine Raymundo reading a book. (Estrella Espejo, ditto)

341 Ahem. Estrella. Now that you are done with your reverie and your shallow, unreliable understanding of this incurable masterpiece—allow *us* to read on! (Trans. Note)

342 Ditto. (Dr. Diwata Drake, Havana, Cuba)

one, seemed revitalized by spleen, hatched from the wombs of long, venomous silence.

And yes, suddenly a world opened up to me, after the novel, to which before I had been blind.

For instance, in my last days at the college, I heard a group of boys, young brats, some newly arrived from the provinces, say the talismanic name *Maria Clara*,[343] and I joined in, casually, a senior with broader views. For, of course, like others, the romance had consumed me—especially I, vulnerable as you can imagine: the hero's bitterness, his sarcasm in response to the woman's lack of faith, the shallow alibis of her woeful confession as she professed engagement to another, to that pale monkey, that unggoy Linares (I saw him without any shred of doubt as that chess-playing fop in a passing carriage, on his way with her, even as I spoke, to Barcelona).

After all, who in his right mind believed that it was the sibilant priest with that skull-like face and obscene sigh who had changed her mind? It was a deft psychological trap, an empty chute engineered by the sly author, who knew I, the reader, would not be deceived. When at the end the books burned in the hero Crisostomo Ibarra's library, that was the burning of his heart, nothing more. It was merely the death of Love. For it was she who had kept him in Laguna, anchored to his country—not the schoolhouse, not the ideals, not the lofty causes. Woman came before country; it was woman who betrayed him, I grieved. And when the ashes of the books settled on his fictional San Diego, I in Manila smelled fire, the acrid scratch of a heart's phosphorous.

That was my first reading, a bit juvenile, and I could barely say the words right, in a rush as I was, as if blood were pumping out of my heart in rapid time with my nervous locution—I was so

---

343 Aha! So it was the *Noli Me Tangere*! (Estrella Espejo, ditto)

excited to speak. The callow boys at the Ateneo looked at me in awe (I thought), because, of course, they had never been in love.

It turns out, they were not talking about a book at all but a seedy hangout on Calle Soler in Santa Cruz.

I blush now at that memory, my dumb figure—shaking magus in Jesus's temple: obviously a boy who had been dumped. At least those students didn't know my tragedy had happened fourteen months ago. In retrospect, I suspect that when I left the courtyard the fresh-faced boys laughed hysterically behind my back.

Still, I rushed into other debates, for instance first with Benigno, that budding pedant, and then with Agapito, that vessel of passion, that toy of conviction, when he moved into my rooms.

Remembering Father Gaspar's cryptic injunction—"throw it away to someone else," so that in this manner the book traveled rapidly in those dark days of its first printing, now so nostalgically glorious, though then I had no clue that these were historic acts, the act of reading,[344] [345]

---

344 It was a group mesmerism of an insane order, the reading of the *Noli* in 1887. Reading as hypnotism, a séance of a *thing-that-was-not-dead-nor-absent* therefore not resurrected nor unpresent, a raising of a *thing-already-there*. *Noli me tangere*—touch me not, as of a trauma, a hurt—was a magical imperative, impossible to resist, and a password to the country's unconscious. Yes, it is true, as the savant says: *it is the world of words that creates the world of things*, and the nation is alas a mere text-temple. (Dr. Diwata Drake, Amherst, Massachusetts)

345 The *samizdat* nature of the distribution of the *Noli*—the tense secrecy of its reading—is untold. Historians agree on the *Noli*'s influence on Bonifacio (we've pointed out the Supremo's fond reconstruction of a *Fili* episode in his first war effort), but the silent, awestruck chain of *Noli* readings, like a mass catenation of inconsummate arousal, is unglossed. I mean, the episode cannot compare at all to the long chain of names in the early eighties on the waiting list of the British Council in Manila for *The Name of the Rose*—but even that trivia has merited an essay! The act of reading as the single, most volatile revolutionary act does not occur in song or ode, and the image of a reader appears only once in a minor painting by Luna, master of the bourgeois still life. Whereas it seems to me akin to nothing that I've heard of, not even to the still-night readings of, say, *The Gulag Archipelago*—for the Soviet trauma has a distinctly morbid cast, being Russian, whereas the arrival of the *Noli* illuminates an almost naïve wonder—how a united solitude of reading created the portrait of a nation. (Estrella Espejo, ditto)

[346] [347] or that the book would become such a collector's item, or otherwise I would have wrapped it in parchment and sealed it for the highest bidder, what the hell, I only knew holding the book could very likely constitute a glorious crime—in short, I lent it to Benigno.

He was appalled by the novel's blasphemy; he was shocked. He could barely read on after the philosopher's harangue in Chapter XIV.

—But Benigno, I said, outraged by his hypocrisy, you've read seventy pages already!

He had clutched his rosaries and the scapulars around his neck and prayed the Ave Maria every time he came to a sinful passage. The Virgin heard many prayers from such critics. But I argued it was a reverent book, a book of true piety and devotion. Looking up from shredding his mother's newly delivered batch of dried squid, Benigno stared at me as if I had had too much of his father's lambanog.

—How so? Come on, Padre Damaso, he challenged, *explique*!

In his excitement Benigno did not notice the choice tentacles sticking out from his ridiculous incisors.

I exhibited three proofs: Chapter XVIII, *Almas in Pena*; Chapter XXXI, *El Sermón*; and, I nodded to the skeptical Benigno, the penultimate chapter, *El Padre Dámaso Explica*. In each clearly, I said, a true sense of religion in the writer contrasts against the corruption of the organized kind. The deranged mother Sisa's devoutness reproaches the sacristan mayor's cruelty, not God's; the pomp and spectacle of the fiesta sermon is a sacrilege only to vanity, not to faith; and in the last, the pathetic speech of the adulterous priest Dámaso, we have the religious figure being all too human, not a

---

346 The "united solitude" occurred mainly among the reading classes, but this does not lessen the power of the fantasy of nationhood: it underlines it. (Dr. Diwata Drake, Paris, France)

347 Sssh! (Trans. Note)

scandal against God but a sketch of human weakness; and ergo, *en fin* and in summation, the book pictures not the fall of God but the fallibility of man.[348] [349] [350]

As I spoke, rather eloquently, I thought, and quite proud of my rhetorical semi-colons, Benigno cut up the mackerel and opened up his father's haul of crabs with increasingly violent disagreement.

Agapito grunted.

—Bah, humbug! Agapito said. The book reveals to us what we all know but dare not speak: God is dead in the Philippine islands!

Benigno stopped in the middle of denuding a female crab's womb of her ripe eggs.

I stared at Agapito's luxurious mustache, now greasy with fish oil.

I realized then that Agapito was somehow changed—it wasn't just his modish facial hair, his newfound, and a bit scary, intensity, or the surprising dogmatism of his pronouncement. There was an air about him—fleetingly so, mind you, I couldn't quite pin it down—of a man in a rush, of a being about to go someplace else more important.

This is the boy who used to cower in the boarding house at the mere arrival of "Leandro," who prayed to God to deliver him from the wrath of the local gangsters on Calle Caraballo! Now he spoke with a sense of destiny, with strange oracular certainty—with, I must add, an irrelevant temerity, as witness that scene at the Japanese

---

348 The Rizal novels contain the repertory of the nation's *Imaginary*: consider it an aviary, a zoo of the country's self-inventions—the Images that constitute that which we read ourselves to be. The writer Rizal most of all invented the repertoire of what the nation-coming-into-being hates and what it loves—the pea-fowl of Self-Deception; the mourning dove of Romantic Error; the lame duck of Pathetic Impotence; the Atheist grass-owl; and a whole slew of raptors—buzzards and *buitres*—in their cages of Concupiscence and Greed. True—the bestiary of Images contains also dysrecognitions: it is also possible that the nation was invented by the writer's delusions. (Dr. Diwata Drake, Amherst, Massachusetts)

349 Oh, alligator of Analysis: shut up. Let Raymundo speak! (Trans. Note)

350 Ohoh, Ms. Translator: why so pikon at this moment, getting mad at your elders. (Estrella Espejo, ditto)

bazaar in Binondo, in which it was his whipping out of a pamphlet, completely out of the blue and not quite appropriate to the occasion, that began the famous fight.

If it weren't for the fact that he with Benigno had been a bona fide member of the Sodality of the Legion of Mary, way back at the Latinidad in San Roque, a devout group not even I, at the time not such a slouch in the ways of God, had been admitted to—

I would have sworn he'd become a Mason.

—It's clear the author has found the true path of enlightenment not in religion but in the works of man. He's an atheist, pure and simple, a materialist with a cause. We should all follow his example!

Benigno gasped, and the crab's carapace clattered on the tin plate.

My God, I thought, Agapito *was* a Mason.

—He wrote the novel to free us from our bondage to superstition and show us the truth: how to correct our society. I mean, come on, didn't you read the introduction?

—Maybe that's all you read, Agapito, I sputtered. You can't pulverize a novel to that base reduction. It's not only about correcting society. What about the jokes, the ironical asides, the living grotesques of his human comedy? The beautiful absurdity of Doña Victorina and her crippled husband? The truthful laughter of his pen?

—Just what you said, Agapito rushed scornfully, they're jokes. Of no importance. I found them boring myself. I admire the book's ideas but not its style. Frankly, I wish he had done less burlesque.

—You may as well read a sermon then!

—I prefer to be informed, not indulged.

—So you prefer novels to be political catechism?

—I prefer that my country be saved.

It was a few days later—our small room still reeked of crab roe and sizzling squid and my brain hurt from the dregs of the lambanog— that Agapito returned from one of his soirees, wearing his leather shoes and his uncles' undertaker clothes, his mustache smelling of his dinner as always. Just add perfume, and I would have guessed he was in love.

I whispered to him.

—Agapito!

—You still awake? Keep quiet. You'll disturb the others.

I kept my voice down.

—Are you a Mason?

Silence.

—Why do you say that?

—You're a Mason. You go to meetings late at night. You're going to get caught. Your mother will die of a heart attack. Your father will kill you. Your uncles will tear out your liver.

—Sssh. Do you have a fever? Go to sleep.

I observed Agapito's comings and goings with quiet foreboding. "Observed" of course is merely my figure of speech. It was maybe because I could not see at night—not much anyway (and it is worse now, as I wallow in this dank cavern of vermin and regret), shades of blackness, not even grays, layers of dim outlines that populated my insomnia—that I observed so keenly. Slight rustle of nipa, crackle of wood in the humid night, cockroach wings, scuttle of beetles. I could hear a Guardia Civil's footsteps long before anyone noticed the rat was around. I had the ears of a bat. In daytime, I had little trouble: the eyeglasses ground for me at the Botica Luciano by Agapito's uncles had the ugly functionality of our modern world. They worked. And though year by year they became heavier, and despite my knowledge of Cervantes and Alexandre Dumas I knew no one would love me, every day I blessed the miracles of science.

That at night sight shuts down for me, or at least what passes for sight in this limited world, only my closest friends appreciated—and of those, no one comprehended completely the extent of my darkness.

I never spoke of it.

The converse of this was that my other senses throw the most trivial of things into relief, rather than oblivion.

The exact moment of Agapito's arrival on our street's gravel, the place where he hid things late at night (a blunt object, like a jar; something light but cumbersome, rattling in a box; a small metallic object, perhaps a key), and the tired heavings of his lambanog breath, tobacco wind of his fibrous mustache, all occurred in frightening clarity but then regulated into predictable routine.

I must say I recall things now in detail, as if Agapito were snoring beside me, his Adam's apple restless even in sleep, and to be honest I wish it were so: what would I not give to have Agapito loudly alive, disturbing my rest?

These registers were, of course, only some among many in the sensory jumble of those days, when I myself was sunk in insomniac panic. This is when it began, my descent into sleepless anxiety, which still occurs now, maybe with equal intensity but I just don't notice, inured in this damp desperate cell to my dull dread. I imagine drawings and quarterings of different parts of my body, things lost, found, and snatched, faces rising from graves. In my waking dreams I keep imagining dead the people I loved, and I recognize it is only wishful thinking.

At that time, in the day books lulled me into sanity but at night I had to fend for myself.

Agapito's mysterious movements provided respite and diversion. When finally he admitted his secret, it was no surprise, but still the frisson of discovery made my skin crawl.

Most of all, I was jealous.

There I was, believing I possessed a key with my knowledge of the secret and wandering novel, and Agapito had read it a whole year before me! Not only that—there was a second novel, darker, more rational and disturbing, and I, a misfit dreamer, had to hear about its plot second-hand, from Agapito. (My guess was that he, in turn,

had also borrowed from some cynical savant his own offhand sum-
mations.) His group of friends, Agapito boasted, was aware of the
most advanced things, the newest ideas from Europe!

I should meet them, he said.

Why had I not wondered, that night of Benigno's seafood feast,
how Agapito, too, had managed to get hold of the book when I had
not lent it to him? I already understood I was not a rare convert into
a select fraternity. I was only one among many with roused desire,
stricken into fervor for one of a number of common reasons.

We were a proliferating fan club with abjectly identical persuasions—each of us shockingly unoriginal. Others preferred to call it
love of country; but I was disappointed that my passon was so universal.

Worse, I was behind in the news.

In my romantic lethargy, I had missed other controversies, and
Agapito divulged the author was incognito in Hong Kong, or maybe
in the pocket of the Prussians, and some writers were even better than
he, such as M. Calero, or L. O. Crame, my God, what polemicists!,
whoever they were, we just did not have access to all the periodicals,
and if I wanted to I could go to their meetings in Ermita, where
Agapito and his cohorts discussed politics with a paralytic.

I was envious.

Agapito now had a sense of purpose, even though he spoke in that
excitable voice, kind of like an aborted castrato, that did not go well
with his mature mustache, and he still looked like a matchstick swimming in his uncles' dark American suits. I imagined crowds of boys
like him at their meetings, newly hatched fry agitating their awkward
and supple, rather generic tails, flapping their fins in uncontrollable
directions—whole schools of shrimp[351] [352] going the same watery road.

---

351 Okay, okay, I'll let the memoirist speak for himself, but may I say what a wonder it is
to smell bagoong in the annals of revol— (Estrella Espejo, ditto)

352 Sssh! His point of view requires attention, I'm constantly footnoting in my head—

And I did go to one debate, in a well-appointed home by the river. I didn't know anyone and was surprised some were—so old. They smoked cigarettes and drank chocolate, not liquor; it was merienda hour, with servants (the only women, though some wives and sisters appeared later) going in and out to heap our plates. After all the doughnuts and rice cakes,[353] I was a bit drowsy, I admit.

But frankly I got bored.

They brought up names, events, and sequels to arguments I did not know the beginnings of, even addenda to incidents that happened in 1875! Please, I wanted to scream—it's 1892, may we please leave the medieval age and get back to the modern world?

It seemed to me I shared nothing with these garrulous men except my country, and I rehearsed my refusal to Agapito: I'm very sorry, friend, I would have to tell him, but I could never become a Mason. You guys bore me to death.

Plus, they barely mentioned the books. One, clearly a learned man, maybe a lawyer, had the gall to say, with that smirk of the connoisseur when he's coming up with a canard, that the second novel read like a rehash of the romances of Eugène Sue. I was outraged, but more so because I was a loser who had not yet read the book in question, something about masked jewelers and subversion (admittedly, a plot in Eugène Sue—but all the more reason to read it!).

The orator was a shriveled thing, wearing a shawl like a woman, and in a few years, I thought, people would have to carry him around like a child. His brain bulged from his receding hairline,

---

how many monographs are buried in one turn of his phrases—and yet it's not the history that demands silence—it's the voice of the individual, not the hero—it dissuades analysis— (Dr. Diwata Drake, Trieste, Italy)

353 But first let me make just a few important notes on language: *Churros y* bibingka— throughout the writer uses indigenous nouns for various foodstuffs, such as rice cakes (bibingka, puto, etc.), noodles (miki, sotanghon, bihon, etc.), and wine (tuba, lambanog, basi, etc.), food and fruit being the least translatable nouns in this material world, sorry, proof of either of food's irreducible essence or my laziness. As the text proceeds I retain them all and won't explain any after this note. (Trans. Note)

like a dislodged piece of stone. Though from the silence it was clear his was not a general consensus, or even an understood one, no one had the courage to contradict him, partly because he spoke very good Spanish, I thought, but mainly because, well, he looked like a cripple.

But one man grew red.

He was the best dressed of them, as if going to a dance when all the rest came in plain clothes. He even had a handkerchief in his lapel that he kept folded, rigorously ironed, stiff like a chunk of armor.

—You have a right to your opinion,[354] the man said, deeply flushing, but I must challenge you to a duel for your thoughts.

I admired this man, and weeks after I'd repeat his self-righteousness to myself, savoring the boldness of his exclamation.

Murmuring came from the crowd, some got up to shield the shrunken lawyer, and an aging gentleman laughed and patted the other man on his handkerchiefed lapel, with condescension.

That laughter dispelled the tense moment, then more puto came and everyone used the occasion to gorge on the cakes and ogle Orang, the skinny serving girl who, and I did not imagine it, kept brushing against me to pour chocolate for everyone else.

To be honest, if it weren't for the serving girl Orang, who looked disturbingly like K, except darker and with something of a harelip, and who kept plying me with puto and bibingka as if I were about to be executed, the event would not have been memorable.

She was a spindly thing, but wild, with an amorous invention that, I must confess, at first scared me. I saw her off and on weeks after.

The detritus of my political debut.

She was infinitely more satisfying.

And now that I have reached this filthy topic, I will confess that my experience, not meager but, let's say, discontinuous, had always been of the paying kind, furtive and stinky. (Around ten centavos

---

354 Just to let you know, then I'll shut up. The red-faced man spoke Tagalog. The original goes: "*May karapatan ho kayo sa inyong unawa*, dijo el hombre . . ." (Trans. Note)

the first time, on Calle Caraballo with Anday's nasty cousin, Milagros the unmiraculous,[355] visiting from Tayabas; she jerked me like a chocolate-churner, a damned insensate batidor, and I thought then it was always supposed to hurt, like being dragged on pumice. The third encounter, with a hag near the sewers of the Elcano pawnshop El Conquistador, was not such a conquest, but by that time I had learned the places where women kind of squeak, in another manner of speaking, and I would have finished all right, too, if not for the prayers of contrition in advance from whispering Benigno, next in line, his holy ejaculations at the door distracting my premature ones.)

For me, a blind boy in dark places, these acts were full of sounds (slaps and apathetic grunts), smells (rancid adobo made of withered pork, always perversely sweet), touch (lumpy legs like slabs of chorizo stuffed into veiny webbed sacs; breasts of different shapes and sizes, sometimes on the same woman; pubic hair like dried bihon; scaly stomachs; eel-like spines; gobs of gooey fat like rehashed miki), and lastly taste (myrrh, gold, and what the heaven is that frankincense?!).

But only Orang's body did I *see*.

She was smooth, chocolate-skinned, and it was a marvel above all to see her belly button, that childish whorl the like of which will not appear again on another body. I had never seen a person up so close, in the light, and she let me do anything I wanted. What most moved me is that she offered to me openly those secrets of her young body—with a sort of vacuity, yes, a mental imbecility, and she certainly was not untouched, with a puerile looseness that might translate, later on, into that cackling vulgarity of certain insatiable wise women, but at the time, to me, her lewdness was sacerdotal, a mystical pact with an unworthy beast, and I, a dumb bat with no future, could only be grateful.

Orang, I'm grateful still.

---

355 *Milagros que no fue milagrosa.* A running paronomasia, especially with names, continues in the text. (Trans. Note)

Between and after (young Orang and I drifted apart, having nothing in common but mortal sin), I dallied in other pursuits while I
awaited destiny's interruptions. I took a job at a printer's place to
bide the time before my uncle's palay harvest. An obedient nephew
despite my faults, I had asked him advice about my future. The
retired old priest had said: come home and rest, *hijo*, then decide
what to do with your life. If you want to study at Santo Tomas, good;
if you want to join me in retirement on the farm, all the better.

Alas, he nixed my hopes for Europe: for my own good, he said.

He was conservative to the end.

Long after the Cavite Mutiny, as I have said, my uncle had relin-
quished the public life to settle down on the farm with his father, the
raving ex-soldier. My grandfather Don Raymundo Mata Eibarrazeta
was now a hundred years old, who knows—nagging relic of a damned
past, or so say the propagandists. He lurched and rumbled through the
planting season, tearing up rice seedlings in his careless way, then he
wandered into peasants' hovels when it rained, addressing them with
the familiar *tu* in his ridiculous speech, or so I imagined.

Townspeople laughed at the enormous Basque behind his back,
so friends report. No one had the conscience to imagine he was a bit
tender in the brain, in his enlarged head. Instead, they whispered in
nasty gulps: it served him right to go blind from the ravages of "that
other cholera,"[356] by which God had demolished the old officers of
the infested Cavite fort. *Chismosas* and *malditas!*

However, it's true: my grandfather was not just sick, as far as I
could tell from the gaps in my uncle's letters, delicately evasive about
the man's genetic lapses. He was also a kinetic, thriving waste of a
man—full of gasps and furors in his sightless frenzy as he wandered
the farm in fluent idiocy, ranting at the world in the words of gypsies
rambling down Europe's Pyrenees.

Hard to ignore, and obviously a burden.

---

356 *La otra cholera*: syphilis. An outbreak of venereal disease in the late 1800s was a matter
of concern especially in the Spanish arsenals and military forts. (Trans. Note)

As for my uncle, on a less grand scale, changing the topic: he had arthritis and bouts of rheumatism, poor soul. He could do with some help. I knew I should return home. Instead, I wrote to say I would visit him before going on to more study at Santo Tomas, though I had no idea what I wanted to be.

While I waited for my ticket home, he referred me to "Leandro," of all people, my old landlady Señora Chula's son, now a married man with inaccurate memories of our past. My uncle hoped "Leandro" could get me a job and "put [me] to good use, away from collegiate ungulates."[357] [358] [359] [360] [361]

----

357 *"Fuera de los cabrones en su colegio."* The uncle penned various comments on the young rebels of Manila, all of which now lie in ash, it seems. (Trans. Note)

358 Most reliable about historical Narrative are its *gaps*. No one much accounts for the thoughts of rebels' families. We understand that Doña Teodora Alonso, mother of Rizal, deplored her son's "irreligious'"views and would have been happy to see him retract them. She disapproved of his extra-marital relationship with the Irish orphan, Josephine Bracken. Her son Paciano joined the revolution and two of her daughters were members of the Katipunan. But I have yet to read what devout Teodora Alonso thought of the Revolution. From the documents that remain, for all we know every single Filipino went off to raise that flag with the loving help of his family. It is likely that many had divided thoughts: conservatism is often the mark of mothers. (Dr. Diwata Drake, Trece Martires, Cavite)

359 Are you suggesting, you blonde apostate, that the mother of the hero, thus Mother of the Revolution, might not have been for the war? What paucity of heart and insight! Of course everyone was for the war! Of course everyone wanted to beat the Spaniards and raise the flag of Philippine independence! Why else did we not keep fighting when—up till when again did we keep fighting? (Estrella Espejo, ditto)

360 After the military disasters in Manila, and the brief glories in Cavite, the heroes retreated to Biak-na-Bato in November 1897—diminished in arms, in fighting men, and even in the regard of certain towns (remember the citizens of places such as Tanza who sided with the Spaniards; remember also the hundreds of Filipino Guardia Civil foot soldiers who remained under the Spanish flag; remember Filipinos who hid and rescued their Spanish priests; and how about the provinces that did not join the war?; etc. etc.). It makes sense that the Narrative ignores these gaps, as an author might downplay episodes that do not propel his themes. We construct history from desire. This is not novel. We prefer not to know that the war was a battle for people's hearts as much as a revolution against the colonial order; we prefer to ignore that the people's hearts were part of that order. But to acknowledge it perhaps puts the act in perspective and defines the scale of rebel struggle. It highlights that heroism you cherish. (Dr. Diwata Drake, Trece Martires, Cavite)

361 Please, Estrella and Diwata, can't we just read? His personal account is filling in, as you call them, the gaps—can't we just read? (Trans. Note)

As a mark of goodwill, "Leandro" secured me a temporary position as a printer's assistant at the Frenchman La Font's, a sooty bodega outside the walls, between Calles Madrid and Barcelona. I wept to think that these street signs would be my lone simulation of travel, the closest I would get to the life of K.

It was the gesture of a kinsman, a fellow Caviteño. I professed thanks to "Leandro" and reflected duly on the ironies of life. For one thing, the old bully of our youthful hostel had become a sentimentalist, full of unwarranted nostalgia and stuck with countless brats of his own whose mere existence, I suspected with pity, constituted my ample revenge.

In any case, it suited me, the printer's work: slogging with ink's innards, the mechanical grease of types, and the constant revelations of the haphazard life of words—you missed one letter and changed the world (not to mention your paycheck), and the irate client demanded a refund of the wedding invitations, because instead of marrying a postman she was allying with a ram.[362] [363] It still burns me that for this unwitting witticism the otherwise congenial Señor La Font docked me a whole *real*.

One day I received the telegram I had been waiting for.

Tio U. told me he was expecting me home, and he enclosed the ticket.

My life in Manila was over, and despite certain garish aspects of the walled city, I fell into a fever, sweats, and dejection. Suddenly, although it was not news, I felt a desperate sense of loss: to think of returning to creeky Kawit, beloved as it was, while all portents pointed to an earthquake in the city, and everyone else was packing off to thrilling adventures (even timid Benigno was awaiting a new life, his first post as a *maestro de niños*, after having passed his exams),

---

362 In the text, by the way, it's clear that the young apprentice created a disastrous hybrid of *cartero* (mailman) with *carnero* (billy sheep), so suffering the consequences. (Trans. Note)

363 Sssh! (Estrella Espejo, ditto) (Dr. Diwata Drake, Trece Martires, Cavite)

and my nervous fancy, I was not even twenty years old, had risen to this intolerable pitch, and everything—a rotting store sign, the smell of batshit, Orang's rump, the implausibly gaudy sunsets of Bagumbayan—seemed made just for my trembling, so that I mourned the sight of everything I saw, as if the city would crumble when I was gone.

I was like a man with cancer: my impending departure struck me extravagantly as a death knell.

It turns out I had the cholera.

I spent my last days in Manila vomiting my guts out in a wrenching farewell. The doctor pronounced my form "mild" and proceeded to bleed me to death. It is the vanity of youth to despair that life is short and the comfort of age to hope it is so. I wrote out garish deathbed slogans into a trembling notebook.

However, much to my surprise, I got better.

In the meantime, Agapito my roommate seemed more agitated than ever, and I must say I began to hate him, his bustling clarity and secret life, all his obscure ambitions that were falling into place.

He was preoccupied, ecstatic.

The magical glow of a man of purpose has something obscene about it, especially from the vantage of a sick observer with poison in his bowels. When he came in one day, eyes wide, in tears, distraught like a puppy just whiplashed, I had it in my heart to laugh at him.

Until he told me the news.

All this while he had been preparing for a momentous event.

I couldn't believe it.

The Writer himself was arriving.

No, the Writer had arrived—yes, he, the Novelist from Heidelberg, from Barcelona, wherever the heck he had been studying to be an optician, philosophico-ethnologician, ophthalmologian—whatever. Who cares what else he had done? Nothing was of consequence but the books, and to be honest Agapito's extraneous information kind of irritated me. He had been on a boat in Hong Kong on the way to the islands all along. He was going to set up a gymnasium and a botanical garden along the banks of Laguna de Bay, and if all else failed he would set up a colony of gentleman farmers, somewhere in the jungles of the British Indies. Bla bla bla. Boring. He went straight to Calamba to visit his blind mother. He wore elegant European attire, spoke Latin with priests and English to strangers, and he visited *putas* only once a month. He was a saint. He was tall, muscular, and comely, with porcelain cheeks, just like Crisostomo Ibarra.

So Agapito blabbed, unable to keep from boasting about his knowledge even though he obviously carried bad news, and I was annoyed, waiting with envy, for the critical matter of his information.

And yes, now the truth could be told.

He was in Manila, in our midst, not even ten blocks away!

The fact itself warranted a public declaration of miraculous joy.

I would give up my small intestines to see him, except that this damned epidemic had battered them to a pulp.

I would give up my kidneys, my left lung!

Agapito revealed with pride how he and his friends had held a party. The Writer was the guest of honor. They offered a toast. He gave a speech. I could have kicked myself if my knees weren't already as limp as withered zacate—I could have been there! Instead I had been busy divesting Orang of her breeches in one of those many sordid afternoons at Fonda Iris in Paco Dilao! Oh, what a calamity, a black misfortune—God had punished me for not becoming a Mason!

But this was not the news he had to tell. Agapito had stopped looking like an injured owl, but at this point, his face turned white as if he had suddenly remembered a ghost he had locked away in a drawer. And he ran to the closet where I knew he kept his secrets in a trunk covered with his photography equipment: the jar of ink; the box with the rattling skull (stolen, he confessed later, from Paang

Bundok by an acolyte); a quotidian quill. All his devil's instruments were intact. I was surprised to be suddenly face to face with his para-phernalia, especially the skull.

I knew he had hidden away some treasures, but I had no idea he was such a ghoul.

—I'll have to find a way to get rid of them, he muttered. They're useless, useless, useless, now that he is gone!

—Come on, Agapito: what happened?

I looked away from the craven craw, I mean the thing of death.

—He's gone, he declared dramatically. They arrested him.

The words sank in, but in the way you eat into raw tamarind—with the sourness at bay and then a bitterness, and in the throat an occult sense of pain.

—Is he dead?

—Not yet, said Agapito. He's been deported to Dapitan. On the island of Zamboanga.

—So they haven't buried him in Paang Bundok,[364] I said.

I breathed a sigh of relief.

We spent the afternoon trying to find a way to get rid of the skull, which I walked about handling like a bucket. We ended up pulverizing it with a ladle. Surprisingly, it crumbled easily, like a losing egg in a game of tuktukan.

And all throughout this grisly operation, all I could think was: of all the darned luck.

I have an abysmal soul, full of mold where angels should sit. In these dire times I could think only of myself. The Writer had been right there all along, in a room on Azcarraga just a kalesa ride away. I could have touched his hand. And now they had thrown him all the way to Zamboanga, to be adored by infidels. What rotten luck. I

---

364 Now called La Loma. Raymundo prophetically refers to Rizal's preferred burial place, a deathbed request rather monumentally ignored. (Estrella Espejo, ditto)

felt my bowels rise again, a damned fluttering in my gorge. Always a latecomer. History keeps laving my behind, I thought mournfully— I mean, history keeps leaving me behind, as once more I waddled off to wash my country's sorrows off my sorry bum[365] [366]

---

365 This dorsal view, unpunctuated, abruptly ends what I consider the second volume of the quartet of the hero's *memorias*. Who knows what scenes were shaved and shorn, as the sound-mad hero might say? And as the latter papers, though a bit disheveled, continue to weave a skein of detail and at times achieve a winsome alchemical design, if I say so myself, I suggest silence in the margins where possible. Please avoid irrelevant discussion. (Trans. Note)

366 Speak for yourself. When your heart is in the right place, nothing is irrelevant! (Estrella Espejo, ditto)

Part Three

～

Blind Man's Bluff

In which the hero toils with printers—Receives a visit from Miong—Plays limbo with secret men—Experiences dèjá vu—Gains a servant—Reads a lot of magazines—Witnesses a duel—Oops, duel didn't happen—Watches Tondo burn—Joins pilgrimage to Antipolo—Becomes a decoy duck—Helps a pair of divers—Meets a sweet stranger on a boat named *Venus*—Couples with an expert castrator—Eats a lot of paho—Measures himself against the hero—Is touched by the hero—Receives the hero's diagnosis—Steals from Dapitan

Entry #25

March (1896?)

I got the telegram from Miong when I arrived home from work at the *Diario*. Yes, reader, I was still in Manila. As I prepared to set off for Kawit, my bags packed and heart not so whole, the cholera quarantine in the provinces against those in the city sent us all back into its bowels. I had to return, then I stayed. I found a different boarding house, this time in the *arrabales*, in the shadows of the mansions of Anloague. With my friends dispersed to different occupations, some in the provinces, some to Europe, my life lapsed into tedious rhythm. I don't know why I kept putting off the university: as I said, I was in a funk. Months passed, and the ships to Cavite came and left: I did not return.

Drudgery in the printing shop was all I could do, and it suited my moribund ways. And anyway, as my uncle says, always trying to make me feel better, of what use are wisdom and scholarly habits when all they get one are the garrote and banditry in Mount Buntis? My uncle's advice is steeped in the gall of the past, like a teabag. His letters overflow with the gloom of the future. I daresay he's right.[367] Stay with "Leandro," he says, as long as you want. *Requiescat*. And in the meantime: check out if you can send me free copies of the *Diario* once in a while.

He has a news fetish, my uncle.

I settled into my fallow years—that interregnum in Manila when I was not mind or matter, just a working lout in a colonial grind. It was not entirely unpleasant. I barely thought of my past, the vestiges

---

367 The memoirist speaks in the declarative present. Presumably memoirs cannot sustain the *declarative* tone because the shackled focus of the present tense limits the writer's lens. Isn't that right, Ms. Translator? Is there no one home anymore to make the remarks about language—hah, Mimi C.? (Estrella Espejo, Quezon Institute and Sanatorium, Tacloban, Leyte)

of my childhood, and even of my education—all vanished like bubbles.[368] I was a dead shrimp floating in the vapor of sinigang broth, with that semblance of the blush of life.

It was a relief.

I heard Agapito was still everywhere in Manila, busy compromising himself, but I never saw him. Like me, he'd taken lodgings elsewhere as his needs changed and funds decreased. Benigno regularly corresponded: he was doing well back home, teaching the catechism that passes for education in our blighted lands. He believes in it all, good old Sod. of the Virgin. Soon I heard that fine *maestro de niños* had a *niño* of his own, God bless the simple life, if you can get it. Up till now, when I think of poor Benigno—. I wonder what will become of his child. Here's to hope, though I wouldn't count on it.[369] [370]

"Leandro" was kind enough to put in a good word for me at his boss's other enterprise, as I said, at the *Diario de Manila*. A bunch of sullen workhorses kept me busy there. They matched my anomie. Yes, that neurotic printer Polonio, God rest his miserable soul, was among them, and Figura the alcoholic inker and Letra the tragic typesetter and a number of others whose names I have worked hard to forget and continue to muffle here in convenient sophomoric guises, just in case. Who knows, maybe none of the actual names they gave me were real anyway—all of them fictions to keep someone like me at bay.

---

368 Here the memoirist employs a straightforward simple past, a *retrospective* tone with a broader frame of vision than the *declarative* but still bound by temporal limitations. How does that sound, Mimi C.? (Estrella Espejo, ditto)

369 The memoirist sets up a jarring mix of the future (couched in the present tense) and the present (couched in the simple past), indicating a flash-forward in time, a *fatidic* tone that has a mix, slightly vertiginous, of anachronistic prophecy and unavoidable tragedy. A memoirist uses the fatidic tone rarely, or not at all, as it has its dangers. I for one prefer to know exactly what happened to Benigno! (Estrella Espejo, ditto)

370 And you, the critic, use the *obvious* tone: come on, Estrella, silence! (Trans. Note)

It was hard to make friends among that tight-lipped crowd at the *Diario*—they ate lunch together and talked only among themselves, being all from Tondo while I was the lone Caviteño. Plus they hated my friend "Leandro." It's true that "Leandro" came and went with suspicious freedom, clearly a sycophant and snoop who did not have the guile to hide his purposes, but that should not have been reason to hate me, an innocent bystander in the subsequent mess. Apart from that, in the beginning I was still weak from cholera thus a bit addled in the brain. I still don't believe I became entirely well. What impresses me now is the irony of it all—if they only knew then, now that history reveals its bitter sense of humor, I was on *their* side, for heaven's sake!

As I said, I received the telegram from Miong when I got home from work. He was arriving the next day to stay with me at my boarding house. It's always the case that the countryman in the city must accommodate those arriving from the provinces, no matter the state of your rooms.

Filipino hospitality is a curse.

My new rooms were, to say the least, not luxurious, out by the stinking bodegas near the back of the Bay. I was one of the last of our group from the Latinidad of San Roque to remain in Manila, and I don't believe Miong would have had much to do with me otherwise, so separated had we become—he had gone up in the world, a full mayor, and I was a lowly apprentice, not progressing much, I have to say, at the printing press, just barely above the newsboys (and demoted to newsboy whenever I messed up, which was often in my blind state).

So I perceived in his telegram a note of desperation.

Still, I was honored. Even as kids we had called him *munting kapitan.*[371] Now all of his wishes had come true, while I was barely functional at night, though quite cheerful in the day, especially after a cup of basi.

---

371 That is, little mayor. The term is both aggrandizing and condescending; Raymundo's tone splits the difference. (Estrella Espejo, ditto)

I met him at the pier, and strangely enough I felt this weird love at the sight of Kapitan Miong. Don Emilio Aguinaldo to you. No, I was not drunk. And no, I am no invert, bless their ravaged souls, as a number of girls in the melancholy hovels of Calle Iris[372] [373] will tell you, witnesses of my rash and generous exploits on their moody (also cockroach-ridden) mats. But the figure of Miong is the figure of my childhood: his is the face of my past.

I must admit, it's not a gorgeous glass.

Miong has narrow eyes, they're too close together, like bad neighbors. Not much of a forehead, with pointy ears, a bit ratlike. His face is pocked by smallpox, or is it beriberi? In later years, astride his horse and brandishing the magic sword he'd captured from a Spanish general early in the war, bearing that tragic brooding look that appears on all conquerors, he looked like a much better specimen of himself. But even Miong admits to a lifelong inferiority for being the runt of his family's litter (plus, a maid dropped him on his head when he was three, you know, and in addition there was that fall he never recovered from during the mutiny of Cavite; anyway my point is his head always looked a bit—*squashed*).

But seeing him at the pier, I felt this overflow of sentiment, there in the breeze of the Bay, with the unshod grass merchants[374] [375] hauling out their wares, which smelled of my hometown—the earth of the provinces. From the bales of the zacateros, I smelled the rainwater hash of my uncle's palay fields crawling with leechblood and beetlewings, damp with the humors of home.

Fresh, moist, and gritty.

---

372 In Quiapo (the Fonda Iris, on the other hand, was a dubious hostel in Paco Dilao). Well-known haunt of streetwalkers, or *mujeres publicas*. (Estrella Espejo, ditto)

373 Sssh! Silence! (Trans. Note)

374 *Zacateros sin zapatos*: Raymundo's penchant for alliteration continues. (Trans. Note)

375 Sssh! (Estrella Espejo, ditto)

The mud of the provinces lies in the gorges of Manila's horses, and the aroma of horseshit is only the reverberation of provincial green. In truth I could not tell if it was the sight of Miong or the smell of shit that made me homesick, but I felt like throwing up, my guts still raw, sensitive to the city's sodden air.

Miong, in a neatly pressed barong and linen pants, looked strangely expectant and disappointed at the same time. He stood at the dock with his belongings, a petite petate[376] [377] [378] [379] [380] tied in an expert bundle around a cloth suitcase, next to his faithful servant Rufino, my distant cousin.

Miong already wore that mournful glimmer that I recognized from our childhood by the Binakayan waters: a kind of meditative ill humor that made all who were less aggrieved throw in their lots with him, just in case.

It was an odd charm he had, the ability to make everyone else fall in with his temper's whims, as if they could for sure right the wrongs against him.

I felt again my boyhood concern over the cloud about his face.

—Bulag! At last!, he growled.

He greeted me with that childhood name, which no one had called me in eleven years. For no good reason it sounded like an endearment, albeit the familial kind: a nasty affection.

---

376 *Une petite petate*: annoying French indulgence here. *Petate* simply means mat-bundle, or portable sleeping mat, of woven straw. (Trans. Note)

377 That's a thought—Emilio Aguinaldo carrying his banig to sleep over at his friend's house. The last time someone did that at my house—when I was twelve—our houseguest had to stay over because of the dictator's martial-law curfew. She ended up giving me kuto, and it took me weeks to get the lice out of my hair. (Estrella Espejo, ditto)

378 That's a charming thought, Estrella, but as we have agreed: let's just read! (Trans. Note)

379 What? How? You can speak but I cannot? Enough of the vow of silence! Our readers need our wisdom. (Estrella Espejo, ditto)

380 Sssh! (Dr. Diwata Drake, Kalamazoo, Michigan)

—What is it? What happened?, I said.

He took me aside and spoke in a whisper.

—Bulag, can you believe—that pilot over there—that starving old fisherman. Acts like the bastard of a Spanish priest, like those sons of devils I knew in Letran. He does not know who I am—a *gobernadorcillo* of Cavite. Didn't he see my cane, with the insignia of a kapitan? Treats me like a servant.

—What did he do?

—He made me move my bags when I got on the boat—told me to take my mat and shove it. Rufino had to carry everything on his lap all the way to the shore.

—But maybe you were blocking the ladder, blocking other people's way in?

—Bah, they'll see. One of these days, they'll know who I am. Make sure you get his name. I will report him. He can't get away with this. I know the owner of that ship.

—Sure, Miong. Sure.

Old Rufino Mago, son of a farmhand of my grandfather, embraced me in the way Miong failed to do. Town rumor had it that Rufino was descended from criminal Mexican sailors who had jumped ship on a trip from Acapulco. He was a Chabacano ruffian whose strange pidgin Spanish endeared him to no one. Now old and gnarly, he held me close to him in a peasant hug, a provincial warmth I missed but could not wait to wriggle out of.

—*Ah, hijo de puto! E tu un buta como paniqui ya!*

Ah, son of a bitch—or rice cake? And I bet still blind as a bat!

Or something like that.

How could you not hug the old man back?

Rufino and I went off to see the surly pilot.

One could see from the pilot's bulging arms that he had worked at this trade from childhood—a growling master of Manila's shoals, a raw talent at the oars. His face was red and wrinkly from life in the open air, and he grumbled about the weather, which portended rain, while Rufino paid their fare for the banca. The cranky pilot, probably a Batangueño, settled at half a *real*, plus so much for the bags. All that fussing over some kusing.

I always turn away from scenes of haggling, embarrassed especially to argue over the skills of men upon whose talents our lives depend. What's your name, I mumbled. Betong, he said. Betong Rivera, from Bai.[381]

Our duty done, we left him.

Soon enough, as our charred old Charon had predicted, it began to rain.

Did you tell him I know his boss?, Kapitan Miong barked.

We nodded, lying.

Settled in the kalesa, Miong directed us exactly how to arrange his bags behind the horses, Rufino and I soaking in the wind. Miong had the knack of a born leader, I always admired it. He compelled action while he remained idle—and dry—and we obeyed everything he said. The pilot Betong gave us a good fare, Mang Rufino reported in the wind, spoken in reproof of his master, I thought, who sat stiff, erect and unresponding, as we got into the kalesa, and the driver shook the horses, and we drove off.

I asked Miong what took him to Manila, but he put his finger to his lips and asked instead about the different *arrabales*—in which direction was Trozo, Tondo, and Binondo, as well as Meisic and Santa Mesa, as if he were here on a tour of Manila's suburbs and had never studied right in its center, at San Juan de Letran. Come to think of it, he had barely been at Letran before he had dropped out to become a *comerciante*,[382] so maybe he was not feigning but

---

381 Silvestra "Betang" Rivera was Rizal's aunt and mother of Leonor Rivera, the hero's doomed fianceé. Was she related to the pilot from Bai? It's tempting to note coincidences, but real life is not so: Leonor was from Dagupan. (Estrella Espejo, ditto)

382 A capitalist at a tender age, Emilio Aguinaldo dropped out of high school when his father died; he became a daring young merchant on a seafaring banca, buying and selling fishing nets and other implements. By all accounts, Aguinaldo was a teenage businessman

genuinely wanted to know. We went by the coast, and the rain made the Malecon even moodier and the walls of Intramuros creepier, but once inside the gates I perked up.

I showed him the stones of the Ateneo, and the majesty of the Palacio, then my old boarding house on Magallanes, that tragic site of adolescent romance, the exact, mortifying details of which I mercifully kept from my old friend (who could have cared less anyway—he's always been pragmatic, impatient with fantasies that were not his). Miong was impressed by the statues and the gardens but like every visitor to Manila he said it smelled.

Rufino, on the other hand, soaked it all up, including the vapor, his mouth open. Down through the Puente de España into the Escolta and its lace-like lamps in the distance, I couldn't help share the old servant's awe, as we passed the colored paper lights and macabre made-up faces of bold European women in the shops. Manila always moves me if I am in the right frame of mind. The rain, just as suddenly as it had begun, stopped—jerky masculine clime.[383]

Now a romantic gauze filled the city, and the sun tippled the skies into mauve. The Bay fell behind us, drunk on its glamor. There where my dashed heart had upset the fruitsellers of Quinta; there where the warehouses of Chinese trade spilled onto nasty bars, such as that of Tagawa, the agreeable Japanese, with its dim cellars suited to heartfelt fistfights; out by the flimsy cascos of the Pasig's bloated cheeks, blinkered witnesses through the centuries of eternal Manila's trite routines—I understood how every city had the capacity for novelty if only you looked at it through foolish eyes.

---

who grew up mastering life's practical arts, which led to his becoming mayor at age twenty, general of the revolution at age twenty-four, and killer of the Supremo at age twenty-five—*bastard*! (Estrella Espejo, ditto)

383 "*Ulang linalaki.*" Were those the words in the original, Ms. Translator? Filipinos apply gender to rainstorms. Softly falling, steady, and long-lasting rain is feminine; shortlived, sharp bursts of rainfall are masculine. Ms. Translator? Come on, speak up—why am I doing your work?? (Estrella Espejo, ditto)

Miong, on the other hand, shared nothing of our wonder, and Manila, I soon saw, left him cold, his interest in the sights a mere feint for the driver, I realized. Once we got off the kalesa and into my rooms, Miong went straight to business. More or less, in not so many words, as you know I am a bit verbose and my friend is annoyingly taciturn, I paraphrase below Miong's agitation.

—Mundo, he said, you've got to go with me, you with your learning, and I with my brawn, to join the revolution.

—What the f—, I said, truly eloquent.

—Santiago's coming for me tonight, pretty soon, and you may as well join me, because, to be honest, you are not living up to your potential.

He looked around at my miserable rooms as if to make the point.

—Well, f— me, I exclaimed, peeved, though I should have expected this backhand compliment.

—Anyway, you'll have to put me up every time I come to Manila for the meetings. I have no idea where they're taking me, Miong added, peering suspiciously out the curtains, but I am confident I will pass their tests, as I am already a Mason.

—Mother of f—, I declared, with amazing erudition.

I was not as surprised as I paint myself to be in the above profane pantomime, but the dashes, I believe, sufficiently underline the drama. Anyone might wonder with me that I was part of the historic moment when Miong joined the Supremo's war, given the fate of their future encounters.[384]

---

384 Readers of Part Four, "The General in the Revolution," keep expecting Raymundo's bat's-eye view of the "future encounters" between Emilio Aguinaldo, first president of the Philippine Republic, and Andres Bonifacio, founder and Supremo of the Katipunan. I'm still searching for those sheets. Ms. Translator—Ms. Translator, hoy! Wake up! (Estrella Espejo, ditto)

Santiago, Kapitan Mariano's son,[385] [386] that tiresome busybody, soon arrived. What can I say about Santiago except that I wish him well? Those two were scions of Cavite, Miong and Santiago, who were born to command, while I was a wiseass bastard. All I had in common with them was that shared fishhook of a creeky landmass, which, come to think of it, was not much, let me tell you.

At the time Santiago was a well-shaven youth whose sincerity excused (but not completely) his pompous air. He was earnest but, most of all, he had an amazing head of hair—I used to call him Señor Brillantina®, but only when he was drunk and he did not seem to mind. I knew him from the Latinidad and had last seen him in that brawl, thrashing Agapito with a toothpick in Binondo.

It was only later that I appreciated the constant anxieties that beset him and erroneously gave him a look of gloom. No one talks about those of us who gave their bladders, nay entire gastrointestinal systems, to the revolution. I have seen Santiago suffer his incontinent malaise with the pent-up agony of Saint Sebastian. Even his stomach was heroic.[387]

We rode in a kalesa to the telegraph office.

There we were blindfolded and bundled into another kalesa toward who knows where. A small altercation occurred, I'm a bit ashamed. I made a fuss about the blindfold. I mean—Jesus Christ—I'm night-blind. I couldn't see anyway, for Christ's sake. But Santiago was firm: no, no, Don Raymundo (he was very polite, calling all of us Don,

---

385 Mariano Alvarez, father of Santiago, mayor of Noveleta, Cavite, and head of the Magdiwang group of Cavite's katipuneros, opposed later to the Magdalo group of fellow Caviteño Aguinaldo, was a relative by marriage of the Supremo, Andres Bonifacio, an irrelevant detail, however, at this point in the narrative. (Estrella Espejo, ditto)

386 If it's irrelevant, can we not get into it? Let us read. (Dr. Diwata Drake, Kalamazoo, Michigan)

387 Is he making fun of the noble Magdiwang hero Santiago's digestive troubles, which may be traced to Santiago's patriotic travails in the Revolution, when rebels had to hold in their guts in the midst of battle and eat the wild forest's shoots and watermelons, foraging like animals in those uncertain days?! (Estrella Espejo, ditto)

though we used to play nasty tricks on each other in our underclothes in San Roque), no, no, you must wear a blindfold, it is the rule.

Fucking stupid rule it is to blindfold a blind man.

But Miong held on to my arm in that firm way of his and said, Mundo—Bulag—cut it out. I kept quiet and let them do it, but I silently chalked down a black spot in the checkbox of insanity, one for the revolution.

I know now we went toward Trozo, but at the time I only knew we drove close by the esteros, because, as I said, I have bat's ears. I heard the river. I mean its rats. And then, not so much the river but the traffic along it, the wooden thud of oars against the banks, muffled bamboo knocking, plonk of paddles and clatter of clogs as people got off and on every so often as we clopped toward our goal.

But most of all the rats—a musical rabble of weak monsters scurrying softly about their dark excursions. And I have to say, in that ancient moment, rattling along in the blind kalesa, I felt one with them all.

When we got off, it was Miong who was a bit discomposed by the blindfold, tripping on everything as he slipped to the ground. I, on the other hand, knew my way with my hands, how to handle the backseat and fall to earth.

It was Miong who was dizzy, staggering into the house, and it was he who had the devil of a time in the oaths. On the other hand, I passed my examination with flying colors, not knowing what I was doing at all. While he—they kept him at it until almost curfew at least, trying to get him to speak the right answers to their tests. I ended up watching this all with Santiago, who whispered to me: Don Emilio has to stop answering like a Mason—this is the Katipunan, not the Oriental lodges, tanga![388]

I know, reader, you are on the edge of your seat, waiting for the details of our initiation. For in imbibing this scene, the reader

---

388 The flavor of the expression perhaps needs no translation: "naïve one" comes to mind as a mild evocation of his sarcasm; "idiot" is more accurate. (Trans. Note)

partakes of the body of our freedom. The holy sacrifice of independence: this scene is the Mass of the nation's redemption. When
blood turns on the initiate's knife, so *indio* turns into Filipino, and
slave transubstantiates into Soul.

Oh History! Oh Fate!

One moment we were Spain's servant and the next we are her
scourge!

But no matter how much I call upon the Muses, pale-cheeked,
preferably naked Mnemosyne, the sober stylus of Memory, the
scratchy glimmer of my recall—all I draw is this blind blur—of step-
ping into a room that smelled of a nauseating mix of kerosene and
bagoong, the shrimp fry a sly whiff off my breath, or maybe that
was the misguided perfume on the arm of the lady who led me. (I
knew she was a girl because she pinched me without ceremony when
I moved too close to her chest: what could I do, even a blind man
could tell she was practically naked under her camisa.)

At some point in the night I heard a shout saying, of all things,
for no apparent reason, Cold! Cold!,[389] in the startling voice of a
shrill Visayan. To be honest, in my nervousness, I was Warm! Warm!
Mainit, mainit!

My armpits were wet.

Then I believe they made me do the limbo.

Oh God that I cannot do more service to the nation than this—
dancing stenography of details, my silly redacted recall: not for some
witty moral purpose, mind you, but just because I'm a dunce. Now
all these guys swear there were, first, skulls and crossbones, then
bloodletting and banners, and then divine decalogues sworn over
dead bodies, all that rot that smacks of gothic fiction.[390] Well, to

---

389 Oh good to hear from you, Mimi C.! Welcome back. P.S., the Katipunan password
was *Malamig*, meaning cool, code for "all's well." (Estrella Espejo, ditto)

390 *El gótico* was the term for certain types of ghostly romances, a genre Raymundo
scorns though it is clear that, like me, he read the tales. (Estrella Espejo, ditto)

each his own. Whereas, what I remember was passing underneath a covered table in the dark, bending low while someone shouted questions, and all I could answer was, Damn you, of course, I love my country, idiot, but as for dying for her can I think about it?

Then Santiago kicked me in the shins.

Finally they took my blindfold off, and under the glare of the oil lamp I recognized him before I saw him: Andres Bonifacio, the Supremo, with a handkerchief in his lapel and a triumphant smile on his face.

The Supremo swore us in.

You know I would recognize his voice even in the wilderness.

I had heard it before.

Only later did I learn who he was, but all along that strange blindfolded evening I kept wondering where I had heard that Tagalog rasp, a low melody of vowels. He instructed me to stop being a poisonous weed, to love my neighbor as myself, unless he's a Spaniard, and don't do unto others what your wife does to you—or was it to stop doing what you don't want done to your wife? Whatever. They had so many *don'ts* but you get the drift—it's the thought that counts. In any case, in that still night he spoke with a haunting speech, as of an echo from the past.

I couldn't place it.

In fact, altogether, there was an impossible conflation in this untidy moment with an incident that had occurred before, and I ransacked the closets of my dirty mind for this solemn event's partner in time. Just kidding. My mind, of course, does not work in such logical metaphors, and time does not dwell in cabinets. What I mean to say is that there was something oddly redundant in the voice of the man before me, and when I saw him, in a flash I recognized his twin. Well, not really in a flash—but you've probably guessed by now to which episode I shall soon flashback.

The handkerchief gave him away.

It's odd to think how he was so well dressed for a workingman, and I understood that—I understood the dry itch, like a rasp in the esophagus, of upward mobility; and sadder still, is it that he had just the one suit?

The man before me was the same man who had defended the sacred novel in that latticed room in Ermita where Agapito used to meet with his radical book club. At least, I thought then it was a radical club only to discover they were mostly a bunch of home-bodies who ate too many *churros*.

I hate to admit this, but in that flash of recognition during my initiation into the Katipunan, by the Supremo no less, with San-tiago prodding me into patriotism and Miong making all the wrong Masonic answers in the background, my thoughts, of all things, flew to the serving girl Orang of Ermita, my erstwhile skeletal love, and I wondered, with an ache akin to that of rapists, to which forlorn fool she was now showing her skinny chest?

Anyway, that man in Ermita who challenged the crippled lawyer over his nasty reading of *El Filibusterismo* was, there you have it, the founder of the Katipunan.

Now you know.

What a difference time makes. Now he was in this poor man's quarters in Trozo, whereas before I had met him smoking with gen-tleman lawyers in a mahogany room.

What had he said to that shallow critic? Quote. "You have a right to your opinion, but I must challenge you to a duel for your thoughts." Unquote.

Sadly for me, it is details like this that buzz like bedbugs in a holding pattern in my brain.[391] [392]

I remember exactly the handkerchiefed man's words, and my shock to see him now before me, ordering me to shed blood for my country, in front of a bunch of pensive farmers and somber

---

391 "... *que charla como un chinche en la cabeza*": a mysterious phrase since bedbugs do not speak nor nestle in brains. (Trans. Note)

392 Oh, hello, Mimi C. Welcome back again!! (Estrela Espejo, ditto)

witnesses, was great, as you can imagine. I agreed immediately, not having much choice as they had daggers. Then someone slit me on my left bicep (tip: it doesn't hurt as long as you don't look), then I signed my name with my blood. It looked like this: *R Mat*

My script was kind of thrifty because I did not want further bloodshed, given that it was at my expense, but even though I left out the final vowel, running out of blood, they were satisfied. Then they asked what I wished to be called in the revolution, and seeing they were serious, not joking, I answered without thinking.

Paniki?

I posed the name as a question, but they took it as fact, and to this day I regret my quick response for sometimes it seems I could have chosen a more masculine alias, instead of a freaky flying beast.

I could have called myself Elias, brawny and elemental precursor of the revolution.[393] [394] [395]

Or, to continue the literary motif, Aramis de Kawit (to be jumbled cleverly into a fighting anagram, Iskrima de Tawa[396])?

---

393 Supporting lead of *Noli Me Tangere*—clearly a better man than the lead character, the Spanish mestizo Ibarra, because Elias was a man of the people, an inspired revolutionary whose avant-garde venom could only have arisen from the oppressed lower classes. (Estrella Espejo, ditto)

394 Please. Okay, I will interrupt my silence to tell you—the family history of Elias belies your one-dimensional analysis, Estrella! Elias was a dispossessed landowner, like Ibarra, thus placing him, like Ibarra, in the class of panginoong maylupa; this dark bandit was educated and (before his fall) bookish, like Ibarra. In fact, the trajectory of Ibarra's biography follows that of the bandit Elias, the two being obvious literary doubles. Rizal regretted killing Elias in the *Noli* but coyly does not note that, in terms of literary economy, he killed him because his book did not need *two of the same*. (Dr. Diwata Drake, Hampstead Heath, London, England)

395 Oh yeah? You know more about the novel of Rizal than I, a Filipino who lives amid the country's sweltering mangroves, suffering with the people, while you are a traveling wombat, fake diwata, a half-baked mestiza whose knowledge of the nation begins and ends with— (Estrella Espejo, ditto)

396 That is, Lance-of-Levity, or Comic Fencing Match. Noting the anagram (minus w), I curse you, dueling pair, Estrella and Diwata: *dami kasi arte*! Sssh! Let Raymundo speak. (Trans. Note)

Or what about Rodolphe, after the hero of the *Mysteries of Paris*?

I mean, why I called myself a blind freaking rodent only an ass can explain. What was I thinking?

In any case, Paniki I was and Paniki I shall be.

In the meantime, they were still trying to cast out Masonry from Miong's soul, while to my credit I was two steps ahead, albeit transformed into a son-of-a-bat.[397] [398]

Later, I reminded the Supremo of our first encounter and asked about the lame critic in the shawl.

Ah, he said, that's just the way he is, old Ka Pule—Don Apolinario to you. He will out-Rizal Rizal.

That's blasphemy, I exclaimed.

The Supremo laughed: Wise men like Don Apolinario are not the same as you and I.

You must be joking, I said.

Who's this?, Miong asked (finally passing his test, and, I might add, choosing an entirely appropriate name, after a saint, no less,[399]

---

397 That is: . . . *'jo de puta* . . . (Trans. Note)

398 Sssh to you, too! (Estrella Espejo, ditto)

399 Miong's nom de guerre was Magdalo, after the Magdalene, patron saint of Kawit. His men were also called Magdalo. Their fellow Caviteños, called Magdiwang, became their rivals in war. Modern-day rebels who invoke the Magdalo brand show a finely tuned irony and sense of history. The Magdalo of Cavite, loyal to Aguinaldo, began as a troop of perhaps idealistic rebels and ended up, well, shortsighted: history rightly judges them with harshness for KILLING THE SUPREMO! (Estrella Espejo, ditto)

[400] [401] unlike some out there who may as well have been baptized by lizards).

Oh, you should meet him—Don Apolinario is sickly, but he has more brains than all of us put together.

I was skeptical and wanted the Supremo to elaborate, but we were running out of time.

It was almost curfew, and after the ritual libations we had to leave.

But, oh, I had so many questions now that I had found him again, the defender of the holy book's honor. He seemed like an

---

400 So this is the crux, the end of my patience. Enough, Estrella, enough. All readers of history are prey to this revolutionary postscript—dueling memoirs that arise from ashes of war. Magdiwang writers jumped the Magdalo to the gun: Artemio Ricarte and Santiago Alvarez, both Magdiwang, penned the first memoirs. Then that elegant stylist, Don Apolinario Mabini, damned Aguinaldo in sublime dudgeon. Miong Aguinaldo never recovered from Mabini's prose style. It took him six decades before he published the Magdalo version of events (though before that the historian Agoncillo did function as his ventriloquist). But he was too late: by that time he was a villain, a schemer, and a murderer in the eyes of many (and to be honest, I agree). The point is: he became so not necessarily because of established fact but because *he did not frame the narrative*. The question of why Aguinaldo took so long to publish—The Mystery of The Tardy Memoir—is thought-provoking. His image as villain was convenient to Americans, the actual combat enemy. In this quarrel, Filipinos forget who their enemy was. Who benefits?! The Magdiwang case, the vilifying of Aguinaldo, suited the eventual occupiers (which does not mean that Magdiwang statements were *untrue*). Aguinaldo's memoirs show he was, *at best*, an insecure egoist who lent his instability to others' schemes. *At worst*, Bonifacio's death points to him, however ambiguously, as party to murder. So the Interesting Case of the Dueling Revolutionary Memoirs may be no postmodern mystery. The first president of the Republic is, as we suspect, less than a hero, and his tardy recollections are acknowledgment of his failures. This does not lessen the following fact: Estrella's agony is symptomatic, a fantasist's angst. The Supremo Andres Bonifacio's death rightly inscribes trauma—it is the emblematic wound of *all Filipinos betrayed by fellow Filipinos*. (One notes that Aguinaldo, in turn, was betrayed, though not killed, by Filipino turncoats in America's pay.) This duplicitous sense of self, the Judas wound, marks the country's notion of its humanity, so potent in its history. We agonize over that which makes us imperfect, most human. For our enemy, we conveniently ignore that war's obvious, material problem: the islands' subsequent occupation by the United States: hello! Why were some memoirs published and not others? Ask that! Only in the story of Rizal is there no Judas kiss, which may explain why, given the country's complex aversion to the past, it clings to the hero Rizal with implacable ardor. Rizal's death is simple: Spain killed him. Filipinos are not complicit in his blood. Emilio "Miong" Aguinaldo, on the other hand, is troubling—he is the man in us whom we prefer not to see: the sinner in our midst who is ourselves. Just as we will never see Rizal as a man because we idolize him, we will not see Aguinaldo as a man because we vilify him. (Dr. Diwata Drake, New York, New York, U.S.A.)

401 Whoa, Aramis de Michigan. Calm down. (Trans. Note)

amiable man, the Supremo, and I thought if I pumped him, he'd tell me all he can. Especially, I wanted to know about that noble sequel in question, which, after all these years, I had still not read. After the Writer's exile, the authorities were brutal, and anyone with the books kept them locked in their trunks. People bragged they owned them but no one saw them around. It's tricky for readers when their favorite author is an outcast. I mean, if you ever tried to get their autograph, it might kill you. I kept getting mixed reviews from different people who, I now realize, were as ignorant as I. Did Elias resurrect (I guess not, unless Jesus Christ turned up)? Did anyone kidnap Maria Clara from the convent? So many cliffhangers that demanded solutions! But the night was almost over, and anyway, they wanted to talk about revolution.

On the way out of the house, I noticed a shelf covered in a scalloped cloth. That was it, I thought. While Santiago and Miong said their grim goodbyes, each looking a bit stunned, with that constipated look of those who're sworn to deathly secrets but can't wait to share them, I took off the cloth and found it: quite a library of novels and histories. The Supremo had a sinful stash. I saw, with a stopped heart, that the fatal book, *El Filibusterismo*, lay under the runner, innocent as can be. And I will confess now, as that time is over and my days are numbered, it was on that evening that I was sorely tempted to commit my first crime. I desisted. Hurriedly, I covered it up again and walked on. I left the Supremo's copy of the secret book on his shelves, unmolested, though I do wonder where history has purloined it, trusting as I do in the mischief of time.[402] [403]

---

402 Dr. Diwata, let me explain the physical nature of my "implacable ardor," as you call it—though you do not deserve my patience! I recall distinctly when my illness began, this withering in my arteries, my stultified knees. It was late in June in the year martial law was lifted by the tyrant, and yet the country was no more changed than I was by the proclamation. I was a freshman in college taking Philippine History and Institutions 101. I had always been a bookworm, an idealist—yes, as you say, a fantasist. As a kid, I used to collect the posters of the heroes and labeled them with their corresponding epithets, because I was a nerd with weird compulsions. When I learned about the political assassination of the Plebeian Martyr, Andres Bonifacio, by the men of the First President of the Republic, Emilio Aguinaldo, I was not only surprised that I had never heard about it before in my high school textbooks: I went into septic shock. My breathing froze in that room at Palma Hall Annex, and my asphyxiated shriek before I slumped sideways from the graffitied desk onto the lap of my blockmate, a pale, kind of palsied kid from Panay, made the entire classroom go still (or so I was told, as I had gone into abasic atrophy, a kind of failure of the nerves). I remember (or fancy I do) the ambulance, the brief blur of flame trees in my rolling vision, the concerned face of my professor (the bifocaled, unwitting perpetrator of my nervous wreckage), as I was strapped onto a trundle, given emergency respiratory help, a blood pump, a pale, camphor mask. My classmates waved at me as if calculating already whether or not they could take time off to go to my funeral. It was a minor seizure whose source the doctors could not fathom—whether I was epileptic, schistempsychotic, or just plain pathetic, it was a mystery to them. I returned home for the rest of the term, and in those months all history books, even komiks versions, were banned. But secretly I read. By the end of the year I was back at college, but this time armed with the weight of history—not to mention all the kilos I had gained from provincial bibingka, lumpia, and puto. In this way I became a vessel of the country's pain, a small price to pay for truth. If this is a symptom, then what is a country? A tumor of ideology?! (Estrella Espejo, ditto)

403 Yes. (Dr. Diwata Drake, New York, New York, U.S.A.)

Entry #26

1896

So many things to remember, so many faces![404]

---

404 Where's the rest? The revolution begins in August 1896, Caviteños led by "Miong" triumph over the Spaniards in September 1896, Dr. Rizal's trial begins in November 1896, then the hero is executed on the penultimate day of 1896, etc. etc. In short, this year in the journal covers a major swath of history. Too bad it's glossed over. (Estrella Espejo, Quezon Institute and Sanatorium, Tacloban, Leyte)

Entry #27

April 30 [1896?]

Pilgrimage to Antipolo. This time Miong's stern brother Mang Crispulo takes the lead, the old servant, my old comrade Rufino Mago arriving with him and carrying the bags of all the travelers. Miong is absent. Once again they sleep in my rooms, eat my bread, and drink my barako. It's all okay, if they told me why they were doing this—attending frivolous feasts when they should be planning for war! I mean, sure the Virgin is a good enough spirit, but the priest of Antipolo is a fat pig who is raking in money on Mang Crispulo's misguided piety. Did no one read *Fray Botod*, or that wit Dimasalang's revelatory vision of Fray Rodriguez?[405] Where was our anticlerical spine: shouldn't we be tossing rosaries into the river instead of brandishing them like sheep?

Santiago, that hypocrite, kept nudging me in the chest to keep quiet. Did he not make me swear in Trozo to get rid of the friars, and now here he was at a priestly carnival with a bunch of praying cows?

I know, I know, when I got on this banca with the traveling devotees from the provinces, I should have trusted my instincts and run away from this herd of fanatics. But I was also their host. And they did bring whole jars of tuba, red-blooded and freshly fermented, splashing amid the scapulars.

I was too polite to decline their invitation.

Out on the waters of the Pasig, our fluvial party floated with the rest of the Philippines—citizens from islands as far-flung as Capiz,

---

405 Since the memoirist is unsure, let me add: "that wit Dimasalang" is Rizal. Readers at the time conflated writers with a number of personages; Rizal himself was often mistaken for some Prussian wit. (Estrella Espejo, Quezon Institute and Sanatorium, Tacloban, Leyte)

towns as craggy as Cabanatuan and sleepy as Pansol. They were singing hymns, playing cards, carrying passive pigs unaware of our plots for their doom.

Fireworks deafened everyone's devotion.

Bands marched on shore in full regalia, oblivious of our loss of hearing. For some reason a squadron of rondalla players floating right beside us seemed to me to possess the stupefying air of a passing dream. And everywhere roosters with a morbid calm sat at the helms of bancas and seemed for all the world like solemn pilots.[406] They certainly looked a lot more sober than the Christians. Women protected straw bins of bibingka from the waves, children tossed marbles, old wise wives spat what looked like chewed red blood—the belch of betel—into the generous, forgiving canals. And the Chinese came in droves as usual, floating restaurants in striped trousers.[407] [408]

In straw hats or European bowlers, barefoot or booted, some women in those ridiculous silk-fretted shoes, the world joined in the watery mood: fisherfolk, farmers, architects, pharmacists, foreigners, laborers, and men of law. Soon enough, I too had that wastrel feeling, that abandoned concupiscence that precedes giving everything up to the Lord, or in this case the Lady, titular goddess of peace and good voyage. I joined in the singing, ate the lechon, and frankly drank too

---

406 Comments from foreign travelers in the nineteenth century always include remarks on the pintakasi—featured cockfights during fiestas. The French found it an amusing natural phenomenon, describing human gestures as they would the plumage of birds; the Spaniards were grumpy about the childish brutality of "the natives." Rizal himself believed any form of gambling was a waste of time, so that his fellow patriots in Barcelona avoided him because he was k.j.: killjoy! During the war, revolutionists had cockfights in between battles, and when they won battles they had cockfights to celebrate them. But let us go on and just read, hmm, Dr. Diwata? Dr. Diwata? Have you calmed down? Okay, okay. We will keep our words to a minimum from now on. Have you calmed down from your dyspeptic attack? Yes, we'll let Raymundo speak. (Estrella Espejo, ditto)

407 My guess, given his previous wordplay: karinderya *en calzoncillos*. (Estrella Espejo, ditto)

408 Sssh. (Trans. Note)

much tuba. I did not notice our growing caravan, the circle of boats swimming beside us, filled with carousing, sharp-eyed men. Cascos, bancas, simple outriggers carried, I soon discovered, a host of my old friends, as well as jackfruit, hay, and tinapâ. Was I cross-eyed from drink, or was that Agapito, still looking mournful and agitated, wearing the same funereal suit he wore the last time we parted? Was he still with his radical book club? Would he laugh when I told him I had joined a secret society, like him? Did he want to join my club? I had so many questions! I sang out his name, but he stared as if he did not know me. Maybe I was mistaken, and wine had overturned my brain. I saw companions from San Roque and a few men whom I recognized but couldn't place. I was getting dizzy, everything unfathomable but familiar. On another boat stood Kapitan Miong, suddenly arrived from Kawit. And where was his brother, the dour Crispulo, I asked him?

—Sssh, Miong said. Crispulo has nothing to do with us.

The last I saw of Mang Crispulo in Antipolo, we had left him behind at the church, lighting up candles to his vested Virgin. Anyway, I thought, Mang Crispulo was a drag, a bit too devout for us drinkers. We called him "Father" behind his back.

But whose sweet image was grinning at me?

There, in a gauze shirt, in festive fungal green and cradling a child, next to Miong, was Benigno, *el maestro*!

I practically leaped out of my boat to hug him, upsetting some drinkers and getting some flak, but hey—I hadn't seen him in years! There we were, Benigno and I, rocking and chatting on his little outrigger when we heard a shout, a loud firm voice I knew in my bones.

It was the Supremo, upright, therefore taller than all, and as usual very neatly dressed, with a kerchief at his throat, shouting the meeting to order.

Miong rapped me on my skull: For God's sake, Bulag, shut up! The meeting's begun!

It dawned on me, and I felt stupid.

Why had I not guessed?

What an ingenious ruse—to hide out in the open among a carnival crowd, to clump in groups next to the unwitting, praying masses.

The Guardia Civil, our lazy dupes, would not question our congregation—like the rest of the Philippines, we carried candles and were dressed for devotion. The river was so swarming with noise, fireworks, and caravels that no one would bother with yet one more holy communion.

Ah, these rebels were smart!

Some were hugging roosters, carrying rosaries—Benigno was holding up his swaddled child!—pretexts for their presence, solemn pilgrims and gambling men, out to honor Mary and plot the deaths of friars.

Even Mang Crispulo, I thought, had been our blissful instrument—a pious sodalist whose sincere purposes had provided honest cover for our sins! As Miong had explained, "Father" wasn't one of us.

A thrill coursed through me at my tardy revelation, and I nodded at Miong and shut up, acting as if I had known all along, that we, the Katipunan of the Sons of the People, Kataas-taasang Kagalang-galang na Katipunan ng mga Anak ng Bayan, were out to hold a riverside meeting with aims more devout than any of these murmuring souls could imagine.

And as the meeting wore on, my thoughts wandered, as they do, to the looks of the men about me, both nervous and alert, the Guardia Civil patroling stupidly on the banks in a vague mist, Benigno's rapt gaze at the Supremo, as if listening to the Holy Sacrifice of the Mass, and the black fingers of Polonio, the printing foreman, whose hands would never recover from their inky trade.

Polonio!

He, too, my fellow worker at the *Diario*!

So that's what you're all up to, I thought, you *filibusteros*: aha! Who've you been trying to fool with your pensive poses?

Except that I, literally speaking, was on the same boat with him.

I gazed at my nervous *confrère* from the printing press and recognized others from my job: Letra, Figura, et al. I winked at them, but none of the rascals got my drift. And though after all this time they were still snubbing me, I had to admire their steely gaze.

I heard a shout.

Mabuhay!

Hurrah, hurrah!

Viva!

I clapped my hands with all of them and kicked myself for not knowing what the commotion was all about.

The Supremo was saying: All right, then we must ask his advice! We will now consider who will visit him in Dapitan.

Dapitan!

My ears pricked up, my head was suddenly all clear.

Was it what I hoped? Were they going to rescue him from exile, did they vote to take him by force from the island? They say he's writing the third novel—will we get to see the last instalment of his hoped-for trilogy, the triple-decker of my dreams?

That's so right, I thought—why hadn't we all thought of it from Day One?!

That should be the first act of the revolution.

Yes! Rescue the Writer from Dapitan!

My God, I thought, if that's what it's all about, I'm so glad I joined the Katipunan!

Despite my straining to hear, I could only get a few muffled comments, the occult words "massage," "duck," and "proctology," what with bandurria players and firecrackers picking away in pesty pizzicato all around us.

But when Miong spoke, I heard it loud and clear.

For one thing, he was right next to me, screaming in my ear.

—And since the honorable doctor Pio Valenzuela needs a patient to go with him, a blind man in need of help, both spiritual and medical, I offer him a perfect decoy, Bulag here—who certainly needs a good doctor's guidance. He's a learned and honest patriot: Don Raymundo Mata.

And he put his hand on my shocked shoulder.

What was he talking about? Was I going to Dapitan? Not me: I cannot kill a fly much less capture a man from the Spaniards. They have guns and cannons. I've never even caught a moth. What? Of course, you can, Raymundo: did I not read *The Man in the Iron Mask*? Did I not devour the *Lives of the Presidents of the United States*, in translation, but hey, I know what they did to the British? Sure, I can learn how to pull a gun in the name of my country. What? Pull a gun! I'm as blind as a bat in the night. Plus, I'm an insomniac, an easily distracted filibuster with a weak digestive tract. I'm a panicky Paniki, not even worthy of the name of Elias! Or Rodolphe. So help me, God. Whoever you are. I can't even make up my mind to be a Mason!

—Don Raymundo will pay for his own passage and bring a leper, if he so chooses. I mean, helper.

Oh really? That's asking too much of my hospitality.

Looking down, I noted Miong's gun in his waistband and kept quiet.

The Supremo then proclaimed:

—Decided. To ask advice and guidance on the matter of war—to resolve our decision on when to revolt—doctor Pio Valenzuela will visit the honorable doctor Jose Rizal in Dapitan. The blind patient Raymundo Mata will accompany doctor Valenzuela to provide cover for the visit.

Hey, hey, I thought: I can still see. I'm only *nightblind*!

The Supremo yelled: *Mabuhay ang Katipunan!*

Then he shot a pistol in the air.

Not to be outdone, Miong took out his own secret gun and exploded it right next to me, in tandem with the fireworks of

Antipolo. Oh *por dios*, have mercy! The explosion was so loud I almost fell off the boat.

Miong exclaimed: *Mabuhay si Doctor Rizal!*

—*Mabuhay!*

—*Mabuhay!*

I almost fainted, and I have no recollection of what happened after. To be honest, I'm not so sure of what happened then, pushed blindly as I was into history—yes: shoved with shotguns like a decoy duck into the blasted fray![409] [410]

---

409 O History! O Words! The story of Raymundo Mata's moment in history is so fraught with alternity—from Santago Alvarez's *Katipunan* to Emilio Aguinaldo's *Gunita*—and this, his own narrative, has about it a confusing frisson, a watery aura of prophetic chance. (Estrella Espejo, ditto)

410 Sssh! (Dr. Diwata Drake, Dapitan, Zamboanga, Philippines)

Entry #28

May [1896]

Meetings, meetings, meetings. Everyone was getting tight those tense months, especially Miong and the Supremo, with Santiago as their *boulevardier*, a man of *camaraderie* and *joie de vivre*: he took great pride in his connections, just as I took pride, as you can see, in a useless book of French vocabulary.

There they were, a band of brothers, *Egalité, Fraternité,* et al., wandering back and forth from Manila to Cavite and talking constantly of stratagems, fired up by conspiracies, fearful, thrilled by all sorts of possible calamities. As for me, I could never get a word in, though they took snacks in my rooms and schemed in my humble abode while Rufino offered them cup after cup of barako. (On Miong's advice, I had taken in my cousin Rufino[411] as my helper, which, despite the old man's Chabacano independence, was a surprisingly good call on the part of Fate.) It seems to me I was the only one with a regular job, and for this I was treated like a lackey. But in truth, and I hate to admit this, I was envious of Miong's easy friendship with the Supremo: they treated each other like blood brothers while I could at best come up with the soulful mien of an idiot cousin, twice removed.

Once, Miong arrived from Cavite in a huff, a sight not unfamiliar to me and Rufino but a matter of concern to the Supremo, who asked, Don Emilio, what is it?

We were resting as usual, lazily drinking lambanog. I remember we were eating the roasted stones of langka seeds; they were not quite done, and I kept spitting out the mealy pith, mentally cursing

---

411 At some point, will the wild Chabacano servant Rufino Mago's memoir appear? Is it covered in the dust of a baúl somewhere awaiting resurrection? I can't wait. (Estrella Espejo, ditto)

out Rufino, who, I'm sorry to say, was negligent about his duties, especially the menial ones; he went lazing about like a katipunero himself, with a morose look of worry.

The telegraph man, Mr. Dizon, kept joking about how he could barely recognize us without the blindfolds. Ha ha, good one, but you said that already last time, and anyway, I thought, why do these people keep making fun of me, their host, but all I did was laugh.

Meanwhile no one could ignore Miong in his cloud of sorrow.

—That purser!, Miong exclaimed. Acts like a katsila just because he knows some Spanish.

—Someone insulted you on the boat? asked the Supremo.

—At the port office. I got his name and badge. Ramon Padilla. He's just a functionary. How dare he look at me as if I were not a *gobernadorcillo*! He will remember me one of these days. I may not speak Spanish as well as he, but did he not see my cane?

—Ah, Don Emilio, isn't it only to be expected?, softly inserted the Supremo. We are not masters of our destiny as long as Spaniards hold sway.

—But Supremo, Ramon Padilla is a Filipino, from Pandacan, not a Spaniard, I exclaimed.

—Scoundrel, said Miong. All the more reason to slap him.

—But Miong—, I began.

The Supremo, however, raised his hand. He shook his head with the sorrow of one who was not surprised.

—The tragedy of our circumstances is that we can only ape the corrupt manners of our superiors. We're a bunch of beasts without redemption. Without freedom, we turn into rude animals with Spanish brutes for our models, and one day to our sadness we will turn out just like them, a brood of monstrous assassins.[412] Daily, under the Spanish yoke, I fear we lose our better angels. You don't

---

412 Prophetic words from Supremo. Hah, take that, Aguinaldo. Assassin!! Bastard! Not to mention the sorrows of our current days! Okay. Now I got that off my chest. Let Raymundo speak. (Estrella Espejo, ditto)

know, my friend, how the specter of this erosion is a constant grief. Brother Emilio, do not worry. We will take care of *Señor* Padilla. We are not blood brothers for nothing. Anyway, we know where he lives in Pandacan.

Quoting all of the above with philosophical license, I will submit here that it's not that the Supremo had a dull-brained empathy, eager to please, which smacks of the undiscerning. In fact, he was a calm, collected man with—and I say this with tenderness—an almost irritating lethargic demeanor.

His introspective gaze and quick disgust struck me as not so much empathic as saddened: as if the world constantly revealed actions too base for him to bear. His frank air of compassion belied, I feared, the moody nihilism that knocks like an imp at idealism's door.

It's this current of anguish that attracted me to the Supremo, that lashed me like hemp to his baleful ark. What optimistic dreams spurred our brotherhood, and yet from what mute pessimism did it spring forth?

I do not entangle him in my melancholy, mind you: he prompted it.

Miong's gambit was not entirely ingenious: Miong had more self-love than he had cunning. I mention this with the regret of a kinsman. *Amor propio* hung like fool's gold on his blighted chest. There was no malice in his constant calling of attention to his personal injuries, no plan to dominate our sympathies by always retelling his awful adventures.

It was just that the world according to Miong was all about him.

Only when the Supremo took on Miong's cause with the resources of a general, calling upon his men to fetch the darned Padilla, to throw the gauntlet of a duel—the poor man's choice of weapons, knife or nightstick—and settle the time and place of revenge, did Miong admit—that his cause was stupid.

It was then, in a flash of insight that had eluded me throughout my boyhood, that I saw Miong in flagrante for what he was—kind of a whiner. Among friends he talked like a bully, but in public he had second thoughts.

His complaint was a trifle and not worth all the fuss, really, he kept saying, while the Supremo's men geared up to back his honor.

For one thing, his eyes said, he would much rather live.

—So, Miong, I whispered, amidst all the commotion, you got your wish. You will be fighting your enemy tonight. Are you happy now?

—Shut up, Bulag.

His face was flushed. I swear I could hear his heart beating from two butakas away. Santiago, too, couldn't help ribbing him, but he did it loudly, because, after all, they were related, by marriage.

—Hah, Don Emilio, why's your face so red?

Miong knew he could not get out of the mess without dishonor, and yet you could tell (from the fingers tightening on his *gobernador-cillo's* cane) his rising tension as the clock ticked away the minutes to Padilla's rebuttal.

I myself was confused by the escalation of events.

Only an hour ago we were laughing while eating old Rufino's mediocre merienda, langka seeds as miserably undercooked as Mr. Dizon's jokes were stale, and now here we were contemplating death.

Like everyone else, I felt both thrill and dread, relishing a fight and not wanting it to begin, rocking restlessly on my butaka. The Supremo waited for Padilla's reply with remarkable composure, though his honor, perhaps more than Miong's, was at stake in this challenge. In fact, the Supremo was almost glacially composed, reading a frayed copy of *La Ilustración*[413] while taking a peek now and then at Miong's giveaway agitation, his feet tapping and hands clenched, telltale sweat as he feigned conversation. I was not sure if the Supremo did not take some private satisfaction in the little

---

413 A monthly magazine favored by the bourgeois classes. Santiago Alvarez in his memoir *The Katipunan and the Revolution*, recalls this incident but unlike blind Raymundo retells it for a noble purpose—to show the Supremo's brotherly love! (Estrella Espejo, ditto)

gobernadorcillo's unease. Our relief was palpable when the seconds arrived with Padilla's answer—his sincere apology for his actions and best regards to Don Emilio. We all clapped Miong on the back for his narrow escape from roasting like langka, and the Supremo barely smiled though he inclined his head at his victory, as if saying to Miong and all gathered, I told you so. It occurred to me such dramatic incidents among the brothers were coded messages for those who were not as blind as I, and if I were smart I would pay attention. Instead, I took the Supremo's magazine and began reading about the topography of Paris through a naturalist's eye, and soon enough I settled into the jaundiced torpor of readers who will never experience the elaborate world pictured before them. And as if suddenly famished by our reprieve, we ended up picking Rufino's already ravaged langka into shreds.

In this way, the sticky leftovers and our late, hastily improvised lambanog carousing diverted us all night from the catastrophe we had just avoided.

When the Supremo's house burned down during one of their sojourns (I believe to Kawit), it was as if our dire prophecies had been answered, though it was an accident, not intentional. From Cavite's heights, the Supremo watched Tondo burn.[414] Incidents like these kept plucking at our nerves. The Supremo bore his misfortune with stoic resignation (as Miong, his assiduous host in Kawit, reported). Okay for the Supremo to be so calm, since he had already read all his books, but I mourned the secret pamphlets I had yet to read, the novels charred to smithereens, and all those hapless things.

I kept thinking of *El Filibusterismo* in the secret bookcase under its scalloped cloth. I volunteered to check out the ruins, just in case,

---

414 Manila's fires were habitual. It's sad. The wooden material and thatched roofs of the ever-crowding, ever-loyal city has always been a hazard. (Estrella Espejo, ditto)

but his friend, the doctor from Bulacan, had already done everything he could, and all I could offer the poor Supremo was a rambling, garbled telegram of distress from my gloomy perch in Manila.

I don't know what came over me as the days advanced. I had the worst feelings of withdrawal—an urge to turn hermit and close out the world.

Who was I to pledge my soul to my country?

On the streets, Guardia Civil officers whipped me when I failed to greet them, and woe to me if I failed to show my *cédula* to any old crank with a badge. True, my situation as an *indio*[415] on the islands was craven, and if my heart were in the right place daily I should cry havoc against Spain.

But really, I was no rebel, no man of arms.

I was a distracted bookworm who would much rather be sailing off to Parma, wherever that was, to drink absinthe, whatever that is, in a derelict abbey of alcoholic Carthusians, whoever those damned fools are. I waited for fires of wrath to burn in me at the thought of my country's sorrows, but mainly, if I were truthful, all I had was a dim passion for irregular verbs.

I remember one afternoon I kept leafing through a French dictionary I had found in a bookstall on Azcarraga. I found in it not companionship but a hoax, a false dream of brotherhood, but still I felt bound to the volume, there in the doorway of the bookstall, wanting to devour—yes, weirdly munch on—the book's dry, uncut pages. Those days, I kept feeling this phantom hunger, a subtle intermittent sensation gnawing crosswise through my spleen. I sat through a book of medicinal plants and a tedious missal in Latin that illuminated the oppression of the Lenten season. The book-seller, a phlegmatic Hindu, had an embarrassed cough, as if he knew

---

415 Just to correct, then I will let the reader read on: he was not technically an *indio*. Raymundo Mata was, of course, mestizo: half-Basque, quarter-Chinese, quarter-Filipino. This acceptance of a single identity for the nation is important. It is the great legacy of revolution. (Estrella Espejo, ditto)

his wares were pathetic; but he was a kind man who let young men like me peruse his trash without trouble.

Random corners of learning were all Manila's stalls had to offer, cursed as they were by censors and an indifferent trade. In these I found cold comfort, but comfort just the same: maps, dusty dictionaries, a rat-gnawed atlas. These were my talismans, not bloody bolos with my blood on it.

Of course, like everybody else, I was left with those articles in stupid Spanish periodicals, nothing but echo chambers of the kumbento, the pulp of pulpits. I don't mean the illustrated magazines, *El Mundo Ilustrado* and such, with their shiny pictures of Madrid fashions (fantastic hombres in ombré, absurd albinos in grisaille); albums of ornate continental hairstyles, smacking somewhat of ornithology; exotic travelogues through Havana, Borneo, and Sarawak, which all anyhow looked like the rice fields of Bulacan.

I will admit: these monthlies gave rise to an insidious self-loathing and were at best an absorbing poison. My uncle, ceaseless castigator of the material world though an avid scanner of its ills, had always said: *those magazines are the devil, worse than taxes!* At the same time he kept them, piled up inside carved mahogany trunks. But I've always been fascinated by those ghoulish European supplements, for instance, which catalogue reptiles in that far-off planet *Jardin des Plantes* and count our own carabao with aurochs and bison of brutish wonders.

I could not bear to see the armchair sights of Madrid, imagining K wandering through its cobbled lures; but I could admire Rome's rotting masonry, houses vaster than the horse stables that the Augustinians kept at Imus. I marveled at the city of Paris, veritable Babylon of desire. True, the Seine was perhaps no more pleasant than the Pasig, but what a view, spanning an area greater than Tanza, Noveleta, and Maragondon combined, even if you included Mount Buntis!

I did note the pompous pamphlets, pustulant tirades in *La Politica* and *El Resumen*,[416] and damned sketches and brushstrokes[417] from those deformed wits, the Spaniards Quioquiap and Retana—they were the true reptiles in our pages; but really, I skimmed over their venom. My interest was sluggish, though persistent. Yes, yes, was it too much to ask that they burn in hell, roast slowly like tender piglets in their own putrid fat? Every night, like everyone else, I prayed to God that those scoliotic rightist cuckolds would die, those clerical leeches. I dreamed of pickling them in posthumous brine, so that their malformed souls could be served with salt and red tomatoes to the masses, and at times I'd wake with an acid taste in my mouth. To be honest, soaking them like *balut* was an insult to the ducks.

Yes, yes, I wished to kill Father Font, Quioquiap, Cañamaque, and every single rabid pervert in *La Política de España en Filipinas*. It was strange, but more than my own daily actual mortifications at the hands of Spanish creeps, it was those poison papers, masquerading as learned epistles about my country from so-called enlightened visitors on the islands, that made my blood boil. Canards about our indolence and swipes at our superstition! Those could rouse my dilatory soul into rank convulsions.

Not bruises but books made me burn.

In my case, those hyperventilating texts did spur revenge, so that if revolution were to occur, as, turning over page after page of continental ignorance, now I hoped it would, how strange that I owed my growing bloodlust to the pulp of trees and ash of words, even though it was my life that was at stake.

Personally, I was pathetic.

---

416 For those who are not in the know, that is, everyone: *La Política de España en Filipinas* as well as *El Resumen* and others were conservative papers popular among the abusive Spaniards of Manila. (Estrella Espejo, ditto)

417 *Esbozos y Pinceladas*: published in 1887, these were compiled articles of the hated Pablo Feced, or Quioquiap, Spanish writer and enemy of the Propaganda Movement. Posterity, remember his name and spit on it. (Estrella Espejo, ditto)

You can imagine what it meant to read those pamphlets of the Filipino *propagandistas* from abroad. I won't tell you how I got them, those yellowed pages hoarded from eons ago, the size of missals, about eight inches' span, the breadth of my puny chest. You could slip one in a hymnbook and so fool the friars.

I'd like to know what became of those scribbling musketeers.

Sadly, I hear that apoplectic genius, Plaridel, is dying of the Filipino plague, poverty, in Barcelona, picking cigarettes off of cobblestones; and such luminaries as Laong-Laan, Dimas Alang, et al., are now scattered to ever-desperate sections of disparate straits: Vienna, London, even America. And where have Carmelo, L. O. Crame, and M. Calero gone, cunning men in anagram masques? Some are plotting utopias in Borneo, while others have fallen to the frail witticisms of Spanish life. (I understand, from those same mongering sources, that K herself has grown stout and matronly in El Raval, though her eyes, I imagine, are still wicked, a trap for fops.) Personally, I never much cared for Paterno or that Lete *de leche*, superfluous Spanish peacocks, though they had their moments. But that Prussian pedagogue, Herr Blumentritt, the saint of ethnologists—what I would not give to offer him with sincere thanks, with my own trembling hands, a cup of steaming barako. And by the way, I would like to know where in the world is the raving statesman, Lopez Jaena, my favorite, a rascal, magician of bile, even more eloquent, some say, when drunk, but what can one do with an Ilonggo? In hindsight, my own attempts here at imitating his lurid oratory do betray, even I will admit, a rather specious, a bit waxen, grace. So be it. I relished them all. They whipped that cur Cañamaque good with the lash of their Latin logic: "Nosce te ipsum!" "Materialiter vel idealiter sumptum!" *Francamente, no me gusta perder el tiempo atacando y luchando con empresas particulares como la del Padre Font, Quioquiap y otros: yo lucho por la nación, Filipinas!* [418] My God, how that blessed

_____

418 A spirit erroneously ascribed here to Blumentritt, these sentiments are Rizal's,

German Blumentritt scratched out Quioquiap's blind eyes with epithets like lances. Quite above the belt!

And as for dear, deported Rizal, who unlike others signed his name to his quips, unafraid of redemption, I mean retribution—I, like many others, could only bow like a cow. That was my problem: my organ of adoration burst to seams on reading such glories as "Missals and Mocking Missiles" and "Stop Asking Me for Poems!"[419] and the froth of my praise was not entirely coherent.

I will confess, now that those gusts of fervent steam have blown over, that I, too, penned my own paeans to my country's future freedoms. My masterpiece, "Pearl of the Orient Pawn-Shops," studded with lurid chess metaphors and metallurgical allusions, was one such stupefying poem: the crappy surplus of veneration. I admit, this is all paltry excuse for my subsequent adventures, but, frankly, it is all I have.[420]

And so I prepared for my voyage to Dapitan.

Reading my old hoard of pamphlets, I tried to get into the spirit of the thing. Soon, I did feel it, full of hope for the revolution, and a bit proud, if I might add, of my coming-soon, cameo role in it.

Carefully I packed, wrapped in tissue and a pair of my lone wool trousers, Father Gaspar's beat-up old copy of the *Noli Me Tangere*, read and re-read and not handed around among my brothers, despite

---

who, in his letters to Del Pilar, expresses candid disdain for propagandists who preach to Spaniards instead of to Filipinos. Other errors: M. Calero, Carmelo, and L. O. Crame are not three men but one—Marcelo H. Del Pilar. Though to his credit, Del Pilar's energies did have the air of multitudes. Dimasalang and Laong-Laan are both pen names of Rizal (Dimasalang was his Masonic name; Laong-Laan [Ever-Ready] is a boring choice though an intriguing comment on rebellion). It should be noted that Raymundo remembers names and titles of the Propaganda Movement as any ordinary reader would—with sloppy affection, idolatry and rumor all mixed up. Who could blame him? (Estrella Espejo, ditto)

419 Mix-up of titles again: *Dasalan at Tocsohan* and *Me Piden Versos* were by different propagandists—Del Pilar and Rizal, respectively. (Estrella Espejo, ditto)

420 Happily, no trace of Raymundo's poetry seems to have survived. (Estrella Espejo, ditto)

what the priest had said. I was still jealous of anyone who had read it, as if the book were written only for me, and except for those early days with Benigno, I kept it for myself.

Finally, I could get it autographed.

Dr. Pio gave me daily missives on what to bring and how to act—he was a moralizing sort with a condescending attitude, but who was I to argue with the secretary, or was he treasurer, of the Katipunan?

Above all, he said, do not carry incriminating material, such as your copy of the *Noli Me Tangere*.

My God—what was he—a spying savant?

I put the novel away with reluctance and packed instead the holy missal that I had bought from the Indiaman's bookshop, an ertswhile gift for my uncle when I returned home.

Tio U., of course, knew nothing of my impending trip.

It was all hush-hush, you know, like Cassius and Brutus among the Romans. My secrecy made me feel self-important, though if you think about it, Brutus's life did not end well. In any case, I never told my uncle, as he had enough troubles at home. For one thing, like a vast joke on the universe, my grandfather simply would not die. The marvelous hound of Jaca—you had to give it to the old man!—barked his blind dominion to the end. Plus, there were my uncle's other tribulations: his bad sugar harvests, chicken coop banditry around Kawit, and complaints of arthritis.

Above all, his affection endured.

I knew anything I did that was out of the pale would both worry and annoy him—remember your father, *hijo*, remember 1872, he would write, and I could hear the mothering quiver of his lisp!

My poor uncle.

Couldn't he get over it already? Like many of us he used the past as crutch in his solitude, and though I had no intention of sharing his despair, I felt guilty. So instead in my letters I mentioned my eyesight, my impending visit to a doctor, an ophthalmologist—one day, uncle, I will be cured! Don't blame me for telling him romances in advance of my fate. I wished to break no one's heart.[421] [422] [423]

---

421 Dr. Diwata? Dr. Diwata, are you there? What do you make of— (Estrella Espejo, ditto)

422 Let Raymundo— (Dr. Diwata Drake, Kalamazoo, Michigan)

423 —speak. Okay, okay. Your silence rebukes, and yet—my heart must speak. (Estrella Espejo, ditto)

Entry #29

June [1896]

In the midst of these preparations, I experienced this one interlude of attachment—I'll tell it now. because I know that that memory, too, will be lost.

A few days before my departure, in the middle of the night, before curfew, I heard his steps—familiar, the solid clop of his soiled shoes.

Agapito's swift gait, like a horse fed molasses without water. He took refuge in my rooms before the Guardia Civil's call; and my reunion with my old friend struck me then—as it does now—as a leitmotif, the plangent chord of war.

Allow me to digress here on tardy prophets, those clever historians who praise in hindsight the glories of Napoleon's birth or young General Washington's first wobbly steps. Craftsmen of Truth, who cobble grandeur out of childish acts, unaware that Historians are mere Tools: hoary handmaidens of what some call Victory, and others Darn Luck, or Genocide, depending on whose side their wits survive. The biographies of heroes are only a conqueror's postscript, anachronistic addenda to battles. Who records the tender curls of Pyrrhus's massacred enemy, or the portentous squalls of the gurgling baby who grew up to be the extremely large Goliath?

Only the Greeks, those classical souls, recall the history of the damaged Cyclops.

While I, dear reader, wish to inscribe here, as warriors monger and scalawags surrender, the intemperate, perhaps insane, saga of Agapito, who will live on, I am sure, on the lips of his countrymen.

Through my efforts, admiring fellowmen will certainly reward him[424] with, if not a majestic tomb against a crabby lawn, at least a

---

424 Silence clogs the arteries of the passionate reader, and I must speak. Raymundo's irony is not lost on me—woe on us for our brief memories. Who remembers Agapito the agitprop photographer, *uno de los trece martires*? No one. The oratorical flourish in these

musical composition by Julio Nakpil, one of those endless habaneras that always puts me to sleep.

In short, let me write about Agapito while I wait for the boat to Dapitan to arrive.

I call this segment "Agapito and the Sailors, or, Notes toward a *Kundiman*," with apologies to Homer.

As I said, Agapito did not flow with the times—he preceded them.

He was always in a hurry, and on that night he arrived in a flurry of chimes—tinkling, tinkling along, carrying his photographer's rack and settling against the door with an asthmatic sigh. Gone were the bobbing Adam's apple, the lavish facial hair. Now he had the haphazard hygiene of one who could barely shave, much less wax a four-inch mustache. His former bohemian look was altered; his eyes were old.

It occurs to me that you measure your age from the faces of your friends, and I am sorry to say his miserable look was not comforting to me.

On the other hand, who knows if my own face gave him that look of pain, as if in me he were witnessing his futile posterity right before his eyes?

I stumbled from bed in the dark, a stark paranoid insomniac, and I was so relieved to find it was only Agapito at that hour, and not the Spaniards out to get me, that I broke some of his photographic mirrors in my joy.

His mission was secret and urgent, something about ocean divers, capiz shells, and Australia.

I cannot divulge its full intent, and so I throw into this list at least one red herring for spies out there who read with malice.

I told him I'd see what I could do, and we slept on it.

---

opening passages suggests Raymundo may have been sharpening rhetoric for a future speech—a bombastic Historian's style that perhaps anticipates (with optimistic error) that one day he might leave the cell in Bilibid and find work uselessly polishing his prose in academia, or *Bulaklak* magazine. (Estrella Espejo, ditto)

Agapito left in the morning, as furtively as he had arrived, with only a few glass shards, unswept on the floor, to betray his presence.

In the afternoon two men came, a pair of strapping mariners who spoke English better than Spanish, and Spanish better than Tagalog. They were on their way home to the Visayas and gave me the money for my task. It was right up my alley, as they say—I was the perfect procurer for their needs.

I knew better than to ask them questions, being a secret revolutionary myself (though I was dying to ask where they got those stupendous biceps—just from diving off of the cliffs of Captain Cook's seas, talaga, hah? And that accent, the burr of the Tagalog like swallowed-up Spanish: how was I to know they were used to speaking a different language—English? On the other hand, when they spoke to each other in their native Visayan, I still didn't understand a thing).

Easily I bought them what they needed, without much haggling: quadrupled quintets of a quintet of vowels,[425] plus a dozen more small letter a's, for polysyllabic good measure.

I knew exactly where to go: Polonio the printer barely batted an eye.

I carried the types home in a ragged mat, as if returning from a late night's work. Not even "Leandro," the *Diario's* bouncer, looked twice, busy as he was with affairs of his own, as we all learned later to our united chagrin.

I am proud to say I was part of the Capiz men's plan to set up a printing press for the revolution.[426] I am sad, however, to note my passing position in the moment.

---

425 Silence fails to underline Raymundo's contribution to reality. Agoncillo, in *Revolt of the Masses*, notes that the Sanskrit scholar and local printer, Isabelo de los Reyes, also sold letter types to the rebels; in his document de los Reyes negotiated with Emilio Jacinto and Pio Valenzuela, not Raymundo Mata. (Estrella Espejo, ditto)

426 Raymundo joins a robust band of diarists on this topic. Other memoirs that retell the chronology of the publication of that elusive legend, much-storied but unseen, that singular radical newsletter *Kalayaan*, precursor of all ill-fated journals in the country that, unlike the phoenix, never arise from the ashes of their first issue, include the frenetic General Jose Alejandrino's *The Price of Freedom* and, of course, the lively tome of General Santiago Alvarez, referred to by fine history buffs as the "Zelig" of the revolution (or alternatively by those less in the know as "our own Forrest Gump"). (Estrella Espejo, ditto)

I was merely their alphabetical pimp, so to speak, all they wanted from me were my vowels. And though I am proud that with just one word (for instance the newspaper's diphthonged title) a stolen tetralogy of *a*'s exposes my fugitive presence, no one explained anything to me, not even the names of the visiting Visayans. All Agapito said was that they were pearl divers from Capiz who had won a lottery in Australia; or that they sold capiz shells to Australians who had won a lottery in the Visayas; or they were sailors from the island of Capiz who worked as pearl divers in Australia. In any case, they wished to give their money to the cause of freedom for their country, for this pearl of the Orient seas.

In sum: to describe them one needed a complicated set of predicates, whereas, in real life, they were a pair of heartbreaking naïfs.

Weren't we all simple-minded, anyhow?

As if one throw of our die—casting off hard-earned cash, or printing up some little newsletter, the vowel-laden, wistfully titled *Kalayaan*—could throw off our yoke, once and for all.

And yes, we did.

I think of Agapito, a precocious organizer: he gave his mustache early to the cause, barely a teenager when he began geometrically recruiting those darned triangles among the outcast Masons. There's purity in his young lust; and something powerful about his persistence: something I don't get, but which tears at one's bones. Because it's the ashes of their early grace upon which our late fates feed.We are the cannibals of their young imaginations. Prodigies die and the whores survive. That's what happens in revolution. Johnnies-come-lately take the spoils, heroes die young. The ones who grow old end up disappointing themselves (I will not mention what they do to others). Our governments are made by leeches, who wish only to live, and who blames them; but we forget when we talk about the glory of our war that it buried the best of us, and the country that outlived them feeds on them like maggots.[427]

I remember waking up to Agapito's shadow before he left my rooms early that morning—haggard in all but his gaze, which was cheerful and quite placid. He enjoined me again to help the coming Visayans then he trudged off, who knows where, his tinsel photographic equipment clanking like armor. I didn't think to thank him at all, to mention the merits of his abstract passion—it never occurred to me that anything any of us did required gratitude. I did not even save his shards, though I should have—

The shattered dust of his mirrors, which I swept under the rug in my *entresuelo*.

I was not surprised when I learned he was executed months later, one of the unlucky thirteen of Cavite, with scarcely a song to recall his name, with not a shadow of a reflection from his vanished glass.[428] [429]

He was only twenty-three.

God rest him.

---

427 Harsh! Set aside like aphorisms in the text, exergasia, that is, the repetition of a thought in different words, is clearly one of Raymundo's favorite tropes, used most effectively when describing the nobility of early revolutionaries, as opposed to latecomers, like the alliteratively named villain, Pedro Paterno, who in Raymundo's mind ruined the country. This frequent duplication of a favored truism may strike some as merely tautological, the equivalent of a rhetorical flea, but here I believe his exergasia is suitably *orgastic*, not *pedantic*. Mimi C., Mimi C., what do you think of my translator's analysis?! (Estrella Espejo, ditto)

428 In this chapter, Raymundo's memoir, this vessel of Memory seems to me a drowning bark in the sea of History, tossing up to our scrutiny one more blight upon its waves: our short attention spans. (Estrella Espejo, ditto)

429 Goddamnit! Silence, Estrella! Your words hold no candle to his flame. (Trans. Note)

Entry #30

June [1896]

We were to journey for at least five days, so I was to prepare food, linen, and reading material for quite a span of shipboard boredom. I was used to the quick hauls from Cavite to Manila on the *ychaustis*, those rickety boats you could not quite call steamers; I imagined that the large inter-island vessels that reached as far as the Jesuit posts in Mindanao must be infinitely more comfortable.

It was not to be so, when I got on. I did not have enough money to book Rufino and me on the passenger deck (for one thing, I had spent my last bits on the dry French dictionary mentioned earlier, one of those impulse buys it's best not to regret—though you can't help but feel stupid, cursed with that post-purchase shame that goes with the satisfaction of owning a useless book).[430]

Dr. Pio, comfortably lodged, with his fine medical bag on prominent display, was already on speaking terms with a number of katsila with whom he played checkers and some Filipino ladies with whom he played quite the gentleman, damn his smug clinical air.

Rufino and I had to make do with the smell of copra and coconut oil in the rancid belly of the stinking boat, sleeping with its cargo of cows and pigs.

Fortunately, we were free to wander the decks, where we observed the mad penchant of ladies, Spanish and Filipino alike, for the game of panguingue at all hours, and the truculent pigments of a quadrille of foreigners who traversed the ship in scowling formation. I followed them in exuberant proximity, aping their furrowed brows for Rufino's

---

430 I, too, have often been attacked by that shame, especially in the leaky stalls of the Avenida, where I have bought three copies of the same Penguin edition of *Justine* by Lawrence Durrell, when in fact the gap in my library was the fat midsection of the quartet, *Mountolive*. (Estrella Espejo, Quezon Institute and Sanatorium, Tacloban, Leyte)

amusement and feeling that manic expansion of spirit that occurs as a ship leaves anchor. But Don Pio,[431] ever cautious secret revolutionary with a smug pistol in his pocket, soon put a stop to that entertainment, and told us to follow him instead in his promenade. This we did, and I soon found in this venerable doctor a gaping cauldron of monotony. My God, it was like walking with a sulphurous well! His vaporous fund of aphorisms was soon depleted, and I envied Rufino his mute status, not having the need to join in chitchat, letting the upper classes play the buffoon in the singsong dialect of their Spanish, or in candid Tagalog when a Spaniard passed by.

Later, we came upon three of the aforementioned ladies of the passenger deck, one of them in mourning, a plump, handsome foreigner.

—Don Procopio, the ladies greeted Dr. Pio.

—I was just relating to these two men the uses of hypnosis.

I was surprised by the doctor's awkward prevarication—he was the worst liar, I thought, coming up with the stupidest possible tales.

Why bring up hypnosis if he could talk about waltzes or sunsets? What a dunce.

The ladies eagerly asked for elaboration.

He had given himself a false name and occupation, a precaution neither Rufino nor I, poor obscure souls, required.

He styled himself Don Procopio Bonifacio, a dealer in medical books, especially of treatises on optics.[432]

---

431 Pio Valenzuela's alternate versions of this trip are available in at least three forms, each new version producing a pall upon the next—and a pox upon history! His first calumnies occur in the official Spanish documents collected in *The Trial of Rizal* by Horacio De La Costa. Next follow his twin, confusing testimonials appended to the yet-to-be-satisfactorily-annotated *Minutes of the Katipunan:* to wit, Appendix A, *The Memoirs of Pio Valenzuela by Luis Serrano*; and Appendix W, *Testimony of Pio Valenzuela in the Trial of Vicente Sotto*. A fourth version, *The Memoirs of Pio Valenzuela*, by Arturo Valenzuela, is a rehash of Appendix A, with minor postwar additions. Why so many versions? God knows, only Hudas not say. (Estrella Espejo, ditto)

432 Ah, but the reader must understand the beauty of this document—how Raymundo fixes the historical facts! In Dr. Pio Valenzuela's *Memoirs*, he cites his false shipboard name, Procopio Bonifacio, but Raymundo's revelation of Dr. Valenzuela's "occupation" as a book dealer is original; no other source betrays this detail! (Estrella Espejo, ditto)

I felt bad for the Supremo's brother, the real, earnest Procopio, a wistful kid from Tondo whose simple image was so swindled by this unctuous persona.

The arts of mesmerism, magic tricks by candlelight, coin-swapping and earwigging and casual disappearing acts with a gun—nothing was beyond this coy counterfeit Procopio with his holster of tricks.

The ladies found delight in his tales of occult shamanism among Sarawak tribes, the medicine men of Patagonia, even the rank foolishness of the Englishman Darwin's Theory of Apes.

I, on the other hand, could only glare at the extravagant fool. He performed for the ladies in a way he had not bothered with me and Rufino, transformed from a trite dolt into a succubus of tales.

—*Tu un daldalero, Señor,*[433] Rufino muttered in his wake, spitting out Chabacano with his betel, splat on the deck.

But flattered by the attentions of the women, Dr. Pio was deaf to our wet compliments.

The foreign lady, I have to tell you, was striking. She looked like Jezebel, if you ever imagined Jezebel in grieving weeds. Or maybe she was Venus, avatar of our rickety ship and in her comeliness an ironic personification of our vomitous vessel.[434] She had long, unkempt tresses, a bit like a mermaid's, sometimes reddish, sometimes gold, and green eyes. She kind of smelled, a bit—a bit sultry, like the unwashed *lavanderas* of my early acquaintance, down on Calle Caraballo. But no, I must have been mistaken—that whiff of the body must have been my own glands of the devil at work. At first sight, in clothes like a widow's, the lady seemed old: but on closer inspection, she was probably barely a teenager, like the third woman, a child introduced as Angelica.

---

433 One of the diarist's favorite phrases, a Chabacano weapon, meaning: *You talk too much!* Get it, Estrella—*tu un daldalera.* (Trans. Note)

434 Dr. Valenzuela's otherwise nondescript memoirs corroborate Raymundo's detail—the ship's name was *Venus.* (Estrella Espejo, ditto)

The other Filipina, who seemed to be in charge, was Doña Sisa.

Soon it was that we accompanied these women on the decks, to and fro in slow pageantry, the doctor with his hands at his back, circling the ship with an easy garrulity, and Rufino and I, sick man and sick man's helper, playing the roles of fine deaf-mutes for all we managed to say during the doctor's hair-raising discourses, about witchcraft and pygmies and demonic amanuenses, as the boat docked first at the island of Romblon, with its white cliffs, then sped on toward Capiz and the southern ends of our languid journey.

Eyes at times green, or a prime blue, then in passing a blurred dash of gray, like those of a motile peregrine. I could not figure out that lady, the Scottish *señora*.[435] What was it that ailed her? The talkative doctor's stories must have influenced my imagination, as I thought she was a witch, a sprite, some kind of ambulant ghost. She wore black all through the journey, and yet, as far as I could tell from the conversation, no one had been buried. All I knew was that, if needed, I wanted to help. Sometimes she held her bosom as if a pain nailed her right at her heart. It was quite a bosom; I mean, it seemed quite a pain. Her mercurial eyes bewitched me, I will confess, but that's because of my inexperience with the hypnosis of their changing colors. She walked with a commoner's air, a swift peasant-like stride, and I noticed she cast her skirt between her legs sometimes in vulgar pique when she did not get her way at cards.

In short, her erotic mix of grieving sweetheart and senseless harlot aroused in me a sentiment I had felt profoundly only once before, in those dim drawing rooms of La Concordia, before that minx who, if I'd only known it then, held all the trumps. But unlike those days in Santa Ana, when I believed I was a hotshot scholar

---

435 May I address the gossipmongers among us? Josephine Bracken, the "plump, handsome foreigner," was most likely Irish-Chinese. The other two women on the boat, mentioned also in Dr. Pio Valenzuela's memoirs, were Doña Narcisa Rizal-Lopez, sister of the hero, and her daughter Angelica Lopez-Abreu, who later became a katipunera, at age thirteen! (Estrella Espejo, ditto)

with a future, now I was a dull printer with a compromised life, my blood pledged to honor, death, and country, a secret revolutionary with no time for the inconveniences of love.

Are you kidding?

On that ship I didn't think for a moment about my blood compact with the Supremo as long as the lady looked my way with some glimmer of recognition that at least I was human, and not just some blind lump this preposterous Don Procopio had taken in under his wing as a specimen of his kindness.

Here's where I wished to God I had not been cursed to be held by the hand at night by a faithful servant, tapping with a kamagong cane along the way to the cargo hold, where we slept with husbandry, not wives, and though I had read a whole library of novels to comfort me in my debility, and I was a graduate of the Ateneo Municipal, and I could have enrolled in the University of Santo Tomas, if not for the outbreak of cholera not to mention the doldrums of heartbreak,[436] and one day, after the revolution, I will travel to Australia like a brawny sailor, or maybe just to Andalusia, and drink of foreign waters with the temerity of a free man, still, the lady looked at me as if I were a mosquito, and sterile at that, without a sting to break her heart.

Not once did she call me by my name.

Instead, Rufino and I slunk back every night into our hold after making ourselves busy to others in the day—holding shawls and purses, pulling back chairs, respectfully doffing our hats, all those asinine kindnesses that never occurred to us we did not have to do. And I swear I could have been a hatstand or a footstool for all the lady thought about me: but this I realized, of course, in hindsight, not then. I lisped and preened and curtsied and, worst of all, accepted all of Dr. Pio's lies. I didn't even stop him when he began

---

436 *El dolor de mis dolores*, I take it. Raymundo gets quite lyrical here, very Rizalian, when talking about his old pains. (Trans. Note)

a tale about my burdened youth, when I was struck in the eye by a wayward friar, such fantasies of terror being apt to please the ladies. Instead, when asked in turn about my calamity, I bettered Dr. Pio and embellished the tale with a cause (undercooking the langka seeds, my master's favorite snacks), specific weapons (a large spiky langka, no a bread knife, no a violent violin blade, including a whole culinary crescendo), curses (but I politely declined to illuminate the most venal), and harrowing denouement (bleeding, mucus-swelling, oh the flow of vitreous humor, and now this ineluctable night, my ravaged eye: sigh).

That was my most satisfying moment, when the lady looked at me with something close to tears, and then she outright sobbed.

We all stood up, concerned.

—It's nothing, the lady said, just leave me. It just reminds me—

I was sad to think that she had perhaps experienced a childhood not different from my fantastic one, and I was almost ashamed to have deceived her, for I was, of course, a cherished nephew, while she, it turns out, was a cast-off child.[437]

So it was that we spent those days on ship, compounding deception with pity as we crept past the archipelago, all of us fooled by fate. For this trip, sleepy and uneventful, in which we docked without incident next at Capiz then in Iloilo, shedding our insipid cargo—pigs, cattle, and tobacco, sugar, goats, and candles—and not a single passenger from Manila to Zamboanga looking back to record our shadows—turned out to be a sensation, retold minutely and rehashed, questioned, quartered, and overdrawn. I wish for the life of me I could have taken care then to cut a finer, more striking swath. I mean, I bet a hundred pesos the doctor barely mentioned my name in his odious confessions, the scoundrel, and instead of

---

437 That Josephine Bracken was the adoptive (or foster) daughter of blind, allegedly syphilitic Mr. Taufer, a patient who had traveled from Hong Kong to Dapitan upon hearing of the famed Filipino eye surgeon of the tropics, is well documented. The griefs of her youth remain mysterious. (Estrella Espejo, ditto)

being a major actor in a historic drama, I'm instead a minor detail in a hysteric's act, doomed to molder in history books as some obscure blind man with a useless passion in the company of that lying Dr. Don Pio Valenzuela, future betrayer of the revolution.[438]

Whereas, in truth, what could history have become, if only someone had asked *me*?

---

438 Horacio De La Costa states in the *Trial of Rizal*: "The key testimony in favor of the prosecution's case [against Rizal] was that of Dr. Pio Valenzuela. Now considered one of our heroes, Valenzuela does not come off well in [this trial's] pages." It's not clear if Dr. Pio Valenzuela's sins were intentional. Did it occur to him that his visit would have fatal effects? Who knows? The Spanish judges cited two damning scenes that convicted Rizal: the novelist's return in 1892, when he organized *La Liga Filipina* (see Entry #24), and the visit of the revolutionaries to Dapitan in July 1896 (see the historic entries that follow). In fact, in analyzing Dr. Pio Valenzuela's life, one learns this honored revolutionary had *never even joined a single revolutionary battle*. He sought amnesty with Governor Blanco at the outbreak of hostilities, completely muddled his testimony about Rizal, and did not join the war against Americans on his return from exile in North Africa in April 1899 (he preferred to remain in jail rather than pledge allegiance to America; other prisoners pledged allegiance, left jail, and promptly joined the revolution anyway). His biographer notes he was "disheartened" by the assassinations of Andres Bonifacio and Antonio Luna—a sentiment commendable in hindsight, but then by that time no one was alive to dispute it. What distinguishes Valenzuela is that he was one of the first to *take up pen and write*—which was easy, since he didn't have much to recall. Raymundo Mata's testimony, on the other hand, provides a compelling counter-memoir. Too bad it arrives so late. (Estrella Espejo, ditto)

Entry #31

June [1896]

As we passed by the Panay coast—Capiz, Iloilo, Antique—I thought again of that mystifying pair, the Visayan divers from Australia who had disappeared after their good deed.

Perhaps I was infected with that melancholy that seems to graze one like a rash among a ship's moving shadows. Those pearl divers now rose with a mythic heft, tanned and muscular angels of freedom—with that ragged eyeful of coconut hair[439] that happens to Filipinos who've been too long in the sun.

Who knows, I thought, I might see them when we all go to war, after the doctor-novelist-hero-ophthalmologist gives the green light to our plans, after our mission in Dapitan.

When will we three meet again?

Maybe not.

Passing by Capiz, the third or fourth day of that journey—did it last only a week?—I recalled our moment of farewell, etched in my brain. The pair had a kind of flatfooted stance by my door, as if, pearl divers, they had just begun learning again to walk on land. I wondered how they were, the hard-working sailors who had gone back to organize triangles of mutineers on their far-off island.

Now there it was, their island, scratched against the dark shore.

So the ship's cook, a friendly sort, told me.

The shell of Capiz.

Try as I might, it meant nothing to me.

The random quality of our islands in the moonlight betrays our brotherhood's tenuous pledge.

---

439 *Mata de lampaso*. I get it. Raymundo uses another pun on his name [*mata de pelo* means mop of hair; *lampaso* means, among other things, coconut husk]. Right, Mimi C.? (Estrella Espejo, ditto)

And yet, one day, I hoped, when we saw each other again, we'd note the marks of our union.

Past Dumaguete, we squeezed through the perilous straits of Siquijor, that sea of witchcraft and dolphins. Mermaids swam there, wrecking boats with impunity. Never proceed under the habagat, or you were destined for death, or at least some form of dislocation. That curve toward open sea, before you sighted Mindanao, was enough to drive you insane—it was as if finally you were lost, amid the endless algae and barracuda, as witless about your destination as the loony flying fish.

In this way, the late, slow arrival of the prow-like shores of Zamboanga had about it the false horizon of destiny.

We approached with anxiety—even Dr. Pio had a fit of nerves, muttering to himself over and over the speech he was going to give Rizal, refining his phrases to make himself look smart.

He had a long way to go.

However, I must say I did not envy him.

Despite my bravado, this is what I knew: I would be terrified to speak to the man. I was glad that I had not brought my copy of the *Noli*—no need to ask him then about an autograph and risk looking like an idiot. "Excuse me, Mr. Rizal, can I please have your signature?" What—was I a debt collector, tanga? "Ehem, Mr. Rizal, please sign this vegetable, I mean cabbage, I mean—*lechugas*!" Oh my gulay, God help![440]

I mean, it seemed incredible, in fact, that he lived on that bobbing nonentity in the distance, now you saw it, now you didn't, in the twilight of our vision looking most discomfitingly like, well, like every other island I had just seen.

The approach to Zamboanga was excruciating, and Rufino and

---

440 The declension of vegetables (*gulay*) that occurs in the text makes no sense, as none of them rhyme with "novel;" the American-era pun extends the mystery. Don't you think so, Ms. Translator? (Estrella Espejo, ditto)

I whiled away our time with the eighth sacrament (after baptism, matrimony, and extreme unction): cards.[441]

—They say he has a flying carpet, Rufino said, throwing down a jack of spades.

—Who? Didn't you see my queen?!

—The German doctor. The one who will cure you.

—He's not German. He's from Calamba. And I'm not sick, you know. I'm just nightblind. Anyway, flying carpets are in fairy tales, Mang Rufino. Or at least the Chinese do not sell them in Manila. Ah, I'll take that deuce.

I was beating him easily at the game, but Rufino didn't notice.

—He can walk on water, you know.

—You're mixing him up with Jesus. That's in your gospel of San Geronimo.

—No, Segunda says so.

—Who's Segunda?

I pretended not to know, though he and I knew full well who she was.

—The cook's wife. The one whom I saw—

—Now Mang Rufino, it was dark and your eyes are old. Old age puts fevers in people's brains.[442]

—No, Don Mundo, I saw—a woman showing—

—Showing what?

---

441 That joke is so nineteenth century. I would add the ninth: *karaoke!* Personally, I prefer mah-jongg over cards; it has a most salutary effect on the senses, the clack of tiles like the sound of *om*. (Estrella Espejo, ditto)

442 An interesting discrepancy occurs in two versions of Valenzuela's memoirs. In Appendix A of the *Minutes of the Katiupunan*, Valenzuela states: ". . . Under the assumed name of 'Procopio Bonifacio,' I embarked on the steamship *Venus* . . . accompanied by Raymundo Mata, a blind man, and Rufino Magos [sic], both residents of barrio Binakayan, Kawit, Cavite . . ." In the later edition, Valenzuela's biographer uses the same language but adds to the facts: "He traveled under an assumed name, 'Procopio Bonifacio,' and was accompanied by Raymundo Mata, a blind man, and Rufino Magos [sic], *Mata's young aide.*" The truth of Raymundo's memoirs asserts Rufino Mago [not Magos] was an old man while he was the young patient. In addition, while they were both from Binakayan, Kawit, they were residents at the time in Manila: further proof of Valenzuela's notoriously unreliable testimony. (Estrella Espejo, ditto)

Rufino tossed his last card on the table, completing my winning hand.

—Showing the rich bat hole of the ace of spades,[443] thus: the fleas of the vulva of the widow of *espadañas!*[444] *Que dios berdugo te bendigo!*[445]

He was right.

May God the executioner have mercy on my soul.

I could not repent, for after all, what with my foolish hankering for an untouchable stranger, my sins were already multifold. And then there was Segunda, with the body of an angel and the squeals of a piglet, who helped in the galley, a kind of sous-chef coquette. She was a seasoned voyager, touchingly proud of her husband the cook, an amiable roughneck. In contrast with the English *señora* in widow's weeds, Segunda the cook's wife was jovial, you might say, almost to a fault: she giggled even when she came. But who can blame her? We were coupling by a cow.

I had met her in my errands for the ladies, going to and fro with glasses of lemonade and hot tea. Segunda used to trill as she butchered live animals, and her breasts' fine trembling did justice to her violent songs. By the third day, she had taken pity on my poor glances, which caught her chest, I mean her eyes as she was mangling some soon-to-be capons, while her husband chewed betel off-duty with the sailors. Ah, her dexterous aggression with those blunted birds was enough to make a fellow feel for his own, to make sure they were there, and this I did with such tender distraction, acting thoughtlessly on my thoughts, that Segunda shrieked and hit me in the face with a basting tool. I bled. Then she brandished her bloody knife and laughed.

---

443 *¡Que rico las pulgas de paniqui de puquis—entonces: las alas de la viuda de espadañas! ¡Que dios berdugo te bendigo!* The spate of spite here progresses incoherently. (Trans. Note)

444 Ah, Mimi C. You're back. Welcome! I knew you'd reappear with the nasty words! The faithful reader will note the allusion to the character from the *Noli*, the fraudulent "Spanish" matron, *la viuda de de espadañas* [*sic*], Doña Victorina, Rizaline quips increasing as the ship nears Dapitan. (Estrella Espejo, ditto)

445 *May the wrath of God the executioner fall upon you*: the ultimate oath, perhaps an ancient Chabacano screed. (Estrella Espejo, ditto)

You might say a scene of carnage, not to mention her despotic glee, was not a good start to our communion. But while the ways of God are mysterious, those of humans are more so. Her gruesome humor turned me on, while she believed I was demented, so it was a good match, if you don't count the adultery. With that nobility that marks her sex, Segunda did not even seem to mind, later on, the bovine nature of my lowly loft, and while you could not quite tell my grunts from those of our companions, I believe they were as happy for our union as we were to be rolling in their humid hay.

Segunda was from Dapitan. Despite a few demonic qualities, she had a knack for belief. She and Rufino, who wasn't called *mago* for nothing, were birds of a feather, a pair of gulls. No matter how much I explained that it was impossible for a man, even a writer-ophthalmologist-zoologist, to walk on water on a handkerchief, Segunda clung to her declaration of his paranormal side.

—You'll see, she said, when you meet him. He's an aswang.

—No, said Rufino: more like a manggagaway.

—All those sick people who come for his magic, Segunda said: *oculto*.

—He's an oculist, you dimwit, not an occultist!

—He can walk on water, Segunda repeated.

—You're both crazy, I said. He's a writer. Only Jesus walked on water, and even that is just hearsay.

—My son, please ask the German to cure you of your blasphemy. It's worse than your blindness.

—He's an aswang, muttered Segunda. He makes bats talk and knows the words that resurrect the soul. You'll see.

Boy, that girl would not retreat. If you think about it, she herself was a kind of devil—she possessed an unconscious witchcraft under which any man would be glad to be victim, if you ask me. She had a fiery innocence, that Segunda: and her blend of foolishness and vigor only endeared her more to me. Sadly, she would not disembark with us but would remain on the boat with her blissful husband, happily mutilating poultry as she crooned her songs with lambent glee.

Meanwhile, the mourning American *señora* had now become more animated. As Zamboanga loomed and we coursed toward Dapitan's inlets, she combed her hair lovingly and hummed songs in public. Josefina, as the grieving Swedish lady was called, now exuded perfume and cast off her blighted aura—that soapless stench of sweat and pubis that had first aroused me, a humid reek, especially when she moved her dirty skirts, was now replaced by banal talc. And yet—her stockings, which I glimpsed often in those wanton accidents that happen at sea, remained what they were: smelly, secretive, and sinful. Doña Sisa, Angelica, and Josefina stood with that impostor Don Procopio at the railing, looking anxiously toward shore though all we could see were the blurred outlines of trees.

She was his favorite sister, Dr. Pio had confided to me about Doña Sisa, as if he were intimate with the writer's affections. So why, I thought, had he named his madwoman character in the *Noli* after this ordinary woman carrying an abaniko like everyone else? Why burden a favorite with the symbolism of deranged Motherland? Beats me. Doña Sisa, with her fattish waist and love for garlic, looked about as ready to fall into suicidal depression as Don Procopio was to speak the truth. She did not look like the image of the degradation of *Islas Filipinas* but more like a portrait of a pious eater of pork. As we approached the shoals, I reflected on a writer's reasons for confusing identities to useless ends, and so missed the thudding moment of our arrival. We got off the ship onto a pilot's banca, to negotiate the shallow waters of this edenic coast.[446] [447]

---

446 Is this another of Raymundo's cunning allusions to the hero's poetry, of which he seemed to have intimate knowledge? Was Dapitan also Raymundo's *"nuestro perdido eden,"* etc. etc? At this point, it is hard to tell apart the hero's words from the reader's mind, a symbolic gambit of a sort. What do you say to that, Dr. Diwata? Are you still there? Or are you expelling your quack exhalations on some other text? (Estrella Espejo, ditto)

447 Dear Estrella, contrary to rumor, I have been reading these entries carefully and formulating some interesting—"symbolic gambit of a sort," is that what you said? I will admit, I have been bemused—I will keep in touch, I am in the middle— (Dr. Diwata Drake, Saint John's, U.S. Virgin Islands)

Entry #32

June [1896]

We arrived before sunset. Rufino, Dr. Pio, and I rowed out on one banca and the women in another. I had already made my goodbyes to Segunda in the galley, where her husband, that gifted cuckold, shook my hand with affable innocence. The heat was sultry but not withering though the sun still blazed: a tribute to the town's mild clime, due perhaps to its open posture against the Sulu seas. I carried my cane, my banig, plus a rosary just for effect. Rufino, even on the banca, was already crossing himself as if at a saint's canonization, muttering prayers of novena. I realized only later that, unlike myself, Rufino had the wit to be scared about the outcome of our journey.

After all, we were visiting an exiled man.

Dr. Pio—that is, Don Procopio—paid a porter to carry his valise and other effects. No improvised suitcases for that suave Bulakeño. The porters mangled their backs carrying his mendacious equipment, that heavy medical bag, a useless burden, if they only knew. He shouted when they almost dropped it into the water—but what was the point? He had not come to cure any ills. I must say he cut a dash—quite cosmopolitan in his fashionable trilby and his European shoes, which the porter took and tied with care to a pole. Don Procopio put to shame the likes of me, with my single camisa and pitiable chinelas sloshing in the banca's shallow flood. Oh, that I spend all my money on filthy novels and smuggled pamphlets! I had the spendthrift ways of a cowardly *filibustero*, and all I could show for them were my dumb decoy eyes and wet feet. As we rode the precarious banca, I was conscious, beside the well-groomed *señoras* and fraudulent *señor*, of my ragged costume, my bent reader's posture, cheeks scrunched to perpetual close scrutiny, altogether a lackluster figure, prematurely aged,[448] under a buri hat. Who was I to meet him, shake his hand, and speak his name? I, Raymundo Mata Eibarrazeta, of Cavite's Kawit, the Basque country's Jaca, and any of the obscure towns of tubercular grief around Leyte: son of a bandit and grandnephew of a minstrel, grandchild of a tyrant and a bleeding actress's orphaned kid. Why, hell yes, I had cause to greet him! I straightened my skinny shoulders, kept a hand on my hat, and held high that brow serene, rufous and scowling in the sun: hell yes, I had reason.

Why not?

A reader has as much to say about a book as an author, if not more, I thought, crossing my fingers in the gliding banca, ready for shore.

That avid bunch that greeted us on shore portended our importance, or their boredom. How many of them swarmed at our arrival I couldn't tell—but it seemed a whole village of young boys appeared to wave us toward land. They took our bags, our balot, our burdens—then they all disappeared toward the huts, a few meters from land, that accosted our gaze with a tidy welcome.

—So this is Talisay, Dr. Pio, a.k.a. Don Procopio, exclaimed.[449]

—He built it all, with the help of his students, said informative Doña Sisa.

---

448 How old was Raymundo? In this document's variable math, in this episode he was between the years twenty-two to thirty. I talk to myself now since other readers have taken a vow of silence. It's odd how you miss even those with whom you initially have nothing in common, except words. I think now of our aggressive jesting, our mismatched wits (some were not as agile as others), our triple jousts—we had some fun, did we not— us three musketeers, *sans* kulot? Those were the days. (Estrella Espejo, ditto)

449 Rizal's "estate" across from Dapitan town proper. In 1892, Rizal won 2000 pesos in a lottery, gave most of it to his father, and spent 80 pesos on the spit of land called Talisay, meaning beachfront. One day, let me tell you, when I regain my strength I will sail to Talisay. It is my dream. And one of you can carry my bags, Mimi C. or Diwata, I'd travel with you if you so wish. Did you hear that? We three can travel one day, as a sign of our old companionship. Please: please speak, old friends. I'm so lonely here in the Quezon sanatorium! *Oh—un horrible vacío en el mundo de mis affecciones.* (Estrella Espejo, ditto)

—Can you believe, all this from a lottery?,[450] exclaimed funny Angelica.

—You must see his clinic, doctor, said timid Josefina.

—No, Josefina, let us eat first, interrupted rude Angelica.

—He eats only what he plants, offered tender Josefina.

—Though he doesn't harvest pigs, countered clever Angelica.

—Well, he also has poultry, a piggery, and cows for pasture, asserted proud Josefina.

—Plus cacao fields, a coconut grove, and acres of abaca, added agronomical Doña Sisa.

And that is enough of characterization via epithets, my clumsy rendition of insights frayed from my hunger. What distressed me was this altogether mundane illustration of my hero—what, he was a pigsty owner, chicken cooper, and cowherd, too? O Eumaeus![451]

What blasphemies await poor readers who gain proximity to their writers!

It was as if, the closer you came, the more gall you collected, this unsolicited information about their lives filling up not a holy grail but a tin-can chalice of murky wine. I don't know how I had imagined him—on some lofty cloud scribbling phantom masterpieces at a desk? From Doña Sisa's details, he may as well join my retired uncle in his reverence for the wet season!

Numerous adjustments to my preconceptions confounded me as

---

450 Oddly enough, Rizal bought a share of the lottery with Ricardo Carnicero, the governor of the island at the time, his oppressor who became his friend. He, too, was lonely. This was a common trope in Rizal's short life: his captors admired him. Another instance is his artistic military guard in Calamba in 1887, Jose Taviel de Andrade, who was more of a fellow painter than a guard. Jose's brother Luis ended up being Rizal's defense lawyer in December 1896. It's possible that his reliance on the goodwill of his enemies rather than on the rash justice of his countrymen was fatal. Instead of escaping with rebels who planned to kidnap him from the ship *España*, Rizal declined and left himself at the mercy of the ship of Spain. (Estrella Espejo, ditto)

451 On Dapitan, Rizal had reverted to his family's primary occupation, farming. He was good at it. When he left Dapitan, he bequeathed quite a bit of land to, of all people, his barber. (Estrella Espejo, ditto)

we moved toward his house. The women chattered about the land's improvements with nonchalance, not knowing they were shattering my illusions. He had planted the langka trees near the beach: the locals told him they wouldn't grow so close to the sea, but look—like a miracle their roots have dredged deep enough to clutch the soil! He has a green thumb, they agreed. You don't say, I thought, looking at the lush earth—he's a goddamn green digital giant! Check out that mango tree: he loves its sour white meat. Ditto the cashew plants, green peanuts, and lanzones. He also loved tinapâ, mango jelly, and guavas, and he kept asking for kesong puti, but only from Laguna, and bagoong, but only from the Ilocos, which they used to mail to him even when he was in Europe.

My God, he was a veritable pig!

And do you remember his obsession over the stockings—his competition with the Chinese vendors to sell European-style hosiery in Dapitan? The ladies laughed, even the loyal Josefina. Oh please, do not add vile mercantilism to his sins of gluttony, I cursed to myself. I mean, will I learn he dreams of trading like a *bombay* next?[452] [453] His first project, said Doña Sisa, had been to import fishing nets from Calamba, to improve the catch in Dapitan. They can't make fishing nets here? I asked. Gee whiz, I thought, what did the people of Dapitan do without him—flap their hands in the ocean? No—they used sakag, about the width of a little rice basket, so he asked us to mail large woven nets from Laguna, the largest pukutan money could buy.

Sadly, she said, he didn't get it.

What darned ache and pain in that information—he only wanted a fishnet and he did not get even that?

---

452 In his last years (did he know they would be his last?), Rizal settled into domestic occupations. By all accounts, he lived the active life of a gentleman farmer, like a placid man in Tolstoy, without the deadly spiritualism, or George Washington, without the slaves, and with a full set of good teeth. (Estrella Espejo, ditto)

453 *Bombay* meant itinerant trader from India: from a Spanish epithet, obviously racist. Isn't that so, Ms. Translator? Mimi C.! Mimi C.! (Estrella Espejo, ditto)

I see in my heart a miserable apparition—the flailing arms of a drowning man, flapping at fish.

The twisted irony of that cruel question, quite unrhetorical in his case: if you were cast away on a desert island, what ten things would you take? Not even to include in the list: 1) the dreams of Rousseau, 2) the pamphlets of Voltaire, 3) the sciences of Rost and Jagor, 4) a pen, 5) one musical instrument, 6) postage stamps, 7) an unfinished manuscript, please to forward from Hong Kong, 8) secret perfumed letters from innumerable lost women, 9) a half-whittled wooden figure, yet untitled, 10) desire.

No, not even that.

Instead. Number One: goddamn pukutan, a fishing net from Laguna.

How the turn of fate had made him—well, human.

And look at that chicken coop—see? Against the hill of lanzones trees. He designed it himself. His patients pay him with poultry. He designed that water system, too—over there, beyond the outhouse. He took two months to figure out how to rig it to reach his home. I ooh-ed and ah-ed as they expected, but privately, my heart was breaking. My God, I thought, when the hell does he have time to write his third novel if he's busy dredging up drainage systems for his kasilyas?[454] [455] Worse, what did it mean if his own beloved sister did not mention—not once, of her own volition—that first principle, his writing schedule? Was it in the morning, after the milking of the cows? Or between noon and twilight, when the pigs and the poultry and the household help were deep in siesta and finally he was all alone, catching words with dismal fishing nets?

The sister went on and on as my heart limped behind. When

---

454 Toilet: from the Spanish *casillas*. Pukutan, of course, means fishing net. Mimi C., silence is golden, but will you at least do your job? (Estrella Espejo, ditto)

455 No. This is Raymundo's story now. Leave him alone. (Trans. Note)

she showed us the carefully sculpted busts of his captors, governor Ricardo Carnicero and his grim-faced wife, those sullen gray guardians of his murmuring water system, I wondered at Doña Sisa's blindness to the symbolism, so apparent to my sore vision I turned away. What did it mean but abject surrender, no matter what anyone else thought? He was whittling away his wits in his isolation. What kind of land was this, where he found comfort in carving out the fulsome cheeks of his oppressors?

His livestock, his coffee beans, his engineering marvels. What else was this man expected to think up next—replicate the sun at midnight? Oh yes, and have you noticed the lamps, Doña Sisa gestured, as we walked up the bamboo stairs and looked back at the path we had taken.

We turned around to gaze at the trim footpaths, a neat maze beyond the beach, sweetly hemmed with garden flowers.[456] Like a pendant microcosmic gem resting against the sea, Talisay was beautiful in the sunset, a lovingly mapped dream. A homunculus universe—replete and whole.

You could rest your weary head here, I thought, if they kept you here long enough. If they kept you long enough, I thought, you could fool even your soul.

Necessity, I thought anyhow, is the mother of invention.

But to my sunken heart invention was also the bastard of despair.

—The lamps blaze even at night, Doña Sisa said proudly, so that the people of Dapitan say he makes day out of darkness.

---

456 A specter from childhood rises. What happened to that cottage industry of educators who codified details of Rizal's entire life in K through 6 reading primers, *Unang Baitang* until *Ika-anim na Baitang*? Their details were both pious and quotidian, moral and trivial, a reverent, gossip-filled annotation of his life. Like many, I happily measured out my life in the Rizal Caravan, and to this day my first memories of reading follow the Stations of the Hero's Cross: Grade One, *His Family*. Grade Two, *His Childhood*. Grade Three, *His Studies*. Grade Four, *His Travels*. Grade Five, *His Exile*. Grade Six, *His Trial and Death*. Raymundo Mata appears, but only implied, in a cameo role, in *Ikalimang Baitang: Ang Kanyang Retiro*—he's never even mentioned in the chapter on Dapitan. (Estrella Espejo, ditto)

—And what is that? Don Pio asked, pointing at a shuttered kiosk on the rib of the hill.

All the women looked to where he pointed.

—Oh that, said Josefina. It's nothing.

—For shame, Josefina, said Angelica. That contains his butterfly collection. He hunts for specimens and sends them all in special jars to Europe.

—And he used to write there, Doña Sisa whispered in an addendum I could barely hear.

—Ah, said Don Pio with fawning unction, the famous lepidoptery!

Will this clown not stop his pandering?

—He helped build that hut himself, said Angelica.

I considered the blinkered place.

I considered the entire tranquil torment that was Talisay.

This was the curse of revelation, I thought—the whoredom of Babylon was nothing but the brutal candor of the quotidian matter of the divine.

—Doesn't he use that hut still? I asked.

—No, swiftly said Josefina.

Doña Sisa stared at her but said nothing.

Well, I thought, I couldn't blame her. *Mama mía.* With all this activity, her husband must be a nervous wreck.

Purbida.

When does he have time to be with her, much less write his third novel?

To tell you the truth, I couldn't quite tell the status of the Austrian lady. From Don Pio's pursed lips at my questions, I sensed it was a sore point, and in her exchanges with Doña Sisa, I witnessed a mutual though guarded affection, at times distressingly condescending on the part of the sister, so much more accomplished and knowledgeable even to my limited eyes than the teenage bride.

But my heart went out to the foreign mistress, for it must be so—she was his mistress, none of us were fools.

For one thing, could Masons get married?

Anyway, where was he?

Dr. Pio/Don Procopio inspected the place with the rapt air of a forger, and Rufino and I followed the leader with matching faces of gawking ardor. In fact, Rufino's mute stupefaction had about it such a look of pure comedy that I was afraid to imagine the moronic replica in my own gaze. If this was our reaction to the sister's introduction of his feats, how would we respond to his actual arrival?

And as if in a trice, conjuring the devil, there he was on the footpath, the giant of our hopes, writer of our sorrows, surgeon of our madness, and magician of Dapitan: I almost fainted in the twilight to hear his sister call out—*Pepe!*

Even his nickname was profane.[457] [458]

Pepe, the writer.

That was he?

How can I describe the moment, what words do I have at my disposal, to speak the unspeakable instant when I finally met him, the Writer, face to face.

Was it possible, could it be?

Ecce homo.

I raised myself to full height to gaze upon the man, and I couldn't help it, I said, gasping out in surprise:

—*Jesus Christ, you're short!*[459]

Jesusmariosep, Jesusmaryjoseph.

I was taller than Jose Rizal.

---

457 I've never liked Rizal's nickname. In Waray, it is profane. Ay, *dios mio*, I can still see Albino, a.k.a. Wild Gamao, and Miguel, a.k.a. Green Muhog, rolling on the aisles laughing at the name. Illiterate first graders—mental cripples! (Estrella Espejo, ditto)

458 Sssh! (Trans. Note)

459 Aah, sssh yourself! Raymundo's expletive has resonance. The cult of Rizal as a martyr Christ-figure is banal and *banál* at the same time. A whole mountain of devotees cherishes his relics and sings praises to his name, even as we speak. (Estrella Espejo, ditto)

Entry #33

June [1896]

He was tanned, gaunt, and he carried a cane. A white handkerchief was pressed in the pocket of his cotton shirt.

He laughed.

He had a slight mustache, neatly trimmed by some fantastic barber, I have to admit—where'd he get him on this forsaken land?

—Who were you expecting, he said, Bernardo Carpio?[460]

The women chuckled and clapped their hands in my direction: I should have bowed. At your service: Mr. Mata, the blind buffoon!

I can't begin to tell you my consternation.

That was it, my crowning moment, the day that marks my spot in history, and the climax to which this narrative, not to mention my life's farce, has been ascending.

I met my hero, and he laughed at me.

My face flushed, I hid behind Rufino as if by that futile action the damage could be undone. But Rufino stepped away, that traitor, pretending he had no connection to me.

Bastard.

But most of all, you should have seen the look on Dr. Pio's face, damn him—he was laughing fit to die, just like the rest of them.

Still laughing, Doña Sisa asked her brother, and now ignoring me as if I was just a wasp flitting by: And your birthday? How did you spend it?

—With ninety milligrams of quinine, he promptly quipped. I had a fever. I never believed this body was prepared to live past thirty.

---

460 The hero refers to the giant of Philippine legend (*see* also Entry #15) whose imprisoned length informs the caves of San Mateo. How interesting to witness here the hero making an allusion to his own novel, *El Filibusterismo*, which famously resurrects the old legend, and so mirroring the image here at least quadruply. Gives me a migraine. (Estrella Espejo, Quezon Institute and Sanatorium, Tacloban, Leyte)

And with a look of pathos, or apology, I couldn't tell which, he glanced toward Josefina, as if about to tell her something, but his sister interrupted.

She introduced Don Procopio, whom she called to my surprise by his real occupation: doctor. And then Dr. Pio did the honors of introducing us.

—Doctor Rizal, this is my patient who awaits your verdict: Don Raymundo Mata of Cavite.

—A fine name for a blind man, eh, Mr. Mata, the hero chuckled.

At first Dr. Pio didn't laugh. He was always late to get the joke.

—Ah, ha ha, good one, Dr. Rizal. Mata. Eye. Mata.[461] I never thought of that.

Oh no, you wouldn't, I thought, you fool.

And thus singled out, still flustered, I muttered my apologies, excuses, a mumbled confiteor. But everyone went ahead up the stairs to the writer's salon, not waiting for my reply.

Not even Rufino glanced at me, muttering *ojo, mata, ojo,* as if stunned by a revelation. On the way up, he turned to me and said: Ha! I never thought of that. *El un genio, aba!* Then he proceeded on his own, ass, leaving me to stumble on the steps with growing blindness as dark descended. So much for having a servant, I thought.

I won't go into the various jokes at my expense, blindness and all, that went into Dr. Pio's subsequent comments on my wayward tongue, bantering remarks before, during, and after dinner. Maybe it was convenient for the revolution to portray me as a dolt. And so leavened by levity, we entered the hero's cool home.

But before the hero could even commence to share its pleasures, a messenger arrived with a letter.

—Ah, the hero exclaimed, he saw you all already.

---

461 Aha! "*Ojo. Mata. Ojo.*" Cf. Raymundo Mata's *bulagtasan* in Entry #2. Mata (Tagalog) = Ojo (Spanish) = Eye. I get that! (Estrella Espejo, ditto)

Looking at our surprised faces, he added: It's a note from the governor. I must go.[462]

He went into his rooms to change into a gray suit, an elegance completed by his fine kamuning cane. He bade a hasty farewell and left us.

It was only Rufino who shook his head with foreboding over this interruption. The rest of us accepted the fruit and hot chocolate from a bandaged, grave houseboy, and we gazed from the sala upon the hero's small boat, a speck in the sunset, rowing off from Talisay for the main town.

—Did we get him into trouble? Rufino whispered to me.

—Eat your mangoes, Mang Rufino, I commanded, still piqued by his earlier snub.

I'd like to say I shared in the old man's worry—his early sense that by our coming we had upset the gods' compass, or, more bleakly, set blind destiny in motion. In retrospect, it was old Rufino, of course, in his anxious simplicity, who possessed prophetic dread, the niggling restless apprehension that escaped us as we sipped sweet nectar from the hero's cacao and bit into sour mango from his trees.

No, my mind was on a selfish tack, still smarting from my humiliation and revising the scene as one's shamed heart does, furiously editing out the blighted parts.

And around me, I looked for signs of the writer in the house—manuscripts, scrap paper, pens, inkwells.

But in the sala, all I saw was a spartan home, touches of the feminine in the lace runners and the trite puka shells for curtains separating the living room from a dim passage, my curiosity unrequited.

---

462 Valenzuela's biographer states: "While they were exchanging pleasantries, a messenger came from the military governor, Ricardo Carnicero." Carnicero was recalled in 1893, replaced by Juan Sitges, a doctor, and later by "the linguist Morales" [Leon Maria Guerrero, *The First Filipino*], then he was briefly restored in 1896. Rizal had amiable relations with each of these captors. (Estrella Espejo, ditto)

The hero returned before we even finished polishing off the fruit. His arrival startled Rufino, as if he'd witnessed a magic trick.

—*Mira ta*, he nudged me.

—What, I whispered.

—*El bini aqui—en banig voladora!*

—What do you mean—a flying carpet? Didn't you watch him leave in his banca, stupid!

But Rufino was gazing beatifically on the hero and did not listen to me.

The hero looked with satisfaction at our appetite.

—Ah, he said, I see you like the paho.

—Don Pepe, replied urbane Procopio, I prefer your pickled mango to the olives of the Europeans.

Coño![463] [464]

Will that charlatan[465] ever stop showing off?

The women and the doctors then took up the merits of Mindanao's virgin soil, its paradisiacal profusions, and so on and so forth, Don Procopio building up to that usual hype about the promised land. Sure, I thought, it's a promised land to you, *coño*—but what about the people who have lived here for ages? Who's promising their goddamned land to whom, idiot? I listened to everything the hero said and wondered at his tolerance of that quack Valenzuela.

---

463 From *hijo de coño* (son of a bitch; *coño* literally means that shy swatch of the female body, best left unsaid), a favored form of address among the vulgar, i.e., Spaniards. In colloquial Filipino, the term means any one of the wealthy Spanish-speaking or Spanish-looking classes, that is, Filipinos of a certain decadent group, i.e., katsila. What do you think, Dr. Diwata, is this a form of historical justice or not—how language metes out unconscious revenge, a transformed truth, as you would say? Dr. Diwata? Filipinos blithely baptize the *españolado* upper classes with the curse the old Spanish classes bestowed liberally, for centuries, upon others, not to mention each other—our just revenge—what would your Doctor Murky Smirk think? (Estrella Espejo, ditto)

464 Dear Estrella, forgive me, I am still re-reading. (Dr. Diwata Drake, Antibes, France)

465 *Charlatan*, from the Spanish *charlar*. *Que charlatán*: that is, what a talktative showoff! I can only guess that's the original, since no one is making *charlar* with me. (Estrella Espejo, ditto)

If anyone had the right to shake this man out of his mug, it was the doctor-writer-hero-butterfly-catcher-gymnast-water engineer. For after all, weren't we endangering his quiet life in exile by our revolutionary trespass, bringing the war right up to his bougainvillea gates, so to speak, whether he liked it or not?

We went on to dinner, chicken tinola, chicken sinigang, and caesar chicken salad[466] [467] [468] [469]—a motley parade of the hapless denizens of the aforementioned handsome coop—and in this way we found our journey's troubles repaid.

Meanwhile at our elbows stood a fine servant, a bony teenager with an eyepatch, ready to replenish our sweet tuba drinks. Then at times from the kitchen emerged another man with a deformed eye. In fact, the ocular motif was beginning to unnerve me, I must say.

Was I the only one who noticed the comings and goings of these creatures, like extras from a Gothic Pageant of the Island of the Lost Eyes?

Everyone else concentrated on the discourse during the courses.

—Is everything all right with the governor? Dr. Pio asked.

—Oh that. Carnicero just wanted to know who you are. I said

---

466 Caesar salad?! (Estrella Espejo, ditto)

467 According to the third edition of *Webster's New World Dictionary*, this salad was named "in honor of (Gaius) Julius Caesar by Giacomo Junia, Italian-American chef in Chicago, who invented it c. 1903." However, the exact origins of caesar salad may predate 1903, somewhere in Giacomo Junia's Italy, where Rizal traveled in 1895, after a stint in Germany where in turn he may have fathered Hitler's great-uncle, and definitely before he arrived in London, where he may have been Jack the Ripper. Rizal invented this delightful dish of goat cheese sprinkled on *lechugas*, with a dash of toasted bread crumbs, creating it quite on the fly even as his fingers tangled about his other invention, developed out of his crafty boredom, a spinning wooden globe upon a string, later called *yoyo*, apparently an ancient Chabacano verb referring to metatarsal actions yet to be fully revealed. (Estrella Espejo, ditto)

468 What the hell, what kind of wikimess is that? (Trans. Note)

469 Finally, Mimi C. Gotcha! I knew food, plus expletive, would make you reappear. You know, it was getting quite lonely, though I was doing fine on my own, if I say so myself. But yes, maybe it was not Rizal who was Jack the Ripper—maybe it was Juan Luna. He fled Paris for London after he killed his wife. (Estrella Espejo, ditto)

you're a doctor bringing a patient to me. It's okay, don't worry. As you can see—there are a lot of them around.

Doña Sisa explained the exile's life: patients from all places, blind men from Jolo, Hong Kong, Jala-Jala, you name it, flocking to Dapitan. Plus there were his abaca farming, irrigation plans, butterfly collecting, physical education, and life saving, all of which eased his monotony on the island.

However, in exchange for his freedom in Talisay, the hero reported to the governor every day, usually at lunch, she explained.

The point starkly came upon us: our host was a prisoner after all.

I thought: the revolution must save him.

We must deliver him from this—from this paradise!

—The governor's just homesick, the hero cracked. I can speak to him about the cities in Spain that he misses.

—Plus cities he's never seen!, interjected Doña Sisa. No one's seen more of the world than you! New York! Hong Kong! Egypt!

—Ah, sisters, the hero joked. They think the world of you in your presence, but you wonder what they say when you're gone.

—That's unfair, said Angelica. You know that Mamá would never say a word against you! Not like—

—Want more paho, asked the sweet Josefina, smiling tenderly at her Jose.

I realized at that moment how inconvenient we all were—interlopers all, including the faithful sister—for wasn't this the lovers' first meeting after a mournful division, as any lover's separation must be?

We turned away, or at least I did, at the spectacle of the reunited couple, a topic too delicate for my inspection.

I had the privilege of noting Doña Sisa's passing discomfort, a slight twitch of the shoulder as the pair exchanged the pleasantries of paho with one other. My own unease was not that of a sibling's misplaced, perhaps unwarranted, sense of propriety, or smart sisterly protection—no, mine were the misgivings of the vulgar, as from my vantage I watched the familiar bosom heave in fine irrelevant show, in her wispy black balintawak.

Clearly, it was time to withdraw, and we got up.

—Bulag, exclaimed the hero as we moved off.

I was startled. Indeed, I was offended at this slight.

Sure he was a genius, and clearly the chosen one between us two—still, did that give him the right to make fun of my condition?

In an instant the one-eyed houseboy appeared, and the hero addressed him:[470]

—Bulag, show you the huts, then cowboys three put away their banig. Me hear you?[471]

It was shocking, to say the least, to hear this absurdity from the poet who wrote pensive poems to the flowers of Heidelberg. But then again, he *is* the guy who wrote Spanish sonnets to German flora.

—The teahouse, *Señor*?

—*Si*.

Wonders kept abounding. You can imagine my deflation to note my common cause, including my childhood nickname, with that patched and in-construction creature, the teen houseboy Bulag.

With a devilish gleam that I could not determine was not merely the effect of his one-eyed-bandit look, he gestured us to follow.

---

470 Was it Rizal who baptized his houseboy/medical aide on Dapitan "Bulag," the Tagalog term for blind man? The word for blind, on Dapitan, is the Visayan "Buta" or "Halap." Later, the houseboy Bulag became a prominent teller of Rizal tales, a separate genre in itself in Dapitan. (Estrella Espejo, ditto)

471 Dear Mimi C., do you think that evidence here suggests the hero-linguist did learn Zamboanga Chabacano, a "pidgin" mix of Spanish and Visayan languages? His letters to the Caviteño patriot Evaristo Aguirre show the hero bantering in Cavite Chabacano as well. *See* also Chapter 28, "*Tatakut*," in *El Filibusterismo*, a sparkling gem in the book's linguistic stew—language being that novel's theme. Chalk Chabacano then to a list of at least ten languages [5 European, 4 Filipino, and 1 dead] spoken by the hero. Plus, he used to pretend-speak Japanese to gullible Frenchmen at museums in Paris. (Estrella Espejo, ditto)

Don Pio approached the hero before we descended. They whispered together. The hero nodded, and so I understood the mission was underway.

The doctors motioned us to go on.

Down the path we walked, Bulag and Bulag & Co., lugging our belongings beyond the water system, through bamboo, guava and acacia, through that eerie swath of baluno trees burdened with its lavish paho-bearing fruit, then up toward a gaslit pair of polygonal huts. And all the way it irked me that here I was, carrying Don Pio's effects like a porter, while he remained behind with the writer. And I had not even had a chance to ask the man for an autograph!

So that night went.

I must say, I should have been content to have witnessed the household's rhythms, its loyalties, rifts, and underbelly, including: the pleasant nature of the hero, but with a wit like a coiled snake's bite—an accommodating brother whose word nevertheless was law. And then there was the sister's possessive affection—perhaps a subtle in-law rivalry, unknown even to the duelists, that in her case blended nicely with the laws of decency, who could blame her. And the sweetheart's situation in this ménage, loved by the brother who in this accidental life had no one else to love, and tolerated by others—adored and yet, who knows, secretly reviled. Anyhow you could tell she was the inferior creature, humble and ingratiating, and in this way, for some reason, her pathetic figure broke my heart (or at least what I believed was my heart, somewhere above the viscera, a bit occluded). And still none of this explained the Greek *señora's* sadness, her mourning gowns. She had the wistful subservience of one inured to sorrow, and her freakish eyes gave away a gray despair. But what the hell. Unwedded bliss, if you asked me, had its own rewards.

And lastly, I hate to say that they creeped me out—my *confréres*, doubles and *semblables*. Those walking wounded, the one-eyed houseboy and men in bandages and others I noticed later in various recuperative stages, one obviously a noble Moro, in her flowing robes, promenading with a walking stick about the blazing bamboo groves. For I kept hearing all these rustling movements in the twinkling darkness, and Rufino, that wit, kept whispering beside me: *Psst, Don Mundo—tu kababayan aki!*[472]

Compatriots, my ass.

In my fantastic anticipation of this meeting, I had failed to envision the writer's clinical preoccupations. These blind apparitions on the island—shadows in my vision, my bumbling brothers—presented, let's say, an unsightly jolt. We deposited our bags among those men in limbo, and then I took Rufino aside.

—Now listen: we must follow Don Pio and the Doctor. For the sake of the revolution. Make sure Don Pio gets it right.

Obedient, nosy Rufino took my hand and led the way.

Bulag the houseboy followed suit.[473]

He was not one to be left out.

A bold malingerer and, it turns out, an irrepressible host, the teenage Bulag led us both down an unbeaten path, and before we knew it we reached the sea. All throughout, the young Bulag talked a reckless Chabacano streak—and between his Zamboangan cha-cha-cha and the Cavite kuracha-cha-cha of Rufino's sister-slang, they fashioned what I could only call a twin tongue-twisting tango of Spanish Babel, marvelous and hilarious but also exhilarating, for some reason. It was as if, with history soon to unfold, the freedom of their tongues paved a magical path. In addition, Bulag was a trove

---

472 *Psst, Don Mundo—your compatriots are all here!* Again, nineteenth-century Chabacano, with variable orthography, occurs in the text. I imagine that the translator left the original in for a reason, and not because she was asleep at the wheel. (Estrella Espejo, ditto)

473 In Don Pio's version, the only other text of this event, Raymundo and Rufino are not even minor characters. They're stick figures who are told: stay—do not go near us when we talk! It is to Raymundo's credit that he refuses and so achieves his place in time, and this trio's walk toward the beach is a sublime moment, as three blind men catch up with history. (Estrella Espejo, ditto)

of fantasy and delusion, but I couldn't tell, in their riotous intra-translations, if his superstitions were Rufino's embellishments or expressions of his own.

When we reached the beach, Bulag climbed a rock like some puny goat. We followed.

—Psst, Bulag said, flagging us away as we, too, climbed. Go back down. He already smelled us.

Nos ti baho!

What were we—swine?

From Bulag's account, if the Doctor found us out, we could be turned to stone.

—Someone's enchanted under this rock, he said.

I thought of the myths of the Greeks and the scurrilous fables of Ovid—men changed into pigs and girls into marble. I looked at the hoary mass and doubted I would find locked in it my Galatea, preferably with sad and slavish Irish eyes.

The stony promontory, dividing us from the sea at this angle, gave away nothing.

I heard a murmur—some voices beyond us.

Was that the writer or just the wind?

—How can you tell it's enchanted? Rufino whispered.

—He's always climbing on this rock, and he talks to it.

—In what language? Rufino asked.

—German.

—Ah. I knew it, Rufino said. He must be talking to the Siquijor mermaids. They travel, you know.

Just my luck to be stranded with mythological coconut-heads. It was enough to make me miss Don Procopio! Where did he go with the Doctor? It was so frustrating not to *see*!

Once, the amiable Bulag continued, he made the students jump from this rock, one by one. Each of them was terrified but still all of them jumped, as if pushed.

—Did anyone die? Rufino said with concern.

—Ah, said Bulag, he put a magic net upon the ground: he turned the earth into a pillow!

—Impossible, I interrupted.

—Hush, Rufino said. You don't want him to get mad. The kapre[474] [475] might hear you.

—He's not a kapre. He's a—a novelist!

—Then how can you explain the magic featherbed?

—It wasn't magic. Maybe they fell into—a pukutan!

But no one was convinced by that stupid explanation.

The voices beyond the rock grew louder as I crouched higher.

I grabbed Rufino as I crawled.

He pulled me up toward the lowering tones.

—Are they there?

—Yes, said Rufino.

—What are they doing?

—Sitting under a langka tree, eating bibingka.

What is it with these heroes, I thought—they eat rice cakes like there's no tomorrow.

—What are they saying?

—Don Mundo, you're blind, not deaf. I can hear what you hear, *tonto*—the sound of waves and cries of bats!

It's true.

The noise of Dapitan Bay made eavesdropping the devil.

But worst of all, the screech of nocturnal creatures drowned out the dreams of spies.

I gave up.

—Let's get down from this rock, I said.

---

474 Here's an expletive, Mimi C.: do you want to break your vow of silence? (Estrella Espejo, ditto)

475 In the round robin of offensive play that marks linguistic legacy, *cafre* is a Spanish term that, unsurprisingly, has roots in a derogatory word for blacks (*kaffir*). However, in Arabic *kafir* means infidel. In sum, for Filipinos, *kapre* is a magical beast—that is, the magical beast that is language. (Trans. Note)

The bats of Dapitan, my brothers, followed us to the ground, swerving about and testing my shaky steps with their whirring, whistling wings. Their paniki moves.

Suddenly, I felt homesick, or what is it you call that humid swell of longing, like a wave in the chest, in my case activated by one creature's passing caress—the whiff of sulfur in his flight, a frozen grist of tears caught in his graveyard wings. The changeling orbits of these creatures' progress, night-scourers of grief, reminded me of the lush caverns of Cavite with its cold groves and banyan ghosts. And the haunting susurrus of their flight recalled another twilight moment—a long time ago.

I wondered at my distance from my hometown: up here by the foreign drawl of this southern sea. If I fell, no one would remember my name. If I drowned, no one would follow. An ancient undertow took me into its claws: a grip of sadness. How did I get here? On top of the rock, I was dizzy, disconcerted. And I imagined, from this vantage, I would never escape this island.

I understood then the weight, the burden in this place—the sour nightbloom of exile and remorse in Dapitan.

Slowly, distinctly, we left the bats to their derangement, and Rufino pulled me downward and downward, to meet smug Bulag, his feet firmly on the ground, who said:

—Aha! Did you feel it?

—What? Rufino said.

—The hand of the kapre, from the rock.

—No, said Rufino.

Yes, I thought, but I did not admit it out loud.

As we shuffled back toward the huts—we heard it clearly.

The hero's voice.

We were standing to the right beyond their ken, under the shadow of the rock.

—And so the seed grows, the hero was saying.

—Still talking about his fruit, the paho, snorted Rufino.

—Sssh, whispered Bulag.

I hate to say it: there was something unconsoling about the voice, its echo of unspeakable remove. I knew I should leave, but I couldn't. A pall oppressed me: a black despair. On Dapitan, if I were not careful, oblivion would swallow me up. Zamboanga was the end of the world, as far as anyone could tell from the top of that rock: and there was nothing, with all the pig-herding, coffee-planting, fishnet-hauling, butterfly-gathering, mango-eating, drainage-fathoming, eye-saving, Spanish-teaching, carpet-flying, even love-making— there was nothing to live for under its stricken, endless stars.

It was disorienting, the pearl of the orient: I could see no horizon against the beach. They had flung us far from the flat world, and anyway what was the point? To retrieve the illusion of wholeness for this random and sinking archipelago, this patchwork of bamboo-and-coconut planets speaking idly and in tongues? From where I stood, what was there to save—a geography as well stitched from the confused leaps of flying fish as from the sole-cisms of foreign lunatics? It was true. Into the dumb chattering world we had been born from the mad mistakes of Magellan and one day, who knows, we'll perish from our own. My doubts blinded me even more than my senses did. Cosmologies built from spon-taneous horror have the virtue of dubious detail, and for a minute I saw the precise outlines of my country's fruitless map, etched in a plot of grass.

Arrested beside Dapitan's sea, I grieved: it was undeniable.

In fact, I was surprised to see, as I looked about, the disjoint yet unmistakable shape of the archipelago in the distance, scraped out and shaped from a careful scrub of leaves.

What the hell—did the man plan out even the topiary of the nation?

From this vantage, the notion of *Filipinas* was at best a fluke, or worse someone else's error.

—The resolutions of the association are just, patriotic, and timely, the hero murmured, especially as now Spain is weakened by the revolution in Cuba.

—So what are we to do?

The hero sighed, an escaped phantom from the chest.

I patched his sounds from the air, sonar gambles.

How distant for him were fights for the *Cortes*, newspapers' propaganda fevers? Europe's museums; straits of Gibraltar and Suez; maidens of Biarritz and lewd London; the scientific nightmare that was New York; and ships of Babel in which, to his misfortune, he alone understood words people used to slander one another. Childhood between the mountain and the bay, all the generic names of putative loves. They were mirages. He pondered daily which of the following most depressed him—to remember the sweet songs of his old yaya and her tobacco tales of mystical lakes, or to admit that those days would never return?

To what end revolt? He had said it already, better than most: he had balanced the syllogisms of further predations, proximal Japan or enormous America, take your pick.[476] Worse—and personally he did not wish to live to see that day: to look at ourselves, in some abject distance, and so gaze: at the hopeless deformity of our hopes.

For the moment he made no answer, his silence drowned among bats.

—In Hong Kong, he said tentatively, I have a library—

But Don Pio interrupted that pleasant thought.

---

476 In his 1889 essay *Filipinas dentro de cien años*, Rizal eliminated a host of other plausible colonists that could come after Spain (among them Holland, Germany, Japan, or China) and at the end of this list deemed America the probable candidate: "it is not impossible [for America to think of expanding in Asia], for example is contagious, greed and ambition being the vice of the strong, and [U.S. president] Harrison expressed himself in this sense of Samoa . . . North America would be a bothersome rival once she enters the field [but] it is . . . *against her traditions* [sic]." In this essay, Rizal was both prophetic—and wrong. America's "traditions," as we have experienced Rizal's prophecy in action, are those of "the strong," and virtues of republican America are an abominations on the Filipino tongue. (Estrella Espejo, ditto)

—The revolution . . . even . . . arms . . . there are over thirty thousand in the Katip . . .

—Precautions, the hero mumbled. Neutralize, he admonished. Horror, he declared.

Huh?

Their words were garbled and buried by the sounds of the sea, the riffling of monsoon foliage, the murmur of swallows and my endless bats; and my testimony has all the clarity of the tremulous sandfall of waves. Did it occur to me, with tingling blood and thumping heart, that, yes, I was eavesdropping on a pivotal moment, and the progress of our history would turn on the knife-point slices of these sentence fragments?

What a shiver of historical thrill should have frozen my deaf brain.

But I was terrified to be found out, knowing somehow I was in the wrong, and perhaps I gathered the ambiguities of our cause through my anxious filter, which explains my lasting sense of failure and unease. Maybe they did parse fortune with foresight and need against anger, weighing risk against bloodshed in careful measure, so that the two men shook their heads as if with the pathos of alchemists, sifting for that key element, that which turns bold adventure into gold, and not just blood—but to tell you the truth, and this egoistic flaw of course does me no good, in the end what I remember most was the charm of my dramatic role.

I couldn't help it.

I was born from the cracked egos of a pair of stage actors. I was in the wings of history, waiting for my cue. I'm sorry to say that I happily anticipated the moment when it would be my turn to face applause. This was a distinctly engulfing feeling—to be stuck in dramatic pause, as if in a starring role—though you couldn't even call me an understudy, and anyway my bit part had no lines. If I were honest, I would say I saw absolutely nothing, but instead I will note: there was my mother, coughing up her blood; there was my father, the young prince, flashing his petard; there were the scent of flowers, leaves, silence—

And it's hard for me to separate out my mind's dim memory from dim desire. Now I blow up what fascinated me (Jose Basa in Hong Kong possesses his books, who the hell is he?). I narcotize the dull (they go on and on about Cuba, who cares!). I catch Don Pio's tactful tactics—I have to admire him in his shining moment. He has a mission. He has focus. At last he's in his element, and I note, with belated respect, the inutile, thankless mission of the Supremo's secret messenger.

For the Katipunan, after all, there is only one right answer.

He waited for the hero's reply. If not now, when?

For the hero's in a bind: the flattery of this trip alone unnerves him. *So the seed grows.* Who sowed it? He did, but that was a shallow answer best left unspoken. Don Pio waits. As for him, the hero, Cantu's fallacy of historical causality has finally caught up with the living, and he's too tired to wrestle with belief. My own perceptions in this matter mix with hindsight, plus fancy, such being the rules that govern recollection. He had as much interest in idolatry as cows have in cud; godhood is tiresome. Exile is a gift. He had tried. I strained to catch it, the unspoken. The man had tried on the island to captivate something beyond the soul: a surplus matter. It was a terrible accounting, and I struggled vainly to comprehend. For one thing, I could barely hear. It was beyond us, vile trespassers. How to say it? The goal? Simply to live, oblive? I could not get the words, I improvised.

To succumb to rascal matter. The risible, fetid completeness of a sac. The secret volcano in a rock. The tumid gristle on a bull, sadly defunct. Castration was no picnic, but what one would give for the tenacity of dumb beasts? My God, the infinite capacities of the rav- ened eye! And a breast was a breast was a breast: neither a lesson in futurity nor the lesions of a mother's love. The world was enough if it was narrow enough. That is grace.

He knew damned well what we were up to: we wanted his signature in blood.

It's true.

His bones did not matter.

We wanted of him what was air and nothing, such as his name, a ghost louse-scratch. As for his novels, his words? Not futile but culpable. Blameless, but still: bloodstained. This pained him.

I was shocked. This is what I got for my crime, arrant listener. Struck dumb: for this must be our Medusa. Worse than a hero's death was a hero's truth.

How could we not have seen it: that he possessed the regrets of ordinary men?

I was disconcerted, and I wished in that moment to turn to stone.

And then, how could we convey what we meant, our profound—? How could Don Pio even begin—? Our mangled esteem. Our symbol equals, yes, the shreds and skein of his body, but quiddities, if we thought about it—yes, just as much, really. It's not fair to discount our concern, though it is true, yes, we preferred blood. It's all we had. It was all that we could draw.

Stalemate.

And then I kept wishing he would talk more about his library.

What again was the address in Hong Kong?

A sudden movement toward stage left, a sandshuffle of feet, where I think they rambled up and down upon the beach, the sea making a fine backdrop. And I swear I saw that wistful gesture, more like an aside, when the hero pointed with his moonlit cane to that cleft of land where the Katipunan's boat would never rescue him.

—Bulag!

Like a clarion he called out, his voice away from us, toward the useful shore. I imagine Don Pio himself had a hand to his waist, ready to brandish his secret gun—but the voice's pistol shot was quicker.

—You behind the rock: get back to the huts! All three of you. And be careful on your way up to help the blind man.

And then, as if he had not interrupted his walk, he continued with Don Pio, hands holding his shining cane: I believe it glowed, a hypnotic snake, its head raised against the sand no matter which way it twirled.

Bulag, as if he had indeed been stricken by a blow from the man's cane, raced up toward the huts, dragging us through the grass. We scampered like beasts in flight, for all the world turned into swine. To be honest, I did not think I would make it up alive, and when I fell on the mats, I touched my limbs and my eyes to make sure my body had not become marble, or worse engristled into the wildness of a boar. I was delirious, feverish, and like Rufino tossed and turned all night.

When he woke up, Rufino said:

—Examine my face, Don Mundo: do I have the whiskers of a dog?

—No, I said.

—Really? Feel my chin: I have the beard of a goat.

—No, I said.

—You mean he did not turn me into an animal for our sins? God bless the kapre! He took mercy on our souls!

In the fresh light of Dapitan's sulky morning, I laughed.

—*Tu un tonto*, I said, meaning both of us, eavesdropping citizens, and in my bewilderment I spoke Rufino's crazy tongue.

Entry #34

[June, 1896]

The sun was barely about, and none of the blind ghosts were up, except for the Moro woman who rose to pray then smack her mouth silly with her favored buyô. The day itself, with that poison spat of betel in the dawn sky, promised oblivion. Not taking the footpaths, I wandered, pretending to seek nature's privies. I noted a number of curiosities along the way, such as: mounds of fruit carcasses by the lanzones grove; a host of burned insects, their limp-brown wisps of damaged wings; a humongous stray pig, pampered beast in the promised land; and the odd detachment of the shuttered butterfly kiosk, obviously unused.

I stopped in my tracks, I hid behind the nearest baluno tree, wondrous source of all things paho. Its trunk wide enough for my tensile frame, I crouched unseen to witness a strange incident.

It was she, the sweetheart.

Half-sepulchral in the foggy dawn, kneeling on the ground by the empty hut.

A wraith, a ghost.

She sobbed wordlessly, and I didn't know what to do: I was only a trespasser, looking for the toilet. Please madam, how can I help? And by the way, is this your kasilyas?

Dressed in black, his love wept like a child. Sure, the hut was a graveyard, dedicated to unnamed butterflies, but did it warrant this sadness, so early in the morning even the gumamela looked gray? Her hands brushed at the earth, then gripped locks of hair, and her whole being's posture of secret, irreparable grief, I knew, was not meant for any eyes. But I did not turn away.

Then I smelled the burning.

A long time ago, I had smelled that smell—the acidic ash of seeds and citrus, fruit trees on fire, a sweet edenic pyre curdling the monsoon air. My knee-jerk recall mixed with memory's hunger. Guavamangolostlanzones, all the debris of childhood tears. What an odd mingling of sensations occurred at this tremor of morning—terror and tenderness both in the waft of cinder. It was a kind of kaingin, but fresh, like a baby's corruption. There at her feet—the mounds of burning lanzones flesh smouldered like an altar and offered morbid ambrosia to this day out of time.

The servant Bulag was sweeping at the ground with a midrib broom, his bandaged forehead nodding away. He didn't recognize me. And before I could move, the Doctor found me.

What fright! What horrible shame and embarrassment! I had not noticed his shadow in the ashen light, and, in fact, recognized him only by his terrible cane.

Its two serpent heads flashed their beastly maw in twin anticipation—monstrous forgeries of each other.

My gut recoiled.

—Mosquito repellent, he said.

Huh? Was he talking to me?

I looked to see if anyone else was around. The sweetheart had vanished without a trace. Bulag, the scamp, was nowhere to be found.

—Lanzones peels are a fine insecticide, he said.

I could not speak.

—Well. Ready for the clinic, *Señor* Mata?

I gulped. I knew I should apologize for last night's intrusion, but I was a coward.

—I see you're an early riser, like me. Did you sleep well? The chickens are a bit noisy, he said.

I shook my head. I nodded. I moved my lips, but I could not speak.

—Follow me then, he said: I was just on my way down.

He strolled with leisure on the path, taking in the cool air, a little mannikin of manhood. Like a trussed insect floating on my spit: I followed. I remember his slippers, a frayed, pathetic affair, leather soles with dust embroidery shaping his heels, and the way he kept flipping his walking stick, the silver-edged snake twirling: a fencer toying with his foil.

It was a curious cane.

As I said, the snake had four eyes and two heads, one at each end. Its ivory contour wove through the dark wood in crafty relief, at both ends a vicious mouth and on each a silver stud that cleft the tongue. It kept darting out at me, as if to eat me. In this way, that horrid amphisbaena reared its ugly head, making awful faces no matter which way the swordsman struck.

Dozens of lanzones fruit lay dashed on the ground, as squashed as my frightened tongue. He towered before me: I cowered. I was as small as a pinned bug, as weak as the stripling trees that lined his home. My arms could not move, as if indeed they had been taped, like unformed wings, to a vitrine foil: pinned. Where were my questions, my sorry notes? My rusty antennae squandered my moment in the sun, in the tepid desperations of their futile flailings. No way was I ever going to turn into a butterfly.

What had I come to the island to speak? I could barely remember the name of his novel—something about tangerines, tamarinds, tangents.

—*Tanga*, he denounced.

I realized that he had discovered my scientific name: *noli me tanga*, a vulgar species of citizen with a vague personal agenda. Now he could seal the data in a jar and send it off to the Hapsburgs of Heidelberg, where in a collection of sacrosanct dust I would molder, a glum figure of terrible redundance, baptized for my foolishness by a careful man.

For some reason, the knowledge of my doom gave me peace.

—And what do you do, Mr. Mata?

—Ah. Aha. Ah.

Slowly, the spell eased, and my wings seemed unglued: weak and weightless.

He stood still and waited politely, his walking cane still.

—I work for the *Diario de Manila.*

My morning voice was strangled, like a cat's.

—A journalist! And what do you write, Mr. Mata?

—No, sir. A printer. Only apprentice, sir. I spell. I mean, I sell! No, I do not write. I like. The alphabet!

When it came to the crunch, I knew it. I was just some *latinidad lechugas*, a vegetable lump.[477] [478] [479]

—So do I, he said.

—I mean, sir—Iwonderhowyouhavethetimetowrite, with everything you do in Talisay?

I blurted it all out in a phantasmic burp.

He wasn't angry. He kept sauntering down the path.

—I mean, sir, you do entomology, ophthalmology, pedagogy, in fact all kinds of *ology—*

I chased him down the path.

—Don't forget pathology, he said without turning to look at me. However, I rarely do apology, he added, moving on.

I hurried to keep up.

—But where do you get the time to write the third instalment? The whole island speaks evidence of your mythic energy: cartography, sculpture, engineering, husbandry, everything but—

—Don't forget wizardry, he said, waving his cane.

—All sorts of wizardry! I said. Hypnotism, mesmerism, telekineticism.

---

477 "*Fue un latinidad lechugas* a vegtable [*sic*] lump." The original translates his idiomatic self-loathing into English. (Trans. Note)

478 Ah, Mimi C. Is it self-loathing that brings you back to the table? (Dr. Diwata Drake, Kalamazoo, Michigan)

479 The better to speak with you, my dear. (Trans. Note)

—Don't forget witticism, he exclaimed.

—You have a host of worlds to suit all types of fancy, but *come stai le livre?*[480] [481]

Briefly, descending, he looked back, as if the sun were in his eyes, though he faced west: he glared straight at me, and I understood what Bulag had said.

His gaze could turn you into stone.

He laughed.

It was not what I expected, but it was the only reply I got.

—Come, Mr. Mata, he said. It's time for your check-up.

We were at the clinic, and I woke up.

The eye has a vitreous humor, mysteriously impervious to the touch, enclosed in sclera and choroid bands. If you cut it, it resists like rubber. If you hold it, it exhales. More fabulous than a mirror, it is less fragile. If you scratch it, it gains the wisdom of renewal. But the eye's atrophy, like any other affliction, admits

---

480 The text is garbled here: this line contains the only instance of Italian plus some French. A solecism, how-are-you the book, instead of *come va*, how goes the book; or is *le livre* in weird vocative, or budding appositive, i.e., icon for Rizal [how-are-you The Book]; or maybe a dyslexic pun, how-are-you the liver, who knows? In any case he sounds stupid, and I kept the mystery intact, untranslated. The rest of the dialogue is a similarly hallucinatory mix of Spanish, Tagalog, and Chabacano, which I smoothed out into more orderly English, sorry. (Trans. Note)

481 Speaking of hallucination, Blumentritt, Rizal's faithful correspondent in his exile, was concerned about Rizal in Dapitan. By 1896, Rizal spoke in passing despair about his waning gifts. And his always admiring Austrian friend began to note atypical parapraxes, for instance in Rizal's Italian—the hero misquoted the opening lines of Dante's poem of exile in an otherwise upbeat missive to Leitmeritz. The grammar school teacher was alarmed, told the hero he must do something, say, apply to be a doctor for the Spanish in Cuba, get out of the island already, for Christ's sake. Such was the effect of Rizal's solecisms. In short, the plan to go to Cuba was a mental health intervention engineered by the good Austrian—not a form of treason to the revolutionary cause! Raymundo's slips, on the other hand, should just be corrected, Ms. Translator. (Estrella Espejo, ditto)

to no reverses under certain states. I have long understood that my situation was that of a damaged soul, an original infection passed on from a cursed breed. That man of mystery and hack from Jaca, my mad grandfather, had been no pristine specimen even in his prime, though he had the miraculous gall to keep on living, immortal in his peevishness. His dimness was tiresomely physical, not just symbolical, though I was prone in my young wrath to find in his blind gestures the proof of colonial disaster. Even my father, *el genio* Jote, was famous for his lack of vision: he declaimed rather than read and dramatized rather than observed. Who knows what failings gripped him even now in his jungle wanderings, if he so lives, out there with my mystical bats? I could tell, from the doctor's sighs in his cool clinic, as I lay under the balm of his camphor, or was it chloroform, that all was not well, and soon he would divine my bleak future.

Of my genetic history, I believe I gave him the above scant clues, and though I hope I did not in my delirium give away undue bitterness, I secretly wished him to pity me.

In short, I have no idea what I revealed. I surrendered to the hypnosis of his cold, Teutonic hands. He wrote in a notebook— I heard him scribbling as if from a drugged distance—and he clipped and prodded me with icy screws, while I lay back in the rustic medical chair, with its hemp bottom and leather scars, and gave up the ghost to the intermittent swivel of its squeaking wood. I believe it was to that unhinged sound that I owed my surrender—or some other creaky pendulum of forgetting. Outside the waft of burning lanzones peels soon fumigated the medical hut. And perhaps it was, as I now imagine, the sway of the snake and the soothing swish of its apocalyptic tongue that unlocked my own speech. In any case, in my version, I proceeded to spill the history of my country as I have done until now[482] [483] [484] [485] amid the distinct smoke musk of mosquito repellent in Dapitan.

I may as well lay it out here in its complete abjection—the last, minute details of my fraudulent adventure with the Doctor, who did the only thing he could do for us when we asked him about revolution: the next morning, he examined my disease. You might wonder that he still deigned to see me, the decoy patient, despite the discovery of our arrival on his island under flagrant false pretences. My heart still races, with deep, irretrievable shame, when I remember with what good nature he rewarded our bad faith. By the morning, I was so completely sorry for our obvious inconvenience and ignorant trespass on his *retiro*, that I preferred to run away on the next boat or flying carpet, whichever arrived first at Dapitan.

Instead, I found myself in the confines of his leafy clinic, the first among a host of cystic polyps, fistulae, vesical calculi, osteomyelites, tongue carcinomas: the mass of patient patients now awake and nurturing their fragrant buyô in the lines beyond his langka trees.

In the clinical act, I believe, he was most at ease.

Tinkering with his implements, he calibrated pulse and heartbeat, then in his impersonal way he asked me personal questions, and for no good reason I forgot the rest, as if I'd fallen into a dream.

---

482 Here is a vertiginous spin in his story, his retelling of his telling, so that the narrative spawns an infinity, a dizzying yarn at this juncture: just as, in the Scheherazade tale, for instance, the heroine-storyteller at one point indulges in infinite recapitulation to avoid decapitation, a literal [in]stallment. The teller's motive here is less obvious, however— to retell his story *in æternum* does not defer his diagnosis nor his nation's. Rather, the story speaks to and remains with the dead hero *ad infinitum*: in a temporal miracle only narrative might engender, it prolongs a meeting that otherwise *occurs nowhere* in Rizal's myriad scripts of his much-recorded days. (Dr. Diwata Drake, Siena, Italy)

483 Well, Dr. Diwata, it's good to hear your voice! Sometimes. To be honest, I have no idea what you're talking about. Again. But so pleased to hear from you again! Welcome back! Would you like some lugaw? Tsokolate-eh?! (Estrella Espejo, ditto)

484 Yes, and how are you, Ms. Mimi C. Magsalin? Is that your full pseudonym? (Dr. Diwata Drake, Siena, Italy)

485 I am as I am, as I've always been, thank you. (Trans. Note)

His bedside manner was sublime, to the point of amnesia. Don't blame me for my inattention, the sciences of the nineteenth century are not my cup of tea. I preferred, of course, full wakefulness, in which I could take down notes, but so much of that fateful morning has the air of shameful smog (a regrettable hypnosis first contrived, I understand, in French and Germanic institutions)—except for sensory perceptions of the wasteful kind, such as the annoying invisible bedbugs in the medical chair, the bloody death-throes of poisoned mosquitoes, and various kinds of glass vessels with vile and fascinating smells—that I labor to write them all down though I do not believe any of my foolish details will be of use.

I don't even know if I spent five minutes or five hours with him, so variable and tainted are my mental reconstructions. All I know is that, with a mesmeric sigh and one final regretful pat on my brow, he said there was no hope for me.

Degenerative macular morbidity, in a lingering dry stage, with incipient retinitis pigmentosa: hence, nyctalopia will only exacerbate. I mean, he said gently, resting a fleeting finger on my eye as if it could heal its phantom hurt, your nightblindness. It will only get worse. Straight lines may appear wavy and objects may appear in the wrong shape or size. In your old age you will experience the loss of correct colors, and while you will note the disappearance of objects in the eye's central frame, who knows, peripheral vision might remain.

You have a dark, empty area in the center of your vision, the hero explained.

My heart understood his diagnosis, and my soul, as if in pathetic agreement, clenched in shame. Unfortunately, his tone told me, there was no cure. It was all too true, and I felt he knew that the weakness was not just in my eyes for he looked at me with an insuperable tenderness that I have yet to be able to portray sufficiently, much less construe—as if he had glimpsed something else bereft in me. For a minute, I felt the comfortless gift of imagining significance in my degeneration. It helped me to think of my symptoms as a portent rather than a waste. The moment passed. And then—and I remember it distinctly—I had this odd satisfying feeling of knowing with certainty that nothing will be of help. Truth, I guess, is always a relief.[486] My fate was beyond my grasp, an organic fruition that even the hero could not cure. Who was I to whimper, curse the gods or the gluttons of tragedy that follow us, poor mortal creatures in the clutch always of some sort of fall? Even he would not escape, though I could not see, blind as I was, the extent of the pain his own agony would cause.

Not that I use such an easy alibi, the trauma of diagnostic despair, as reason for my subsequent actions. My lightness of mind, I will admit, did not leave me when I left the clinic and joined the populace of polyps out in Dapitan's sun. It was as if, now that my misfortune was settled, I was free to commit errands of distraction, missions of obscure mayhem in who knows which and whose direction? I felt the liberty of a leper and the fulsome feelings of a bandit recently released from jail.

I met again the blind Moro, first in line in her wondrous gown, and resisted the urge to embrace and swaddle her ample body with my affection—which was a good thing, as you know such fine thoughts could promote aggressive responses in unsuspecting persons. And *hers* is a suspicious tribe as we who've never lived with them ascribe. A crippled pair playing checkers, a tall boy praying with webbed fingers, and a palsied chorus of abridged disasters: plus a slew of blind mice. I passed them with the mute portions of my pity, distributing through my glances my useless form of love.

—What! Stop staring at me, *coño*! Haven't you seen a man without balls before?

---

486 The creeping unconscious of Raymundo Mata's debility bubbles into a pool of "knowledge." So much is at stake in our blindness, and so slight is the fulcrum of our release. Is that not so, Ms. Mimi C.? (Dr. Diwata Drake, Mesmer, Ohio)

Before the atesticular indecent Spaniard could kill me, I raced down the path beyond the sand.

Thus I wandered Talisay in a mania of inert passion, ready to give away my heart if anyone so pleased. Sure enough, I passed by Bulag, and my double's sanguine look of disrepair was enough to make my tears overflow, and I tried to pass off the sentimental moment by pretending I had kaingin ash in my eye. He said, as if he had not ignored me in the last hallucinatory hour: how'd you do, and all that, before hurrying on to the clinic—I realized he was also the medical orderly, bringer of ointments and hygiene commander—and good luck to us.

Adios ta, he called out to me, running: he was late for his job.

I passed the *buyera* with her weapons of forgetting, both the betel nuts and their slimy lime, and if only I had the money I would have bought a pound of her beat-up poison. She offered me good day but no credit in the cheerful generosity that marked Dapitan's folk, and I choked a grateful greeting in reply. Up past the beach I walked, straying so far I could now barely snatch the sight of sand from my screen of fruit-fallen trees. Everything was so lush out here in the promised land the mangoes lay rotting. Ditto the lanzones. Like the flies, I filled my lungs with their decadent perfume. I washed my body in a random stream, and I checked out my face in its pure mirror.

I was surprisingly unchanged, given the significance of the moment. I was exactly as I had been—reddish and wrinkled under my straw hat, with a small hill of a nose like my uncle's and my grandfather's crazy, wide-open eyes. Nothing special, except for my extravagant, admittedly bulbous brow, like my father's, which made my head look precarious, like his. In truth, I was nondescript and looked like any old mixed-up Filipino circa 1896, fresh from a bout of self-discovery and therefore bitter about fortune.

He had given me a receipt, an RX of rueful pablum in his tidy script. All through my walk, I clutched it in my hand, like an amulet.

Potassium iodide: 3 grams. Distilled water: 100 grams. To be taken one spoonful each morning. Signed. Now I looked at his signature. Finally, I had his autograph. For some reason I began sobbing like a baby, the way I had never sobbed before, the way I never would again. I felt my body rush out of me, and it sneezed out my soul. I wheezed and burped, and in my sorrow I exhaled the offal of rank fruit. The sounds and fruit pulp, the dregs of paho, that came out of me were pathetic, and to this day I have no idea why I wept.

There by the lanzones grove, I loitered. I wish I could say I passed it, that shuttered spot against the hill. I wish I could say I collected my senses and moved on. I didn't. I climbed the stairs of the closed kiosk.

Unlike the other constructions, it was a square affair, not pentagonal, diagonal, contrapuntagonal: just a squat straw box, barely five feet by five, natch. It looked more, in fact, like a halfway shack, a temporary fruit stall or one-night stand. I unlocked its useless door, bent my head, and went in.

Cobwebs, ants, the crumbly remains of formerly moist grass, a pile of grimy glass frames, papers. A dusty old bowler on a nail. A European umbrella. Papers. My livid eyes reverted to the sheaves of paper, a film of dirt already settled into a close reading of its fine lines. I walked over, as thoughtless as a marionette, and I recognized the slanted scripture, the clean sweep of his RX *r*, the critical *j*, his showboat *z*, medicinal *p*, and his liberal and garrulous *l*. An insect buzzed, and I swear, that index print on the dust, my first violation, was not intentional—I was only swatting at a fly. And my second touch, an awkward sampling, as of a brief, hesitant pinch, was only because, as you well note, one day objects may appear in the wrong shape or size and I will experience the loss of correct colors— though, who knows, peripheral vision will remain. Oh all right, I did: with index and thumb, I held up a dog ear of a page. I didn't lick it, I admired it, holding it up close to my ruined eyes the better to ravage a phrase. Then I read on, and on and on. I took page after page in my criminal hands. I perturbed and caressed and, sheaf after sheaf, word for word, I devoured. I penetrated and entered and sated my lust. There. Are you satisfied? I violated the pristine state of the hero's third novel. Not only that: I kidnapped it.[487]

---

487 Oh my God. *Brujo*. Is that true? Did he—Is that— (Estrella Espejo, ditto)

Entry #35

Even now, I feel them on me: a pair of bleak gray eyes. As I tucked the papers in, awkward and beribboned against my loins, into my finally useful, rapacious karsonsilyos, I felt the gaze of the weeping woman. But nothing, not even my silent conscience, would deter me. The clumsy sheaves themselves indicted my guilty ribs. I did note the fresh mound, a clump of earth with flowers about it, a memorial corona shaped like a cross on an interstitial grave that almost obstructed my path. It was situated—let me see if I remember this right, just in case the details of that purloined hour might one day be of use, though I doubt it—it was by the steps, in an opening beneath the hut just small enough for grieving. I remember the keening woman of my morning dreams, and I wasn't sure, in my delirium of flight, if those brazen eyes were in fact watching. I stumbled over it, the flowered patch of earth.

In my blindness, I almost, almost stumbled over it as I fled.

And now I return with lost foreboding to that moment back on the ship—when finally after my sawdust breakfast and faithless good-bye, the formal exchange of pleasantries and jars of preserved paho (plus secret gifts) between the two doctors, and our forlorn launch from that betrayed beach, we all climbed aboard our returned-to-sender ship, gaggle of revolutionaries carrying the weight of their finished business and already missing the mystic peace of the vanishing isle—I finally escaped their accusing eyes.

True, no one noticed my agitation nor the lumbering stiffness of my movements: each of the doctors was wrapped in his separate dilemma. Come to think of it, even in the best of moments, no one would have noticed me. Even Rufino brooded in his own manner, following Don Procopio and his new twirling cane.

I hid down in the hold where the cows bore me no grudges: and there, I threw my project on the straw. A pillow of magic. The

sheaves jumped from my tainted hands. I gazed at my catch, my pilfered fish—these were my grace, my curse, and my bounty. I'll show
them all, I had said, all those mestizos and priests and ladies—all the
astounded host. I'll show Lady K (but I will avoid the gaze of the
other's weeping gray eyes). What did I have to show? My shadow
sheltered those orphaned sheaves, now lifeless on the straw. I gathered them all again, in a bundle: burrowed in my petate. For those
five days, they breathed under the cows, explosive as kindling.

Up on the passenger deck, as I said, Don Pio walked about with
his new, fine kamuning cane. It was the hero's gift, exchanged for
Don Pio's pistol. Good riddance. With awe, Rufino looked out for
the *mago*'s cane during the entire trip, as if the stick were God's
subaltern.

He did not dare touch it.

Back on the shore of Manila Bay, when we got off the banca
and quarreled again with the criminal pilot, who wanted more than
his share of the passage as usual, being a Batangueño, all Don Pio
needed to do was rap on the boat's side with that kamuning cane—
its garish mouths swearing their silent oaths—and, swear to God,
the pilot was struck dumb.

So Rufino Mago tells the story.

Don't you know, Rufino crowed to the nonplused Don Pio, that
cane is *encantado ya*—that cane is magic!

The pilot took our small change, and without protest, without a
word, he left Don Pio to his not-so-scientific stupefaction.

But I was preoccupied, I did not notice. I understood something
had turned on that intolerable portage—as we sailed back through
Cebu, Capiz, and Romblon—this time devoid of the flatteries of
ladies, even of the smiling Segunda of our old *Venus*, who had abandoned ship around Jolo, we learned, but not without leaving (her
form of affection) an entire crate of castrated feathers to her faithful
castrated cook. For some reason on that journey the wind, a ceaseless unseasonal storming, burdened our days with a sense of failure,

though our mission, or so claimed Don Pio, hoping against hope amid the din, was not really entirely lost. Or maybe it's true that even in such details as harsh weather my conscience betrays me into imagining a damned deluge.

And yet—lash myself as I will, whip and batter that imp, my soul—still, I felt at the same time, yes, an odd terrible lightness. Even as I withered on that benighted ship: I carried in secret, against my bosom, that fledgling being: a novel. It scratched against my chest. It crackled as if alive. It breathed with me. That portage was intolerable—the way the absurd tempest of being is intolerable, the way the emergent hatchling of words, the slow reading of a story, is at times impossible to bear, and it's best to put it down. But I didn't. Across the country on that boat, I carried upon me, I guess, a pack of words: my own troubling war.

Part Four

﹌

The General in the Revolution

In which the hero chooses between Polonio and Patiño—
Contemplates virtues of pakwan—Receives a message from
"Leandro"—Escapes from Binondo—Comes upon ichthyological
Father Gaspar—Witnesses a zarzuela—Meets a milkmaid—
Arrives in Balintawak—Receives news from the bandit Matandang
Leon—Fights in the "Battle of Balara"[488]

---

488 More accurately, Raymundo fought in the Battle of Pasong Tamo, several leagues
away. His kleptobibliomania insisted on Balara because it is *alliterative*. Bastard! Klepto!
(Estrella Espejo, Quezon Institute and Sanatorium)

Entry #36

Like a novel revolution is never finished[489] [490] [491] [492]

---

489 The above is the statement as it appears in the original, in English, unpunctuated. Some interpretations, provisional, awaiting final edit, are the following:

a. subject-puzzle, fill in the blank: *Like a novel revolution, [ ] is never finished.* Trans. Q: Find the missing referent of the modifier "novel revolution"? But why?

b. convention, use splice: *Like a novel, revolution is never finished.* A comma should pierce the first two nouns, to correct the awkward notion, "novel revolution," which anyhow, without one more noun, renders the line ungrammatical. Trans. Q: Is the speaker speaking as i) a novelist, ii) a reader of a novel, iii) a revolutionary, iv) none of the above, v) all of the above, vi) etc.?

c. colloquial, annoying: *Like, a novel revolution is never finished.* Trans. Exclamation: *Basta!* (Trans. Note)

490 Nonsense. There is only one logical sentence. *Like a novel, revolution is never finished.* Period. How brazen! What gall! The blind criminal refers without shame to the novel he has just kidnapped: *Bastard! Klepto!* (Estrella Espejo, Quezon Institute and Sanatorium, Tacloban, Leyte)

491 And yet, come to think of it, is it true—*like a novel, revolution is never finished?* Maybe that explains why they call them *plots?* In short, the scourge of police states and props of fictionists are connected, at least in dictionary entries? Ay, Raymundo: *basta na!* (Estrella Espejo, ditto)

492 Aha! Just as I thought. English keeps creeping into the memoir. Excuse me once again if I disappear from these pages *for a while* until I finish re-reading with a fine-toothed comb, a magnifying eye, all the Entries presented so far. *PS: If you send me an email, please do not be offended by my automatic out-of-office reply: I'm re-reading.* (Dr. Diwata Drake, Kalamazoo, Michigan)

Entry #37[493]

Plot I: Two Pesos

The plot of Polonio took everyone by surprise though everybody knew about it. How could you not, when Polonio and his men all had the same bloody wound on their biceps and kept speaking in hand signals, like deafmutes, though none of them were deaf? That group of printers moved about for all intents and purposes like a tight-knit barkada, but in their case with dim Morse code tics.

No one would have minded their exclusive ways if they were a bit less—well, let's say, sensitive. They were a thin-skinned bunch who brooded over their afflictions so that each bruise was always raw, worse than Prometheus's liver. From my point of view, they celebrated their brotherhood with rancor that was a bit too vigorous. They would have nothing to do with me even after seeing me at that boat meeting in Antipolo.

They kept apart because I was friends with "Leandro," the boss's stooge, but what could I do? He was a pro-Spanish creep with a dozen children to feed, and he had given me the job. Sure, he had favorites, such as that weasel Patiño, he with the slick brilliantine hair and airs of an *ilustrado* (his sister was cute, though). In any case, I always knew I would never be their friend, because they were from Manila and I was from Cavite, which did not bisect it seems with any point on their triangles. Or maybe, as I began to consider it, it was I who was weird.

---

493 A series of entries in what seems like katakana, or Sanskrit, or who knows a wandering ancient Gaelic appeared crumpled up in the bin in which the Mata manuscript was rotting. Fortunately, I kept intact every piece of garbage in the tin, including cobwebs, two dead spiders, and a number of rusting Coke tanzans, circa the American postwar period. After lengthy study, sleeplessness, rationalization, I deciphered the mystery, inserted in this section of Part IV, The General in the Revolution, which otherwise contains mainly a number of finely handwritten pieces of a meandering sort, undated, though any student of history can tell the sequence of time.

The long-crumpled, newly deciphered message appears above. Oddly enough, Estrella, the writer named these aborted sections *plots*. (Trans. Note)

When I returned from Dapitan, I could breathe nothing of my adventure to any soul, to no rebel nor relative—no nothing, not even to a *puta* of Paco Dilao—Don Pio made me swear. There was no need to twist my arm. I had my own cross to bear. I did not dare to confide even in Rufino—and anyway, he went back home to Kawit, where I understand he's retailing a pack of tales about magicians, coming up with one fable after another for a few sticks of *La Insular* cigarettes.

Mostly, I kept to myself, more so now than before, though none of us at the *Diario* had ever been friendly. There's something about being a member of a secret society that makes you, well, secretive, surly, and morose. Or maybe morose men seek the comfort of cloaks and daggers. It's true that once Polonio, in a rare burst of curiosity, asked about "the visit." I showed him my druggist's receipt for potassium iodide. It was the medicine, I said proudly, that the writer-ophthalmologist had ordered. He was impressed. I, on the other hand, knew the vanity of my placebo, and I went home depressed.

I wonder what I looked like to men in those days. Did my bleary eyes give me away—I was sneaking off during siesta and returning with my disbelief under constant suspense. I was a nervous wreck, and I had the habits and heightened introspection to prove it.

I avoided my colleagues.

I was reading.

I kept trying to read the disheveled pages with the scarce daylight that I had, and it was enough to make anyone irritable. In addition, I was terrified of getting caught. At work I was clumsy and forgetful, and every time I misprinted a page or blotted some ink, I knew any kind of promotion was beyond my grasp.

The fuss over the appointment of a new foreman meant nothing to me, therefore—I could care less who was going to get ahead of whom, and how many measly centavos it meant to his daily bread. I was reading my stash in bits and pieces, and it was driving me nuts! I was in a state of arousal like one of those louts touching wild women in the market without proper reward. Those first days back at the *Diario*, I was spent in the passion of my labors with the secret novel and to be honest forgot the point of my existence.

I only grasped vaguely that something was up when one of Polonio's brothers (and mine, too, for I kept forgetting, in that wasteful time, that I, too, was a Son of the People) took me aside and asked me which man I chose.

—For what, I asked, confused.

—To be foreman, tanga! To get the raise from eighteen to twenty pesos a month.

—You mean, for two pesos more?

—Yes. Who do you pick? The katsila boss's man, that show-off Patiño, or Polonio, your brother who is more worthy?

—My brother, of course, I said.

I had no idea what he was talking about, and I thought fighting over two pesos was dumb, no matter how much lambanog it would get, plus, our boss was French, not katsila, but I didn't bother elaborating.

However, I had given the right answer, and he allowed me to leave for my break.

When I returned, "Leandro" took me aside.

—Who's the better man, he asked, the guy Polonio from Tondo, who has nothing to do with us, or the pious daily communicant Patiño, the choice of your countryman from Cavite?

—The choice of my countryman, of course.

I gave the right answer, and he let me go.

In that way, I could go on calmly reading the pages. I will admit: with a folly that to this day I cannot fathom, I had begun taking a few sheaves with me to the shop, and I read in the warehouse where I hid them in what I believed was a clever decoy pile amid mounds of soiled newsprint.

Now I remember the period in the newspaper bodega as a time

of mystical elation: I was wrapped in my halo of criminal reward. Mice, cockroaches, and lizards coexisted with my vermin understanding; dust, cobwebs, and ink-gas oppressed my breathing; and in that pulpy cave of papers, I was disturbingly conscious of being alive.

In reality, it was itchy, smelly, and unhygienic, and actually wasn't any good for my lungs.

All hell broke loose that afternoon, of course, and how was I to know my reply to my brothers was of such moment? I was about to leave. My stash was almost done. It had been harder to decipher the script than I had thought—especially since I did it in fits and starts, emerging from the dazzle of my abstraction into the drudgery of the printing shop; and by the time I was ready to set off for home, to which I could literally walk blind, such being the blessing of routine, twilight was falling, and it was impossible to read by gaslight. I admit I was getting reckless because my labors would soon be over. I was almost done with the novel. And most distressing of all, and I hate to say this—I felt dumb.

After all this time, I had no idea where the hero's story was going.

It seemed to me that the confused state of the narrative echoed the perilous conditions of my reading: a tenuous unraveling and a distracting multiplication of scenes and voices, even, to my annoyance, of languages and genres, as if the author had yet to settle on the merits of which attractions.

Not to mention: my eyes hurt.

Patiño arrived at the shop in a rage just as we were about to close. His hair's lunar sheen sparked with his madness, his saliva compounded with his pomade to send out oily satellites of his venom.

—Who's the thief? Who's the secret stealer from this shop?

My heart grew cold.

I froze in the middle of adjusting my trousers.

This was the question that, each day, I expected.

Who had discovered me, who knew my plot?

—What? Polonio's men cried to pale Patiño. You're the thief! Trying to be foreman when it is not your due!

As if at a signal they all began to clump together, joined against the greasy, raving printer.

It seemed to me a kind of ludicrous denouement was about to erupt from an invisible crisis that had completely passed me by.

—Liars! screamed Patiño, so agitated that tears streamed down his face. You'll get it for this!

Polonio, Letra, and Figura just smirked.

A broad figure appeared at the doorway: fat "Leandro," my countryman, who was waving an incriminating sheet of paper.

—Who wrote these lies, "Leandro" bellowed.

—Yes, who wrote the boss calling me a thief? Patiño screamed. I never stole blocks of types, especially vowels, and sheaves of paper from the press! Liars and schemers! I'll show you who's the secret conspirator in this shop! I know what you've been doing all these months. *Filibusteros!*

At this, people surrounded the plastered madman with the plastered hair. But before the rumble could begin, I snuck away, breathing freely.

No one knew, I sighed with relief: the pages were safe against my chest.

I was already in bed that night when I heard the knock at the door—his heavy breathing clued me to his presence.

I let him in.

The outlines of his figure, like an incipiently roasting pig, exuded sweat and gristle. He was panting.

—"Leandro"?

—I know you're part of their secret, he said.

—What secret?

—The lists. They found evidence of a secret society. Your printing stones, your ledgers, even the sums of your donations. God, what were you guys thinking—that you could win a war with one sikapat a month? Twelve centavos! A half of a quarter of a *real* among fools! You all make me want to cry. Hala ka, Mundo. They know your name.

—What are you talking about? I'm not with them, I said.

Technically, I was not lying.

I was signed up for the Kawit chapter, under Emilio's lead.

I had nothing to do with Polonio.

Miong and his men claimed my dues: twelve cents and a half[494] whenever I could hack it.

—Don't lie to me. Tonight the *veterana* confiscated the records your group hid in the printing shop. Stupid! Why a secret society would leave their papers *with names*, for God's sake, in a goddamned public place of business, only the devil knows! Padre Gil, the confessor of Tondo, reported you—with information from the pious daily communicant Patiño. That's what you get for sending poison letters when it's you who poison the land!

And he sounded—I could barely discern it—ineffably grieved.

—What are you talking about? "Leandro," get a grip!

"Leandro" looked ready to shit his pants.

—That damned Patiño!, I couldn't help add. That's what you get from going to church. Daily communicant, that dirty mouth! Daily informer is more like it! Anyway, my name is not on those lists! My name is on the lists of Kawit!

—Purbida! I knew it, Mundo. You know I didn't see the names, but I thought you were part of it—with your secret movements during siesta and those pamphlets you keep reading in the bodega when you think no one can see. *Hala ka!* You better get back home. Leave Manila. Go back to Kawit. They're arresting your people all

---

494 This is the sum of one sikapat. One kahati was twenty-five centavos, one salapi was fifty, et cetera. In January 1896, a few months before war began, the Katipunan raised the monthly contributions of its members from twelve and a half cents to fifty cents—see Entry #33 and Entry #38 for possible explanations. (Estrella Espejo, Quezon Institute and Sanatorium, Tacloban, Leyte)

over the place. Your poor uncle. After all he's done for you. You will break his heart.

He was practically crying, that good-hearted stooge. "Leandro" left as crazily as he had come. Even today, I wonder about him: how he had jeopardized the lives of his fourteen children to warn me to escape—loyal to his countryman to the end.

Of course, now I know it was "Leandro," along with that lout Patiño, who told on Polonio and his men (with the help, of course, of the cute sister). And that's how the government found out about the secret society, and that's how the revolution broke out before its time, before we could get the guns from the Japanese.

Over two pesos. And a pair of poison pens.

"Leandro" was right. It's enough to make you weep.

Entry #38[495]

Plot II: Twelve Melons and P14 Worth of Mangga

Okay, I was party to the following incident—but really, I partici-
pated only in the guise of one and a half melons. It was Santiago
who came to my door a day or so after I had disembarked from the
steamship *Venus*. He was carrying a bulging paper bag, soaking wet.

—What's that? I asked.

—It's the bloody head of the parish priest of Tondo.

—Padre Gil!

I had heard the rumors of the priest's possible assassination a
few weeks before—in the covert way secrets traveled Manila: like
the open rot of overripe fruit. *Chismes*,[496] as defined among revolutionaries and civilians alike, is a chronicle of deaths foretold or at
least hoped for. Everyone knew of the evil Spaniard who terrorized
his parishioners about infidel Masons and revolutionary bandits and
through the confessional bedeviled docile women into becoming
betrayers of their own (e.g., Patiño's cute sister). There was constant
debate even among the lowly brethren about which rat to kill first
when war broke out—Padre Gil of Tondo was a favorite.

—Did you kill him? I asked.

—Gotcha! that bon vivant Santiago answered, fondling the
paper bag. It's just a pair of pakwan, he laughed.

That joker Santiago, I have to tell you, was a connoisseur of
melons, figurative and otherwise. From the paper bag he took out
two mouthwatering gourds, one of which was already breaking apart
and spreading a red trail in my kitchen. I took out the bolo, my

---

495 This, too, was written in squiggles and aborted types—mostly numerals and what
seemed like semaphoric code and other odd morphological devices. I tried my best.
(Trans. Note)

496 Gossip: popular Filipino pastime. (Estrella Espejo, ditto)

ever-ready all-around weapon—I always kept it sharpened to perfection, you know, just in case. Just in case I have to defend myself
against the *cazadores*, or weed the garden, or go to war. You never
know.

I call my bolo *The Supremo*, a fond appellation.

I was about to hack the pakwan in half, but Santiago held up a
hand.

—No. These are for the Japanese admiral, from the boat that just
docked in Manila Bay. Want to donate? We're chipping in for gifts
to give the Japanese in exchange for their goodwill.

—You mean their guns?

—Well. Yes. We hope they'll sell us some arms for the revolution
once we scrape up the money. Didn't you get the memo—they're
raising the monthly contributions. To buy our arsenal from the Japanese. That's what the hero said—get guns, isn't that right, Mundo?

—I have no idea, I said, though flattered by his question, as if I
were in the know like a member of the Secret Chamber.

In fact, among certain circles, it seemed, I had at first held a privileged position when I came back, because I had been touched after
all by the hero. But when I refused to divulge any secrets (I acted as
if I knew it all, of course, and then afterwards kept up my silence for
my own good), they all dropped me like a warm watermelon.

—You know the Japanese are now fighting the white men
of Russia, Santiago explained. They're making us Asians proud.
They're sure to help us. Tagawa will introduce us.

—You mean the skinny waiter from the Japanese Bazaar in
Binondo?

—He'll get us on the ship.

—Good. Be sure to give him a nice tip. But your pakwan gift is
breaking apart. It's seeping from your paper bag.

—I know.

—The flies are all over it.

—I know.

—You may as well cut that cracked one into two. I mean, better one-half pakwan sliced nicely, rather than a whole one that looks like a mess. The Japanese are picky, you know. They're neat and tidy people.

—You're right.

—Well, we might as well eat this half. No use crying over one half of a watermelon.

—I know.

—Ah, the Japanese will love this gift. A tropical aphrodisiac. Do they have pakwan in Osaka? One piece of this paradise is sure to merit at least, I think, a third of a rifle!

—Who knows?

—And one half of a pakwan should be, let's see, two and a half pistols!

—Only two and a half? That's not a lot, said Santiago.

—Well, including the flies—maybe less.

—You think?

—I don't know. Only if this tastes as good as the other half.

—Well?

—Excellent! Fit for a Japanese admiral!

—You think?

—Well, maybe only for a first lieutenant.

In this way, I believe, we denuded the pair, dismantling barrels, cartridges and gunpowder, piece by piece, until only one sikapat of a pakwan was left, looking a bit wistful. And that, too, we demolished.

Santiago came back later in the day, this time with empty hands and the following announcement:

—Oh Mundo: it cannot be!

—The Japanese did not like the pakwan?

—They accepted it—twelve watermelons, plus a basket of mangga, worth fourteen pesos from our brother from Kawit, Kapitan Miong, plus a pleasant sculpture from the laborers of Laguna, among other gifts. We scraped as much as we could from our scattered brothers, who gave with all their hearts, God bless them. But they want—

—What?

—The Japanese want ten million pesos for a shipment of arms.

—Ten million pesos? Oh my sad rebellion![497] That's a lot of pakwan, I said.

---

[497] *Ang kawawa kong himagsikan.* Imagine the Tagalog is an irreparably more profound cry. (Estrella Espejo, ditto)

Entry #39

balimbing balanghoy baluno balete baloto balato bamboo banyan
bangungot bathala bahala bahal bohol betel bigti bugtong bagting
bagol bagaman bagacay balangay baluktot balintawak barumbado barasoain bungol buta bukaw buot buyog buyag bayag bulak
bulaklak bulan bungaw bangaw bangin bingi banga bungo bulaga
bulag[498] [499]

---

498 Raymundo's manic mumbling stumps me here, so I kept the original intact, above.
A charitable notion is that it's another of his word puzzles. Some patterns one might
note are: the vowel mutations [*i, a, u, e, o*] following the triad *bal* in the first five words;
the multilingual triplet [*buyog, buyag, bayag*], in which a testy bug transforms in vowel
increments into, well, a testicle; in short, one will find any number of patterns limited
only by the reader's cunning. It's the interstitial connections—what connects one pattern
to another—that baffles me. Most of all—why is he doing this when at that point history
is in the middle of the Cry of Balintawak??! (Trans. Note)

499 In the middle *is* the Cry of Balintawak—between *baluktot* (crooked) and *barumbado*
(troublemaker), toward Barasoain. In short, he traces in manic progress the wayward path
to the First Philippine Constitutional Assembly in Barasoain Church, Bulacan, in 1898,
which, as every scholar agrees, leads straight from the Cry of Balintawak, the opening shots of
revolution: which thus set up the first Asian republic, however shortlived. *El Grito de Caloocan*:
a.k.a. Cry of Balintawak, or Cry of Pugad Lawin (both Balintawak and Pugad Lawin are
place-names in the city of Caloocan) is the first event of the revolution. The Philippine
republic predates the Irish Uprising, the Bolshevik Rebellion, and inspired every volcanic
event in the colonial reaches of Asia, so there. Exact location and time (and even weather) are
still in dispute. Circa August 1896. Some people might simply prefer the more rebel-like Cry
of Pugad Lawin (literally, *Cry of the Hawk's Nest*) to the sissyish Cry of Balintawak (literally,
Cry of the Lady's Shoulder Vestment). However, whatever, the symbolism is clear. This is when
Bonifacio's revolutionaries begin the war, after the Katipunan's premature discovery following
a labor dispute in a printing press. Classic imagery has the cornered katipuneros gathering in
a rice field and crying out against the dogs of Spain while they brandished bolos and tore up
cédulas (residence certificates—similar in egregious function to identity cards required of blacks
in apartheid South Africa or immigrants in modern America). In reality, some memoirists
have pictured them soaking after swimming in swamps, no *cédulas* mentioned. Etc. etc.
    As for the other busy *b*'s above: I have one word for you, puzzler—b--s--t [*buwisit*].
(Estrella Espejo, Quezon Institute and Sanatorium, Tacloban, Leyte)

Bugtong:[500] what did the idiot call poems that repeat the sounds of initial consonants? Answer: Illiteration.[501]

Another bugtong: Into what language can you not translate a work translated from the Spanish? Answer: Spanish.

---

500 Bugtong = riddle: a form of indigenous Filipino wit. (Trans. Note)

501 Bugtong sated a thirst for mystery, wordplay, and philosophy. But what's a riddle doing in the middle of the revolution? (Estrella Espejo, ditto)

Entry #40

Even now when I recall my tossings and turnings that night, a fist of anxiety clenches in my chest and I feel winded. I left in the morning. Just to be safe, though I believed my name was not on their lists, I wound my way through Manila in the masque of a wandering laborer, carrying only a woven petate, papers stashed into it along with one pan de sal, and a pen. I wrapped [ ]⁵⁰² in my rags as I imagined fleeing Romans wrapped their cursed crosses.

The minute light crept down the esteros, I crept along with the silent hue, my slight figure one with the sonar tune of *lecheras* and *buyeras*, whistling guides whose untroubled faith in their routines' immortality gave off a creepy serenity to the morning. Happily, I followed the charms of one maiden, sleeve of her cotton camisa flopping over her merry pails, showing a tanned and lacquered arm, a burnished shoulder.

Sunlight warped her golden figure like a medieval mandorla about her dress and suggested, in its caress, the innocence of Filipino womanhood. Just kidding. That's in the portrait book *Tipos Filipinos*, full of stereotypes. In truth, this lady had sores on her legs and shoulders and face, like the ravages of midnight sin—worse than a trail of mosquito bites, even from a distance.

"*Leche!*"⁵⁰³ she yelled at the morning.

How is it that one's loins perk up at the most inconvenient times, even at the unlikeliest sights, shooting up like little muskets? Things fired up inconveniently at her hustling cackle, but I sensed she would have nothing to do with one who looked like an escapee from the

---

502 A crossed out phrase blots the manuscript here: "my sacred belongings"? "my Sacred Heart"? Something sacred. (Trans. Note)

503 I.e., *milk*: a Spanish curse. Just as Filipinos might have a hundred variations on the word *rice*, Spaniards play infinitely on the nuances of the word *milk*, and who knows why Spaniards hate their mothers?! (Estrella Espejo, Quezon Institute and Sanatorium, Tacloban, Leyte)

polo, though she herself looked like a guest from the *islas de conva-lescencias*. Anyway, I couldn't waste my money, not even for one nip of her creamy, I mean tip of her dreamy—oh, what the hell, she was gone before I could unscramble my cheek from my nasty tongue.

There is something about the empty roads of a bustling city that presents fake balm to troubled hearts. When I stepped into the café at the corner and saw him, I knew, however, that fate had a plan for me.

—*Hijo*, he said.

A dark scrawn, a bit humpbacked, or finned: in the shadows, a lone abalone drinking barako.

It was my old Latin teacher, Father Gaspar of the Ateneo Municipal.

He was, as I said, a sad ichthyological shamble, and I swear it was as if he had not moved from the suspicious shallows of our last meeting, when he had offered me the book.

What had happened to him since? I had heard rumors of him here and there, disparate conjectures of his allegiance depending on the politics of the dubious source. Whether he was a spy, a brother, or a double agent, a few claimed to know for certain though none had any proof. He was an obscure person of privilege, and his status as a native priest of Butuan in the Jesuit conclave still gave off that odd conjunction of both pathos and pride.

But at the café he looked simply the person he was, an addled professor: wizened, with glum fishy eyes. I understood that he still shuttled back and forth from the Jesuit dominions of his native south, and his long overdue book on Philippine fishes of the Sulu Sea had finally reached *bacalao*. Now the astronomical tower in Intramuros kept him busy, where he with a bunch of other mad amateur explorers scanned the heavens from an increasingly tenuous perch in the Spanish walled city, trying to gain perspective from the seat of power: a doomed project, in short, though some say their science was decent enough for men who believed in God.

The fact was, I felt guilty about not having looked him up at all in the years after school, after the book—but then my life had turned so different from my expectations. Instead of a scholar, I'd become a skunk. I stood before him a stinking paragon of slime: stealer, klepto, ravisher.

But I felt this déjà vu, a whip of recognition.

—*Balangay*, I said to the old man on a hunch.

—*Marikit*, he replied, without skipping a sip.

It did not surprise me when the waiter announced, fist pumped in the air: *Malamig!*

And then in chorus, raising their cups, a pair of *polo* laborers in workers' fatigues, sang: *Mabuhay! Viva!—GomBurZa!* (Repeat 3x)[504]

They kicked up their feet in unison, scattering some coffee beans.

A slapdash portrait, more an impression than an image, rose curtain-like against the café's walls. A somber man in European clothes, mustached, top-coated, in a three-piece suit, gazed down at me with an ethereal nod, already missing his kamuning cane.

He had that diagnostician's look, the shrewd accusing upturn of his lips, and at that moment, I fell into a swoon.

I woke up to the faint smell of crème brûlée. Women were dancing about, their dresses merging to unfold a flag, panels in gold and gules with the hoist of a Spanish crest (crowned lion by gilt masonry) that dissolved into pirouettes of stars and stripes that blinded my watering eyes. Then in a trice, confounding my guilty eyes: a can-can flourish, and I raised my spectacles to see. The ladies posed in adorable *plié* to show peekaboo bloomers in

---

504 *Balangay* (ancient Tagalog term for unit of community); *Malamig* (cool); *Marikit* (pretty); and *GomBurZa* (Gomez-Burgos-Zamora): all Katipunan passwords. In addition, a portrait of Rizal in a three-piece suit adorned Katipunan places of ritual. Shows you that no matter what they say of Rizal as American-era hero, it's the katipuneros who made love, or hay, with Rizal! (Estrella Espejo, ditto)

piquant ruffles—and before I could grasp at them they blazoned: the scarlet ground of a secret flag, with the letters *K* in triplicate, argent against bloody field—one letter each on a showboat triplet's showboat rump!

I will admit it was a rousing play, punctuated by gongs from gamelan, kulintang, and other exotic forms of random percussion, with Muslim geishas swishing gigantic abanikos, creating useless movement, as fans do, like roosters in abortive death-moves. A head-hunter going out of his head lunged in staccato irrelevance and soon enough wild painted men in yodeling poses stretched out their arms to the unfurled flag, now gyrating amid a row of bumping behinds, while to the side women with bizarre candles on their heads displayed the perfection of their balance with enchanting nonchalance.

So much was going on in the pantomime display I was dizzy from the demands on my praise, and once again, I swooned.[505]

When I came to, all I could do was applaud, but the chorus drowned out my feeble noise.

Damn, damn, damn the insurrectos!
Cross-eyed khaki ladrones!
Underneath the starry flag,
Civilize them with a Krag,

---

505 I enjoy those anti-American zarzuelas, don't you? My golly, but why is he in the American era already? The Cry of Balintawak of the First Phase of the Revolution hasn't even happened. Anyway, I want to say our ingenuity gives me pride, how we used the old colonist's spectacle of song-dance-and-drama to meet our needs—especially since in the American era you could not raise the rebel flag, and so actors enfolded it in dancing vaudeville skirts. And then how Filipino flair indubitably improves the thrilling conventions of Spanish folk operetta! The pandanggo sa ilaw is the acme of Filipina dancing talent, don't you think? *Isputing!* That's grace under pressure for you—balancing candles on your head! Don't care much about the fans; they're Southern. But where's the tinikling, delicate boogie with bamboo, the epitome of talent of Filipinos on tiptoe? And the dance of the ricebird, what a romp! However, planting rice is never fun—you can say that again! Whoa—why does that racist hymn occur amid this fine display? Oh stuff my ears with a kundiman, won't you, and dress me in a patadiong and balintawak! (Estrella Espejo, ditto)

And return us to our beloved home![506] [507] [508] [509]

A bit of a panic ensued on stage, as it occurred to the singers that they had the lyrics to the wrong song. A flurry of scripts and operatic gestures, accusing fingers pointing at the bewildered strings, the rondalla (infantile rotund bandurria, and passive octavina, and guitar gazing at its navel in indifference, while bass attempted, in vain, to blend in without calling attention to itself). The rondalla struck a note of anguish, rapidly squashed under its own steam. The chorus resumed:

Damn, damn, damn the *cazadores,*
They say they come to crush the lawless
But no crime-fighters, they—

---

506 This is the racist refrain from the racist "Soldiers' Song" sung at least three years later by racist American GIs in the Philippine-American War, one of many racist wars in that racist country's history, and who knows when those racists will ever stop. (Estrella Espejo, ditto)

507 Calling a spade a spade, aren't we, Estrella? *PS: If you send me an email, please do not be offended by my automatic out-of-office reply: I'm re-reading.* (Dr. Diwata Drake, e-mail, out-of-office reply)

508 Calling a bolo knife a bolo. The American war is out of place in this section, for after all Raymundo has yet to join the Supremo at Pugad Lawin; get mixed up with his old friend Santiago in Cavite; with the Magdiwang take the towns of Noveleta and Imus but not his native Kawit (taken by rival Magdalo, led by old friend Miong, whose band by rights he should have joined); live with horror through the Supremo's murder by old friend Miong's men; guide Miong's men along the bat caves on the path to Biak-na-Bato; become a general with the remnants of the Katipunan for his spectacular ability to creep into all the recesses of Cavite's caves, just like a bat; live in seclusion in Kawit until the Americans invade; join the millenarian colorum with his old prious friend Benigno; and lastly fall to the G.I.s, one of whom seems to have secretly provided paper in Bilibid jail for this story.
This song "Damn, Damn, Damn the Insurrectos" is the touchstone of tragedy in the Philippine-American war. Two hundred thousand Filipinos dead in the American war, and that's just civilians, not soldiers. Aha—I get it. Raymundo's going nuts in that American jail. I guess it's true that he was victim of both Spaniards and Americans, and as he is being tortured by G.I.s he comforts himself with sugar plum visions of Filipino culture dancing in his head. (Estrella Espejo, ditto)

509 Hold on, Estrella: I'm re-reading. I'll get back to you on this when I'm—
PS: If you send me an email, please do not be offended by my automatic out-of-office reply: I'm re-reading. (Dr. Diwata Drake, e-mail, out-of-office reply)

Really, they're chicken stealers and cow-rustlers, hey! (*Repeat 2x*)

Refrain:
Call them *cazadores*—that's a lie:
Saviors and law-enforcers, my eye!
Sock it to me, *sacadores*—
You're just a bunch of extortionists and whores![510] [511]

Hey, *sacadores*—give us back our cantaloupes,
Tomatoes and watermelons! *Cazadores*: you leave us
With nothing—not even a shred
Of dignity.[512] [513]

---

510 This metaplasmic wit—*cazadores* (i.e., Spanish law enforcement figure; literally: hunters) sarcastically turned into *sacadores* (extortionists, but also implying plain *akyat-bahay*, petty thieves)—seems lifted from the Supremo Andres Bonifacio's classic poem "The Cazadores," through which his Tagalog's elastic playfulness shines. Maybe Professor Estrella can expand? (Trans. Note)

511 "Seems," Mimi C.? Ehem. I'm going through Entry Number— *PS: If you send me an email, please do not be offended by my automatic out-of-office reply: I'm re-reading.* (Dr. Diwata Drake, e-mail, out-of-office reply)

512 Gladly, Mimi C. The Tagalog poetry of the Katipunan Supremo, the Great Plebeian and Martyr Andres Bonifacio has a folkloric wit that mirrors the authentic voice of Filipinos. His was an idiomatic force, an unadorned candor that spoke directly to the ordinary man: "*Mga kasadores dito ay padala/Sanhi daw sa gulo'y lilipulin nila/Ngunit hindi yaong kinikita/Kundi ang mang-umit ng manok at baka.*" The pungent verb, *mang-umit*, is comically mocking—and untranslatable: it evokes the pettiness of Spanish *cazadores'* banditry and grievous constancy of that larceny. Bonifacio understood that the war was as petty citizen revenge against petty officials as it was an august ideological battle. His emphasis on common matter—watermelons and other gourds—to talk about centuries of grievance is a stroke of revolutionary wit aimed at the gut to get at abstract tissue: nationhood. Despite what *ilustrado* scholars say—*damn damn damn the ilustrados!*—I submit that it is Bonifacio's Tagalog, much more than Rizal's Spanish, that stiffened revolutionary fervor. One might even say that Rizal's brooding poem, *Mi Ultimo Adios* (not yet written at this point in the plot, but anyway—ultimately *Mi Ultimo* was a text of individualist languor and indulgent sentimentality, with apostrophes in the end not to the Motherland but to the mistress!) fired up revolutionists because of Bonifacio's Tagalog translation. Sure, the authorship of the Tagalog version is disputed by disgruntled foreigners—but who cares about them? (Estrella Espejo, ditto)

513 To resurrect the Tagalog of Bonifacio, do we need to denigrate Rizal's Spanish? Just asking, I'm just a grad student, not yet even a.b.d. (Trans. Note)

And then, in the midst of this ebullient potage came a voice: I tried to gather the source of grace—where amid the pageant's scuttling shadows did the brief note arise? I could not, the instant I heard it, trace its pure trajectory, and perhaps for that reason it seemed to emerge from the awful tremor of my own bones. The voice was sweet, pained. It spoke dirge and demand. It ordered my confusion. It was as if, in the moment of its expression, an aimless hope came into shape.

You've heard the words before: you've sung the song. It asks a simple question: *Aling pag-ibig?*[514][515] You have no reply, not because the question proposes your answer. It is precisely the speaking of it that creates grief: the need to speak is the sorrow. These were not, of course, reflections I pondered while the voice rang, ending in a kind of sepulchral echo in my heart's chamber.

I was a runaway printer, after all, carrying a straw mat stuffed with stolen papers. I had no right to be moved. And yet I stood before Father Gaspar on that morning with a burst of love. Abstract, unfamiliar. It was, to be honest, an intolerable thing; I was a fatling in patriotic lard, a rice cake simmering in the saturated oils of a congested heart. It was a not so healthy state and yet the only one in which, at the moment, I could exist.

---

514 "Which love—?" The statement, in Tagalog, occurs in Raymundo's text as an anacoluthon: an interruption suggests the reader's knowledge of what follows. Perhaps Professor Estrella can expound? (Trans. Note)

515 Gladly. The Bonifacio poem, "*Pag-ibig sa Tinubuang Lupa*," popularized in a copy of *Kalayaan*, the Katipunan paper that sadly went through only one issue, aborted by the secret society's discovery, and now who knows where all those vowels went, begins with the question: *Aling pag-ibig pa ang hihigit kaya . . . Gaya ng pag-ibig sa tinubuang lupa?*: "Which love is greater . . . as love for the native land?" A beautiful plaint, yet to be answered. *Tinubuang lupa*, a reflexive construction, strictly translated as "land [ ] grew up in" or "land [from which one] grew," is the newly uprising Nation, the cult around which revolution springs. As I've noted: this explosion of feeling, worded in poem and acted in battle, in 1896 is unprecedented in Asia's colonized lands, and I still have no idea exactly how we fostered it. Except that, when I was a child during the Marcos regime compelled to be a "fatling of patriotic lard" daily during morning flag ceremonies at school, I, too, loved that feeling in my heart and wanted to kill communists or something. (Estrella Espejo, ditto)

—*Hijo*, repeated Father Gaspar. What brings you here?

He was reading the morning's papers with the apparent look of a professor extracting rhetorical silver from difficult propositions. One could sense his tense suspicion. As I said, he looked a bit like his fishy obsessions, a grilled tuna or lapulapu, with dead eyes and peeling skin; his veins pulsed about his forehead as if he were in simmer, glimmering in a pan.

—What's the news, Father?

—At twelve midnight, on August 30, the country will erupt in revolt. The Supremo's men will move to take the powderhouse of San Juan. You must look for the Supremo now. Lights will go out in the Luneta at precisely midnight, to signal the men of Cavite across the Bay to take up arms. Find the Supremo, but don't go by the roads: the Guardia Civil is on the lookout for foolish men like you.

—Bless me, Father.

—Move on. Go. Remember, my child: nothing exists without an observer.

Entry #41

The *lechera* kept going about her business, and I followed.

I did not go by the horse carriage roads. As Father Gaspar had instructed me, obedient, I crawled by the ricefields and swam under mangroves.

And I went by cover of night.

Yes, I, Raymundo Mata, with degenerative macular morbidity, and the nyctalopia will only exacerbate: I wound my way through the wilds of Dulumbayan, Calubcub, and Bilarang-hipon, the oasis of Balic-balic and groves of Manggahan—I went my way without sight. I edged beyond the kalesa paths, across palay harvests, sapa, and streams. I ranged like the Cyclops and roved more or less like three-legged Oedipus; I did not sing like Homer. I have a dark, empty area in the center of my vision but an acute sense of sound. No, it's not that. I don't know if I can call it sound, or even sense—how do I put it?

It was not my body that had the ability to hear. It was the world that revealed itself to me.

I can hear the touch-me-not close. It shudders, a brief pitch that sends with pain its signal of shyness. And the shattering ripple of the dragonfly as it touches the timid plant that closes in on itself like a book: that, too, announces itself to me. I hear not only the swish of wings, but the width of places, the secret measures of my walk. And it is in this way the world becomes itself as I move. Gust of wind, crackle of stone, and there—the lightness of her walk.

—What are you doing?, she asked.

—What are you doing?, I asked.

—I'm minding my business, she said.

—I'm minding mine, I answered.

I followed the wisp of her skirts toward a clearing. No one was around.

Leonor the Lovable reeked of lime and tobacco, the residue of her full day's work. Her tongue was gastric red from the acid of her buyô, and there was something itchy about her. Neither of us had washed. An old woman, or maybe a girl withered to a lifetime of calamity: her body was this scrabble of scabs. She was soft in hidden places. She took me into her, she did not struggle. Her skirts smelled of piss and her blouse of cow. I smelled worse. Before sound turned into morning I was already a pig.

I don't know what it is about me that I contain nothing but semen and words. Because the writer died while he was writing. My lechery with the *lechera* inflames me even now; we had no doors to lock, and she moaned in the moonlight with the milk in her loins completely free. That rare and radiant maiden, whom the angels named.[516] Maybe she was sixty-three; maybe she was twenty. In the nighttime she was wrinkled, like the score of lines on a mother-of-pearl; in the daytime I wished her to look young, like my mother. She didn't. She had the look of the woman she was: a pockmarked soul, I thought.

And I was a humping hunchback.

Once more let me digress, admit one last thing: I would never have found him, the Supremo, if not for that *lechera*, rare and radiant, whom the angels. On that morning far away in Binondo, after I stepped out of Father Gaspar's dim bar—it was her gait that had called me, but in the end it was she who took me home. Leonor lived in Sapang Palay, though her routines and her resourceful modes of living splayed her skirts all over—through Tutuban, Sulucan, and Uli-uli, through Caloocan, Mandaluyong, and San Juan. As I said, I had left Father Gaspar to his erudite mysteries, pumping him as much as I could for information, and getting only enough, not much.

I understand a few days later the Spaniards tried to do the same, but that's another story I'd rather not inhabit, as it seems that if in

---

516 . . . *la doncella rara e iluminada, por los ángeles llamada* et cetera. A free translation. (Trans. Note)

fact I have a soul (whatever is left of it now in this numb ravening dungeon), I feel, that mite, my soul—I feel it tear up in little pieces when I remember what the Spaniards did to Father Gaspar.

When I woke up and saw her, my lost Leonor—I leapt up from the grove—one more body among the banyans after the Battle of Balara.

Entry #42

I was not a literal hunchback, of course. Where am I? No, it was later, after I met the rare Leonor, that I carried the suitcase of the Katipunan shaped like a medical bag. Like Dr. Pio's mendacious kit, the one he carried on the trip to Dapitan. Right—why should you remember? That doctor, Dr. Faust, the one who irritated me no end, carried this quack doctor's bag all around Dapitan. Well, not really: the porters and the servants carried it. His mimicry of the other one, the Doctor to whom we traveled, for whom I traversed, was so patent to me he could have been carrying a banner along with his kit: *Where he is there shall I be!* What a buffoon. God, I hated his guts. Anyway, there I was, carrying that bag like his on my back, like a man with gout, an inverted glut, like a uterus, behind me. Who knows whose it was?

A child *a posteriori*.

How did I get it? Where am I? I fell into my grave with a witch. Or in a ditch with a brav— Whatever. When Matandang Leon fell, Captain Carbuncle, as they called him, in the battle of Balara, the first battle, by the way, of the revolution,[517] albeit accidental, but then all of them were accidental, now that I think about it—I caught this weight falling upon me. No kidding.

We had just come out into the sun, kind of drunk, for what does one do after tearing one's *cédula* and crying out Fire before jumping into the goddamned frying *pandemonio*, you said it, of freedom?

One drinks.

Where was Leonor?

Anyway, our throats were dry from all that crying, we needed the refreshment.

---

517 Various commentators have already noted this error: Pasong Tamo is more likely the first battle, when the soldiers of drunken Matandang Leon were surprised by the *veterana* soldiers near Tandang Sora's farm; it was days later that Bonifacio fled to Balara. Why Raymundo persists in this error is obvious: he was losing his mind, drowning in his excrement and being lapped by dogs in the G.I. prisons of Bilibid, *damn damn damn damn etc.* (Estrella Espejo, ditto)

On Father Gaspar's orders, nay, his faith, yes, I had gone off and finally joined the Supremo—when, where, why, what the heck, who wants the details, since so many others have already provided their versions (at least seven, if you don't count the liars) of the reunion, which none of them got right.

Father Gaspar's directions, though sketchy, were sufficient. After all, I was a man of the *Diario*, an all-around man—before you even touch the Minerva machines, you start off as a paper boy with the routes of the city on the back of your hand. Where else could people hide but in places we didn't reach, among farmers and laborers beyond the walls? The perisylvian canals and thatched palay penumbras could only lead me to the swamps and leeches of their gallant dens.

I knew where to go.

Sure, it is best, in the annals of revolt, to make shortcuts and cut out the crap—apostrophes to the divine, expository introductions of brave men who heeded the call to arms, classical-like enumerations of Achaean ships, plus the boring roll call of names that retell the lives of their fathers, semi-literate though classical thugs, with too many causes, as well as all the tragic epithets on the sad provincial provenances of the soon-to-be-dead.

But still it would be nice to introduce a few sterling men with rhetorical flourishes, and not simply a brief, opportune sigh for Matandang Leon—obscure and, as you've noted, unpremeditated in my story.

But to return.

I came upon him, the Supremo, in the middle of a meal, of all things, like Jesus Christ amid his disciples, except Christ had only a dozen. While *he* had a few hundred, some well-dressed, some barefoot, all welcoming me as if I were exactly who I was—not Barabbas, the other one.

It wasn't really a supper, as you know the word—some smartaleck had hacked a wandering nag, or was it a castrated bull of a carabao, into pieces, and we ate scorched horseflesh, or some irredeemable hijacked hide, upon wet banana leaves. Another fine son of the people had "found" a jug of tuba.[518]

I was moved by my welcome. At that point none of us hungry and hunted men, after that discovery of names in the La Font printing press, knew when our next meal would be, and still they gave me rest and food without a word. They were barefoot and filthy, soggy and unarmed. They were scared, tired, and intolerably happy. You know, I have survived on kangkong and insects, the fruit of the narra and one bat, and once I had lived in the ruined boardinghouses of genteel Binondo, where Señora Chula treated dinner as not so much a meal but a religious rite, and at home in Kawit my uncle used to be an assistant priest, with a fine table and always at least two lechon at fiesta, and only a few months before I had dined on pickled paho with the gentleman hero in Dapitan.

But when I came upon the men of the Supremo once more, I felt like weeping. I felt, well—really really hungry. And as I dug into the hide and ate the flesh, it was the only time in my life I understood the meaning of communion.

Don't ask me about how I got on with the sons of the people.

They got me drunk.

—Your father was a good man, Matandang Leon said, his tongue slurring, his face a blur.

It was late at night, and I had no idea who this horse-faced general was.

---

518 Raymundo seems to conflate two incidents here, the "feasts" before the Cry of Balintawak, and the haphazard rustling-cum-butchering of stray animals and other forms of theft during the starvation-ridden, swamp-swimming escapades of the rebels as they ran and hid from the Guardia Civil. In truth, between battles many of the rebels went back to their hometowns, kind of going on recess, to resume their duties as tax collector or plowman, and rejoined the war *kapag tumawag ang himagsikan*: when revolution called. A grueling schedule, and honestly few could hack it; some just stayed home, hiding with their carabaos, which by then were dying of the rindpest, an incidental plague that also contributed to the failure of the rebels' war. (Estrella Espejo, ditto)

—But the man was an odd one, Matandang Leon said, *el genio Jote.* All of us bandits respect him, don't worry.

I know that in any knot of Filipinos, bound by one thing or another, in our case Masonic-type rituals of bloodletting, reverent displays of skulls, and distinct notions of masculine valor, et cetera, it is possible for your genealogy to produce, I mean proceed you, and it is as a preexisting condition that you arrive, full-blown in your familial tumor, so that everyone embraces you into the fold and wonders when you'll turn out crazy like your dad.

The drunk old bandit Matandang Leon, he of the flaming carbuncle and the fearless march, insisted that he knew my father.

I should have trusted this strange man's confession, a monumental revelation fit for its own paragraph and best enclosed in a glass case.

But I hate to say—Matandang Leon did not have a look of probity. I mean, he was a bandit. True, he dominated the old lady's yard[519] with his muscular bulk—a well-hewn man of above average endowment. God, I wondered what it was like to be him—how many women could he have on his good nights? But this was not one of those good nights. His eyes were bloodshot, and his notorious *carbunco*, sure to be written up in song, if the fates have any sense, glowed like a red glistening jewel on his forehead and blinked at me like his third evil eye. Veins and dried pus festered at his wound as if the carbuncle were some geological mass, a dormant volcano, and his veins were the prehistoric clusters that witnessed its age. The unwashed wildgrass hair, the betel breath, the way he tore into the horse's hoof like a tikbalang, a repulsive cannibalistic sight—I know these details are irrelevant, but they grossed me out.

Matandang Leon turned out to be one of those susceptible

---

519 Some say the host of the revolutionaries in the days leading to revolt was the old lady Tandang Sora, a generous farmer; others say it was some unnamed gentleman with a huge granary near what is now Quezon City. Here, Raymundo adds his two cents. (Estrella Espejo, ditto)

alcoholics—one drink and he was gone, as if drunkenness came from auto-suggestion, like a curse from a manggagaway.

When as a boy I longed to know of my father, I imagined the news reaching me as a bugle call from noble messengers, telling me the *principe* of Asturias had knighted him for his deeds. Not really, but still, I wished for a better news service, not this drunk with a bukol.

Why the Supremo chose Matandang Leon to lead us was a mystery, though I bowed to his intelligence, of course. I can't tell you what a relief it was to see him again, the Supremo, and to show him my stash. No matter the shame. But he was kind of busy, what with starting the revolution and all—I could not get a word in with him. Even now I wonder, after all these years, what the hell he was thinking when he went off to Cavite in November and left these men from Manila—who loved him, loved him, loved him so?[520] I stood apart from them, that's true, carrying my ragged straw bundle, a bit like those pictures of the disciples' last dinner, with the irrelevant, hungry dog in the foreground, and divinity recessed.

But that night in August we crowded round him like locusts, or bees driven to their maker, dancing in their hive.

Yes, I would never have found him, the Supremo—where am I?—for whom do I write?—to what does my mind regress?—if not for that *lechera*, rare and radiant, whom the angels. Some would say Leonor the milkmaid wasn't much to look at, that morning I found her in a ditch, after the meeting with Father Gaspar, before I heard the clarion of Matandang Leon. No, not much to look at, I will admit—plus she had a nasty temper, worse than a wife's.

It's true, our first coupling was not worthy of a man, and even less of a woman, given that, technically, I would call it, without her urging, rape. I followed her, and she let me, but even so I am a craven ghoul. Even now I am not sorry, though even then I knew I was no

---

520 Sure enough, outside Manila, in Cavite, they ate him up alive. (Estrella Espejo, ditto)

good. The hounds of war at my heels, the roar of semen—ah, it's all semantics, *technically*, a pretty drooling of words that disguises that raw burst of freaking manhood as other than what it was, my brute failure at being a man.

I followed her that morning because—because—I preferred to get lost. I confess. I didn't think so then, because I was busy spilling it, but it makes more sense to spend seed than blood. I'm not much of the hero type. I mean, I'm fucking blind. Being with Leonor, with her leper body and her milky wounds, was by far, if you think about it with any kind of rational thought, an infinitely better alternative to killing other people. Really. I'd rather fuck a leper than go to war. That's just common sense. I know, I know—the Spaniards were our enemies. But I'm just not a killer. I'm not even much of a rapist, as critical Leonor later smirked.

Really, I'm just a reader.

To be honest, I do not know if I would have gotten anywhere in this story if Leonor had not, in the end, kicked me out of her house.

Let me say, once more. With injustice I call her, lime of my life, slip of my tongue, light of my dungeon, a leper, when it is I who should hold this awful sign—*do not touch*.

I'm a wordy, worthless beast.

There is only one whose happiness I think of in these dying hours—in this dim bat cave of a jail, this prison of our last solitude— let me not kid myself, these days don't look good, what with my friend Benigno laid out like a cross on a watered floor, somewhere in this maze of torture chambers that we share, here in the American hell.

My powers are waning but my memory engorges in terrible moments, especially when I smell my blood, crunch of salt on my chin in this churlish cell: and my spleen does not feel so good either. Oh, Americans of easy fame, we of easy faith: and here I am of uneasy fortune, waterlogged, mangled, and so they say losing my sight if not my mind: oddly enough, I see more clearly now than I ever have before, remembering Leonor.

More paper, please, G.I. man with the fat and thin weapons, skinny rifle on my skinned skin, fat pistol on my fatted scars: I throb but write.

It's my own rebellion.

I like to imagine she sits somewhere in the sunlight out there, in Pangasinan or Panay, mixing tahô or selling planggana, hawking all kinds of harmless mixed-use wares out by Balintawak. I wish her among a brood of children and a good man by her side, preferably clear-eyed.

Leonor, here's looking at you, if I might be allowed to use that verb: I hope providence, though blind, treats you well.

It was not I who told her my secret: the blasted woman goddamned stole it from me.

She'd gone through my belongings as I lay asleep, and as if in a dream, she thrust the papers at me like a sword.

—*Sonomagun! Ispichoso!* You're one of them—you're carrying secret papers and rebel documents! *Plibestiro!*

—*Filibustero*, I corrected her.

Of all people, it is the *lecheras* and the *buyeras* and the *putas*, and it wasn't clear to me if Leonor was one or all of the above, who know of the comings and goings of furtive men, who understood clues of suspicion like goddamned sybils.

Leonor and her companions must have understood the inevitable outbreak of war months before we all recognized it ourselves. The secrets of the sleeping city are laid bare to those who trek through the labyrinths before we awake and after we lie in bed. And even now I am not sure if Leonor was one of the above some of the time or all of the above most of the time—I only know she had a walk and a look that marked her as a marvelous, ambiguous wreck.

In any case she had an understanding finer than that of a spy, who's a mere pawn in the business, after all, while she is a powerful invisible eye: she's a woman.

At first, when she discovered the manuscript, she would have nothing to do with me.

—Tell me what these are? she screamed.

—They are the hero's pages, I said in a panic as she beat me up in her sad hovel.

—How dare you—endanger—my poor mother!

I didn't even know she had one, and worse that she had all along been that limp hump in the corner of the room, never stirring, like a sack of copra, while we did the nasty thing!

—My ma does not need more pain!

But she's barely alive, I thought, my God, she's as animate as a bandehado, sleeping through your racket! How much suffering can a corpse take?

—Please don't twist the papers, Leonor, please. That's the hero's novel.

—What hero, you worm, you thug, you pimp?

—The hero. Doctor Jose Rizal.

—Oh. My. God.

I thought she would pummel me right then when I said his name, maybe even drag her sleeping rag of a mother into the fray, to beat me up with the lump of her ma.

—Don'tyouknowtowritehisnamedownisacrimeandtospeakitisac urse? Toownhisbooksisstupidandtoreadthemisworse?

And so on and so forth in a burst of mellifluous malediction, and I could have mentally corrected her unforeseen prejudice or at least praised her rhyming run-ons if I had not been in such a bind.

Leonor held the sheaf of papers hostage in her mad hands.

I did not keep my eyes off them for a minute as she wailed and flailed.

I waited for the moment to snatch them, but it was a delicate issue, as I had to do it without harm to my quarry. I tried not to move as she cried, so as not to provoke the wrong gesture. My God that lady had a temper and a tongue. She was quite magnificent, if you discount her missing teeth and garlic breath, plus the way the buyô had coated with a reddening rust the rest of her dental squalor.

But you know, even her sores to me had an odd luminescence as I watched her fury, as if each scab and pockmark had some glory, and all I had to do was connect the scary dots and find my way home, or at least trace somehow, even if only by phonemic dabbling, her crooked symmetry into stars.

Then she calmed down and asked:

—So what are we going to do?

It did not occur to me then that the sweetness of the word—the word "we"—would be my undoing. The life of tenderness is best left to non-combatants, husbands and cowards and other lucky bastards who prefer to survive. It was not my life, as I had a commission from Father Gaspar, to wit, quote unquote, nothing exists without an observer, and anyway I had sworn an oath to the Sons of the People, with a little slit of a scar on my biceps to show for it, which I revealed to her later, and she kissed it awkwardly so that I felt her stubbly chin on my armpit—a curiously domestic affair.

She held the papers still in her lap, and I finally took them from her.

She watched me smooth out the sacred corners and pat down the wrinkles.

She had scarred some words, and her spit had damped out some inkblots. What words of the hero had been erased by her madwoman's saliva, lachrymous lacunae to be deciphered by dumb scholars in our dim future? It was all my fault. I put the sheaves back in the creased square of the straw mat and again she asked:

—So what are we going to do?

If I had known Leonor then as I know her now I would have understood that to a woman of action questions are rhetorical and a plan was already in place.

She told me she had witnessed in her wanderings the escape of the katipuneros from their homes in the dead of morning, she had witnessed arrests and horrors. One man was torched in his hovel.

Another was blinded by the Filipino guardia's lash: whipped by his own neighbor. I won't repeat the stories here, as even in the retelling the tales slit me up, find fresh places in my cut-up flesh, gained from the pity of Leonor. Most of all, Leonor repeated the tales of women, weeping women, women dragging at their men's bodies, women clinging for their sons' lives. Leonor had a peculiar quality of remembrance—I recognize now with lame wisdom that this was because, of those tales of pain, easily she imagined her own.

She had an ear to the ground for the whispers of the hawkers, and later she left me alone with her oblivious ma, who scared me to death in the middle of the afternoon when she suddenly sat up, and then all she did was roll cigarettes all day and smoke in peace.

When Leonor returned, it was she who told me where to go: toward the fields of Caloocan.

Father Gaspar had a key. It was Leonor who had a clue.

No war could happen without women.

Father Gaspar only had the script.

She kicked me out to get me on the road.

But bless me, Father, for I have sinned:

I did not want to leave.

I was seeking the Supremo because I believed he was the only man I could trust. I explained everything that day to Leonor, as if I were talking to my own self, because she had an odd way of taking on the expressions of the story, as if her face were a narrative mirror, and to be honest if Leonor had ever learned to read, she would have been a damned magician[521] at it.

I told Leonor, only the Supremo will understand—like me, he loves the writer, not the hero.

Hadn't I seen him defend the book, to the shawled cripple in Ermita?

I am sorry, but I must challenge you to a duel for your thoughts.

---

521 *Una maga maldita* (Trans. Note)

Leonor's shy look of admiration for the Supremo's polite bold-ness won my own silent praise.

I told her, the Supremo will tell me what to do.

She nodded with the anxiety I felt, the underlying question—but what would the Supremo say to my crime?

How would *anyone* respond?

Leonor's face fell as it would in that ghost minute before the expectation of another reader's horror.

Well, think about it, I said to her, the Supremo had read all of the *Filibusterismo*. Curse my life that I have yet to read that second novel, and what am I doing, wandering around with the thir—

And Leonor went into a reverie, that lingering mood that shadows base acts for which one fails to summon up regret.

And as a last confession I told Leonor, almost as an aside, as if it were the least of my worries, I still don't know what came over me, why I walked into the hero's hut, that kiosk on the rib of that cursed hill, with the garland of flowers outside it, a corona of color around a grass mound—and my disheveled mind still puzzles over one thing.

The witness of the weeping woman's gray eyes, the melancholy lady who watched me take his book.

Leonor's meditative pity as she dwelt upon the weeping woman gave me hope that she, finally, might fill the reader's gap.

Leonor spoke.

—She wasn't looking, Leonor concluded with the superior wisdom of women.

She was looking at her grief: not you.

And it struck me then that it was true.

The slight damp mound bordered by flowers in the lanzones hill in the exile paradise of Talisay—it was the width and measure of a child. An infant's wildflower tomb. The hut was the burial grave: there where he had abandoned his aborted novel, her still child lay.[522]

---

522 Austin Coates, the most empathic and elegant among Rizal's many biographers,

Entry #43

With the third in the bag, I mean. The one on my back, in my goat
like a bag. Oh you know: *a posteriori*.

—He's living in the mountains of Maragondon, Matandang
Leon added.

Like that shiver that occurs when a passage in a book happens
exactly as you had imagined, so my body responded to Matandang
Leon's words. My heart spoke other questions, but my mind kept
staring at his carbuncle. Is my father one of us? Did he speak of
me? And where in the hell did you get that bukol? But in the course
of the night, it turned out Matandang Leon knew everyone else
as well—including the Count of Monte Cristo, the juggling dwarf
of good old King Alonso, the bold but well-mannered *principe* of
Asturias, and even Jose Rizal.

—Ah, Rizal. I met him, you know, when I had the hideout in
Makiling. I didn't know so many others would be joining me there. If
I knew people would be fleeing Calamba left and right, whole families
with straw mats and children, after the case of the Hacienda that was
a disaster, I would have set up shop in Banahaw instead! The *veterana*
tore down the farmers' homes, and the friars drove them out of town,
and they kept coming to me in droves, clamoring to become bandits.
Hey, I told them, you can't become a bandit just like that—you have
to work at it! But anyhow, there I was in Makiling. I heard rumors of
the German doctor who liked to take hikes and walk about with the
Spanish fellow, that guard of his with the mustache and fancy uniform
and a habit of painting watercolors, who followed him around. I knew
it was the doctor the minute I saw him.

---

notes that in Talisay in 1895 "[Josephine] gave birth to a stillborn child—a boy. It would
seem that at the time of the shock, no one was in the house except for Maria's [Rizal's
sister's] infant son . . . in any event help came, and Rizal was able to do what was necessary
to save her life. The same night he took the tiny body of his son and went alone to a
secluded part of the vale, where he dug a grave and buried it, so concealing the place
before returning to the house that no one ever knew where it was." (Trans. Note)

Tell, the men at the Supremo's table demanded, tell how you knew.

—Because the security guard with the fancy uniform and the bag of watercolors was with him, you idiot.

Tell, the men at the table asked, tell us how he looked.

—He was tall and fair, like a German. Taller than that painting Spaniard, who was just a pygmy, an unano in a uniform, next to Jose Rizal. Rizal wore a salakot hat and a purple jusi shirt and spoke to me in my own language. So polite. He was a polite man, that doctor. He bowed to me when he saw me, as if I were a *señor*.

Tell, the men at the table intoned, tell us what he said.

—Good morning, he said, and I said, Good morning. We are looking for a good banyan grove, so I can show this gentleman how roots can grow out of branches, instead of the other way around, he said. It would be a nice subject for a watercolor. I said, over there. And I added, since he was nice, whenever you get a toothache, you can take a piece of banyan bark and just rub it on your gums, that helps. He answered, my old yaya used to tell me so: she lived near here, he said. He thanked me for my information, bowed again and went on his way, twirling his walking stick. And as he walked off, guess what?

Tell, the men at the table chorused, tell us what happened next.

—The grass turned purple as he passed with his cane—purple just like the shroud of the tabernacle during Santo Pascua!

Leche, someone said, he's just like the Christ! And the Spanish want to kill him.

No, said someone else, they'll never get him. He has magic powers, German potions.

What do you mean, magic powers? Ulol! Didn't you hear he wants to become a doctor to help the Spanish in Cuba? He's on their side now.

You shameless—want to fight?

It could have come to blows, except that we were tired. And anyhow, we still had to start the revolution the next day.

As I said, Matandang Leon was our troop's leader, that rascal.

Lying old bandit. The hero was taller than the unano, my ass. Still, when I slept, I had happy dreams on the strength, I believe, of Matandang Leon's news of my father's existence. And once more, I swore, I would speak to the Supremo the next day.

But the next morning, I slept late, and the Supremo had left to join the troops in San Juan.

When I woke up he was gone.

I didn't even have the chance to say goodbye, much less mention. I was groggy. I still had the papers on me. I had no idea what to do with them, or why I had done it, what had come over me in Dapitan, and now I was the guardian of this albatross.

And if that weren't enough, soon they would be sending me to war.

Matandang Leon took all of us into the sunlight, to exercise us. He showed us smart military tactics he'd learned from spying on the Spaniards when he used to rustle horses.

His face was red-cheeked, like a baby just born. In my memory what strikes me now is the smoothness of his red-cheeked face—red like an areca nut, red like a newborn babe, red like a general of the revolution.

Santo Santo Kasis!
Santo Santo Kob!

Well, all of us liked Matandang Leon's tactics.
They were just exercises of vocal cords!
We followed:

Santo Santo Kasis!
Santo Santo Kob!
Susuko, susuko—
Sumuko ang kalaban.

It was the kind of thing, I guess, meant to keep our spirits up, even though we were already quite spirited, if you know what I mean, but it was fun making a clamor, fit to raise the dead. That was the band, of course, which finally woke up, those moochers. They were all borrowed from pieces of a church choir in Trozo, and following the code of religious fiesta they had slept soundly after the lambanog. But once they got started, I understood why wars cannot exist without marching bands.

The horns fired up our lungs, and the drums loudly admired our moves. We followed Matandang Leon's wild gestures, *Santo Santo Kob!*, and the castanets jingled in happy chorus. The band major, a boy not even old enough to have a *cédula* to tear, waved our sanguine flag. His color troops, a pair of gawky Bulakeños, marched behind with a cumbersome medical bag, one skinny hand each holding a leather handle. If this was war, I thought, count me in—it was just like being in a fluvial procession, minus all the praying and the old ladies mumbling the novenas.

This must be heaven, I thought, where all the angels and drunkards fall into place in single file.

No one expected the arrival of the Guardia Civil.

It was so early in the morning, and anyway the Supremo, who had gone ahead with his chosen men, had scheduled the battle for later in the afternoon, conveniently somewhere else.

I tell you this was the story of the war—all mixed signals and crossed destinies and aborted plans. The war was supposed to happen in the next *arrabal*, not in this nondescript fork between a banyan grove and a Chinese bodega in an unnamed barricade near Bilarang-hipon!

You could tell the guardias were just as surprised by us as we were by their arrival. They, too, had probably just had barako, tsokolate-eh, and pan de sal. At first I thought they were part of another balangay who had come to find us. The men's dark and startled faces mirrored the surprise on Matandang Leon's, and when one of the guardias spoke, he shared our tongue.

That was my other trouble with the war.

It was so goddamned annoying.[523]

I couldn't tell apart my brothers from the other brothers, the guardias who were Filipinos like us, even when they wore uniforms. Some were deserters, some were not. It was only the arrival of the *españolados* in the bunch, always holding up the rear, that cleared up the issue.

And then—and this surprises me even now, because it was as if my heart already understood—my heart beat double at the sight of the leader of the Guardia Civil even before I saw him in full.

The *españolado* stood uncertainly by the Chinese warehouse's rusting gate, staring at us, the sons of the people.

He wore the uniform of my grandfather Don Raymundo Mata Eibarrazeta, the one in the framed picture in my uncle's home. The *españolado* had my grandfather's unseeing face. Most of all, he had the same scary gray eyes of my father in the other picture on my uncle's mantel.

It seemed to me that finally I was face to face.

With *el genio* Jote.

I was so surprised I stood like a dumb decoy before the parley, open to everyone's guns.

Like a moment long ago—I waited for him to recognize me.

Was this what had become of the bandit who strode the mountains of Buntis swaddled in women's clothes?

Paniki, sabi ko.

The smooth-cheeked face of interchangeable fate gave me a sting of nausea.

Two chickens came out of the warehouse and pecked at the *españolado*'s thick brown boots, and he bent to shoo the fowl away.

Sugod, yelled Matandang Leon.

At that moment I understood why the Supremo had chosen Matandang Leon to lead us—and not, for instance, me.

---

523 *Nakakabuwisit talaga*: bursts of Tagalog occur frequently; here, much of the text is a mix of colloquial Tagalog and obscene Castilian. (Trans. Note)

Because Matandang Leon was a crazy son of a bitch.

The tulisan forged ahead of us, even on such short notice, and he cast his raw courage at the startled guards.

The rest of us, I mean, me, I froze.

I mean, look at us. Look at us in the pictures of the U.S. Army Corps of Engineers, bootleg copies of photographic curios that survive of our war. Even the Filipino guardias wore shoes and, lucky bastards, a uniform, with stripes and pockets. Plus they had guns. *El genio* Jote, or whoever this lifesize double was, with his precarious head and fantastic katsila nose, wore the arrogance of a man who had not only a gun but a silver, gleaming sword.

Matandang Leon was barefoot, not to mention hung over, and all he had was a bolo and a reconstituted pistol. God bless that intsik merchant who had sold us back our pistols, which our fine brothers had stolen in turn, in parts from the Manila arsenal, a round-robin of stealing and reconstituting and selling that marked our ingenuity at least—at least with the single pistol we had one chance.

Matandang Leon hoisted a weapon and lashed out with the other, and sure enough instead of shooting with the gun he fired with the bolo. The *españolado* shot him dead. Bulls-eye at the carbuncle, an easy target.

Chaos followed.

How can I describe the battle? Don't ask me because my brains rattle in my guts and my toes move upward toward my spleen when I think of the moment.

I ran.

I was bent and breathless as if something were breaking in my chest's bony cradle, amid the flesh and ganglia of my nerves and despair. I was weeping. I was weeping and running and I lost my step and got entangled somehow in someone's feet, and I didn't care if he were a son of the people or the son of the Lord, something in me was dying and on top of that I was scared to death.

I fled.

I saw him.

I saw him die.

Matandang Leon was my first—he was the first katipunero whom I saw fall.

I wished never to see another again.

Those staring eyes on the path toward the banyan grove, looking up to the sky in surprise, as if to say somehow nothing had prepared him for this particularly ignominious story. Then he was a nothing—gone—he was a nothing of himself. In that minute, I saw how easily it goes, and a weight fell on me.

As I said, it was that buwisit medical bag.

The skinny Bulakeños were nowhere in sight, and the band major with the red and white flag was gone. The flag sat on a chicken's carcass, a scarlet inflammation, one with the blood, and the bag had fallen first on my head then at my feet.

The Spanish reinforcements had come, a bunch of Filipinos still picking their teeth, and in the mess I don't think I ever saw him again.

The unseeing sharpshooting *españolado*.

My unnamed enemy.

The mirror of Spain who mimicked my father.

But who cares about him?

In the mess of my retreat, I retrieved it, our poor three-letter flag, missing a digit to round out our curse.

Running on, I picked up the fallen medical bag.

—He's living in the mountains of Maragondon, Matandang Leon had revealed to me. He's respected by all the bandits.

In retrospect, when I think of it, I must believe it was a kind of truth, an act of kindness, Matandang Leon's revelation. The clairvoyant drunken old knight had in fact answered the questions of hopeful sons. Who knows if any tale, any tale at all, were not so much an invention as a charm, created for the comfort of a child? I take his words now as a memento: something to remember him by—not my father, no—but to remember that livid old codger Matandang Leon.

In that way storytellers live forever.

I don't think I ran—I rolled into the grove, and I squeezed myself through the banyan's grave roots, bag flag and all, to dwell in the ghost-shape of the banyan's host—

Entry #44

I lay there, looking at a crack through my damp burrow, at the hanging fingers of the banyan tree, its branches looping about the heavens like a maze of fantastic bat wings. Soon, I knew, I'd hear the bats, the geckos, and the owls. We used to play in groves like these, out by the creeks of Kawit.

Long ago.

Entomological fulmination in immobile rectitude.

Guess what the tree branches look like, tanga!

The banyan begins not as a tree but a mass of strangleholds, tentacle-roots choking its unsuspecting host, say a fruitwood—langka or guava. The roots start out innocently enough, fine epiphytes of pulp. It's only later that it turns woody, a semblance of its origins. In a grove of banyans by the bat caves in Cavite that I used to climb, one could hide perfectly still among the branches and listen to the sky.

The best groves are those with the oldest trees, with their gnarled roots upon roots. It was fun to squeeze through its cannibal contortions until you traced the whole of the vanished form into which the banyan tree had become.

The banyan above me, the one that chanted, spoke as if it were the voice of many, perhaps bees or locusts, united in a single drone:

—Because encryption is a way of burying, the banyan said.

I lay in the depths of a phantom shape, against shards of damp wood. It was cramped but cozy, and trapped with me were my proliferating personal effects, now a bit bulky, all of us in a cocoon beyond the battle.

I lay in that gap in the banyan grove, and I heard her steps go by the dark path. It was over. By that time it was over. And as far as I could tell it was stalemate, and the flies and the beetles and soon the rats were perhaps the victors. The fields and streams of Balara were quiet, and even the remnant chickens were asleep, out by the unhusked grains of the Chinese bodega.

She felt me staring at her—Leonor has the intuition of a witch.

I got out with difficulty: the bag hoist on the petate—I mean, of course, the other way around: I swaddled the bag with my unraveling mat.

Without a word, I followed her down the paths of the banyan grove.

It did not surprise me that Leonor would appear at that point near the climax, which is an image in my mind that looks anyhow like a figure hanging perhaps at the edge of a cliff by its fingers, or maybe by a rope, whereas a denouement looks a bit like a flat planggana.

It was Leonor who put it together, in the post-amble of a lover's walk.

Because nothing exists without an observer. Because the writer died while he was writing. Because encryption is a way of burying.

Still, I said, there was something missing.

Leonor turned to me and nodded.

God, I thought: we really smelled.

Entry #45

Cash.

Pesos, reales, pesetas, kusing.

Centimos, sencillos, small change, coins.

Sikapat, kahati, salapi, piso.

Years and months and weeks and days of contributions from the Sons of the People, twenty-five cents here, twelve cents there, when most of us could barely eke out a peso, and two pesos were a godsend, enough to betray the revolution.

Those scraps and scrapings squeezed from the lives of our men rained out of the bag in the dead of the banyan grove.

When I opened up what seemed innocently enough Dr. Pio's leather medical bag, I thought—no, this was not the destiny I had hoped for.

This was not to be my footnote in the revolution.

There were ledgers, signatures, and pens. There were memos and calculations and IOUs. *Vale*: one lamp jar. Signed, Genaro (a.k.a. *Pato*). It was just my luck. Curse my fate. I had the cash of the Katipunan on my hands, the damned bag of the treasurer of the revolution. Why they had put it in the charge of Matandang Leon's army, who knew; and why they gave it to a starving pair of Bulakeños who had barely the strength to sing *Santo Santo Kasis* and do the hokey pokey with their left and the right, much less smuggle out the goods in a heavyweight medical bag—I could curse the Secret Chamber, or the Most Respected, Most High Association of the Sons of—if we weren't cursed enough already.

Now where to put it? Where to hide the sums so I could stuff the papers into the bag instead? I buried the money under the gnarled roots of the banyan. Somewhere in Balara, in a grove by a ditch and a Chinese bodega. One day, I hope the nation finds it.

Part Five

Aftermass[524] [525]

---

524 Both the title and what follows occur completely *in English* in the original text, most of it neatly typed. (Trans. Note)

525 English? But why? Is it the American period already? Just as it was getting interesting. But now as the G.I.s bombard deserted and tranquil Manila Bay (the 1898 Battle of the Bay was a farce, cousin to the sinking of the irrelevant *Maine*, Admiral Dewey charging decrepit Manila warships barely armed by Spain!)—I feel my skin turn a bluish bile-swarmed hue. I know soon I will descend into rash and burning eczema, a creeping conflagration in the flesh, a familiar itch—whenever history befalls, I mean befouls me. My mouth is beginning to swell, a dumb numbness in my jaw. What about the Battle of San Juan, the successes of Cavite, our valiant wars against the troops of Camilo Polavieja, even against that young future fascist, Primo de Rivera, not to mention our sad yet heroic Republic of Biak-na-Bato and, later, Malolos? Where is that treasured narration of our rising action, in which we beat back scattered Spain, before G.I. benevolence occupied us with terror? A congestion spews in my lungs, an abasic symptom, I need my inhaler again, let me breathe. (Estrella Espejo, Quezon Institute and Sanatorium, Tacloban, Leyte)

Entry #46

And rising up to the balconies, a touch of spring, an infusion of scents and heat. On leaning out, she saw the figure of the young nephew of the assistant priest. His name was Ysagani. The young man passed, their eyes met, she smiled, the young man raised his hat. Cecilia [Marcela] felt a blaze in her cheeks, wished to withdraw, her feet would not move, she strove to look indifferent, but her eyes looked down upon the garden the better to watch him as he walked away.[526]

[This lay upside down in folder, typed:]

If only he had witnessed the slight strain as she gazed, the way she bent to look down with too forward a glance: a movement scandalous, one must admit, for the innocent citizens of the town of Pili—so that she was lucky only a blind bee and a few oblivious gumamelas witnessed her bold regard. But alas, his own vision was not perfect. At times, straight lines appeared wavy, and some objects appeared in the wrong shape or size. For instance, once he attempted to open up his straw hat like an umbrella, and at odd moments he mistook flocks of birds for banners with written messages, saying fragmentary things in foreign languages, like sic transit *or* glory be, *and in one hallucinatory incident after a locust storm, he had actually picked up the fallen pests, believing he was gathering bullets for the war. The war was always on his mind anyhow.*

---

526 My flesh moves toward twilight, or is it a kaingin shadow, and I note a few odd details, amid my hallucinations: Cecilia and Ysagani, the couple in *Makamisa*, she of the unimaginable wealth and he—well, so it is said Rizal never finished that novel, if one might call those fragments a book, and in fact couldn't decide on the couple's names (he sometimes called Cecilia *Marcela*, and Ysagani *Crispin*) and before we could foretell any part of that young nephew of a curate's fate, the story ends in blurry aporia—a nimbus of truncated folios, erasures, abandoned revisions. (Estrella Espejo, Quezon Institute and Sanatorium, Tacloban, Leyte)

Cecilia felt a vague infantile irritation with herself. What? Was she enamored of this nephew of a priest who used to criticize with enormous hauteur the comings and goings of old friends?

It's true that the pusillanimity of her father and the ambitions of her mother had separated Cecilia from the townsfolk of Pili. She had passed her childhood with her aunt in Manila, her mother's sister, the famed lawyer Doña Orang, she of the unbending views on virtue and love. Ever since she could remember, Cecilia had spent only two or three days a year in Pili, during its fiesta.[527] When she was young, her father Kapitan Panchitong had been reluctant to send her to school, because the expenses incurred for educating her brother were heavy losses he already regretted. Her mother Kapitana Barang thus sacrificed her own maternal pleasures for material ones, giving up her only daughter, and through the years of her daughter's absence, little by little, bit by bit, Barang had managed to silence and kill what remained of a mother's tenderness, which used to catch at her throat at times, like a poor man's scarf.

[This crossed out in bold pencil, still surprisingly legible:]

> *Ysagani, on the other hand, was the seed of unsung trouba-*
> *dours, the type his young country never failed to abandon, so*
> *his uncle, a romantic coadjutor who would never rise to vicar,*
> *would say, with the extravagance of certain off-putting, gre-*
> *garious men. Ysagani, like Cecilia, knew not his mother nor*
> *his father, though perhaps he had better reason: they were dead.*
> *Unlike Cecilia, he had spent his youth in Pili, growing up in its*
> *fruit groves, its streams full of fish and washerwomen, its fresh*
> *lake breezes, its crafty geology of hills and caves. In his small*

---

527 Dear Mimi C., before I regress into my astasic inertia: enclosed herewith is Rizal's third novel, *Makamisa* (after the Mass, as one might say in English), a mix of Tagalog and Spanish, rediscovered in parts and translated—by a Benedictine—or was it Augustinian— my memory's failing—anyway, some scholar in monkish garb. (Estrella Espejo, ditto)

area of ambition, he had built his own renown, gaining public advantages for his fine calligraphy, his skill at memorizing entire swaths of Tagalog poetry or Spanish legal phrases, his quick, flowing hand, and the ability to develop a mustache with brooding panache. People sought this distinguished-looking but rather mute youth to write out their documents, encode their love affairs, and all in all provide a satisfying means of expressing their most secret, binding, and lawful or illicit desires, albeit through the counterfeit of his gracious pen.

There was no doubt: Cecilia was interested in this young man, of whom she had heard even while in Manila. Cecilia had been educated by her formidable aunt. The society of that extraordinary woman, the lady lawyer Orang, an opinionated lady who could play men's games, and the world of the chosen in which Doña Orang moved, formed the habits and graces of her young niece: Cecilia's strong character and imagination. It was Doña Orang, when her ward came of age, who created the image of the ideal, the type of man whose virtues the fantasies of severe virgins sculpted out of whole cloth. Thus, Cecilia had imagined an idol contemplated by the single-minded inquietude of her unmarried aunt. He would possess the rarest qualities of brilliant men. Valor, youth, generosity, heroism, and disinterest were his natural attributes; and the result was that, when she woke to reality and heard her suitors' bleating pastoral phrases and witnessed their vulgar acts, she would close her eyes and smile secretly to herself, a bittersweet smile: she would close her eyes as if to sleep, the better to dream a virgin's dreams. The richest youths of the best families were not men enough to rouse her from her illusions. It was to him, the taciturn figure of Ysagani, enigmatic, silent, and incomprehensible, that she would entrust her destiny and confide her lasting hopes.

[This written on reverse of previous sheet, atypical:]

Ysagani crossed the garden with no more thought of the girl on the balcony. He knew who she was—la señorita. *Señorita Cecilia, the urbanite, the Manila girl who had abandoned Pili for the distractions of an education in the city. Every year, during the week of fiesta, he would hear of her comings and goings—the flurry of preparations in her father's home before the stranger-daughter returned; the pageantry of the arrival of the horse-drawn carriage, fancier in haunch and style than that of even Father Agaton's carrosas; and the sad annual replications of the family's introductions to their changeling child, who grew up to be (by all accounts) as whimsical in spirit as her imperious aunt. When news had come the month before that the* señorita *would be arriving in clothes of mourning, this time without her benefactor, Ysagani heard without comment the speculations and rumors about the young woman's newly bestowed wealth, her unbelievable good fortune, and the host of young men from the best families of the walled city (and beyond) who vied for her lavish hand. All this was nothing to the youth, whose only thought was to return to his uncle's rooms, to sit in the company of that most angelic of man-made implements, the Minerva press. Even its name was mythological, befitting its intransigent gifts.*

As she watched his figure disappear into his home, across from hers, near the parish priest's convent, she imagined she saw him dragging his feet up a steep mountain amid pale shades, or dancing and smiling yet laden with anxiety and the dread impulse of a powerful will. She looked away from this disagreeable picture and fixed again on the fading image in her mind of taciturn Ysagani, enigmatic, silent, and incomprehensible. Farther up the summit, sitting like a sovereign, he seemed an imposing figure, menacing with his feet those crawling on the ground, disdainful and arrogant like a triumphal lord.

She closed her eyes and smiled, a bittersweet smile.

"That is a man," she thought.

[This handwritten in green ink:]

Ysagani climbed up to his small room with its spectral windows. Even the capiz shells were decayed—cracked, opaque lozenges, some warped vitreous slivers sliding out from their wooden panels like so many stiff eyelids opening into a void. He always kept the windows shut, not minding the heat or the representation of a subtle entombment in the wood-lined room's enclosed coffin air. He preferred to minister to the machine in complete privacy, away from all the prying eyes of Pili, which were not inconsiderable, mind you—his uncle was the least dangerous of them, but even he, despite the touching depths of his love, did not look with favor on his nephew's obsession. In fact, he refused to speak of it at all. The young man took off his hat, exchanged his jusi shirt for his cotton camisa, took off his pants, and strung upon his languid waist his limp calzoncillos, and in a minute he was on the floor, cranking up the machine.

She saw the flowers of her country lime-washed in blue and red pots, arrayed in a line along a wide balustrade that ended in a low wall on the edge of a small canal, which served to irrigate the garden. Thin reeds crowned with eggshells to protect them from rain gladdened the flowers, adding a ghost touch to the roses and leaves: the cactus flourished, growing large and white flowers that compensated for the ugliness of its stalk, and the Easter flower tinted its branches a crimson red. By a natural course of thought, from the blush of spring flowers Cecilia dwelt on her new life in Manila: her dear aunt had left, upon her death, an immense fortune, sums of money in several banks and estates that, upon her coming of age, would fall upon her to nurture, just as the gardener tended this sweet arbor.

[This handwritten in pencil, with letter doodling in margins:]

He cranked the Minerva both with his foot and his right hand. He understood that some of these machines could now be run by electricity, in those countries favored by a crude optimism; Ysagani himself could not imagine the act of printing without the pressure of his moving hand and the slow prophetic pedal of his reverent feet. He preferred to imagine the atoms of his own rather lugubrious (even he had to admit) body transferred into the formerly sleeping machine. Now it was awake to an awkward clacking, to a clunking and pedantic rhyme. The sounds of the machine were a bit hoary, no matter how he oiled—a hoarse onomatopoeia of tongues. That, too, he believed, was a blessing, not a curse. It provided music of distraction that prevented the calumnies of the outside world from penetrating his dominion. It kept from him the shrill neighing horses of the Guardia Civil. It shut out the indecent shouts of Father Agaton in the convent next door, cursing out his maligned maid, the pitiful Anday. It kept him from the poor miserable weeping of the abject and cursed Anday. It shielded him from the dueling novenas among the ignorant women of the various Legions of Mary and the ignoble prayers of their rivals, the Sodalists of Mary, gathered in the vestibule of the church beside his home. It kept at bay the daily lashings and the boyish wails from the latinidad across the plaza—the harsh rewards of education in an enlightened land. It silenced the vacuous roar of the cockfight, the murderous chaos of masculine games, and the street hawker's melancholy ardor on dismal and sleepy afternoons. And it muffled the beating of his vengeful heart.

Voice.

Cecilia heard it and wished to withdraw.

It was Father Agaton, the parish priest. The Curate, as they called him, had free entry not only to all the homes of Pili but also to the private chambers of those homes.

Even before he appeared, she shivered with disgust.

—What beautiful flowers you have, he said from the garden below.

[This lay uspide down in folder, typed:]

> *Once a week or so he came up to crank up the press and so complete his project. He had to do this in spurts and starts, not knowing which day of week would be free, or when someone would call him out for some emergency hackery, for his work as the town's unofficial secretary, calligrapher, and designated lover (at least in pen) demanded a laborious mimicry of others' lives that exhausted him. Acts of translation were the worst. He always ended up duplicating the same sorry yearnings, as if all of humanity were the same depressing series of endless desire, and every man's wish seemed the theft of another's. He could not wait to get back to the halting progress of his machine. It was the typographic process, to Ysagani, that seemed always a reinvention, not just eternal but constantly novel, and every time he began printing, the product seemed unutterably strange.*

Leaning out the balcony above the little arbor filled with flowerpots and hanging trellises of disparate forms, Cecilia wished to distract her thoughts from the apprehension of the Curate's voice: again, she looked upon the flowers—but now their freshness only reminded her that they were destined to be raised to praise the priest at the Lenten mass.

—Tuktukan!

Down below she heard the cries of the town of Pili, from the galleries and playgrounds the mob cries of men in duels marked the time of fiesta. While the fathers played with their fortune in the cockpits, the sons with a sense of admirable proportion played with eggs. The only difference was that in the cockfight, the disgraced lost money, while in the childish battle of eggs the winner gained absolute power over the vanquished. She reflected: this follows history, as Darwin noted. In infant nations, the weak become slaves; while among older systems, the loser only pays her fine, and each citizen has control even over her corpse: such logic is the law of nature.[528][529]

[This lay upside down in folder, typed:]

Everytime he began printing, the product seemed unutterably strange. And even as, at his feet, he contemplated the work he had already done, a thickening bulk that seemed at times autobiographical and sometimes fanciful, and at some points historical and factual, though admittedly partial (and then maybe to some degree hysterical, not in the meaning of comedy

---

528 I'm reading through the text Estrella Espejo offered me. I read here this passage from Brother Ambeth Ocampo's careful transmission of *Makamisa*, which the Benedictine monk believes was the last in the trilogy of Rizal's novels. The following is from fol. 70, the original version in Rizal's hand and "discovered" by the monk in 1986 in a mislabeled folder in the National Library: ". . . *La unica diferencia era que en la lucha de gallos el desgraciado perdia su dinero, mientras que en la lucha de los huevos el vencido pasaba a poder del vencedor. Cuestion de historia como diria Darwin: en la infancia de los [naciones la] pueblos el debil [era] pasaba a ser esclavo; entre las naciones viejas se paga la indemnizacion y cada uno se queda con sus cadaveres: la logica es la ley de la naturaleza.*" Mimi C.—what do you think? May I have your cell phone number? Let's talk. (Dr. Diwata Drake, Diliman, Quezon City, Philippines)

529 There is indeed resemblance between Rizal's Spanish and Raymundo Mata's English. Though one might attribute the modern allusion to Darwin to the latter text, it's clear here that the long-entombed and antique Rizal was the original modernist. (Estrella Espejo, ditto)

but of pathology, but then, he hoped, not indubitably so), he couldn't help reading it as if it were the first time.

And then the oracular machine, which sideways looked (he thought) like a Cyclops's eye, a one-wheeled wonder of Ysagani's mechanical times, scrawled out the next page:

love my father's yellow stream buttnaked green coconut open to surprise cuckoldroaches-dancing-in-a-cone Porkrind-Chronicles saltweep of fish Emilia Christmas lights Padre Mariano Gomez (r.i.p.) my gonads! indios Jorge Raymundo Mata scabs lanzones deeply ripe mangoes navel-orange thighs

[end of Raymundo Mata's papers]

Afterword
By Estrella Espejo

I would like to express my gratitude to Raymundo Mata and his heirs. It's a miracle—I mean, a miracle happened to me. Capital *M*! If you recall, there I was, falling into necrotic sleep and inertia, a familiar nightmare when I contemplate the history of my country. My spleen was twitching beneath my ribcage like a poisoned bantam chicken, and I was swooning into horror. My ganglia and gorge, my nerves and nasal hoar—I was shaking toward that fatal torpor, a malaise I know so well—not just of the body, but of desire, of memory and mind.

Oh country, oh fate!

When suddenly apprehension broke, like a fever.

What I apprehended was this: it was the voice of History.

It spoke.

I swear it was him, Raymundo Mata, a trembling lisp of a nation's desire. Arise, Estrella Espejo, he said as I lay prone in my bed, breathing through a plastic apparatus. You hold in your hand the mirror of your race. (To be honest, maybe he said "face," I could barely hear through the inhaler, and my ear, stricken with the same old abysmal abasia, long-dormant, still has its problems. Anyway, as I said, he had a lisp.)

But his pitiable message was unmistakable.

You must publish or perish, he said. This is a monumental paean to History. When the word is made flesh, he breathed: you will be well.

Sure enough, I have been sitting up in bed for days, eating special bibingka from Hotel Alejandro, not needing my lugaw, and soon I will be leaving this haven on Magsaysay Boulevard, this trap, this refuge, and even now am scribbling ideas for a new paper on my findings in the manuscript, this blind man's history of the revolution.

Who knows: maybe it is true. One day I will be well.

I would like to express my gratitude therefore to Raymundo Mata and his heirs.

This work is a monumental paean to History. It encompasses (through limited means and blurry vision, it is true) a sweep of time otherwise slipped under a rug. The two mysteries Raymundo Mata unlocks, with his signature modesty and aplomb, foreground two serious gaps in our knowledge. The first, the key to the mystery of the Katipunan's lost cash, long a bone of contention among now deceased rebels (may they rest in peace in the unjust oblivion of their tombs), will enliven business among certain sections between Tandang Sora and Balara—perhaps the same motley stampede of optimists still looking for General Yamashita's gold.

The second, the mystery of the hero's last hour in Dapitan, has occupied the memories of that town's pious folk for more than a century and enamored armchair dramatists of more prurient dispositions for years (but intermittently, given the nature of our attention span). It's a passage in history that has always moved me, it brings pangs beyond my capacity to diagnose, or quell—that description of Rizal's last moments in Dapitan before leaving on the steamer *España* that would take him (he supposed) to a free man's post as a doctor to the Spanish troops in Cuba. (We know that instead he ended up in the overnight travesty of a window-less cell at Barcelona's Montjuic Fortress—incidentally, the same cell occupied three decades later by Lluis Companys, the con-demned president of Catalonia, as Orwell must have reported in his *Homage*. As Rizal himself said—perhaps with bitter sacrilege—of his saga in 1896: "This is but the First Station.")

A British biographer of Rizal, the astute Austin Coates, writes of that brief moment in Dapitan in his book *Rizal—Filipino Nation-alist and Patriot*:

In the afternoon of . . . 31 July, nearly the whole town of Dapitan walked and boated to Talisay to bid farewell . . . He came to a window of his house to find the people gathered in hundreds outside beneath the trees, the elders of the town, their wives and families, indeed everyone in Dapitan with the exception of the priests . . . On a flat-topped rock beside the sea the town band, pride of Dapitan, had installed themselves to take their part, too, serenading him on his way.

"He came down the steps of the house, made his adieux, and with the whole gathering walked down toward the shore. The boat in which he was to be rowed out to the steamer was waiting, the band was waiting.

"But he did not at once embark. Bidding no one follow him, he mounted the rib of the hill leading to the kiosk, symbol of his personal life in his own country, and stood for a few seconds deep in thought. Then, striking a match, he set fire to it. Within a few seconds it was a mass of flames. Turning away and never glancing back, he came swiftly to the boat and embarked.

Any reader would be no less struck as the entire town of Dapitan was struck—a whole mystery of families and gaping citizens—by Rizal's final puzzling gesture in what turned out to be his final home. Not even the hero was to know (though he may have guessed) that these fateful people, on that crosswise slipper of land, that spill of rock and abaca, would be the incidental witness of his *ultimo adios*. (It is this moment that the ashen imagery of his celebrated poem merely postdates.) To the people of Dapitan, the riddle of his actions seemed both tender and disturbing: it provoked years of pity and bereavement in the townsfolk's memory.

And now it is through the unearthed diaries of Raymundo Mata that one might find a slim shard of understanding—as of the Magdalene explaining Jesus's acts (but only in the haze, of course, of his posthumous glory).

That the tomb of the stillborn child, his son, lay under the kiosk's kindling—yes, the people of Dapitan have long held that ceaseless view, with the kind of tact and appropriate gravity no other place in this avid archipelago has been able to muster, as there are only two things that unite Filipinos: gossip, and the life of Jose Rizal.

But that the secret kiosk on the rib of the hill—long ago smelling of lanzones coil, a site yet to be fully determined even to this day, so say the curators of the estate—surely contained the other strangled child (no less terrible a death, and for some perhaps more terrible, for after all books are immortal while children break your heart), few have gleaned.

Rizal's ritual act of burning recalls the burning of the fictive Crisostomo Ibarra's study—of Ibarra's own history and letters—in the town of San Diego, in that text that some consider the precursor of the hero's myriad biographies: the prophetic *Noli Me Tangere*. The hero, in those last moments of his innocence, believed in Dapitan he was also burning a book. And in his Orphic angst, not taking a backward look, he understood he was burning not only the child of his loins—in burning the book, so burned his spirit.

Fortunately for the history of Filipinos, that book, unknown to Rizal, was already absent from its tomb. How was he to know that an obscure crook— blind, impulsive, and ridiculous—had purloined his text from its dusty grave? Only the flat-topped rock, fortunately mute, in Dapitan remembers the shadow of the crime.

(In my case, I will always recall with affection the image of the budding larcenist meditating on that flat rock in this memoir's pages: the memoirist's haunting solitude as he gazed down on the ocean's blank page.)

Nowhere in the recollections of the hero's family or of the wise men of Dapitan does it appear that Rizal worked again at the kiosk after the death of his child. There lay undisturbed the twin ghosts of his genius. The hero's numerous letters, postcards, and other ephemera ascertain that he never discovered, or at least spoke of, the manuscript's loss. And so it is that the Philippines owes to the perfidy of that nightblind thief Raymundo Mata the preservation of what one might call a limb of its patrimony—or maybe some other organ: a distorted lens, a partial eye.

The actual state of the hero's manuscript—as preserved here in a circular loop, with same beginning and no end, in bits and unfettered pieces, promiscuous and confusing, an omnivorous mad shedding of words, as of some kind of ecdysiast eccentric taking off all her clothes without much ado—is not for me, a mere historian, to evaluate. I leave that to literary upholsterers and cultural quacks: those critics and amateur hypnotists whose words must inevitably follow.

An Epitaph
By Dr. Diwata Drake

Excuse me for my long silence.

I was reading.

I have been re-reading *The Revolution According to Raymundo Mata*. I encourage you all to do the same. Sure, the beginning is a tatter of mangled texts, all of which one could skip without anxiety (although I daresay without them the rest would not exist). And then there's the matter of the leaning tower of commentary, so that the document seems not one but two—or who knows three: one a waspish intertext of witches, another a disarmed combatant's confession of misadventure, and yet another (the most revolutionary document of them all, perhaps) the abominable pulsing void in which the intramural wrangling and all that awful mess, the *pasticciaccio brutto* of voices, intersect and must converge.

But one clue among the excursions of the translator, Ms. Mimi C., led me on a chase, and in the last few weeks I've had to drop the usual effusions of theory, and even praxis. My own unfinished work, now titled, *Why, You Lovely Symptoms: The Structure of the Filipino Unconscious, Not Really Lang(ue), or Even a Parol(e)*, has been abandoned.

I've worked as a detective.

I found a few wild geese, a bronze, or at least mestizo-type golden fleece, and some cut-up kusing, plus one centavo. In short, I've picked up stray cues (or should I use a fishy metaphor instead?) from the trail of little red herring left by this monumental paean to History, as my esteemed colleague Professor Estrella Espejo puts it.

The fossil evidence of Raymundo's words, especially the conclusive Entry #46, seems to indicate a curious interlacing of the blind hero's memoir with the ophthalmologist's third novel. It is as if the doctor-savior and patient-crook were looped (Estrella's words, not mine), tangled in knots of each other.

I congratulate Estrella on her reprieve from history: I hope it lasts. However, Estrella accepts the ghostly state of the text with too much goodwill (I only hope the voice she heard was figurative).

In her last passage, she seems to concede, without directly saying so, *that Raymundo's memoir and the hero's third novel are one.*

Without questioning at all the oddness of her point, its vertiginous trap, she . . . accepts that Raymundo, that ecdysiast eccentric, has taken on the emperor's clothes, so to speak—and thus Rizal's naked bones, that is, his sentences, lie like a dark fitted overcoat upon Raymundo's memoir, a circular loop, with same beginning and no end.

She does not bother to disentangle one from the other.

Various scholars have already argued the pros and cons of the two conclusions that instantly arose when advance copies of this text were indiscriminately mailed out by an anonymous crank (I had nothing to do with it). I shall not go into the ideological specifics of the scholars' tirades but will gloss on a few points.

One: certain renegade Rizalists, alleged escapees from Mount Banahaw, argue that the "loop" in Entry #46 tells us this—Raymundo Mata of Kawit's memoir is part of the lost third novel of the hero, as told in the Minerva press sheets rolled out by the young curate's nephew, Ysagani. To these devout and balding apostates, Raymundo Mata's memoir is a text within Rizal's recently discovered novel *Makamisa,* or *After the Mass.*

One of these escaped Rizalists, perhaps driven a bit deranged by his own lost years on the mountain, has gone so far as to declare: *the memoir is the lost third novel.*

If so, Rizal in his last days turns out to be a sore parodist; ventriloquist to a purloiner and, perhaps, a rapist but also, oddly, a rampant plagiarist of himself; clearly a heretic against his Jesuit God; and a bit inattentive when it comes to plot. This rather modern Rizal, I must say, has his admirers, among them a coterie from Queens, New York, who lists a number of "postcursors" of Rizal, such as the hero of the Frenchman Raymond Queneau's *The Blue Flowers,* and one sentence in a paragraph about bat wings in a story by the late symbolist Franz Arcellana.

The Revolution According to Raymundo Mata is seductive because it implies resurrection, which is a desire that unites all humans, even those who are not Filipinos. Somehow in this memoir a lost novel rises from its grave, and with it its author. The execution of Rizal by the Spaniards (curiously omitted from Raymundo's plot[530]), the eternity of the hero's pathos and injustice, has perpetrated all too many deceits and delusions in his countrymen—and I am not just referring to the sectarians of Banahaw, although they are a special case.

The many seances and tableaux calling up the ghost of Rizal are innumerable in the Philippines, his child-republic, which seems to exist only as a remorseful postscript to his name: the monuments in the plaza of every single town in the country, the sad caricature on the matchbooks (the absurd hairline, the fine mustache), the yearly bouts of remembrance that dissuade no violent tyrant and soothe no one's daily woes—in these images is the hero reproduced by a desperate country, an ironic denouement for a stubborn man who left not a single trace of the ashes of his own son's grave.

The more vehement critics, those who man the barricades of truth, a numerous tribe, curse the renegade Rizalists and say: *pwe!* The mere notion that the text can in any way be attributed to the noble and long-suffering poet sickens these scholars.

The travesty is Raymundo Mata's alone, they chorus: he has desecrated and appropriated Rizal beyond forbearance. The "loop" in Entry #46 is brazen proof of Raymundo Mata's horrible sacrilege, his tampering and revision of a holy text. He dares to enlace his

---

530 A student in my course, Psych 401: The Writer on the Couch, has written a thesis, unfortunately full of run-ons so I'm not including it in my bibliography, in which she posits that, in the way that Mark David Chapman, perhaps, would have been incapable of including in his own timeline of universal incidents the death of the first Beatle, Raymundo Mata was not capable of explicitly conjuring the death of the writer whose identity he had embraced.

own words—interpolate his vile witticisms—with Jose Rizal's! *Que verguenza*, not to mention *barbaridad*. It means nothing to these scholars that in doing so Raymundo Mata the thief, that Barabbas, recovered the lost novel and, however feloniously, resurrected the hero. That last fact only adds to Raymundo's errors.

To these diocesan faithful, this text commits a crime punishable by death (in any case, Raymundo Mata seems to have vanished in time, derelict and hallucinating, water-tortured but somehow sublime, in that cell in Bilibid, under the custody of American G.I.s, so that takes care of that). To these fastidious readers, this memoir, this fantasy, is cousin to all other vibrant forgeries and textual ambiguities that have plagued this fervid democracy's highly imaginative history: e.g., the sadistic delusions of the prehispanic Code of Kalantiaw, a bunch of bark documents wrapped in wax, written in cuttlefish ink, and stuffed in the horn of a six-legged bull; the laborious stenography of the *Minutes of the Katipunan*, cursed by an over-earnest, too-detailed banality; the ignoble contretemps over the ignominious so-called Retraction of Rizal, in which the hero allegedly confesses in his last hour his return to God, like some poor modern Chaucer—a spurious document perpetrated (so the scholars say) by no less than the Archbishop of Manila and the head of the Jesuit order; Aguinaldo's apocryphal writ commuting the death sentence of Bonifacio, smacking more of wish-fulfilment than fact; and the still-disputed translation by Bonifacio of Rizal's posthumous poem found in a lamp, *Mi Ultimo Adios* (but anyway, they add, who cares—what matters is that the translation was memorized, word for word, and gave the rebels heart).

The list of textual deceptions underlines without a doubt the eternal trauma of the Philippines: like everyone else, it is a contingent being, born of words.

And it soothes none that their own flagrant sense of self is perhaps recast in the miracle of Raymundo's language, in the strange way that words conversely enact magic tricks of being.

But as for me, I have no wish to deny Raymundo's story.

Indeed, I prefer to give him ballast.

I hope, I fervently desire, to give witness to his truth.

I know. I know.

You know.

That there is a shadow on my cheek, a wisp of a pinch and a palm on the face, along with the breeze of the beach (in Antibes) that perhaps surges with this desire—

I admit my own personal regret: the way I failed to follow my folly, my love, Pedro Ménàrdsz, who prophecied as he escaped with his minions from the just wrath of Claro Mürk—

It is the world of words that desires the world of things.

As I said, I have combed through *The Revolution According to Raymundo Mata*, I have retraced and retrod and gone through clues like Edgar Allan Poe's Prefect G— (to recall the allusions of Mata himself).

I have come to some troubling conclusions.

Among my (hundreds of) clues are the following, to wit: the use of English in Entry #36; the names lifted from Rizal's student diary in Entry #19; the entire section on Lady K in Entry #22; a mysterious signal of textual finality, *consummatum est*, in the middle of narration in Entry #23; and the faithful translation into English (from the Spanish) of fol. 57 of *Makamisa*, as found in Entry #46. There is one interesting, provocative statement, a line in Entry #21, in which the hero cryptically declares: *I enjoyed the act of copying*; but in that case I may be overreading. (I'm not even going to mention the soup of other texts that indelibly stained this memoir, from balagtasan to bugtong— all of which otherwise sustain the Filipino soul.)

Each of these clues shares a linguistic deviltry, an almost incandescent reflexive trickery—the kind perpetrated by agile liars, or translators.

I wish to call on the single witness of the actual text—the sole reader of the so-called original papers of the memoir: the Translator.

Mimi C.—where are you?

As our correspondence reached a climax, I tried calling upon her in person, Googling her address and phone number, but in vain. Has she fled the country? The publisher Trina Trono keeps her itinerary under wraps, stalls whenever I try to get at least her cell so I can text her, and now refuses to return my calls (and then my server keeps sending back "undeliverable mail"); all this even as Trina Trono graciously extends full support for this publication—since pretty soon she can pocket its modest profits.

The translator's hoax—yes, I use the word boldly, Mimi C., wherever you are—only stokes the fires of a cruel illusion:

That a nation so conceived, from the existential exigencies of a young man's first novel, will find redemption in the phoenix of his lost words.

And if so her enterprise preserves the country's painful paradox: it is full of writers who believe a text will save it, even when they know barely anyone will read it. (Perhaps this explains her effrontery.)

And so I demand in the name of Raymundo Mata: *habeas corpus*. Give us the body.

It is the Translator, Mimi C., alone who can answer the questions of the critics. Where are the original papers?

True, there is one reader out there, a voice in the wilderness, who has already declared with the ardor of a broken heart that she does not care: to her, this living testament, this book, of Raymundo's world, is enough.

She insists: *It is the world of words that creates the world of things.*

But not for us.

We wish to peruse for ourselves Raymundo's childish Spanish script, his Chabacano escapades, his incidental Visayan locutions, his Latin vulgarity, his schoolboy codes, his English lapses, his Tagalog tricks. Or is it possible that the Translator, the pseudonymous *Mimic*, has had us in the trap of her infernal arts all along, and history is only a blind alley of her imagination?

I hope not.

Translator's Postcard
[sent from an island in the South China Sea]

Mi noamla: ra puada vimgoes am at

References

Spanish passages from the following texts occur in translation in Entry #22 and Entry #46 (English translations by the author):

P. Jacinto (Jose Rizal). *Memorias de un estudiante de Manila: autobiografía escolar inédita del Dr. Jose Rizal Mercado, durante el périodo 1861–1881*. Manila: s.n., 1949.

Rizal, Jose. *Makamisa*. In *The Search for Rizal's Third Novel* Makamisa, by Ambeth Ocampo. Pasig: Anvil, 1992.

English translation of Voltaire's *Candide* taken from:
Voltaire. *Candide*. http://www.gutenberg.org/etext/4650

The following are some books consulted in the writing of this novel:

Agoncillo, Teodoro. *Revolt of the Masses: The Story of Bonifacio and the Katipunan*. Quezon City: University of the Philippines, 1996.

_____. *The Writings and Trial of Andres Bonifacio*. Manila: Manila Bonifacio Centennial Commission, 1963.

Aguinaldo, Emilio. *My Memoirs*. Trans. from the Tagalog *Mga Gunita* by Luz Colendrino-Bucu. Manila, 1967.

_____. *Saloobin/Sentiments*. Trans. and ed. Emmanuel Franco

Calairo. Dasmariñas, Cavite: Cavite Historical Society, Inc., 2002.

Almario, Virgilio S. *Panitikan ng Rebolusyon(g 1896)*. Quezon City: University of the Philippines, 1993.

Alvarez, Santiago. *The Katipunan and the Revolution*. Trans. from the Tagalog *Ang Katipunan at ang Himagsikan* by Paula Carolina Malay. Quezon City: Ateneo de Manila, 1992.

Anonymous. *Doctrina Cristiana*. Ed. Edwin Wolf II. Facs. of the copy in the Lessing Rosenwald Collection, Library of Congress. http://www.gutenberg.org/etext/16119

Anonymous. *Minutes of the Katipunan*. First English Edition. Manila: National Historical Institute, 1996.

Bellessort, Andre. *One Week in the Philippines*. Trans. from the French by E. Aguilar Cruz. Manila: National Historical Institute, 1987.

Borromeo-Buehler, Soledad. *The Cry of Balintawak*. Quezon City: Ateneo De Manila, 1998.

Calairo, Emmanuel. *Cavite El Viejo: Kasaysayan, Lipunan, Kultura*. Dasmariñas, Cavite: Cavite Studies Center, 1998.

_____. *Cavite in Focus: Essays in Local Historiography*. Dasmariñas, Cavite: Cavite Historical Society, Inc., 2001.

_____. *Liping Kabitenyo*. Dasmariñas, Cavite: Cavite Studies Center, 1999.

Camagay, Luisa. *Working Women of Manila in the 19th Century*. Quezon City: University of the Philippines, 1995.

Castro, Modesto de. *Pag Susulatan nang Dalauang Binibini na si Urbana at ni Feliza.* http://www.archive.org/details/pagsusulatan-nang15980gut.

Churchill, Bernardita Reyes and Francis A. Gealogo (eds.) *Centennial Papers on the Katipunan and the Revolution.* Manila: Manila Studies Association and National Commission for Culture and the Arts, 1999.

Churchill, Bernardita Reyes (ed.) *Revolution in the Provinces.* Quezon City: Philippine National Historical Society Inc., 1999.

Coates, Austin. *Rizal—Filipino Nationalist and Patriot.* Manila: Solidaridad, 1992.

De la Costa, Horacio (ed. and trans.). *The Trial of Rizal.* Quezon City: Ateneo de Manila, 1996.

De los Santos, Epifanio. *The Revolutionists: Aguinaldo, Bonifacio, Jacinto.* Manila: National Historical Institute, 2000.

Duc d'Alencon. *Luzon and Mindanao.* Trans. from the French by E. Aguilar Cruz. Manila: National Historical Institute, 1986.

Guerrero, Leon Maria. *The First Filipino.* Pasig: Anvil, 1998.

Guevara, Antonino [Matatag]. *History of One of the Initiators of the Filipino Revolution.* Trans. from the Spanish by Onofre D. Corpuz. Manila: National Historical Institute, [1988].

Joaquin, Nick. *A Question of Heroes.* Pasig: Anvil, 2005.
Lacan, Jacques. *Écrits: A Selection.* Trans. from the French by Alan Sheridan. New York and London: W.W. Norton, 1977.

Mabini, Apolinario. *The Philippine Revolution*. Vol. II. Trans. from the Spanish *La revolucion filipina*. Manila: National Historical Institute, n.d.

Majul, Cesar Adib. *Apolinario Mabini, Revolutionary*. Manila: Trademark, 1998.

Marche, Alfred. *Luzon and Palawan*. Trans. from the French by Carmen Ojeda and Jovita Castro. Manila: Filipiniana Book Guild, 1970.

Medina, Isagani. *Ang Kabite sa Gunita: Essays on Cavite and the Philippine Revolution*. Quezon City: University of the Philippines, 2001.

_____. *Cavite Before the Revolution: 1571–1896*. Quezon City: University of the Philippines and Cavite Historical Society, 2002.

Nakpil, Julio. *Julio Nakpil and the Philippine Revolution*. Filipiniana Reprint Series Book 26. Manila: Academic, 1964.

Nobus, Dany (ed.). *Key Concepts of Lacanian Psychoanalysis*. New York: Other Press, 1999.

Ocampo, Ambeth. *Aguinaldo's Breakfast*. Pasig: Anvil, 1993.

_____. *Bones of Contention*. Pasig: Anvil, 2001.

_____. *Bonifacio's Bolo*. Pasig: Anvil, 1995.

_____. *Looking Back*. Pasig: Anvil, 1990.
_____. *The Search for Rizal's Third Novel* Makamisa. Pasig: Anvil, 1992.

_____. *Rizal Without the Overcoat*. Pasig: Anvil, 2000.

Quibuyen, Floro C. *A Nation Aborted: Rizal, American Hegemony, and Philippine Nationalism*. Quezon City: Ateneo de Manila University Press, 1999.

Ricarte, Artemio. *Memoirs of General Artemio Ricarte*. Manila: National Heroes Commission, 1963.

Rizal, Jose. *El Filibusterismo*. Trans. from the Spanish by Maria Soledad Lacson-Locsin. Makati: Bookmark, 1996.

_____. *Letters between Rizal and Family Members*. Manila: National Historical Institute, 1993.

_____. *Miscellaneous Writings*. Manila: National Historical Institute, 1992.

_____. *Noli Me Tangere*. Tercera Edición. Manila: Librería Manila Filatelica, 1908.

_____. *Noli Me Tangere*. Trans. from the Spanish by Maria Soledad Lacson-Locsin. Makati: Bookmark, 1996.

_____. "The Philippines a Century Hence." In *Political and Historical Writings*. Volume VII. Centennial Edition. Manila: National Heroes Commission, 1964.

Rizal, Jose and Ferdinand Blumentritt. *The Rizal-Blumentritt Correspondence*. Volumes I-II. Manila: National Historical Institute, 1992.

Rogers, Annie G. *The Unsayable: The Hidden Language of Trauma*. New York: Random House, 2006.

Ronquillo, Carlos. *Ilang Talata Tungkol sa Paghihimagsik nang 1896–1897*. Trans. and ed. Isagani Medina. Quezon City: University of the Philippines, 1996.

Schumacher, John. *The Propaganda Movement, 1880–1895*. Quezon City: Ateneo de Manila, 1997.

Scott, William Henry. *Prehispanic Source Materials for the Study of Philippine History*. Revised Ed. Quezon City: New Day, 1984.

Valenzuela, Arturo. *Dr. Pio Valenzuela and the Revolution*. Manila: National Historical Institute, 1996.

Villacorta, Wilfrido, et al. (eds.). *Manila—History, People, and Culture: Proceedings of the Manila Studies Conference*. Manila: De La Salle, 1989.

Villaroel, Fidel P. *Jose Rizal and the University of Santo Tomas*. Manila: University of Santo Tomas, 1984.